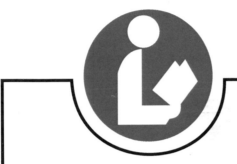

ENTER PALE DEATH

ENTER PALE DEATH

Barbara Cleverly

SOHO CRIME

Published by Soho Press, Inc.
853 Broadway
New York, NY 10003

Library of Congress Cataloging-in-Publication Data

Cleverly, Barbara.
Enter pale death / Barbara Cleverly.

HC ISBN 978-1-61695-408-6
PB ISBN 978-1-61695-617-2
eISBN 978-1-61695-409-3

1. Sandilands, Joe (Fictitious character)—Fiction.
2. Aristocracy (Social class)—England—Fiction.
3. Murder—Investigation—Fiction. 4. Family secrets—Fiction. I. Title.
PR6103.L48E58 2014
823'.92—dc23 2014019274

Interior design by Janine Agro, Soho Press, Inc.

Printed in the United States of America

10 9 8 7 6 5 4 3 2 1

For Eleanor and Gordon

pallida mors aequo pulsat pede
pauperum tabernas regumque turris.

Pale Death comes knocking as loudly at the door
of the poor man's hovel as at the gates of the king's castle.

—Horace, *Odes*, 1.4.13-14.

PROLOGUE

ENGLAND. APRIL 1933.

"Gingerbread? You're sure it was gingerbread she asked for, Gracie?"

The odd request was the very last thing a housekeeper wanted to hear at this moment. Mrs. Bolton stood in the centre of the heaving kitchen overseeing her troops with a discipline firm enough to have impressed the Duke of Wellington himself. But, ever alert, the Iron Duke would, like her, have had his attention snagged by an unexpected detail.

"Don't run!" Mrs. Bolton swept a teetering pile of dirty dishes from the hands of an exhausted fourteen-year-old kitchen maid, straightened them, waited until the girl was steady on her feet again and then handed them back. "Put these in the sink and go upstairs to bed, there's a good girl. You've done well tonight, Elsie." She turned her attention back to her ladyship's maid. "Now, Grace. You see how we're fixed. It's half past eleven. Twelve sat down to dinner. Twelve have to be cleared up after. That's before we start setting for breakfast. And you come swanning in here telling me her ladyship wants gingerbread served with her bedtime cocoa?"

The two women exchanged glances. They were getting dangerously near to implying criticism of the mistress. The other servants were bustling a little less noisily. Mrs. Bolton sensed that ears were being cocked in her direction and she finished diplomatically: "You must have misheard, Gracie. She doesn't eat gingerbread. Take her a slice of nice plain Victoria sponge if she's still hungry. Can't see why she would be—she cleared her plates as usual and had a second helping of Pavlova pudding."

Grace smiled and shook her head. "No, no, Mrs. Bolton. She was very particular. Just tell me if you've got gingerbread in the pantry and I'll do the tray myself. I won't get in your way."

Mrs. Bolton led her over to the larder. "If you're sure then. But I warn you—the mistress can't abide anything spicy."

"Ah . . . women can change their minds sometimes, you know. And their fancies," Grace confided. "For undisclosed reasons."

"Oh, ho! So that's how it is!" Rolling eyes and a quick intake of breath indicated that enlightenment had struck the housekeeper. "It's true then, the murmurings I've heard? Well I never! You and she have kept that one dark, Gracie! I doubt even the master knows his good news. Is that so?"

"Shh! I've no idea what you're on about Mrs. B. We don't want to spread silly rumours do we? Now if you'll . . . ?"

"You'll find some in the Jubilee biscuit tin behind the pantry door. I keep it for the servants' tea. It's a bit stale, but if I'm guessing right and this is by way of being a craving, she probably won't notice. I've known fancies for stranger things than stale gingerbread at midnight. Oh, and by the way . . ." Mrs. Bolton wiped all expression from her face as she added, "Bearing all in mind . . . she might like to hear that the master has retired to the snooker room with Master Alexander and the other gentlemen and two bottles of his best Napoleon brandy. It looks like being a long session. She should have an untroubled evening."

"Just for once, she'll be glad of that," Grace replied, winking.

The housekeeper smiled. Grace Aldred was always quick on the uptake and discreet with it. The very best lady's maid you could hope for. Mrs. Bolton thanked her lucky stars for Gracie, who covered as best she could for the inadequacies of a not universally popular mistress. Her ladyship couldn't always—in fact, couldn't often—be depended on to make good decisions, but in this case she'd done the right thing in offering the delicate and demanding post to what you might call a "home-grown" girl off the estate. Not like the personal attendants the lady guests had brought with them for this house party weekend. A heap of trouble they were! Demanding fusspots, hating each other, hating being cooped up together in the country in unseasonably Arctic conditions. Unlike their ladies who, for the most part, were as good as gold and content to gossip in corners over their embroidery.

Except for the fifth female guest. The one who'd arrived late. She'd turned up by taxi all the way from Cambridge, if you please. Gadding about the country like some Zuleika Dobson! Who on earth was she? No one seemed to know.

"No friend of the *mistress*, that little Miss Mystery," the footman had reported knowingly when called on to shed some light on the problem at the end of dinner. Leaning close to ladle out the soup, the footmen were always the first to assess relationships and get a breath of scandal. "You're wrong about that, Mrs. Bolton. At each other's throats through the last four courses, they were! All her ladyship's fault—you know what she's like. Did her best to bomb the poor little person out of her trench. But when she finally managed it between the sole and the cutlets, she wished she hadn't! Got as good as she gave! Better! But watch out—you wouldn't want to get caught between those two. Trouble! With a bit of luck, the lassie will pack her traps and buzz off back to Cambridge before we get to the hair-tugging and eye-scratching."

A puzzle. A young, unrelated, single girl of undeniable attractions could not possibly be here as a guest of the master, and yet she appeared to be at daggers drawn with the mistress. Most unusually, the young woman had turned up unaccompanied by male escort or lady's maid. When Mrs. Bolton had offered the services of young Rosie to do the necessary, she'd declined them. Oh, politely enough—there was nothing wrong with her manners—but had there been a touch of supercilious indulgence in her tone as she'd added, "I can tie my own shoelaces and brush my own hair, thank you"? She'd shaken her overly short London haircut and laughed. Mrs. Bolton marked her down as something of a renegade. One of those Bright Young Things. Even the Bloomsbury set when they visited—and they were odd enough— at least brought their maids with them. Maids! *Their* girls were not required to wear cap and apron, and expected to be called by their Christian names. And those would be borrowed from some Greek goddess, like as not. All that nonsense set a bad enough example, but this latest guest, trailing an atmosphere of unease and defiance in her wake, looked even more disruptive, Mrs. Bolton calculated. A Modern Miss Independent. Might even be a Socialist. She'd bear watching.

Enid Bolton sighed. Three French maids, two warring women and one bemused housekeeper to keep the peace. Tin hats on, she reckoned, should be the order of the day.

"DID YOU GET it? You did? Good girl! Let me see." The voice was bubbling with eagerness and laughter. Grace's mistress, sitting in silken pyjamas at her dressing table, put down her hairbrush and examined the contents of the supper tray. She tilted her nose in exaggerated scorn at the square of brown, spongey cake. "So that's gingerbread. Are you supposed to eat it or bathe with it? I'll take the cocoa, thank you, but this offering you can put over there on the table by the window. That shall be our laboratory, our home pharmacy. I want you to do the mixing—I can't be doing with the stinks. Spices always make me sneeze. Now, let's check we have all the ingredients."

Grace unlocked a drawer of the bureau and took out four small blue packets bearing the label of the local pharmacy. Her mistress took a crumpled scrap of paper from her jewel box, smoothed it flat and, putting on a country accent, read out the four items scrawled on it. The affected voice was meant to convey the roughness of the handwriting done in indelible pencil: "Rose Mary, Finnigrig, Sinnimun, Oil of Cummin." She handed it to Grace for inspection.

"All present and correct, ma'am, though the chemist spelled some of them differently," Grace commented and put it away in her pocket.

"Right-oh. Now you have to mix them all into a paste and spread it over the piece of cake."

"But they're mostly powders, ma'am," Grace said, peering into the packets. "How'm I supposed to make a paste?"

"Oh, don't be such a weed! Think of something!"

Grace looked about her. "Your cocoa, ma'am? If there's a drop left in the bottom of the cup . . . It'll add to the flavour."

"Of course! Here, take it. Why don't you combine all the ingredients in the cup? There, that's the way. Urgh! How simply ghastly!" Her ladyship held a handkerchief to her nose. "What was that you just put in?"

"That'll be the cumin. Smells worse than a pigman's old socks. This fenugreek isn't much better. Took me ages to get it out of the chemist. Old Morrison pretended not to know what I was on about when I asked for 'finnigrig' as it says on your list. 'It's a mite special,' he says, 'and not for putting about the place.' And what did I need it for anyway, he wanted to know. He's a suspicious old cove! I told him cook had requested it to make a curry. Indian gentleman expected at the house next week. That shut him up."

"You think of everything, Grace. Now mix it all up."

"Yes, ma'am. Anything else you'd like me to slip in there while I'm at it? 'Eye of newt? Toe of bat? Adder's fork?' . . . How does it go?"

This was greeted with a shriek of laughter. "That's 'toe of frog,'

I think you'll find. And, no, I shan't be needing any of that rubbish. Not when I'm in possession of *bone of toad*! That's the real stuff! Here, Grace, I want you to stir the mixture with this. Careful now! It's precious! I'm not sure how strong it is. It looks a bit ancient to me. And I've sworn to give it back to its owner again in one piece." She took from amongst the silver toiletry implements on her dressing table tray a three-inch-long piece of bone, the colour of old ivory and forked like a chicken's wishbone. She handed it to her maid, who took it with a shudder of distaste and stirred the mixture gently with it.

"Now, set the bone to one side to dry out and check in the morning that I've got it safely hidden away in my left pocket. It has to be the left because that's the side the Devil favours or some such rot. The bone's the important bit of the magic. Absolutely crucial! Nothing works without it."

Grace dropped it onto the supper tray, turned her back on her mistress and made the sign of the cross over her chest. "Didn't much care for the feel of that old toad bone in my hand, madam. Cold and soapy. It fair gave me the creeps." Her voice was pitched unnaturally high with the strain of daring to disagree with her mistress. "Not sure we ought to be fiddling about with magic. It could all turn nasty."

"Nonsense! *Untested* magic I would have no truck with, but I've seen this work with my own eyes. Magic? It's practically science! I have my information and instruction from the very best practitioner. Neither of us must breathe a word, though, or we'll have the clod-hopping peasantry of this whole benighted county vowing vengeance. Mum's the word, Grace!"

Grace bit her lip and bobbed to show her understanding. Her city-bred mistress forgot—or didn't care—that her maid was of Suffolk stock herself. She tinkered about for a few minutes more, the homely activity of spreading and slicing the gingerbread calming her. She began rather to enjoy herself, like a child at a dollies' tea party. "There, that's all done. It's neat and in a hand-sized lump, but it's a bit sticky. I'll put it into one of these empty chemist's bags so it won't spoil the inside of your pocket."

"Thank you, my dear. Put it away in the closet for the night, will you, and spray my pillows with rosewater. Then you may retire. It's almost midnight! Leave the door unlocked so that you can come straight in without knocking in the morning. We don't want to wake the whole house. Just be sure to wake me well before dawn."

NIGHTTIME SHOWERS HAD left the ground sodden, and Grace was glad she'd had the forethought to search out a pair of gumboots in her mistress's size in view of her destination. It was quite a hike down to the Home Farm, and at crack of dawn on a misty April morning, the stables were likely to be a bit nasty underfoot. The wind had turned at last, sending rainclouds racing away in tatters, and a slash of pink on the eastern horizon promised a fine fresh morning. In the darkness, Grace could only just make out her ladyship, but she could hear her clearly enough and cringed as she heard her hailing the two stable-boy escorts in her hunting-field voice. She was wearing a sensible riding outfit over which she'd flung a baggy waterproof cape with two large pockets.

The lads, blinking and bleary, answered up shyly, assuring her that all was ready. She turned with a triumphant smile, patted each pocket in a pantomime of exaggerated care for Grace's benefit and gave a playful farewell flourish of her riding crop.

Grace, from the back doorstep, watched her mistress march off into the morning mist to perform her magic. The maid's body twitched as training did battle with instinct; dutiful obedience helped her to fight back an almost uncontrollable urge to chase after her and somehow find the words that would persuade her to give up her mad scheme. Resentment and anger flared, and thoughts beginning with "Serve her right if..." had to be quickly censored. The woman had no idea what she was dealing with, the danger she was running into. Grace had done her best. She'd always had her doubts but, this time, she'd taken advice from one who would know and acted on it. It wouldn't be the first time the maid had deflected harm and criticism from the mistress and always without acknowledgement, let alone thanks.

A last flurry of rain came from nowhere to slap her face with cold reproof, and she hurried back inside to seek out warmth and companionship in the kitchen.

THE HORSES WERE already awake, stamping and neighing gently, listening for the sounds of their grooms. The horsemen were as regular as clockwork and would be here to feed them their first bait of the day at five o'clock. The two lads collected gear from the tack room as they'd been told to and presented themselves, ready to harness the horse their mistress had picked out. She led them past the lines of saddle horses and through to the farthest corner of the cobbled stable yard where the farm horses were billeted. Eight magnificent Suffolk Punches, the pride of the Home Farm, held court here. Four matched pairs—expensively matched, all being of the coveted bright chestnut colour—would, by seven, be fed, brushed, harnessed up and turning out to work the fields.

The men were behind by a full week with harrowing the winter wheat, waiting for the chill east wind to stop scything in over the North Sea from Russia. The heavy horses, too, had had enough of this long winter. They had sensed the change in the wind and, raring to go, stepped up to their half-gates. Sleek, noble heads peered out, red-gold with intelligent eyes, welcoming the sounds of humans in the yard with a gentle whickering. The boys had grown up with these animals. They knew them as well as they knew their brothers and sisters. They started to count the familiar faces: Boxer, Scot, Jolly, Joker, William and the two mares Blossom and Gypsy. Seven heads. The lads exchanged glances full of foreboding.

Number eight was refusing to show himself.

Her ladyship stopped in front of the last stall in the line. She held up a hand, and the little procession came to a halt.

They'd been praying that something or someone would intervene before she got this far, but here she was, only inches now from the Devil himself and half an hour to go before the horsemen came whistling down to work. The moment had come and the boys, brothers Sam and Tom Flowerdew, stood ashen-faced, twitching with a fear they were unable to express. They would normally not have ventured to say a word to their mistress on any subject and, if addressed directly, would have reddened and stumbled over their answer. Even so, pushed beyond the limits of reticence, the older of the two, Sam, burst out: "Beggin' your pardon, missis, but 'es a right terror, that 'oss! 'Es new. Master not long bought 'un. We nivver so much as got a halter on 'im. 'E done for 'is leader, owd Jonas! Bit 'is 'and clear off to 'is elbow."

"Terrible great yeller teeth 'e 'as!" Tom breathed in support of his brother.

"Then 'e put Reuben in 'orspital. Don't you go near, missis!" Sam finished and fell silent.

This was the longest speech he'd ever made in his life, and he was horrified by his own boldness. The lady was well known in the county for her horsemanship. She was a fearless rider to hounds. No horse under her was ever known to refuse a fence, and all returned from the field in a lather of exhaustion. Just like her poor old husband, they joked in the village pub when they'd had one too many of Martha's ales. Sam had gone too far, and now she'd probably sack him and his little brother for impertinence. Would her anger extend to their father? The old fellow held a tied cottage on the estate. It went with his job on the land, and if he lost it, they'd all starve. They remembered what had happened to old Walter's widow and her kids when she'd crossed her ladyship. The old bat had waited until the Master was away, then thrown the family out without notice.

But the lady didn't seem to have retribution on her mind this morning. She was glowing with confidence, putting on a show, you might say, and the boys were her puzzled audience.

"Enough of that defeatist talk, you two! Jonas and Reuben clearly didn't come properly prepared. Now, get behind me if you're nervous. All you have to do is stand ready to put his harness on when I've finished speaking to him. What's his name?"

"We call 'im Lucy, missis."

"Lucy? I understood the new horse to be a stallion?"

"'Es that all right. Got all 'is bits and pieces. It's short for . . . Lucifer." He muttered the name under his breath. "But 'e don't answer to it, 'cos we don't say it out loud—it'd be like calling up . . . you-know-who, missis. We dussn't go near. We 'as to lower 'is fodder and drink through the roof. Until the vet come with 'is gret big gun. Due tommorrer, Mr. Hartest is."

"Well, Mr. Hartest and his great gun will find their services are no longer required. I want you to watch carefully what I'm about to do. In a few minutes we will have the head halter on him and he'll be stepping out following me like a poodle on a lead. I intend to take him for a little promenade right up to the front door of the Hall to parade him for my husband and his guests. Such ones as are gathered at the breakfast table." Lavinia peered at her wristwatch. "Good. We're slightly ahead of ourselves. That will give me and Lucifer time to get acquainted. The gentlemen will soon be coming down to breakfast—there's to be a shoot later on this morning." She gave a laugh tinkling with good humour. "You boys will be the first to witness a Lady charming the Devil. You have my permission to pass the story round the village. In fact, I insist that you do—none of your usual Suffolky bashfulness! Ready? Then draw back the bolts, stand clear and prepare to be amazed."

The boys shot the bolts and hurried to obey the second command. They watched from behind the corn hutch as their mistress patted her left pocket, then fumbled about and extracted something from her right. Holding out what they took to be an offering for the horse, she moved confidently forward, cooing, "Come on, Lucifer, my beauty! See what a treat I have for you . . . Oh, don't be shy . . . I won't hurt you . . . Here, take it . . ."

The expected furious charge forward with pounding hooves and snapping teeth did not occur. For once, the horse hung back in his stall. Snorting and clattering, he appeared, if anything, to be moving backwards to avoid the cooing advance.

The boys flinched on hearing a shriek of protest as piercing as the unearthly screams you heard on butchering days round the back of the knacker's yard at the end of the village. But their mistress paid no heed to the stallion's distress and took another step forward, thrusting her hand towards his flaring nostrils. From the depths of the stall came the flash of eyes rolling in fear, a neck arched aggressively, ears flattened to the skull, the huge head stretched out parallel to the ground. The whole fury of the one-ton, seventeen-hand body seemed to be channelled through the bared and vicious teeth from which foam dripped in gobbets.

Tom began to sob. Sam put a protective arm round his brother's thin shoulders and called out a last desperate warning.

A further harrowing scream followed, human this time, and the scream ended abruptly in a gurgle. The stallion appeared at the door of his stall, wild-eyed, the body of his mistress clamped by the neck between yellow teeth that opened a source for the runnels of blood and froth coursing down the folds of her cape. He shook her once, twice, as a terrier shakes the life out of a rat at the harvest hunt, and dropped her onto the wet cobbles. For good measure, two massive, iron-shod feet reared up and smashed down on the already lifeless form.

CHAPTER 1

The card arrived at the breakfast table sealed in an unassuming brown business envelope delivered with the morning post. Catching sight of her name on it in handwriting she recognised as she sorted through the pile, Lily fished it out and put it with the rest of her mail. This consisted largely of unwanted advertising material coyly addressed to "The Lady of the House." While her husband grunted and exclaimed over his own morning's haul, Lily read her message, eyes widening briefly in excitement. She passed a hand delicately over her mouth to smother a deceiving yawn.

"Everything all right, Lily? You're letting your egg congeal."

"Not quite awake yet, darling." She slipped the card back into its envelope and shuffled it in with the rest. She shrugged one shoulder. Nonchalant. Bored. "Here's another invitation to buy one of those floor-cleaning machines from Harrods. Nothing personal—they seem to be targeting the housewives of Hampstead," she murmured, passing over a flyer singing the praises of Mr. Hoover's latest invention. "It beats as it sweeps as it cleans, apparently."

Her husband sighed, took it dutifully and favoured it with a cursory look. He gave a sharp bark of laughter. "Have you really read this, Lil? Look—it claims to work according to a new cleaning principle: *positive agitation*. It beats out the dirt and extracts the whole unpleasant mess, leaving behind a fresh home you can be proud of. I'm all for a little positive agitation! I shall adopt it as my motto." He returned, still chuckling, to his own correspondence.

"We could do with a new cleaner, but they are expensive. I'll see what Emma thinks. She's getting a bit cronky—had you noticed?—and could do with a bit of extra help." Lily peered across the table at her husband's copy of the *Times*, lying open at the sports page, and read the headlines upside-down with no difficulty. "Gracious! Can Middlesex possibly have lost to York-shire? Again?"

She listened with half an ear to the genial huffing and puffing and the sporting explanations that followed her attempt to distract, preoccupied by the words she'd just read. In black ink, chiselled characters on a white card:

My office. 9:00 Tuesday. I have a problem I'd like you to help me with. S.

Waylaid by memories, Lily fought back a smile and lowered her eyes to her plate in case they were shining with more emotion than could reasonably be accounted for by a congealed egg.

Her husband rumbled on companionably, reminding her quite unnecessarily of his imminent business trip, as he called his secretive forays into Europe. "Packing coming along is it? . . . Good . . . I say—it's beginning to look more like ten days now with this excursion into the Black Forest. Ugh! Pop two extra ties in, will you, love? Oh, and shove in a pair of long-johns—we're promised a flight in an aeroplane. Nasty, draughty things, aeroplanes."

"Yes, dear. Will six pairs of underpants do? There's bound to be an in-house laundry service. Browning or Beretta? I wasn't sure, so I've left that for you to decide."

"Oh, Browning I think. I'm hardly likely to use it, so I may as well impress them with the bulk. German military tailoring hardly minimises the size of the opposition's bulges; in fact, I think that's the point of it. They'll be eyeing up my Browning while I'm admiring their Lugers. Both useless for close-up work. On second thought, I'll pop the Beretta in there as well. Don't bother with hats, darling. I'm planning to buy something suitable when I get to Berlin. Bit of local cover called for—don't want to be taken for an Englishman on holiday. Would you find me fetching in a green felt Tyrolean with a feather in the side? What do you say, Lil? Lil? Are you listening?"

She gave him the cheerful mechanical reassurances he expected.

"Well, I have to dash now . . . Look, my dearest Lily . . ." He came round the table and took her hands in his, suddenly earnest. He gave her the devastating smile that had knocked her for six so many years before. "Just go and get one of those machines . . . those vacuum thingamies . . . you know what I mean . . . I see the very idea of one brings a flush of excited anticipation to your damask cheek." He winked and caressed the damask cheek. "Now I wonder how Harrods could possibly know I've just had a pay rise?"

He'd guessed. Of course he had. That was one of the penalties you paid for being married to the smartest man in the kingdom. She handed him his briefcase, put her arms round his neck and kissed him. He bit her ear.

LILY WENTWORTH (AS was) entered the reception hall of Scotland Yard at ten minutes to nine on Tuesday morning and announced herself. She acknowledged with annoyance that her knees were trembling and she was breathing fast. The formidable building still had the power to intimidate, however often she ventured into it. Everyone else was walking purposefully up and down the tiled corridors wearing a police uniform or a business suit with bowler hat and briefcase. In her lady-heading-for-Liberty's outfit, she felt herself doubly an outsider. Staff changed swiftly at the Yard, and no one called out a friendly "Wotcher, Lil!" How long had it been? She calculated that it was eleven years since she'd received the first of his summonses. Each one had changed her life. Some had left scars, on flesh and spirit.

The young copper assigned escort duty took her up to the top floor in the lift. Sharing the confined space with a stranger was always awkward and, after an exchange of pleasantries, they fell silent. Out of the corner of her eye, Lily watched him doing exactly what she expected a young officer would be doing with a new subject in a lift. He was filling in his mental portrait form. Page 22 of the trainee copper's handbook. She followed his glance as he made his top-to-toe clandestine observations:

> *Subject: Female.*
> *Nationality: English.*
> *Married status: Unknown (gloves worn).*
> *Height: 5' 6".*
> *Build: Slim.*
> *Age (conjectural) . . . mmm . . . thirtyish.* (She flattered herself.)
> *Hair: Fair, short and waved.* (What he could see of it.)
> *Eyes: Green.*
> *Distinguishing features: Surgical scar to right jaw, not totally disguised by a layer of Leichner's shade number 2: 'Porcelain.'*
> *Purpose of visit: By invitation, to attend Assistant Commissioner Sandilands.*

Lily sensed that his exercise became trickier when it came to evaluating her outfit. He noted her smart cream linen two-piece and matching cloche hat, she thought, with quiet approval. The gloves and shoes were impeccable, but his eyes snagged on the one jarring note in her appearance—a leather satchel she carried slung from her shoulder. Unlike the neat purse just about able to contain a penny coin for the loo and a cologne-scented handkerchief that London ladies clutched to their bosoms, this capacious and battered object was decidedly utilitarian. Lily sighed. Time perhaps to exchange her old friend for something classier from Vuitton? The copper frowned in puzzlement and, sensing his unease, Lily reassured him in her best Mayfair voice that her bag had been checked at the reception desk.

It hadn't.

The desk officer had given it a cursory look and waved her straight through without bothering to search it. Lily didn't want to risk a sudden panicking lunge from her dutiful escort in the confined space of the lift and she gave him a broad, disarming smile. He was right to be watchful. She knew she didn't look like a Sinn Féin gangster's moll, but there was a chance she could have been one of those demented society women the Mosleyite Fascisti cultivated and cajoled into doing their bidding. It wouldn't have been the first time an apparent innocent had walked into Scotland Yard with a hidden explosive.

As the lift lurched to a halt and he opened the doors with a flourish, she eased under the young man's outstretched arm murmuring a word of thanks and added, "Suit is from Monsieur Worth and perfume from Mademoiselle Chanel, Officer."

This was greeted by a shout of laughter. "And smile from Heaven, miss!" he told her gallantly. "The assistant commissioner's a lucky chap! Don't know how he does it!"

"THERE'S A BOMB in there!

"*Bam! Splat! Bam! You're strawberry jam!*" Lily announced in playground Cockney, slamming her bag down under the Assistant Commissioner's nose.

"Always ready with the warm greeting, Lily! But no need for

concern. I told the desk inspector to pass you straight up, unmolested."

"Then you're losing your marbles . . . getting slack. Your modern anarchist doesn't go about with a smoking bomb under his cloak, twitching and frothing and muttering Ruritanian curses. It's quite likely to be some posh lady with a bee in her silk bonnet and a hand grenade in her crocodile-skin purse. How do you know I haven't started an affair with the dashing Oswald, King of the Blackshirts, since we last met? He's cutting a swathe through Kensington, I understand. Breaking more hearts than limbs. Oh . . . sorry! Hello! So pleased to see you again, Joe! How are you doing, old thing?"

"Apart from the onset of senile decrepitude you've just identified, I'm fit and well and very happy to see *you*. Shall we sit down and I'll introduce you to my problem? . . . Ah! Here comes our coffee! Thank you, Constable Smithson. You set a lovely tray! On the side table, if you please. Now, buzz off, lad—we'll wait on ourselves. Here you are, Lily . . . Blue Mountain in Worcester china . . . nothing but the best for my favourite flatfoot. Oh, and a gypsy cream or two to nibble on . . . So there you are. It comes with a warning, Lily," he said after a brief outline. "What I'm putting before you is covert and unauthorised. I don't think it could be dangerous . . ."

"When did you ever offer me an ice cream in the park? Do I need a gun or will a hatpin do the job?" Woman Police Constable Lily Wentworth, as she had been a decade earlier, spoke with sunny disregard to her old boss. "I sharpened my claws before I came. Though I'm surprised there's anything I can still do for you in your new elevated status, Commissioner." She looked around with exaggerated appreciation at the large top floor room with its windows open to the river and the Victoria Embankment below. The impressive desk across whose polished surface they were exchanging delighted grins carried only a severely stylish pewter pen tray and inkpot. Scottish by the look of it and Joe's own choice, she guessed. The absence of files, notes and memos at this hour told of a team of secretaries and a pool of typists at work early somewhere about the building. The empty wastepaper basket and freshly polished floor were further indication of others unseen ministering to the needs of the top police brass.

He was looking the part, she thought, in his well-tailored suit and quiet tie. Far too young for the job, but then he always had been ahead of his time. She remembered that, at her first interview with him, the freshly appointed Commander Sandilands, dishevelled and disorganised, had greeted her with papers spilling off his desk and a face haggard with exhaustion and despair. Alarmingly, his hands and clothes had been damp and still stained with the fresh blood of four gunshot victims. His reputation, his handsome looks and his battle scars had combined to render her practically speechless in his presence. Now, the sleek surroundings and the equally sleek appearance were reassuring. Surely, at last, she could let go and ignore the urge she had always felt to rally round and protect him.

"I'm listening. Tell me what you're really up to, Joe." He'd never liked to waste time, and his pace was her pace. They worked well in harness.

"Getting to the bottom of a mysterious death in high places. So high, people dare not even gossip about it. Nothing ever reached my desk until last week and, unless I've been remarkably slow on the uptake, I don't believe I've ever been passed a hint over a whisky in some concerned gent's club, which is the way these things often start."

"Has it been reported in the press?"

"No. Apart, that is, from an unremarkable mention in the obituary column of the *Times*." Joe fell silent, sunk in thought. "She merited four lines, Lily. Just four lines. The problem, you might say, has been buried six feet under and left to rot away. Unnoticed. Unmourned. To all appearances."

"No police involvement, you say?" Lily asked, eager to hear more. She'd learned to pay attention and give weight to Joe's suspicions over the years.

"Initially, yes, there was. A token enquiry. The county police force involved—efficient fellows, I'm told—have pronounced themselves satisfied there's been no dirty work at the crossroads. 'Death by misadventure,' the coroner announced. I can't imagine why I'm letting myself be drawn into all this. The nearest anyone comes to suggesting that all may not be well is an occasional hissing intake of breath, a quiet shaking of the head and—of all ploys!—an attempt to squeeze a comment from *me*! I who know less than anyone! What really cuts me to the quick is—I fear people actually suspect me of involvement in the cover-up. I won't have that, Lily."

"Gawd! It's the Prince! He's in trouble again? I thought he was safely off in Africa shooting things."

"If only it were so simple! That would be much more easily settled. His every move is recorded, preventive measures in place. At home or away, he's only a danger to the beasts. This enquiry, if my worst fears are well-founded, could involve stepping into unknown territory strewn with man-traps and mines."

"And you want me to tiptoe through the tulips ahead of you?"

"Not quite as bad as that! In fact, it might be just what you'd enjoy. Two nights of luxury, staying at a very discreet, expensive and well-regarded hotel 'in the heart of clubland,' as they advertise themselves—the Castlemaine. Just off St. James's—do you know it? Invent your own cover story—single woman up in town for the shows, the museums, that sort of thing. Here's your subject. You're to keep an eye on this gentleman. A fellow guest." Joe passed a photograph over the desk.

"He looks smooth. Powerful." Lily looked at Joe anxiously. "Sure you know what you're taking on, Joe?"

"No. That's the whole point. I don't. There are things I need to know—relationships I need to understand. I've been having this chap covered by officers from the Branch, with little to show for it. I can't tell you how bored they were. They report everything ship-shape and Bristol fashion—a man leading an impeccable and busy life. I can come up with no further justification for continuing the surveillance of one exemplary Englishman, and I've had to stand the men down. You know how tight my budget is. We need all the men we can muster to get in amongst these Blackshirt clowns who are making our lives a misery."

"But a couple of nights at the Castlemaine will make a bit of a hole in your expenses for the month, won't it?"

"Yes. And tricky to account for. I shall enter it as 'specialist consultation fee.' The formula's held good so far. And worth every penny to the State!" His voice was warm with pride and encouragement. "I've made certain that the people who need to know these things are aware of what you've saved the country in embarrassment, hard cash and lives . . . starting with the Prince himself. Inestimable—that just about sums up your contribution, Lily, to Britannia's well-being. No one's going to raise an objection."

"But the State—I'm inferring—is so far unaware that it is in need, again, of such service as I can offer?" There was a trace of doubt in Lily's voice as she foxtrotted jerkily around the subject, then she plunged in and asked, "This isn't something personal, is it, Joe? You must have enough authorised, official enquiries on the books to keep you busy? All that civil unrest . . . Communists, Fascists, Hunger Marchers, demanding your attention."

"To say nothing of the 'Mothers for Clean Living League.' They cause more damage and use up more police time than any political faction. I won't tell you what they got up to at the Dorchester! But, Lily, I will always investigate the suspicion of murder. I spend a great deal of time sitting on committees and signing forms these days, but I still know which questions should be asked, and I have the energy to nag away until I get an answer."

"The ferret still likes to get his paws dirty? You're not letting this one go, are you?"

"No. I can't. What's more, I know that a clever, well-trained woman can sometimes get further down the rabbit hole than I can. Lily, I want you to stay under the same roof as our gent this weekend and just watch him. That's all you have to do."

"Something special about this weekend?"

"I think so. It's an aberration in his schedule. He's a man who doesn't take time off. It's out of character for him to go quietly to earth in this way. He's booked their best suite. Under a false name. Well, not very false! He's booked in as 'Mr. Fitzwilliam.' He used his mother's maiden name, would you believe?"

"Hardly a seasoned conspirator?"

"You'd say. But that's all we have."

"Is *Mrs.* Fitzwilliam expected to be joining him?" Lily asked carefully.

"No sign of a lady. So far. It's his contacts I'm anxious to identify. I want you to note who meets him, goes to his room, shares a drink with him, passes him a newspaper . . . lights his cigarette . . . You know all the tricks."

There was concern in Lily's voice as she pointed out the obvi-ous: "Joe, you must recognise this setup? It's a divorce case in preparation. I don't mind mixing it with murderers or spies, and I'd cheerfully knock the stuffing out of a Blackshirt or two, but I won't be involved with divorce cases. I'm not that sort of agent. You know that. I get enough psychological drama at home."

"Divorce is certainly not an aspect of this case, Lily. I say again—murder may well be."

Joe's old officer listened to her briefing, asking a few quick questions, and he nodded in relief when she accepted the task.

"You never thought I'd say no, did you?"

"You miss the work still, Lily? Oh, I know you're happily in the married state, but I do note the sparkle in your eye when you catch the scent of the fox! By the way, Bacchus doesn't know anything about this."

Lily gave him a pitying look. "Bet he does! That husband of mine knows everything about everybody. Including you, including me. Start from there. It can be frightening, but that's how it is. You've conveniently sent him off to Berlin, sniffing out British Nazi sympathisers—or so I'm guessing ... Bacchus tells me nothing—leaving the little wife to get up to all kinds of naughtiness."

"The children, Lily? Can I offer ... ?"

"Taken care of. Aunty Phyl's always glad to ride to the rescue and is well backed up by our Emma, who can always sleep over. Dick and Hattie send their love and wonder when they're going to see their godfather again."

Joe smiled broadly. "Summer holidays coming up next month! I'm planning a children's party—or at least, my sister's planning a party—down in Surrey. Swimming, camping, tree-climbing, cakes and ice cream ... that sort of thing. They must come."

"They're very fond of you, Joe." Lily looked at him with affection and concern. "You're used to my bluntness, so I'll say it: time you had kids of your own. Anyone on the horizon who might oblige?" She knew she was the only one who had ever been close enough to Joe to ask searching personal questions. His sister, Lydia, was very dear to him, but she received only edited and optimistic summaries of his London life. Lily, on the other hand, had never suffered from upper-class delicacy, and she reckoned that if you never asked, you never found out. He'd saved her from a nasty end in a swirling Thames whirlpool early on in their acquaintance and that had put him, paradoxically, forever in her debt. A life you've saved is doubly precious, and she knew he would grant her any favours. She would do the same for him and hoped he understood that—he would never have allowed her to speak the words.

She was puzzled to see that a frown and a long silence preceded the smile as he replied cheerfully enough: "Oh, yes there is. The unlucky girl is Dorcas Joliffe. She's well on this side of the horizon, in fact. Sailing into port, you might say. I don't believe you've ever met her, though I'm sure you've heard me speak of her?"

Eyes wide with astonishment, Lily could only nod.

"Yes! That Joliffe!" he said, answering her thought. "And before you ask—she's twenty-one these days, soon to be twenty-two. I tell people she's the daughter of a neighbour and dear friend of mine, which she is. She's also by way of being my sister's ward. She's been away . . . I mean, out of my life for seven years and only came back into it again in January. We were last together in . . . April, I suppose it was. The Easter break before she went back up to college for her final term. She'll be wanting to tell us all how well or otherwise she did in her finals. She's been trying to call me with her news for the last two days, but . . ." His voice trailed away as he heard himself turning querulous. "You know how it is."

"Good lord! Well, I never!" And, doubtfully, "Are you sure?"

"Well, there you have it, Lily. No, I'm not sure. I mean about the future. She loves me, I love her. Always have. We're having a very happy time and it's all going to end eventually in marriage. But, but . . ."

"You haven't asked her yet, have you?" Lily said shrewdly.

"Hole in one! No, I haven't."

"Why on earth not? It's not like you to be reticent. You can talk your way into or out of anything." Struck by a sudden thought, she added: "Have you two . . . ? I mean . . ." Lily failed, for once, to summon up words acceptable enough to disguise her intrusive question. "Er . . . plighted your troth?" she finished with an awkward attempt at humour.

"Troth well and truly plighted, I'm glad to say," Joe replied comfortably, picking up and running with the euphemism. "Though Dorcas would fail to recognise the phrase—she's a very modern young lady. She's not your average English Miss, Lily. Something of a free-thinker. In fact, 'bohemian' is probably the kindest word that comes to mind to describe her style."

"Then I can't see what's holding you up."

"The problem's not with me. It's difficult. She's quite the academic, you know. She won't let me use the word 'bluestocking' but that's what she is these days. She was a late starter on the degree business but took to learning like a duck to water. Most girls her age are either married or snatching desperately at the few good men left standing, but Dorcas doesn't seem to care much about domesticity. She speaks scathingly about friends she's made at the university, girls with good brains who work away for three years and then give it all up because they've met and got engaged to another undergraduate with wonderful prospects, or none. Dorcas has made it plain that's not for her. She's planning a few more years of research into her subject. And this is where the problems arise. Now—if she were fiddling about writing a thesis on, oh, the disputed authorship of *Titus Andronicus*, I'd tell her to put her pen down and let it remain a mystery, but it's not ivory tower stuff she's involved with. It's scientific enquiry which could benefit mankind, she tells me. It's difficult to set one's unworthy self up against the Good of Mankind."

Lily sighed. "Oh, dear! I can understand why you haven't fallen to your knees yet then. Might as well ask Marie Curie to stop stirring that filthy pitchblend and go and put the cabbage soup on. Poor Joe. Poor Dorcas. There's no entirely happy solution. I didn't find it." More hesitantly, she added, "Though I think you ought at least to put a proposal before her. Perhaps she's just waiting for you to come out with it? You know—putting on a show of couldn't-care-less independence in case the offer's not forth-coming. That was my situation exactly with Bacchus."

Joe grinned. "Was I the last one to twig that you were con-ducting an illicit affair for two years with my top Branchman right under my nose?"

"Yes. And the only one to object to him making an honest woman of me. 'Over my dead body,' I remember you said."

"No—over *Bacchus's* dead body—you misremember! Reduc-ing my two best agents to one at the peal of a church bell was never going to please *me*."

"It wasn't easy. We knew we loved each other but he knew I loved my job just as much. That's why he held off asking me to marry him. James is a thug—I can't say you didn't warn me. He'll beat a man senseless, put a bullet through him if he has to, but he's not entirely insensitive. He could see I was having a ripping time and thought I might choose to stick with the police force and reject him—choose danger over domesticity. Because that would have been his own choice if he'd had to make one. His own *masculine* choice. He couldn't grasp that I might be willing to give up all this"—she rolled her eyes with humour around his office—"for a lifetime of cooking and cleaning. But I loved him," she finished as though that were explanation enough.

"How did he get around to ... er ... ?"

"He never did ask me. Oh, he intended to! He took me out for a romantic dinner at the Savoy and all the signs were there that he was working up to saying something important. But he dropped me off on my doorstep at the end of the evening with not a word spoken. He kissed me good night and turned to go. I lost my rag. I grabbed him by the ears and said some very unpleas-ant things. 'Cowardly stinker ... Conscienceless seducer ... What a waste of an evening ...' That sort of thing. I finished with an ultimatum. He had twenty-four hours to ask me to marry him, or I was off to Paris to manage Aunty Phyl's new dress shop on the Rue St. Honoré."

"Seems to have worked."

"Not then and there. He still couldn't find the words. A bloke fluent in half a dozen languages, and he couldn't come up with the four little words I wanted to hear in any of them! In the end, he had to get a little help from Dickens. I got a note pushed through the door next morning. It said: 'Bacchus is willing.'"

Joe snorted with laughter. "You were lucky you got a joke in English! It might have been something pithy from Pushkin. Now, what was *his* contribution to the Sighing Suitor's Manual? *Habit makes the heart grow fonder.* That always clinches it for me!"

"Anyway—do it properly, Joe. You don't want to overhear Dorcas telling an unflattering story like that in years to come. Give her something to look back on with pleasure. Some romantic tale to thrill or amuse her friends with. There's three things that'll fix a proposal in any girl's memory: A special place, an unexpected gift, some silver words." Lily gave him a sideways glance of mock assessment. "A bloke like you, living in London in June, not without a bob or two, with a tongue that can charm birds out of trees . . . There shouldn't be a problem. But do it straight away. When are you seeing her again?"

"Very soon. She's been away, but she'll be back home in Surrey this coming weekend when her term ends. My sister's laying on a family welcome-home knees-up. I'll be sure to make time at some stage of the junketing to come out with something memorable. 'Sandilands is certain,' I shall say. Or: 'How about it, old gel?' Which do you advise?"

Lily smiled her approval. "That's settled, then. I shall think about you on Saturday night while I'm sipping my Sancerre in solitary state, one beady eye on this exemplary Englishman of yours, watching him toy with his lobster."

Joe was suddenly concerned. "Hang on a minute! Not quite

sure I like the scene you're conjuring up. You're a very attractive woman, Lily, to be out and about in the West End by yourself. A potential target. I think I'd better arrange for back-up."

"A police chaperone? Not on your nellie! Not unless the lovely sergeant on reception happens to be free. He had a bit of a twinkle, I thought. But quite unnecessary. What could go wrong? You *are* worried about this, aren't you?"

"It occurs to me—belatedly—that Englishmen, even pillars of society, have been known to crumble under the influence of wine and the allure of a smile across a candlelit room. If you add in the sense of security a discreet establishment offers—well—a powerful fellow like this, with all the good looks and wealth you could wish for, might just throw caution to the winds."

Lily raised her eyebrows, exasperated as always by his delicate circumlocutions. The only concession he made to her sex.

"I mean, in a state of unbuttoned ease, he might just be minded to offer himself a little well-earned distraction," Joe elaborated.

"It'll make a nice change from fending off the plumber then. Joe, you know how I deal with drunken chancers . . . or, as you'd put it, an excitable bloke with designs on my virtue."

"You seize him by the ears and demand marriage, evidently," Joe said. "Sorry, Lily! It irritates you, I know, but I can't help fretting about your safety. And that reminds me . . . Look here." He reached into the top drawer of his desk and took out a small, neat handgun. "Just in case you come across any excitable blokes this weekend. It's your old Beretta. Licenses all up to date and in order, but I wouldn't want things to get to the point where someone had to check."

"Nor would I. I'll take it in the spirit in which it's offered," Lily said, unbuckling her satchel. "Spare ammo with that? Thanks. I'll get some practice done before we kick off. Just the weight of it in there is reassuring. Let's hope they don't spring awake and think of frisking me as I try to make my way out of here. I'm sure I won't need to use it. The setup you describe doesn't bring to mind either of the two things that have me reaching for my gun: villainy or politics." She pursed her lips and frowned. "Now, the best suite at the Castlemaine . . . that'll have a luxurious bathroom attached, two double beds, a sitting room, possibly a study . . . room enough for an orgy, in fact, if he were so minded. No, it's pretty clear your subject's looking forward to a weekend of steaming romance. Perhaps with someone as shy of being recognised as he is himself. Now—which heartthrob can we think of who's in London at the moment? Lolita Benevente? Marlene Dietrich? Ivor Novello?"

And, with the gurgle of amused irreverence that had always lifted his heart, "Perhaps if Noël Coward's in town too, we'll find we've uncovered an after-the-show get-together of the Naughty Set? A spot of sinning in St. James's? I'm going to enjoy this one, Joe!"

CHAPTER 2

Ten minutes after Lily left, the reception officer was greeted by a gentleman requiring an immediate audience with the Assistant Commissioner. The officer, unimpressed by the urgency of the man's manner, checked and rechecked his duty log.

"May I ask if you have an appointment, sir? Assistant Commissioner Sandilands appears to have no further appointments scheduled for this morning."

"No, I haven't, but if he's in the building, he'll see me," the gent told him confidently and passed his card over.

Sir James Truelove, it announced, giving a home address in Suffolk and a town address in Albany, Piccadilly.

The desk officer was an inspector working light duties while recovering from an injury. He was experienced and aware enough to fill in other details for himself. Truelove. Minister for Reform and Education. Generally expected, in the course of his ascent to the highest office in the land, to become the next Home Secretary with overall responsibility for the Forces of Law and Order. Police, Special Branch, Secret Services, the keys to the Tower of London, all in his hands. Sandilands' future boss? His own future boss? The inspector's voice took on a more respectful tone.

"I'll let Commissioner Sandilands know you're here, sir." He picked up the telephone and kept an impassive face as Sandilands barked back at him.

"You've got *who* down there? Truelove? Hell's bells! No . . . no . . . quite right, Hawkins. Bad timing, though—I've got a meeting with Flying Squad in ten minutes. Darned nuisance, but you'll have to show him up, I'm afraid. Yes, yes. Right away. Just make time for me to order up a couple of mugs of tea and straighten my tie." A throaty Scottish expletive accompanied the slamming down of the receiver.

"The assistant commissioner will be delighted to see you directly, sir," the inspector said with unctuous formality as he signalled for an escort. "But first, your briefcase. Would you mind passing it over, sir? And the keys? A necessary nuisance, but it shouldn't take long. Charming weather we're having, wouldn't you say? June can be so uncertain . . ."

"ALWAYS A PLEASURE to see you, Sandilands," the minister murmured, shaking Joe's hand. Again, Joe was taken aback by the workaday roughness of the hand, which seemed at odds with the suave appearance of the rest of the man. "We don't meet often enough. Both busy men, of course, but we must make time. I'm back in London for the next four weeks and insist you meet me for lunch at my club."

A constable appeared with a tray while the two men were still on their feet exchanging pleasantries. "Ah! Thank you, Smithson," Joe said. "That'll be all. I hope you can drink Assam, sir?"

The minister grabbed a mug, helped himself to two lumps of sugar, stirred, sipped, exhaled with pleasure and sipped again. "Nothing like a pot of Typhoo at this time of the morning!" Grasping his tea with the casual assurance of a stonemason, the spoon tucked away behind his thumb, he strolled over to the window and looked out, admiring the view as Lily had done an hour earlier.

"Third floor, is this? Not much higher to go! Got your eye on one of the turrets, have you?" His grin was quizzical, his tone light, his meaning all too clear.

"I don't really care where they put me, so long as I can see a tree or two," Joe said, shrugging away the challenge.

The minister peered out at the full-canopied ranks of greenery below. "Quite agree! Country men like us—we take our spring, our vigour, from growing things. We have a physical need for green arteries across the city, the parks which are its lungs. Whoever decided to plant London plane trees along the Embankment last century certainly knew his business. Coming on well!"

"You're right. Of all trees, they have the knack of surviving all the city can throw at them," Joe murmured blandly, wondering when the man was going to get to the point. Was it possible that he'd just turned up at his office to say, "Hello, I'm back in town, why don't we have lunch together"? An unlikely waste of time. Still, you didn't rush a minister.

"It's all to do with the bark, don't you know," the time-waster went on, apparently preoccupied by the view. Or was he simply avoiding looking Joe in the eye? "That dark, dappled, camouflage colour they develop is due to the pollutants in the air. They absorb the nasty bits and when the moment comes, they shed the infected bark and leave a gleaming pure trunk underneath. Clever stuff, eh? I love the plane. Hardy, resilient, useful. And, you know, they have a certain air of authority—some might say magnificence."

"Just the right tree to plant outside Scotland Yard, then," Joe remarked. "The Met would seem to perform the same function as the London plane."

This sally was greeted by a shout of laughter. "Cleaning up the filth while remaining unsullied by it all?"

"That and the magnificent authority you mention, sir."

"Well, don't worry. I'm not imposing myself on you this morning to test you on your arboricultural knowledge. Or to invite you to dabble in further pollution." He left a pause in deferential recognition of Joe's recent sticky contact with the underbelly of English society. "My business is a personal one, Sandilands."

It was always likely to be. Everything was personal with Truelove when it came down to it. Joe recognised that his foreboding was about to be justified. The affair this man had involved him in some months earlier had proved a sensitive one. The minister had emerged with an enhanced reputation and a further department in his portfolio of power. The police officer had just managed to hang on to his job. And there was always the nagging resentment that the man held a place of authority and, Joe admitted, regard amounting to affection, in the life of the girl he loved. Dorcas talked unselfconsciously of her patron's interest and support, acknowledging—without resentment, it seemed—that she owed her budding career to the Truelove family endowment; his good will and his cash were essential for paving the way to her academic goal. It was more than resentment that Joe felt towards this charmer. He didn't deceive himself. There was a heap of jealousy and a dash of impotent rage in the mix. The perfect scenario for a clash of antlers.

He put his head on one side and wondered if the Lord of the Glen would ever stop pawing the ground and declare himself. He hadn't until this moment realised that the man had been chattering on to hide his unease. Wondering what earth-shaking crisis could make this man uneasy and alarmed by the admission that it was of a "personal" nature, Joe feared the worst.

Fancifully, he waited for the minister to smack him with a glove and suggest they throw their wigs down on the duelling green in the square outside Parliament. At dawn. "First blood," would he demand, or "*à l'outrance*"? Joe was already choosing his second and deciding that cool, ruthless James Bacchus would fit the bill admirably.

"Fact is . . . I need to ask a favour of you . . . No, nothing at all

untoward," Truelove added hurriedly, catching the slight narrowing
of Joe's eyes. "It amounts to two hours of your time—at the most."
And, with an awful echo of the comforting phrase Joe had just used
to Lily, "It's a small task and—who knows?—you may even enjoy
it. Do you know Christie's—the auction house in King Street?"

"I do indeed. I've spent many happy hours there over the years.
My old uncles collected—and sometimes sold—works of art,
antiques, valuable books there. They took me along as a young
thing and trained me in the art of survival in the shark's pool that
is an auction house. I still dabble occasionally. Yes, I know it."

"I'm glad to hear that. I was well briefed." The glancing look,
complicitous, humorous, was meant to suggest that his informant
was Dorcas and invited comment. Joe gritted his teeth and wondered how much more the wretched girl had confided about his
life and character. He glowered and maintained a cold silence.

Truelove took a catalogue from his briefcase and handed it to
Joe. "Page twenty-seven."

Before opening it, Joe inspected the cover and read:

> *Messrs. Christie, Manson & Woods*
> *respectfully give notice that they have been instructed by*
> *Mr. J. J. McKinley*
> *to sell at auction his renowned collection of Miniature*
> *Portraits at the*
> *Great Rooms, King Street, London SW1 on Wednesday*
> *June 21st 1933*
> *at 11.00 A.M.*
> *This collection makes one of the finest galleries of minia-*
> *ture portraits formed in modern times,*
> *comprising over three hundred examples of the best works*
> *by British and Continental artists*
> *from the sixteenth to the nineteenth century. There are*
> *examples of the work of Nicholas Hilliard,*

Samuel Cooper, Richard Cosway, George Engleheart,
J.H.Fragonard and other eminent artists.
    The collection will be on view throughout the week preced-
ing the sale and for one hour before
    bids are taken.

"Wednesday the twenty-first? That's tomorrow," Joe commented in puzzlement. "Thinking of taking a punt on a Hilliard,
are you?"

"No indeed! Nothing so grand, I'm afraid. If you'll just turn
to page twenty-seven . . . There. Well down the listing. Thrown
in at the end with no fanfare. Unattributed, you see. Artist
unknown. What do you make of those two?"

Joe looked carefully at the matched pair. Watercolour on
ivory, the description said. The illustration was in black and
white, but the quality of the oval portraits set within simple gold
frames shone out. The lady on the left was a beauty. Fair hair
curled naturally around her forehead, pale eyes—blue?—held a
touch of mischief reflected in the slightly curving mouth. Pearls,
lace, satin and plump silken bosom seemed all to have found
favour with the anonymous artist. The lord on the right, presum-
ably her husband, had an equal glamour. He wore his own dark
hair sleekly combed about his neat head, his eye was commanding,
his mouth firm. A velvet coat, a swagger of gold epaulette, a flash
of more shining braid on a striped revere framed a froth of expensive lace at his throat. A diamond pin glinted in its depths. Joe
was enchanted and intrigued. He remembered Truelove had
thrown down a challenge. The man *would* do that.

What did he make of them? Not difficult to return an answer.
"Delightful," he said. "I advise going straight down there and
putting in a bid. Unattributed as they are, some lucky devil could
get these for a song. Portraits, miniature or full-size, are not
exactly going like hotcakes in today's market. It's all photography

and cubism these days. One does rather wonder at the wisdom of unloading an entire collection on to the market in one fell swoop. The whole exercise in itself risks further devaluing the art form."

"I dare say." Truelove clearly didn't share Joe's concern about fluctuations in the art market. "But the standard of the painting? And the sitters? What do you make of them?"

"The quality is of the very highest as far as I can make out from these reproductions. The sitters themselves, husband and wife, I'm presuming, are people of some rank. They would naturally have employed the best talent Europe could offer to take their likeness. No wigs, you see—hair not even powdered—and by the style of the clothes and the jewellery, I'm guessing Regency. The second decade of the 1800s. There is an artist—and the best available at this time—who sometimes failed to put his signature on his work . . . Um . . ." Joe searched his memory.

"You're thinking of George Engleheart. The chap painted nearly five thousand of these things during his life. You'll find his name on the back, mostly, but it wouldn't be surprising if he failed occasionally to sign his work, particularly when he was getting on a bit. By the time he painted these, George would have been an old man of nearly seventy. It's my theory that they were done by a much younger artist. Any more thoughts?"

"The sitters themselves are intriguing. Very attractive pair. Young. The fashion of the times was to have one's likeness preserved on ivory as a betrothal or a marriage gift. I'd guess that's what these are. Betrothal, most probably."

"Why do you say that?"

Why *had* he said that? Truelove was listening with flattering attention. Joe plunged on, with a strong feeling that he was running in blinkers. He tapped the face of the young man. "The girl looks too innocent and happy to have been long in harness with this sour-puss opposite. Oh, handsome, certainly, but . . ."

"Grim? Forceful?"

"Not someone you'd choose to down a pint with. Look, sir, if you really don't know the identity of the gentleman, I can give you a clue. If this jacket should prove to be red—" Truelove nodded. "— and the edging a dark blue grosgrain striped in gold . . ." Another nod. "Then he's wearing the uniform of an officer in the East India Company. An army man who's served in India. He's either married, or is on the point of marrying, an English heiress. If you look carefully, you'll see through the open window in the background a piece of bravura miniature painting." He produced a magnifying glass from his desk drawer and handed it to Truelove. "If I'm not mistaken, that's a freshly planted avenue of lime trees marching off into the distance. The kind of landscaping you often see defining wide acres of opulent estates a century or two ago. I don't recognise it, but I think *you* might. I'd say an inquisitive man could stroll along to the record room at the War Office and check the army lists, collating names of officers serving in India and match one of them with that of a Suffolk landowner of the period."

Truelove grinned. "Someone told me you were a detective, Sandilands. I shall heed the warning. It is, indeed, in Suffolk. The lime avenue is still there. And the lady and her gentleman are my great, great, I forget how many greats, grandparents."

"Congratulations, sir! Are you going to tell me how your ancestors have fetched up in a London auction house on view to the world and on sale to the highest bidder?"

"They disappeared from their display case at the family seat before the war. One of those long golden Edwardian summers: 1906 was it? Something like that . . . I wish I'd paid more attention. I was a boy, just home from Eton, more interested in snaring rabbits and popping off my airgun than works of art, but I can just remember the hoo-ha and the excitement of having the Plod on the premises. The pictures were assumed to be stolen, by person or persons unknown. But all that unpleasantness is behind us. It was investigated, of course, without result. No one was ever arrested or even came under suspicion at the time. Family members, staff and a company of friends assembled for a shoot were present, among whom, a royal personage."

"And you don't rush about the place shrieking, 'Stop thief! Let the dogs loose and bring in the Bobbies!' with King Edward on the premises. Too embarrassing."

"No. You wait until the guests have departed and then you invite the local force to attend and allow them to grill the servants. There are hoops to be jumped through for insurance and other purposes. Tedious stuff. But it was thought better to make light of the loss. Whoever did pinch the pair was employed by the family, was known to them, perhaps even *was* one of the family. Really—kinder and more discreet not to find out."

"The local force, you say?"

"No, in fact." Truelove shrugged. "Apple-scrumping and poaching are as bad as it gets in the peaceable county of Suffolk, Sandilands. We are stirred by the odd outbreak of fisticuffs in a dockside tavern in Ipswich at the other end of the county occasionally, perhaps. Anything more demanding is dealt with by the Cambridge force. The city's only twenty-odd miles away, they have a smart detective section and a well-equipped crime laboratory."

"I'm surprised they were prepared to take an interest in a small-scale inside job."

"They weren't! I think they knew my father had no intention of bringing charges, but they went through the motions. They were glad to get away back to the city. They had an outbreak of murders on Midsummer Common on the go at the time. Much more their style!"

"What were the findings in the case?"

"Not sure it amounted to 'a case.' Notes were taken but

nothing so formal as a file ever came out of it, I'd say. Father wouldn't have wanted that. Whatever it amounted to, it was swiftly wound up."

"And your father's requirements cut some ice with the city force?"

Truelove gave a dismissive grin. "You know how it is. He was at school with or in the same regiment as the Chief Constable—the old Chief Constable. I believe the station's under new management these days."

Joe's suspicions were confirmed. He'd observed the progression of affairs like this before. The servants must have had iron-clad alibis; otherwise a dutiful country police force would have made arrests. One of the sons of the household, having open access to the artworks, could have snatched something small enough to put in his pocket. If Joe had been in charge of enquiries, he'd have determined which offspring had made a sudden dash abroad in the ensuing days or weeks. A nifty bit of arm-twisting at the local bookies and a consultation with the Yard's expert in the Art Theft and Fraud Department would have settled the matter.

"Sir James, if you want me to pursue this crime after two decades and a world war, I don't offer much encouragement. But we do have an excellent art affairs department here at the Yard. I'll introduce you to its head and you can tell him what you have in mind. I'm sure we'd all like to know how these came to be in the possession of . . . who was it? . . . Mr. J. J. McKinley. Never heard of him. Christie's are meticulous on verifying ownership and provenance. They wouldn't knowingly be involved with stolen goods."

"Not what I want at all! I'm not interested in unravelling the past. I live in the here and now, Sandilands. No, I just want your discreet self, Commissioner, for an hour or so on Wednesday to slip along to Christie's and put in a bid on my behalf. These are mine! I want them back, and I'm prepared to pay whatever it takes. I have a particular purpose for them. They couldn't have surfaced at a better time, in fact!"

Joe paused for a moment to consider the man's deeper motives. He could have chosen anyone as his agent in the matter. His lawyer, his secretary, a trusted colleague—there must have been dozens of men whose names came to mind before that of Sandilands. So what special trick could *he* possibly bring to the party? Joe thought he knew and the thought didn't please him.

"Not sure who you think might be bidding against you, but I'm guessing that the mere presence of a top policeman sniffing about and showing a warm interest might well scare off any opposition? Is that what you're calculating?"

The man didn't deny it. In fact, he hurried with disarming relief to confess to manipulation. "Exactly that! The man I fear may turn up and bid against me is an international art expert and purveyor of dubious goodies to rich collectors. Almost certainly known to you. Name of: Despond. Guy Despond! He pronounces his Christian name the French way—'Guee.' Despond as in 'slough of.' He's in town with his family. This includes a pretty daughter and two brattish sons. The father is of Eastern European origin, I believe. He speaks English with an American accent. His children speak in any language you care to name. They are all much travelled. Do you have anything on him?"

Joe pretended to consider this. "Your plan would be for me to feel his collar and heave him along to the clink to cool his heels until the sale is safely over? Sorry, can't oblige."

"I say—could you really do that? I must admit I hadn't thought *that* far but—yes—it sounds like a corking idea to me!" Joe was surprised to hear Truelove chortle with boyish glee. "Shove him in the Bow Street nick for an hour or two! Sure you couldn't . . . ? Oh, well. Pity! You must be aware of his reputation?"

"I know what the world knows from the newspapers and

society reviews," Joe said, noncommittal. "Tough opposition in a sale-room. He just has to show his face and people tear up their bidding cards and withdraw. Bottomless purse and a queue of rich customers on both sides of the Atlantic. He buys in Rome and sells to New York. Then he buys back in New York and ships the goods over the Atlantic again to London or Paris . . . The hold of the Berengaria is stuffed with goodies on almost any trip, I hear. A sort of floating Tate Gallery. I don't like to imagine what would happen if she ever sank!"

"He'd make another fortune from the insurance companies. He's careful. He's very influential too. A self-promoting former of taste. Whatever Despond decides will be the next craze becomes exactly that—with inevitability." Truelove was amused, if not admiring. "He's not a man to just happen on clients. He seeks out rich men—women, too—and he cultivates them with the care of an obsessed grower of rare orchids. He educates them in his own tastes, he instils in them a thirst for a particular art form or artist, then dangles the very objects they now desire in front of their eyes. With a hefty price tag attached. I've seen less professional acts on stage at Wilton's Music Hall," he finished with bitterness.

From his tone, Joe wondered whether Truelove might be speaking from personal experience of Despond's machinations.

"You'll just have to hope he isn't planning that this shall be the Year of the Miniature, sir," he said lightly.

"I never place much store by 'hope,' Sandilands. Crossing fingers, pestering saints, tying ribbons around trees—not my style. I plan for what I want. That's why I'm sending you in. I think you know what must be done. Will you do it?"

Joe had no intention of becoming the minister's minion. He should have sent the upper-class chancer shirtily on his way, muttering darkly of the dangers of abuse of authority; should have delivered a flea in his ear, a kick up the derrière. Why wasn't he showing him the door? He recognised that he'd been captivated by a mystery, charmed by an ancient beauty and caught once again on the hook of the man's ambition. All that, he could have resisted. No—more important—he was unable to turn down the chance of digging up more information on this unknown who threatened so much that was dear to him. Information Joe might store away and use to his advantage, should it ever become necessary. The more scurrilous, the better. Would that amount to blackmail? He rather thought it would. Perhaps, after all these years and all the bad examples, he was learning a lesson from Dorcas. She would have called it "taking sensible precautions against disappointment."

"It's a personal matter," Truelove had announced.

"Too right!" Joe growled silently. But he heard himself saying: "I'll see what I can do. I shall need to know your upper limit."

Truelove smiled in satisfaction. "Good man! Tell me—how are you planning to . . . ?"

"Don't concern yourself. I'll just say—no need for clanking handcuffs or police whistles. There are quieter ways."

"Ah! A touch of your sophisticated shenanigans? I can see I've come to the right shop! Oh, there is one thing more. I'm making it quite clear to the management that in the event of a successful bid I want possession of the goods at once. They are to hand them straight over to you after the sale. There won't be a problem—I've dealt with them many times before. They're aware of my impatient nature. I'll collect the goods from your front desk. I'm assuming the front desk of Scotland Yard is a reasonably secure place to leave a pair of miniatures?"

"More secure, apparently, than your country seat, Sir James. Melsett, would that be?"

WHEN HIS GUEST had completed his briefing and left, Joe telephoned down to the inspector on reception. "Well, thanks for that, Hawkins! What a treat you sent me! Look, I'm going to have to cancel the rest of my morning and my lunch hour. I shall be back at my desk at two o'clock, should the Prime Minister decide to pop in for a chat."

He went to stand by his open window, breathing in lungfuls of air freshly filtered by the stout London planes below him until he felt calmer. The future Minister for Law and Order had just told him two whopping lies. He was only aware of two, it could well be more. The portraits? A smokescreen, a glittering diversion, Joe was quite certain. The man was clearly spending too much time at Wilton's Music Hall. Joe grinned evilly. His lordship wasn't to know how many hours his pet plod had spent in the line of duty, watching magic acts from the wings of seedy theatres in Soho. Joe knew all the tricks.

CHAPTER 3

With a hasty glance at his watch, Joe rang for his secretary and warned Miss Sturdy that he was going out and wouldn't be back until after lunch. He took the time to make one or two phone calls himself to cancel the rest of his engagements and spent a further five minutes studying the catalogue Truelove had left with him. Only then did he ask to be put through to the Art Investigations Department for a consultation with its head, Superintendent Pearce.

A little reassured by what Pearce had to say, Joe prepared himself to take advantage of the advertised viewing time. One day before the actual sale, he reckoned he had probably missed the most fruitful moment to make his appearance, but he had to work with what he'd been given. He might not be lucky enough to be caught showing an interest by that smooth villain Despond himself—a busy boy like him was hardly likely to stick around personally in the sale-room for the whole week— but he would have his spies out at all times, observing and noting the names of anyone paying more than passing atten- tion to any item he'd marked down for himself. Comment and gossip to the point of hysteria were rife in this world, and Joe was confident that the show he was about to put on would raise eyebrows and be the talk of St. James's before lunch.

Christie's would not be pleased, but there was little they could do about it.

He smiled to himself with mischief. Truelove's brief had been short on information and shorter on tactics, but the required outcome was very clear. Joe would have his hands, by fair means or foul, on that pretty pair by the sale's end the next day. Yes, having committed himself to Truelove's mad scheme, he thought he might even begin to enjoy himself.

THE ELEGANT YOUNG man on reception was astonished. At the sight of Joe, he took a step back. He adjusted his lilac tie. He began to stammer. "Um . . . er . . . I beg your pardon, sir . . . but are we expecting you this morning? I mean, should you *be* here? Is anyone aware?"

"Well, my mother knows I'm out," Joe said genially.

He stood before the assistant in the entrance hall, holding his catalogue, his face alight with anticipation. He was aware of the reaction his appearance in full Assistant Commissioner's dress uniform was causing. The navy suiting, the excess of silver braid, the smart peaked cap were all in place. He'd even gone as far as hunting out a medal or two. The DSO and the ribbon of the *Légion d'honneur* still caught attention, even in these weary-of-war times. Joe wore this eye-popping gear with the straight shoulders and aplomb of the professional soldier he had been some years ago.

"Don't worry! Not here on police business. Just dropping in between fixtures to take a look at a pair of pictures that have taken my fancy. No time to slip into civvies." He handed his card over. "Perhaps it would be polite to advise your director that there's a friendly Scotland Yard presence in the room?" He leaned forward with a conspiratorial smile and suggested, "He may want to rush out with a screen."

The assistant gulped, took the card and excused himself, hurrying off to find a higher authority to deal with this nuisance.

While his back was turned, Joe took the opportunity to nip into the viewing hall.

He stood in the doorway to the Great Room to get his bearings and assess the crowd. A second or two's pause was long enough to absorb the atmosphere which never failed to excite him. He breathed in the warm scents of wood, leather, oil paint and polish and caught a passing high note of Penhaligon's Hammam cologne. The room was well lit by natural light, and Joe raised his eyes to the high ceiling, as he'd always done, to watch in fascination the golden motes dancing upwards in the shafts of sunlight. His child's imagination had made them out to be a precious mixture of slivers of gilding, specks of gold and silver and oil paint, but with his present knowledge of forensic science, he was ready to believe this fairy dust was in reality no more than flakes of human skin and possibly dandruff.

He glanced at the assembled company. Dapper city gents, suits from Savile Row, ties from Jermyn Street, haircuts from Raoul at Trumpers. No, perhaps no dandruff. Raoul didn't permit dandruff.

Joe strode forward to the centre of the room and stood, taking in the scene. He slapped his gloves against his thigh and wished he'd had his officer's swagger stick to hand. A thin crowd of no more than a dozen here, he decided, but enough to get the handle of the rumour-mill turning. And, at least, they were all looking at him. Conversation had stopped and speculative glances were being exchanged. He referred to his catalogue, checked the sale numbers of the miniatures he was interested in and made straight for them. All eyes followed him.

The portraits did not disappoint. He was instantly absorbed by them. Joe checked that his identification of the young officer's uniform had been correct, nodding with relief to see the rich red colour of the velvet coat with its contrasting blue and gold flash. A fine young fellow.

Only then did he allow his gaze to fall on the young lady. In colour she was even more appealing. The eyes were—as he'd assumed—blue, the hair had the colour and thickness of an August corn-stook. Her green dress was of a silk whose lustre the artist had seized on to express the undulation of a high and rounded bosom. The pearls encircling her neck were lavish. How painters enjoyed their pearls, Joe was thinking as he leaned closer to admire the glancing highlights. But the special quality of the portrait which, after more than a hundred years, leapt out and seized him by the heart was the expression on the girl's face. The smile, just fading—or being suppressed—betrayed an intimacy between the sitter and the painter. Though almost certainly amounting to no more than a moment of shared merriment given the circumstances of the encounter, it yet revealed an understanding of character that no photographic image was capable of replicating, Joe thought with regret.

He yearned to hear replayed the badinage that had just passed between them. What had he said, the painter, to leave those periwinkle eyes glinting with mischievous challenge, the red lips straining to hold back laughter? In contrast, the second subject's features were lacking in emotion, dour and watchful, his attention directed away to his right. For him, the painter hardly existed; he was a necessary means to an end, a time-consuming interruption in his active life. The kind of restless subject who, in a later age, would have appreciated the swift clunk of a camera shutter.

Joe became aware that he was sharing the viewing space in front of the items with one other interested party: a quiet man, and, like himself, totally absorbed. This suited Joe very well. He would be able to start up a perfectly natural conversation with the stranger, a conversation which might well be overheard by the room in general if he spoke in a cleverly pitched police voice. Joe exchanged a smile with the second miniature fancier, liking what he saw. The man was Joe's own age—perhaps a year or two older—dressed in a grey city suit with the tie of a Cambridge college. Clean-cut, handsome features were framed by abundant light-brown hair, which sprang out in all directions in defiance of recent attempts by a barber to exercise some control. The healthiest moustache Joe had ever seen adorned his upper lip. The sharpness of his eyes was accentuated by the honest wrinkles of a man who liked to spend his days outdoors. Large gnarled hands clutched his catalogue; large feet, comfortably rather than elegantly shod, were fixed in the military at-ease position. Difficult to place. Joe decided to hear the man's voice.

"Do you suppose they had a happy life?" Joe hazarded the first comment.

"Assuming he survived the plagues of India and the Napoleonic Wars and that she survived childbirth and boredom, I see no reason why not." English upper-class. Deep, smooth and confident, was Joe's first impression.

"Unattributed, I see." Joe changed tack.

"There's nothing on the front, but so often there isn't. It takes a complete egotist or an exceptional talent to clutter up the tiny space available with his own name, I've always thought. Would you scrawl your name across that glorious bosom? I wouldn't!" He shook his head and sighed his admiration. "In any case, I think I know the artist responsible for these. Beauties, aren't they? Wish I could afford them." The man held out his hand. "Adam Hunnyton, impecunious art-lover. How do you do?"

"Joseph Sandilands, similarly handicapped. Are you thinking of at least making a starting bid for them tomorrow?"

"It's not done to ask, Commissioner, and you know it. But I'll tell you anyway. Sadly—no. They will go for vastly more than I can afford. Though I did take the precaution of leaving a modest reserve bid with the auctioneer, in case by some chance they were to escape the notice of the public. Late in the day and unattributed—it was worth a punt. But I see from the presence of various luminaries of the art world, to say nothing of the presence of the

Law, all poking their noses in, my plans have come to nothing. I just wanted to take one last look. I can only hope they will go to someone who will truly appreciate them and not be stuck away in a bank vault for years waiting to increase in value."

"Ah, yes. I understand there may well be a certain international dealer of repute ready to scoop them up."

Adam Hunnyton's face flushed with a dark emotion but his voice was level as he spoke: "This young couple lived but sixty miles from here. They've been away in Italy for a quarter of a century. Time to come home. I don't like to think of them crossing the Atlantic but I fear that will be their fate. Unless . . . unless you're prepared to take steps, Commissioner? Does the Yard have any information on them? Anything that might scare off the bidders?"

He fell silent abruptly at the approach of the director on duty.

Joe smiled to see they were wheeling out their biggest gun. Clarence Audley came shimmering towards them in a pale grey morning suit and old-fashioned stiff collar, arm outstretched in greeting, a beaming smile lighting his way.

"Commissioner Sandilands! Welcome! My goodness, you're looking quite splendid today! We all risk being dazzled by the sun glinting off your frogging! We catch you between parades, I hear? Not come to arrest me, I hope!" he said archly. "It must be three years since we sold you the Italian primitive. I thought we'd got away with it! Is she still giving satisfaction, your Madonna? Glad to hear it! You got her for a snip!" He lowered his voice to just-audible and added, "Now we all know the painting to be Quattrocento . . . a Filippo Lippi? Can I have that right?"

"A lucky find," Joe said modestly. "The Madonna and Four Children all showed happy, smiling faces when I scrubbed them up."

Professional concern won out over the director's social preoccupations. He actually clutched his heart to convey sudden distress. "My dear fellow! I do hope you employed the very best—"

"Oh, a bit of spit on a hanky usually does the trick, I find."
Joe relished the crumpling of Audley's puffy features before put-
ting him swiftly out of his misery by adding, "Though in this case
I took advice and used Malleson to undo the dirty work."

Audley began to breathe again and recovered sufficiently to
grit out a playful, "No better spit and polish merchant in the business, we'd say. A good choice of restorer. Now, Commissioner, if
you should care to offer up your Madonna again, I think you
would be surprised to find how much she would realise in today's
market. Fra Filippo Lippi? A native of Florence, I believe. I'm
sure the Ufizzi would be interested. Do give it your consideration."
Mr. Audley's voice was a loud, warm purr. It announced to the
room that all was well. Joe was a valued and knowledgeable client—on teasing terms—and perfectly at home here. No threat to
anyone, least of all the auction house.

First round to Audley, Joe thought, admiring the man's skill
and regretting what he was about to do. Time for a bit of by-play.
He took Audley by his lustrous sleeve and urged him closer to
the portraits. He looked over his shoulder, checking that no one
was within earshot then lowered his voice. The audience shuffled
closer, straining even harder to follow the action. The policeman
could just be made out asking police-style questions regarding
the authentication process by which these lots had come into the
gallery. Joe listened carefully to Audley's earnest and—from his
previous enquiries at the Yard, he knew—honest answers. Audley
opened the catalogue, pointed to the description of the pictures,
and held out his hands clearly in protest of some sort of accusation. His replies were growing more concerned, more flustered by
the minute. At one of Joe's comments he stamped his foot in rage.

Glancing around the room again, Joe saw that two young men,
by appearance brothers in their early twenties, had crossed the
room to join each other and were whispering together.

At this point, Adam Hunnyton decided he'd heard enough

of the embarrassing exchange, which had interrupted his quiet contemplation of the art. With a harrumph of disgust, he turned on his heel, tore his catalogue dramatically in two and dropped the pieces on the floor. He levelled an accusing finger at the director and announced, "In the circumstances, I must ask you, Audley, to withdraw my reserve bid on those items, if you please!"

He stalked majestically from the room, followed by the admiration of the crowd.

Joe noted that the two men he took to be the "brattish" Despond brothers Truelove had referred to were sneaking out quietly by a side entrance. Joe reckoned that his job was done. Bidding Audley a friendly farewell and promising to return, he made his way to the door.

The moment he stepped out into the midday sun on King Street, a heavy hand of authority fell on his shoulder from behind.

"'Arf a mo! If you wouldn't mind, sir? I'm taking you in charge for impersonating a police officer, attempted fraud, confidence trickery and bloody bad acting."

At Joe's start of surprise, Adam Hunnyton released his grip, smiled broadly and growled in his ear, "Fancy a pint, sir? There's the Fleeing Footman round the corner, or, if you prefer it—the Grenadiers?"

"I think the Footman had the right idea. Let's flee with him, shall we? I expect they've got a nice little snug round the back where we won't run into any art lovers. And you can tell me, over a pale ale, how an honest country copper like you got caught up in this shaming display."

CHAPTER 4

The interior of the Fleeing Footman was dark, cool and welcoming. The style of the gentleman behind the bar was similar. His glance flicked for the briefest moment over Joe's uniform, making the discreet assessment of a good butler, before settling back on Adam Hunnyton, whom he seemed to know.

"Good to see you again, Mr. Hunnyton. Your usual, would that be?"

"Yes please. Make that two pints of India Pale Ale, Mr. Pocock. We'll take them through to the back parlour if that's convenient."

"I was about to make the suggestion. You'll find you have the room to yourselves and I will divert any further comers, unless you are expecting . . . ?"

"No, no. It's just me and the gentleman. We won't be infesting your belfry for long. We'll be gone before your first steak pie rolls up."

At the mention of steak pie, Joe realised it had been a very long time since breakfast and was about to extend the order but here was Hunnyton waggling his eyebrows in disapproval and muttering, "Put your money away, Commissioner. My round. Here, you are my guest."

They simultaneously drank a hole in their tankards of

cellar-cold foaming beer and carried them through to the snug parlour. They settled down on a red velvet-covered bench at an oak table and Joe looked about him, admiring the ancient space which had clung on in the Jacobean building, miraculously avoiding being swept away by three hundred years of constant redevelopment and a dozen changing architectural styles. The landlord had, gratifyingly, failed to fall for the temptation of cleaning off the years of brown tobacco smoke from the ceiling and decorating the walls with horse brasses and sporting prints. Though he seemed not to have availed himself of any of the goods from the local auction house to raise the tone either. A homely, moralising print of a drunkard, reeling around in sorry state in the style of Hogarth, was nailed up on a beam next to a more modern caricature of Harry Lauder, the Music Hall singer, offering the room "Just a wee deoch an doris." A last whisky for the road. The entertainer had left the pub his own "one for the road," Joe reckoned, a calculating stare convincing him that the drawing (on the back of a menu) was the work of Lauder himself. He'd signed it and smudged the brown whisky ring with his sleeve.

On the wall over the fireplace, in pride of place, was a framed maxim executed in superb calligraphy in gold letters.

Fit in dominatu servitus
in servitute dominatus. Cicero.

Joe translated freely for himself: "In every master there is a servant; in every servant, a master." Some sort of nod to the name of this pub, he supposed, and wondered from what or from whom the eponymous Footman was, by tradition, fleeing. Content with his surroundings, he sighed with satisfaction and raised his glass to his companion. "Your good health!" he said. "We've earned this!"

Both men sank half their beer in contemplative silence. Joe

judged the moment to say, "Thank you for your support back there in the sale-room, Hunnyton. That unscripted display of disgust was very convincing—and unexpected. But you were going to tell me how—"

"No. You have the advantage. I'll humour you. I'll let you tell me how you guessed. Was it the size twelves? Flattened by a year of pounding the streets?"

"That, yes . . . But you recognised my uniform and addressed me correctly by rank. I don't think anyone outside the force could do that with conviction. It was your name, though, that told me who you were. Not surprisingly. It's unusual. It's the name of an officer of a County Constabulary who has recently made enquiries of the art crimes section at the Yard. They keep extensive and meticulous records down there in the basement. And I do my homework! Your name came up an hour ago. I love what some call 'coincidences,' don't you?"

"I share your scepticism, Commissioner. I'm Superintendent Hunnyton, Cambridgeshire CID, and I'm very pleased to meet you. And entertained! I must say, I thought I'd blow a gasket when you winkled Audley out of his sleek shell. I've never encountered anyone actually stamping a foot outside of a romantic novel, but he did it! Well, it was more like a petulant tap of his little patent-leather-shod toe, if I'm being honest. It'll be all round the coffee-houses by now."

"Oh, dear. Yes, I regret upsetting the man. A manipulative, plausible rogue as all will tell you but he's very good at his job and I admire him. He's always dealt straight with me." Joe sighed. "Fences to mend there, I'm afraid. I feel especially guilty since my interest in the affair of the portraits, I'll confess, is peripheral. It's certainly not professional and it's not even personal to me. I'm just acting as agent on behalf of a . . ." Joe paused. What the hell was the minister to him? "An acquaintance," he finished lamely.

Hunnyton grinned. "Truelove ensnares everyone unless they're fast on their feet. Will he care if he's curdled your relationship with Audley? Not in the slightest! Get your long spoon out if you're supping with *him*, sir." Correctly reading Joe's astonished expression, he went on: "He's using you to get hold of them for him on the quiet, isn't he? Having scared the opposition off first." He began to laugh. "Clever bastard," he added genially. "How high are you instructed to go?"

"A hundred was suggested. Though he did say I could use my experience and judgement to exceed that if I scented victory."

"He certainly trusts you, then? I can't think of anyone *I'd* send into a saleroom for me with an open chequebook. What hold has he got on you?" And, to soften the boldness, a hurried and embarrassed: "Look here, Sandilands—sir—if there's anything I can do . . . Forgive me—you don't seem entirely at ease with all this. I'm a useful pair of hands and perhaps we coppers should stick together in the face of exploitation. Just say the word."

Joe smiled back over his glass at the troubled eyes and the leathery knuckles nervously swiping a springy quiff of hair from his forehead, glad that the mask was off and that he liked the bluff countryman's face beneath it. "The word is 'thanks!' But sadly, swiftly followed by 'no thanks,' Hunnyton. A hold, you say? My instinct is to splutter into my ale and deny he has any such thing. But the fellow is likely to take over the Home Office before we're much older and by that, become my boss." Hunnyton gave a sympathetic growl and Joe ventured to say, "Your boss, too. Apart from the political power, he holds the financial strings that the girl I love dangles from and he pipes the tunes she dances to. The Truelove Foundation sponsors research in her department at the university. The man has a scientific interest. He rolls up his sleeves and involves himself at the laboratory level. They work well—and all too frequently—together. He fancies his chances—she rebuffs him in a good-humoured way from time to time." Joe fell silent. This was a confidence too far.

He blamed the draught of excellent ale on an empty stomach and the sympathetic understanding of a stranger. All the same—loose words.

"Gawd! It's worse than I thought. Would you like me to push him under a bus for you?"

Joe laughed, glad of the invitation to make light of his confession and he replied in kind: "Don't you worry! I have several trained killers on the books who might oblige. I'm sorry to ruin your chances of possessing the miniatures but at least they'll be 'going home' as you said they ought. To Truelove's place in Suffolk. He has an ancestral home out there—not so very far from Cambridge. I expect you know it?"

Hunnyton nodded.

"A good and right outcome, I think you'd say?"

"Yes. None better," Hunnyton agreed. "If that's really where they're going," he added mysteriously.

They came to the end of their pints at the same moment and Joe prepared to take his leave. They solemnly exchanged cards, promising to be on hand for each other in any future emergency. Joe thanked Hunnyton for his hospitality and declared a polite intention to visit the pub again and stand his round.

"Ah. Might be some difficulty there, sir," the superintendent murmured as he handed Joe his hat. "You see, it's more of a club here. You have to be a member to buy the drinks. It's the headquarters of the Federation of Domestic Servants—the 'Narcissus Club,' as it's known. Named for the Narcissus who was slave, secretary and later freedman to the Emperor Claudius. He ran the Roman Empire in the name of his old master for many a year. Not to be confused with the self-regarding youth of legend who liked to peer into pools. Membership is granted to anyone of the rank of senior footman or above. And, of course, you have to have been in service in the family of a gentleman for a minimum of five years."

"Good Lord!" Joe said. "There are some strange establishments flourishing within the douce confines of St. James's!"

"This is a long way from being the strangest! Have you enquired into the 'Slippered Orchid' four doors down?" He shook his shaggy head in disapproval.

"Can't wait! Well, it was a pleasure, Superintendent. See you at the sale tomorrow perhaps? It should be quite safe. I don't think the Minister for Mischief will be making an appearance himself. Have you met the devilish Truelove? Do you know him?"

"I wondered when you'd ask me that." Hunnyton began to turn the brim of his bowler through his fingers, deep in thought. Joe didn't press for a response but let him take his time, mindful that people were very much divided in their opinions of the minister and quite often took a while to think of something polite to say. "I can't say that I know him. Though I certainly ought to. The man's my brother."

"Your *what*?" Startled, Joe dropped his fedora to the ground.

"My younger brother. Half-brother to be precise."

Joe snorted, hurried to the door and yelled, "Landlord! Two more pints in the snug please!"

He returned to the table, glaring at Hunnyton. "I never walk about town without a pair of thumbscrews in my back pocket. Shall I need to use them?"

Hunnyton held out his hands. "I'll come quietly. You can pull rank rather than fingernails. That'll do."

"I always find confessions slide down more easily with a steak pie," Joe said. "I'm sure I heard you mention . . ."

Hunnyton went to the door and called, "Confirm order for ale, Mr. Pocock, and will you add to that a couple of steak pies if they're ready? With horseradish, mustard and mash." He settled back in his seat. "You'll enjoy this, sir. Albert in the kitchens used to work for the Duke of Northumberland."

CHAPTER 5

Joe had picked up some relaxed phrases and refreshing attitudes from the American officers he'd worked alongside in the later months of the war. One of his favourites was: Once is happenstance, twice is coincidence, three times is enemy action.

He reckoned he was well into the stage of enemy action.

"I'm sure I shall," he said. "It's a Tuesday. You save me from the Police Canteen's version of not very Hot Pot."

He'd decided that Hunnyton—if that was his name—had recognised him, had even perhaps been lying in wait for him, and had drawn him here for a purpose. Joe had shared his information on the superintendent's interest in the portraits but was keeping silent on the second and more interesting record of the name Hunnyton that he'd turned up on police files recently.

The steak pie was all that had been promised, served swiftly and correctly with a flurry of starched white napery and good silver cutlery laid out on the table between them. By unspoken consent both men held off from serious conversation, content to enjoy a work of culinary art when it was offered.

"There's lemon syllabub or Eton mess to follow, or just strawberries," Hunnyton invited. "The Cambridge Favourites are in season at the moment. New variety."

Joe was glad he'd taken the hint and declared for the

strawberries; the plump miracles of summer magic were duly served on Delft-patterned dishes with a matching pot of yellow Devon cream so thick it had to be spooned from the jug. Finally, comfortably bloated, relaxed and unharried, Joe calculated that his subject must be feeling much the same and decided to come at him crabwise. "Tell me about your name, Adam. Truelove? Hunnyton? Should I guess at a mother in common?"

"Not that." The idea seemed to amuse him. "No, it's a father we share."

Joe absorbed this and was wondering how to frame his next question without giving offence when Hunnyton continued bluntly, "Illegitimate. That's the word you're skating around. You could—well, perhaps not *you*, Commissioner—could say by-blow. Wrong side of the blanket. Baseborn. Bastard. I've heard them all."

"And I've heard it said, Hunnyton, 'There are no illegitimate children, just illegitimate parents."

Hunnyton managed a smile. "Well, the guilty parties in my case were the old Sir Sidney and one of his domestic servants. Before his marriage to James's mother, the then young and spir-ited Sidney had an affair with a young and spirited upstairs maid. My mother. She had red hair—a big beauty in the style of Boa-dicea, Queen of the Iceni, who gave the Romans such a bad time. I'm just surprised she let Sidney get away with it undamaged. No one else ever got the better of her. Sorry, sir, it all gets a bit pre-dictable from now on and I risk boring my audience."

"Not at all," Joe said. "I'm all twitching ears and attention."

"The inevitable happened. In those days, and I'm not so sure it wouldn't happen now, the girl would have to leave the village for good or perhaps go and spend a month or two with her aunty in Ipswich. She'd return having mysteriously lost all that weight she'd been putting on. Childless, of course. But in my mother's case, the pregnant girl was married off hurriedly to a by no means unwilling man on the estate, the whole arrangement sweetened by the offer of a cottage on the village green complete with a half-acre potato patch and bake-oven. I was a six-month baby. 'Popped out just in time for a slice of his mother's wedding cake,' as they say in the village."

"And in Westminster!" Joe chortled. "Quite a few of those about, in all ranks of society. No names, no pack-drill, but I can tell you that one or two of our politicians have surprising dates on their birth certificates."

Hunnyton grunted. "They can keep it quiet. It's harder to hide in a small village. Especially when the child is unfortunate enough to grow up looking the spitting image of his real father."

"Good lord! Must have been difficult for Mr. Hunnyton, whose name I take it you bear?"

The craggy features softened in affection. "No. Nothing ever flummoxed the old feller. Head Horseman by trade. That's a pretty stylish thing to be in Suffolk. It has a certain standing and my stepfather lived up to it. No one would be disrespectful to him or his family, whatever that consisted of. He knew what he was taking on; he loved my mother very much, I think, and he was never less than kind to us. No—he was no Mr. Murdstone." He grinned. "Dickens would have found no inspiration for a heart-rending family saga in *my* early situation. Freud wouldn't have known what to make of a child with a loving mother and two caring fathers."

"Two? Old Truelove kept himself in the picture, did he?"

"He did. I think he took his inspiration from Charles II, whom he much resembled. Charming rogue but affectionate to all his offspring including the illegitimate ones. He had me educated. I outgrew the village school pretty quickly. When he noticed this, he put me into private tutoring alongside his other children. This led to three years at the university. Strings were pulled—perhaps money changed hands—and I was offered one of the eleven 'poor boy' places at Trinity. Reading a subject useful to my position in life, of course. In the good old tradition, Sir Sidney was having me raised to become steward of the estates. The land and the house were his passion and he was pleased to find, in me, an equal enthusiasm. I'd been keeping the accounts from the age of sixteen, buying stock, helping to run the farm. I was on the payroll from an early age."

"A position which gives you access to the best pies in town?"

"It's an honorary extended membership these days. I gave up my position of servitude—like many others—when the war broke out. I joined up."

"The Suffolk Regiment?"

"Second battalion. It was quickly mobilised, not short of volunteers, and sent off to France. We were there from Mons to the Armistice. The army changed my perspective. By the end, my mother and stepfather were both dead. I was twenty-six. I wanted to spread my wings. There were openings everywhere for big, healthy chaps like me with a degree in economics and a commission, and I chose the police force. For much the same reasons as yourself, I expect. Once I'd done the basics, promotion was quite quick, and I enjoy the work."

"Have you maintained your connections with the present lord of the manor? Sir James?" There was no sign in Joe's polite enquiry of his intense personal interest in Sir James.

"We were never bosom pals. I always felt he resented my relationship with his father. Looking like him, thinking like him, did me no good in Master James's eyes. 'Stop bossing me about, Adam! You're as bad as Papa!' he used to squeak. James favoured his mother. He's got that family's dark, handsome looks. And their talent for manipulation."

"To say nothing of their political clout and family money?" Joe suggested. "Perhaps the younger brother would provide more interesting material for Herr Freud?"

"There's no overt bad feeling between us any longer. We began to get on better after the old man died and he inherited. I've always admired his energy and intelligence. In fact there is—and always has been—a level on which we meet and understand each other. Under that glossy layer of sophistication there're some pretty rugged characteristics that he gets from his pa. Just tell him there's coppicing going on in the twenty acre wood and he'll be down there like a shot, wielding a bill-hook, and wielding it well. He can layer a hedge, grallock a stag and sink a pint of cider with the best of 'em. I taught him to ride myself. Picked him up, dusted him down and popped him back on his pony whenever he fell off."

Joe noted the unemphasised implication of Hunnyton's horseman's skills, learned from his stepfather no doubt, and he remembered his own older brother performing the same service for him as a three-year-old beginner. He remembered also the gratitude had been mixed with a much stronger emotion—a resentment that he was less skilled, less strong, less mature. Infantile frustration had so consumed him on one occasion that Joe had burst into tears and hit about him with his whip. Not at the horse, of course. His older brother Tom had borne the brunt of it, holding the squalling, thrashing child at arm's length and laughing until the rage subsided.

"Horses!" Joe said, shaking his head. "The stupidest animals ever invented, I do believe." He asked carefully, "Does Sir James still require a little dusting down?"

After a silence, an equally careful, "He finds me useful on occasion."

"Your half-brother begins to sound like the perfect English gentleman. Yet you recommend, I remember, the use of a long spoon when supping with him . . ."

"I do. It was perfect English gentlemen who carved out our Empire, let's not forget."

Joe smiled. "And how many of those devils would you turn your back on?"

"James is ruthless. He gets what he wants. Because he's able to ask for it with a charming smile, and thanks you with every appearance of heartfelt gratitude when he has it in his possession, doesn't mean he ought to have it in the first place."

"Hunnyton, this wouldn't be, by any chance, a roundabout way of getting me to foul up Truelove's bid for those portraits? I have worked out that they are *your* ancestors, too."

Adam laughed. "Nothing so obvious! I'd have just put such a proposition to you straight out. And been ready to accept a refusal. Sweetening with strawberries, were you thinking? Corrupting by confidence? No! Not my style. I'm not seeking any favours. But I may be doing *you* one. It's just a friendly warning I'm giving you. It may be all rubbish, the product of a suspicious copper's mind, but I wanted to plant the notion in your head that he may have an undeclared reason for getting his hands on these pictures. A reason that might not please you." He stirred uncomfortably in his seat. "Oh, I should learn to mind my own business. It's just that I can't sit back and watch him do another fellow down. I never could put up with a rigged fight. But suit yourself."

Hunnyton bunched up his napkin and put it on the table. It was clear to Joe that he'd said as much as he was going to say. Perhaps even more.

It had been enough.

Joe sat on, sunk in thought, cursing himself for a fool. His back was rigid and his face set in the mask of dread and resolve that precedes a battle.

Hunnyton, disturbed by the intensity of the reaction to his warning shot and uncertain what to do, reached over and tidied away Joe's napkin. He patted him on the shoulder. "Did I just hear the whistle blow? Time to go over the top, old man?" he murmured. "I'm right beside you."

CHAPTER 6

The auctioneer raised his gavel and cast a last inviting glance around the small number of potential buyers remaining in the sale-room at the end of the afternoon's proceedings. The sale had gone like a dream, faster than anyone might have expected, and now, in the dying moments, he could afford to relax and leave them all with an impression of unhurried professionalism. With a huge number to get through, it had been a good idea to mass most of them together into random lots—some more random than others. Baker's dozens, some wag had rudely called them. But no one had seriously protested. The true collectors had secured what they'd come for at a fair price and gone off to Fortnum's for tea. The good-natured crowd had been seemingly of one mind and mood: shift the stuff as fast as possible at the lowest price. An entertaining afternoon had been spent getting their hands on some precious works of art for a song. And the seller? Mr. J. J. McKinley would now have room in one of his mansions to accommodate his latest passion, whatever that was, and a few thousand pounds unrealised was neither here nor there to a man of his wealth. Everyone happy.

The auctioneer surveyed the crowd over his pince-nez and, with an all-embracing sweep of his ivory gavel, called them to attention. Belatedly, he would turn this bargain-basement rummage-hunt into a serious and possibly exciting piece of auctioneering theatre. The main players, he'd observed, were both still on stage. "Your last chance, gentlemen, to acquire a pair of betrothal portraits. Unsigned but undoubtedly the work of a master. And who would not wish to have this delightful lady available and constantly in the palm of his hand?" So near the finishing tape he could afford to be unstuffy, even playful. "I have an opening bid of fifty guineas from the discerning gentleman in the back row. Surely worth twice that amount! Any advance on fifty? Come now!"

Joe held his breath. Why didn't the man just bring down his hammer? What the hell was he waiting for?

He knew perfectly well what the auctioneer was waiting for.

His attention, like Joe's, was constantly, though surreptitiously, drawn to a balding, moustachioed man standing at the side of the room. Meticulously dressed in the style of a gentleman from a previous age, he could have just strolled in from the Champs-Élysées. Guy Despond looked at Joe, smiled with great civility and eased his bidding hand from his pocket.

Joe had studied his style through several bids. No raising of eyebrows, no twitch of a little finger signalled intent for this man. He wasn't in the least concerned to hide his bids. He stood erect and motionless throughout the proceedings, only his eyes flicking back and forth, taking in the opposition. When he was ready to make his play, he took his right hand from his pocket and signalled clearly with an emphatic downward chop.

The auctioneer had not missed it. His eyes instantly focussed on Despond and his gavel hovered in space, waiting on the movement of the lilac-gloved right hand. "Going . . . Going . . ." he said, enjoying the suspense.

The hand went up to chest height and Guy Despond's fingers fluttered outwards in Joe's direction in a gesture of mock-Elizabethan elegance which he was meant to interpret as surrender and congratulation. In his relief, Joe considered for a moment blowing the fiend a kiss but decided that an acknowledging tilt of the head was all that was required. He'd blotted his copy book already in this auction house and didn't want to worsen his situation with a show of music hall frivolity.

Quick to read the by-play, the auctioneer regretfully brought his hammer down. "Gone! Sold to the *cognoscente* on the back row. For the paltry sum of fifty guineas, the lady's all yours, sir."

Joe sighed with relief, relief quickly followed by suspicion. What was behind the overtly generous gesture? Despond had no intention of acquiring two pieces so effectively tainted by the Yard's very public interest and he could mischievously have raised the price higher and higher only to pull out at the last moment. Cynically, Joe recognised that, by the concession, Truelove was now—as this tight-knit world would see it—in his debt. A favour was owed. The whole charade was becoming ever more distasteful to Joe and he hurried to extricate himself as fast as he could.

HE'D PREPARED A bag suitable to put the pictures in and he'd addressed it to *Sir James Truelove. To be collected.* As he left it with clear instructions for the hand-over with the duty sergeant at the desk in Scotland Yard, Joe paused, smiled and asked the officer for a sheet of paper.

Sir James, he wrote. *Success! Despond out-foxed. These are yours for a meagre 50gns. A word of warning! 'Betrothal portraits,' as the auctioneer had it, can be a bit tricky. Anne of Cleves and Henry VIII? That all turned out badly on the first night, I recall, and the show folded. J.S.*

As he attached his note to the bag, the sergeant spoke to him. "Glad you called by, sir. There was a phone call for you. From your landlord. Half an hour ago. He wants you to ring him back. You can do that from here if you like, Commissioner." The sergeant handed over the telephone.

Joe grabbed it and asked the operator for a number in Chelsea. "Alfred? I'm here at the Yard. You wanted to speak to me?"

His landlord, a retired police inspector who lived on the ground floor of the ancient house that was Joe's London base, only ever rang him at the Yard to announce tersely: "Under attack! Am launching whizz-bangs!" He was quick, on this occasion, to reassure Joe that his business was not official. "Nothing urgent," he said. But, Joe reflected, his self-appointed guard dog would never ring him unless something was troubling him.

"It's your . . . it's Miss Joliffe. She was here looking for you. Her term's just finished, she said, and she's off down to your sister's house for a week or two. She said she'd tried the Yard first and they couldn't or wouldn't say where you were. She called in on the off-chance you might be sciving off down here. Anyway, she said she'd be seeing you at home in Surrey this weekend and would explain all then."

"Explain? Explain what?"

"Didn't confide. She just said, laughing-like, that she had a bit of a problem."

Joe groaned. "And we all know what that means, Alfred."

"Yers. Sorry to bend your ear with all this guff, Joe, but . . . there was something . . . she's a strange girl, anyways . . . I mean, out of my experience . . . Gawd, what am I saying? The lass is in a spot of bother, I thought. Twitchy. I told her you'd give her a call this evening. All I could think of."

"Don't worry about it, Alfred. She's always in a spot of bother. Bother sticks to her like chewing gum. She's probably run out of cash again and needs to buy a hat. It's Ascot week after all," Joe said with a lightness he couldn't feel. "But thanks for the warning. I'll do as you suggest."

He put the receiver down thoughtfully. He wondered if the wretched girl would ever call him with nothing but sunny good news. If only she were to ask him for cash, flowers, a night at the theatre, a hat for the races, he'd have been thrilled to oblige. The only help Dorcas ever asked for was in dealing with the baggage of death and disaster that she seemed to drag around after her.

A warning cough and a flick of the head towards the doors from the sergeant snapped Joe out of his gloomy thoughts. He followed the man's gaze and recognised Truelove about to enter the building. Drawing a finger swiftly across his lips, Joe took a few swift strides and ducked out of sight round the nearest corner. He felt foolish listening in to the conversation that ensued, telling himself that he was a detective and whoever he was, this man was not his friend. Spying on him was a legitimate, though uncomfortable, activity.

Truelove breezed up and stated his business.

Caught with his hand still on the package, the sergeant responded with aplomb. "Well, you timed that perfectly, if I may say so, sir. The Assistant Commissioner left it with me a moment ago before he went up for his meeting with the Commissioner." His eyes went automatically to the stairs with such conviction that even Joe thought he might catch sight of himself halfway up them. "If you'll just show me some identification . . ."

Truelove could not wait. The moment his hands were on the package he tore it open and examined the portraits. Only then did he read the covering note. Joe could not catch the expression on his face but he was intrigued to see him read it a second time and slip it into his jacket pocket. The portraits disappeared into the safety of his briefcase. Lastly, his hand went out and passed a square of white paper to the sergeant. Murmuring his thanks he turned and walked out.

After a safe interval, Joe strolled back to the desk, trying to look dignified. The bemused sergeant was still peering at the five-pound note he'd been given. He held it out to Joe. "You made the gentleman very happy, sir. What am I meant to do with this then? It's a fiver!"

A week's wages.

His face creased in sudden suspicion. "I say, sir . . . not handling anything we didn't oughter be handling are we?"

"Stolen goods, you mean, Sarge? Not at all! Quite the reverse, in fact. Sir James was so careless as to lose his possessions some time ago and I have just reunited him with his great-great-granny. But I agree—that's a lot of gratitude to show. However—it was a gift, freely given, and I'll bear witness to that. You can do one of two things—shove it in the Policemen's Charity box or take your wife out west for a slap-up meal. Your choice. I'm not going to stand about checking what you do. If anyone else calls I'm down in records for the next hour or two."

"Oh, sir, nearly forgot with all the hoo-ha . . ." The sergeant reached under his desk and pulled out a brown jacketed file. "This came by messenger from Cambridge. Do you want me to have it sent up to your office?"

Joe snatched it from him. "At last! I'll take it down with me. Thank you, Sarge."

AFTER AN HOUR'S feverish work involving two phone calls to the *Suffolk Advertiser*, he put in a third call to his old friend Cyril Tate in Fleet Street.

The ex-airman shot his targets with flash bulbs these days, his charm, tact and reassuringly good breeding getting him the close-ups he needed in the glittering world of débutantes, duchesses and divas the public wanted to see and read about. Cyril was trusted. "The soul of discretion, darling! You can confide anything and it never gets out. Unless that was the purpose of the confidence in the first place, of course. His photographs are flattering, too. He goes instinctively for one's better profile." No one man knew more about the intrigues at the highest stratum of English life, and his insider's knowledge, though clasped to his bosom, was occasionally shared with his contacts at the Yard. Several personages, one or two of them royal, owed their reputations or even their lives to Cyril while remaining entirely unaware of the debt.

"Hello there, Cyril! Still dishing it up for the *Daily Dirt*?"

"Joe? No! I'm contributing to the piles of *Fortnightly Filth* these days. I'm moving up in the world. Hear you are, too. Congratulations! Hadn't realised an honest copper could make it so far up the slippery slopes of Mount Olympus. What have you got for me? I can spare a minute or two but be sharp about it—I'm up to my ears in Ascot outfits. Big weekend coming up."

"I'm rather hoping you'll have something for me. I find myself involved with one or two dubious characters presently strutting the London stage. You know me—I always perform better when I know the other players' lines."

Joe put his questions, listened to the answers and made notes. Finally he could detain Cyril no longer and, promising the usual exchange of information should things resolve themselves, as Cyril always delicately put it, he rang off. He sat on for a few minutes reviewing the case he was building until the unease of the records department staff filtered through his concern.

With a brittle smile, a lady clerk brought him yet another cup of tea and a sergeant asked him politely but pointedly if there was anything else they could possibly supply. They didn't expect and didn't welcome the sight of an Assistant Commissioner down here in their dingy but busy space, commandeering a desk and a telephone, rolling up his shirt-sleeves and setting to work. Especially this Assistant Commissioner. Sandilands was a new broom and they said he missed nothing. "Watch it! He's going through the departments like a dose of liver salts. All fizz and pop and we're told we'll all feel better for it in the morning. But watch you don't end up down the pan. You heard what he did to Flying Squad!" the sergeant had muttered to his fellow officer.

They were watching him out of the corners of their eyes as

they sorted, stamped and filed, demonstrating a quiet efficiency. Acknowledging their discomfort, Joe got to his feet, gathered up his things and apologised for his intrusion.

The sergeant had expected peremptory formality. Disarmed by Joe's smiling thanks for the staff's assistance, he hurried to hand him his jacket and asked, with some relief: "Did you get what you were looking for, sir?" His interest sounded more than polite—it was a genuine enquiry and he was waiting for a reply.

He deserved one. Joe had not failed to notice the intelligent anticipation with which the officer had accepted the irregular tasks Joe had set him once the wider objective had been sketched out. One of the files he'd thought to hand to Joe had been outside the prescribed area and had turned up a vital piece of information. It would certainly have been missed had not the Assistant Commissioner been sitting, an anxious and demanding physical presence, amongst the troops.

Joe found himself answering with less than his usual reserve. "Oh, I got it, all right. It's all here. Wrapped up neatly in closed and separate files. No reason for anyone to re-open them and connect them; the information I needed is spread across county boundaries and three decades. Trouble is, Sarge, instead of the one dead woman I was chasing after, I find I've got *two* on my hands. Now—I have to ask myself: do we leave these files closed, look the other way and let sleeping ladies lie?"

"Not you, sir. Not you." The young man's voice took on a tone of almost fatherly concern for his superior officer as he added, "You just finish your tea, sir, while I get these signed out and you can take them away with you. We'll hang on to the flimsies. Oh, and good luck with the ladies, Commissioner."

OF COURSE, WHAT you did was send at least an inspector, at best a superintendent, up to Cambridge to confront the Chief

Constable. Having first cleared the delicate matter with the Commissioner himself.

Joe tried out a possible brief for his most senior and most trusted man, Ralph Cottingham: "Introduce yourself to the county force, Ralph, and tell them you've been sent to pick up and take over a case of theirs which is officially closed. A 'death by misadventure' three months back that no one has questioned. Until the Assistant Commissioner received an anonymous letter last week suggesting that closer scrutiny by a more alert force is required. While you're at it, you'd like to rake up a twenty-five-year-old possible theft for which no complaint was ever made and, for good measure, a further and unassociated pre-war suicide. If they will be so good as to make the usual formal application for assistance, the Metropolitan Police will be pleased to offer their expertise in re-opening the cases."

No. It wouldn't do. It couldn't be attempted by anyone but a complete idiot who was maniacally sure of his ground. Joe recognised himself and silently volunteered. He recognised also the impossibility of ever getting the Commissioner's blessing in the matter. He wouldn't even seek it.

Provincial constabularies were not so reluctant to ask for help from the city as the public seemed to think and were often relieved to shunt their more complex cases on to a force with more extensive forensic enquiry resources and manpower. Not least important—a force providing a wider selection of scapegoats to carry the blame if all went arse over tip. MET CALLED IN TO SOLVE SLAYING was a headline that brought excitement and a certain perverse status, not shame, in these days of banner headlines. But three closed cases having this in common—they all had taken place on Truelove's family estate—amounted to a non-starter. No one would think of harassing a man of Truelove's position by digging up the tidily buried past. Writs for disinterment, actual or figurative, would not be contemplated, particularly those requested by an Assistant Commissioner who was acquiring a reputation of being something of a trouble-maker. A reputation wilfully exaggerated by the men of high status and low principles who'd crossed his path. Joe was without authority and on his own.

Perhaps not quite alone. He looked at his desk calendar. Today was Wednesday. Two days before he was expected down in Surrey. Time enough. He took a card from his pocket and picked up his phone.

"Hunnyton? Back in harness already? Good man! I'm ringing to tell you I got the portraits which, as we speak, are crossing London in the new owner's briefcase."

He listened to the chortles and congratulations and found himself being drawn into a richly embroidered account of the sale-room dramas. Tentatively, he put forward his own plans for the coming two days, adding quietly, "I thought—while I'm over in Suffolk—I might pay a visit to the grave of Phoebe Pilgrim. It's the twenty-fifth anniversary of her death this summer—1908, wasn't it? She was sixteen years old when she drowned herself in the moat. I wondered if you'd like to come with me. After all, she was known to you. Went to the same village school. Worked for the same master."

There was a very long silence over the line and then: "You'll be needing somewhere to stay. Can you get aboard the five-thirty train from King's Cross? Get a taxi at Cambridge station—don't think of walking—it's too far from the centre. I'll book you a room in the Garden House—it's a hotel down by the river. Quiet at this time of year. I'll see you in the bar at nine o'clock."

Joe was only surprised he hadn't added, "What took you so long?"

Ralph Cottingham was the next to hear from Joe. The Super agreed readily—seemed even keen—to deputise for him for a couple of days. And why not? Joe would have been the first to proclaim that Ralph would have made a much more careful and committed Assistant Commissioner than himself. "One more thing, Ralph. If you wouldn't mind . . . I'd like you to put the screws on this firm of solicitors." Joe read out a fashionable London address and gave precise instructions for information he wanted Ralph to relay. "I'll get in touch with you—I can't be quite sure where on earth I'll be this weekend. I'll try to avoid annoying Julia."

He grabbed from his cupboard a suitcase he kept to hand at all times, packed and ready for a weekend. After a moment's hesitation, he picked up what his men called his "murder bag" with his other hand and made for the door. If he took a staff car he'd just make it to King's Cross.

He was on board the train before he remembered he hadn't contacted Dorcas.

REMEMBERED? NOT THE right word. It wasn't that she'd slipped from his mind. She was there at the forefront, she was there in the background. Dorcas was the mainspring of this whole enquiry, though the word flattered the muddle he was stirring about in. He'd temporarily suppressed her name; wiped it from his consciousness. He wondered what psychological jargon she would have used to describe his shock and anger when he'd come across, in the Cambridge bundle, a list of guests present at Melsett Hall on that April night. The night of the death by misadventure.

Miss Dorcas Joliffe had been peacefully asleep in the Old Nursery under Lavinia Truelove's roof at the moment when a dangerous young stallion had torn and pounded her ladyship to death in the stables. Joe prayed that Dorcas had indeed been asleep, alone, and in her own bed.

CHAPTER 7

Joe was at the bar and halfway through his first scotch when the superintendent arrived. His offer of a similar was readily accepted but, seeing no need for time-wasting, Hunnyton suggested at once that they take their drinks out into the garden.

"I always feel easier where I know I'm not overheard," he explained. "My bailiwick, this. More people know me than I know people. Not that there's much danger of running into someone tonight. The place is half full of respectable couples up from the country to watch their offspring getting themselves photographed in gowns and mortarboards. Followed by a lift home in Daddy's Bentley."

"Well, it's not exactly a garden," Joe said as they stepped outside into the summer evening, "but there's a very pretty bit of greenery out here. Do you know this place? It's quite extraordinary! A river-side country house surrounded by meadows full of hairy brown cows up to their udders in buttercups. Just a stone's throw from the city centre. Let's stroll along the bank of lawn that goes down to the river. The landlord's put out some tables and lit up some lanterns along the towpath. Listen! You can hear people out there on the water, laughing and singing. Very romantic! Shame I find myself sharing a whisky with a hulking great copper instead of a champagne cocktail with my sweetheart."

"And there's plenty of light in the sky," Hunnyton nodded. "It's Midsummer, after all. Longest day of the year on Saturday. You can still catch a few flannelled fools on the water punting their girls about. Heading back to the college boathouse, I should hope. Most of the razzamataz passed off last week—the degree awards, the May balls, punting down to Grantchester for breakfast . . . all that stuff. But you always get the odd ones left behind, finishing off research, unable to cut the strings."

"Lingering over a romance? Trying it on with the local lovelies?" Joe wondered.

"That too. The local lads as well sometimes come out, nip down Laundress Lane and hire a canoe from the Anchor boatyard, bent on reclaiming the river once the straw boaters and college scarves have cleared off." The policeman in him added, "There's always a nasty couple of days when they clash. Dunkings and de-baggings and other low-grade mayhem. Town and Gown have never been easy neighbours and we always put our strongest swimmers and liveliest lads on beat duty down here in June."

They watched as a punt drifted by, both men enviously amused to see the lithe young scholar poised at his punting-pole entertaining with his chatter three girls in white dresses who lounged like decorative sofa dolls along the cushions in the centre of the flat boat, fluting and chirrupping and sipping from champagne glasses.

The girls caught sight of the two men watching them in silent admiration and, from the safety of their mid-river station, raised their glasses and shouted saucy invitations to come aboard and even up their numbers. Joe chortled, returned the salute and called back his acceptance. Would they pull over and pick up or should he swim out? He handed his glass to Hunnyton, strode to the edge and began to take off his jacket, miming eager intent. With shrieks of tipsy laughter from its cargo, the punt gave an elegant swish of its tail and swept off downstream.

Joe stared after it, sighing in mock disappointment.

Hunnyton handed him back his glass, commenting starchily, "You look like Mr. Toad when he caught sight of his first motor-car. Sitting dazed in the middle of the road murmuring 'Poop, poop!' as it disappeared in a puff of smoke. I must say, I can never see the attraction of a punt."

"Oh, I don't know. It's hard not to look heroic, playing captain and crew at the same time. Towering over your girls, poised on the stern, chin raised, teeth to the wind, muscles cracking."

"River water running down into your armpit." Hunnyton grinned. "You may manage to look like Odysseus resisting the call of the Sirens but you can never leave go of that bloody nine-foot-high pole! Nowhere to park it. You're lumbered. Both hands fully occupied for the duration of the whole chilly uncomfortable event. All you can do to impress from back there on the platform is look noble and spout Homer. If you really want to make some serious progress with your girl, you'd get further in the one and ninepenny double-seaters on the back row at the Alhambra. The city lads all know that much. For them, a punt is some old fenland boat you ferry the cows across the river in."

"Don't spoil it! I was just considering bringing my girl up here to stage a romantic moment," Joe said.

"She's not a stranger to East Anglia, then?" Hunnyton suggested tentatively.

"I had thought so, but you, I'm willing to wager, know better," Joe said drily. "Shall we stop pussyfooting about and put the few cards we have between us on the table?"

Hunnyton laughed, shrugged and plunged in. "Miss Dorcas Joliffe I understand to be known to you in some way or other. Mind telling me in what capacity exactly?"

"I'd love to tell you exactly but there's no exactitude about our situation at all. Wish there were." Joe gave him the few unadorned facts about his relationship with Dorcas. It occurred to him, in his dry account, that he'd never once discussed the matter with a male friend or relation. It came surprisingly easily when face to face with this bluff, unquestioning, apparently all-knowing fellow copper.

"So, after a seven-year absence, so to speak, this girl comes back into your life and lays claim to you? She'd sort of marked you down as a subject of interest when she was still a whipper-snapper?"

"Dorcas was never that. She's what some would call, fancifully, an Old Soul. Experienced beyond her years, uncertain in some things, over-confident in others . . . But you've got it just about right. She attached herself to me when she was fourteen—looking about ten at the time so I didn't see the dangers. Terrible family background. Mother absconded when she was a baby. Father never bothered to marry any one of the succession of mistresses who flowed through his life. His children, of whom Dorcas is the eldest, ran wild, occasionally whipped into some sort of order by their fearsome grandmother, who disowned the whole brood."

"Lord! How'd you get involved with that mob? Couldn't you have cut and run?"

"Hardly. I was firmly in the middle of a murder enquiry to which Miss Dorcas held the key. A pest, a burden at times, but never less than entertaining, is what she was for me." Not much liking the incredulity blended with pity on the superintendent's face, he tried to explain further: "Look, Hunnyton, some people find themselves claimed by stray *cats* and before they know it their lives are taken over."

At last Hunnyton grunted his understanding. "Can't abide cats but I've got a dog. I rescued it from a gang of tormenting kids when I was on the beat. It loves me and I can't persuade it otherwise. Funny thing—I never picked him but I'd go through hell and high water for Tommy and he knows it, curse him!"

"Tommy?"

"He reminded me of us lads in the trenches. Us Tommies. Mongrel. No value to him but he was fighting for his life. Giving as good as he got and going down snarling."

Joe laughed. "Well, imagine the potency of Tommy's desperate situation and engaging characteristics wrapped in the allure of a very pretty girl and you appreciate my situation. No!" He caught himself in an easy throw-away response and applied a correction. "I'm being ungracious and unfair. In a strange way, Dorcas anchored me. I've been pretty footloose ever since the war and never been the sort who sent home postcards. Until she declared herself as the one person in my life who expected to have them. She was right. She's always been the first one I think of when I fetch up in a strange place. Would Dorcas like it here, is what I ask myself. I shall send her a card tomorrow morning. Who do you send the first postcard to, Hunnyton, when you're away?" he asked lightly.

Joe looked with curiosity at the clear blue Saxon eyes squinting at him over the rim of his glass. Eyes that missed nothing but gave little away. So—the man had a dog called Tommy. Joe realised that he knew very little else of Hunnyton's circumstances. "How are you fixed?" he persisted. "Have you a wife? A fiancée? Sweetheart?"

"None of those. I have a landlady."

"Oh, dear. I'm sorry."

"Why? You shouldn't be. She's the best cook in Cambridge. But you've sussed me out! I'm totally unqualified to offer marital advice. Though that's not going to stop me. I think you'd do best to take it slowly. Make a new beginning. Probably you don't need to hear this, especially from a stranger. But from where I stand, I'd say—treat it as though she's just a few weeks ago come drifting into your life as a fresh possibility. Assume you know nothing about her yet."

The old-fashioned look the superintendent gave Joe told him that this was a politely veiled warning. Joe had no doubt that areas of Dorcas's life were unknown territory for him and it was perfectly possible that this man had greater knowledge of some of them through his investigations. An uncomfortable situation. Joe had never been content to stick a plaster over a festering wound. He decided to hand Hunnyton a scalpel and brace himself for the ensuing unpleasantness.

He took a breath and asked, "Are you able to tell me what the girl I love was doing on the guest list at Melsett the night Lady Truelove died? The list I'm sure you've noted in the file you sent down?"

"It's a puzzle. Where she fitted in . . . A lady turning up by herself like that—it's always a bit of a bother for the servants. It unsettles them. It was an evenly balanced party, you'll have noticed."

"Yes. A dozen sat down to dinner in all. Small house party. Not down for the shooting I take it?"

"No. Game bird shooting season well over by then. But there was some shooting planned. They were hoping to take a few deer—more of a cull than for sport I'd say—and there's always a few hare and rabbits. The men like to tramp about the place with a gun over their arm. It pleases them to think the meat on their plate for dinner is their contribution. The dogs enjoy the stir-about, too. But this was rather more one of those political power groups, I'd have thought. The ones that seem to convene when their host is up for promotion of some sort."

Joe caught the bitterness in the tone and wondered whether Hunnyton was showing his hand at last.

"At least six—three married couples—could be judged to have political interests, the men being MPs of differing persuasions, in fact," Joe recalled. "That's one thing that impresses me about James Truelove—he's open-minded, with friends and influence with all parties. That's not easy to achieve. Then there was the inevitable newspaper magnate and his wife. And Sir James and Lady Truelove . . ." Joe hesitated.

"Leaving the last two—whom I won't describe as a couple. They were put to sit next to each other I understand from the butler—Miss Dorcas Joliffe, Sir James's protégée and student researcher, and, by her side, his young brother, Alexander."

"How young?"

"Not that young. Mid-twenties. Alex was an afterthought and no one was more surprised than his mother when he made his appearance on the family tree after James and two daughters. Still, a spare is always a useful addition to the heir."

"I blush to air such an obvious matter but I suppose I should ask: What are his chances of succeeding his brother to the baronetcy?"

"He'll have to outlive him and count on James's not producing a legitimate son. So—the chances are not good when the incumbent's youthful and vigorous as James is. Still, James had been married to Lavinia for some years and produced no children . . ."

Once again, Joe felt himself prodded into drawing a conclusion: "The smart thing, if Alex had some scheme in mind to inherit, would have been to encourage an infertile situation to run its course."

"Right. With Lavinia dead, Sir James is on the loose again and could well remarry. Time enough to produce an heir to dislodge Master Alex."

"What is Alexander currently up to?"

"He's living at the Hall at the moment, taking a year off after his banking job in the City before he goes out to Africa or some other spot unprepared as yet for his attentions."

"He gave up a banking career?"

"Ah. Good question. He'll tell you himself—he got out

minutes before he was booted out. Brags about it. Gift of the gab, like all the Trueloves."

"Seating him alongside Dorcas—was that an attempt at matchmaking by any chance?" Joe managed to keep his voice steady.

Hunnyton fought back a guffaw. "No chance! You'd hesitate to match anyone you liked or respected with Alex," Hunnyton said gloomily. "They probably let him down to dinner to make up the numbers and the two misfits found themselves next to each other. No—Dorcas Joliffe was there at the specific, though last-minute, invitation of her ladyship."

"Eh? What? Lavinia Truelove?" Joe was astonished. "The silliest woman in the Shires? She didn't even know Dorcas. And Dorcas wouldn't have bothered to exchange more than a dozen words with her. Asking for trouble to put them at the same table." He bit his lip.

"Well, it's a blessing that it's a wide table and they weren't in hair-tugging reach, the butler says. A right ding-dong going on. Sir James was embarrassed, her ladyship was 'a trifle over-excited,' in butler terms. In other words even worse than her usual overbearing self. But that's just my interpretation of what was said. You can't fault the servants. They know how to keep quiet. They only opened up as far as they did because it was me asking."

"Did you manage to find out what they were quarrelling about?"

Hunnyton drained his glass and looked back uneasily to the bright lights of the hotel behind him as though wishing to evade the question. "Well, of course . . . social occasion and all that . . . there was no way even Lavinia was going to shrill, 'Keep your thieving little hands off my husband.' If that was the compulsion behind the rivalry. What they were ostensibly arguing about was horses," he finished and looked down at his feet.

"Horses? What horses?"

"Any old nags. Lady Truelove may have been a ninny but what she was good at—the only thing she was good at—was riding. She was raised in a midlands hunting county so you'd expect it. Hunting, point-to-pointing . . . she could go faster, jump higher, stay on longer than any man, they say. I think your lady-friend saw straight through to what I've always suspected—that Lavinia had absolutely no feelings for the horseflesh itself. She'd arrive in the stables booted and spurred, climb aboard and ride. Ask her the name of the horse whose mouth she was wrecking and she wouldn't have a clue. Never tended them, never even took them a carrot. She wasn't tuned in to them in any way. Really she'd have been happier at the wheel of a sports car if she'd ever been bothered to learn to drive."

"Ah. That wouldn't have impressed Dorcas. She's a damned good rider, too, but she tends to go about the place on shaggy ponies without a saddle. They follow her around like dogs. Trot at her heel in an obsequious way. I've seen beasts cross fields to come and nuzzle her neck. I think she prefers animals to people. I'd make faster headway with Dorcas if I were a deer-hound or a hairy-heeled Shire horse. She spent too many of her days with her father yarning around gypsy campfires when she was a little thing and she picked up some unusual skills. Her father's a painter. A very good one, too, but he went through a stage of imagining he was Augustus John. You know—caravans, corduroy britches and clay-baked hedgehogs." Joe shuddered gently.

"I see. Not a meeting of minds planned, then, in this invitation of Lavinia's."

"Not if she knew anything about Dorcas, no. I'm sure you've guessed correctly, Hunnyton, that this was really a rivalry over an imagined interest in or influence over Sir James. Imagined by the man's wife, I mean. But how the hell are we to guess at the contents of that lady's head on this occasion? She may have exaggerated the dangers of the situation." Then, in a rush of confidence and a copper's seeking after the full truth he added: "No, let me be clear. I have to say in Lavinia's defence that her fears may well not have been entirely the product of hysteria and jealousy. Dorcas has confided to me that, though Sir James's attentions to her have never been less decorous than would befit his position of mentor and sponsor, nevertheless, he has made it known that . . ." Joe hesitated, aware that he had plunged into a whirlpool of circumlocution to disguise his awkwardness.

"He wouldn't mind at all getting into her knickers, like. Men! Buggers! I don't know why women go on putting up with us. Got it. What we're saying then is, as I suspected, all this horse stuff was a bluff, a diversionary tactic, an exchange of snowballs when bullets are not appropriate."

"That's exactly what I'd guess, knowing Dorcas as I do . . ." Joe fell silent.

"And knowing Lavinia as I did . . . I'd agree with you that the two women under one roof was an explosive situation. But, Sandilands, what are we on about? There was no explosion. Let's hang on to this—Miss Dorcas had only just put in an appearance and was nowhere near the stables that night."

Joe was soothed to hear the quiet good sense.

"It really was the horse that did it! He was caught red-toothed, you might say. The whole nasty business was witnessed by the most credible witnesses in the land. Two Suffolk boys. No one got pushed off a roof, bashed on the head with a candlestick or stuck with an assegai. It's all right, sir. I'm sure you've no cause to fret."

"I've always fretted!" Joe spoke through gritted teeth, trying to smile. "Cause or no cause, Dorcas is the hostage I handed over to Dame Fortune eight years ago and neither lady lets me forget it."

"I can see why you'd want to get to the bottom of it."

"Hang on, Hunnyton. Before we go inside and pick up the

rest of the bottle to help us get through the notes again, explain that comment, will you. Tell me: Is there a bottom to get to?"

"Yes. I believe there is. And there's a lot of murk to sink through before we touch it. It sounds quite mad but I'll say what I'm thinking: Lavinia Truelove was murdered."

"Murdered, Hunnyton? You've read the pathologist's report. She died of sudden copious blood loss from a severed neck and shock producing cardiac arrest, probably only a second or two before her head was smashed to a pulp by the hooves of a very heavy horse. There was no one else about but the two young stable lads hiding behind the corn-hutch. They raised the alarm and made contact with one of the house footmen who happened to be in the environs and he it was who organised medical attention." Joe noted but did not comment on the way Hunnyton kept reversing his position to test him out. He'd done the same thing himself in interviews. "Hmm . . . it might be interesting to ask this footman what he was doing in the vicinity of the stables before dawn."

"Agreed. But think, Sandilands. Imagine, let's say, Captain Hook makes a sailor walk the plank. The poor soul shuffles to the end, drops in and is chewed up by a passing shark. Who's to blame? The shark? What I'm saying is that I believe Lady Truelove's death was engineered. Someone wanted her to die and the horse was just the instrument. About as culpable as the candlestick or the dagger that comes conveniently to a murdering hand in a twopenny whodunit."

"We're left with the eternal problem of: why, how and who? Any suggestions?"

"Plenty. Too many. I thought we'd sort them out together. Two heads are better than one even if they're sheep heads, my ma used to say. We'll go off into darkest Suffolk at crack of dawn tomorrow and poke about a bit. Tweak a few ears. I've hired you a motorcar from Simpson's car hire firm down Mill Road. Nothing too showy but smart enough to impress those who like to be impressed. I thought, in the circumstances, we'd avoid using police vehicles and back-up. We'll interview the medical expert, who was never asked to hand in a report—no, I wasn't directly involved in the case when it first came up. Close member of the family and all that, the Chief Constable thought it better if I kept out of it. And he was right. Though it didn't stop me from making subsequent off-the-record enquiries, of course."

"Medic? I read Frobisher's excellent autopsy account."

"Well, that's not without its puzzles but I'm talking about the report on the body by the *animal* doctor. The veterinary surgeon, I hear, was on the spot faster even than the local doc. He shot the beast dead but he took the trouble to stay around until daylight and then carried out a careful examination of the horse's body before it was carted off to the knacker's yard. I have this information from the lads. 'Doc weren't easy about it,' they told me. 'Muttered an' cussed. Found something he didn't like the look of.' I've not had a chance to speak to the vet myself yet. We'll see him together. He can see us in his office at eleven o'clock."

Joe smiled to hear again the undisguised evidence of pre-planning. Should he have felt resentment or pressure at being so manoeuvred? Undoubtedly. But professional efficiency to a good end never irritated him and his dignity was not so fragile he had to strengthen it with bluster. "Sounds good to me," he said agreeably. "What about the staff? Are we booked in to see them? And the Dowager Lady Truelove—is she putting the kettle on?"

"It's all taken care of. You don't ask, so I'll tell you—James will not be present. He always spends four weeks after term's end in London. He has a flat in London and that's where he's going to be until he goes north to a cousin's estate in Scotland for the shooting. I checked with the valet he keeps down there. But then, I expect you checked, too."

"Same result. Sir James has a full appointment book. Sir James is hardly the grieving widower it would appear. His life continues as busy as it ever was. Which means he's conveniently out of our hair. What else have you set up?"

"I asked the management here to put you in a room with a big desk."

"They did. Let's go up and cover it with documents, shall we. Leaving a corner for the Glenmorangie."

"FROM A COUNTRY doctor, this death certificate and autopsy report are impressive," Joe said.

"It was a double-handed effort," Hunnyton explained. "If you look at the signatures you'll see that of the local doctor, Thoroughgood, who attended at the scene, and also the name of the pathologist, Mr. Frobisher, here in the hospital in Cambridge where the body was brought for further inspection—at the insistence of Thoroughgood himself. He stayed to witness the procedure and helped draw up the statement, which they both signed."

"Unusual? The doc could, in a clear case of misadventure which this was, have just dealt with it and got a colleague to provide the second signature on the certificate. No fuss. No one would have questioned it."

"Obviously the good doctor had a question in his own mind to make him go to this trouble. It *is* a trouble. Transporting bodies about the place, hospital involvement and all that, it's time-consuming and appears fussy. Truelove himself might well have been a bit miffed."

"He was. At the first suggestion. He quickly changed his attitude to one of resigned acceptance, I hear. Look, Sandilands, you can make your own enquiries, get your own answers. I just pass on to you as impartially as I can what was said to me."

"Understood. In that case," Joe said, riffling through the sheets, "have you an explanation for this? Which page was it now?

Ah, here we are . . . I'm wondering why, when the victim has suc-
cumbed to the most appalling and evident wounds, the doctor
advised the surgeon—'at the request of Dr. Thoroughgood'—to
investigate the lady's internal organs. Heart, liver, blood tests
done—just as you'd expect in a case of suspicious death. He further states that the victim was not pregnant. I'd say this is a
matter the local doctor wished to have clarified."

"The old feller had a suspicion that she *was* pregnant?" Hunnyton suggested.

Joe's voice conveyed a grim satisfaction. "Nothing like a suspicion of pregnancy to stir up trouble with the various males in a
woman's entourage, we find in the Smoke, and I expect it's much
the same in deepest Suffolk."

"Worse," was the unadorned admission, and Joe could have
kicked himself for his ineptitude. Hunnyton's shake of the head
and his knowing grin forgave him and dismissed the idea that Joe
should be ever on the alert for potentially offensive remarks.

Joe grinned back, reassured, and poured out more whisky. He
was beginning to think Hunnyton was a good bloke to be in harness with. He just hoped together they could plough a straight
furrow and avoid careering off into the ditch. "Right. Let's read
through the whole lot again and share insights, shall we?"

HE WOKE AT three in the morning to the sound of a cracked
college bell sounding the hour and stayed awake long enough to
allow into the conscious front of his mind the thought that he'd
shoved to the back when he'd gone to bed well after midnight.
How much information of a personal nature had he divulged to
this stranger with the receptive gaze and the disarming country
growl? In a moment of clarity he remembered he'd bared his soul
regarding his feelings for Dorcas, he'd even revealed that Sir James
had admitted only days before his wife had died to having intentions below and beyond intellectual support for the wretched girl.

Joe remembered her words to him one April afternoon: "He wants to take things further and I'm considering it." Delivered with a cool insouciance. Joe had been too devastated to demand to know what precisely was implied by "things" and "further." Any attempt to spell out to her the habits of men like Truelove would have been greeted with a sophisticated sneer. Dorcas was no ingénue.

But the next week Lavinia Truelove had died and Joe had been left with those tormenting words creeping into his mind, where they'd lodged and festered. He recalled them at the most inopportune moments. Lord! Surely he hadn't been so indiscreet as to confide that? No. Even faced with a professional hypnotist in a Harley Street consulting room, he'd have managed to censor that much. Certainly. But he'd hinted at—no, it was stronger than a hint—Dorcas's special powers with animals. And the superintendent had listened, nodding his understanding, quietly making connections while Joe had blundered on forging handcuffs for the girl he loved.

Too late some baleful words of—was it John Dryden? Or was it his mother?—sneaked into his mind to trouble him. *He who trusts secrets to a servant makes him his master.* Perhaps he should get it made up in poker work and offer the sentiment to the landlord of the *Fleeing Footman*?

CHAPTER 8

FRIDAY 23RD JUNE.

C hrist! He was right behind her!

This was awkward. Your target was supposed to be in your sights at all times, not breathing down your neck. Lily managed to disguise her start of surprise and fixed a smile on her face. She finished the sentence she'd been addressing to the reception manager at the moment Mr. Fitzwilliam had bounded into the hotel and come to a halt, an impatient presence waiting his turn just behind her right shoulder.

The manager took in the situation at once and made an evaluation. "Mr. Fitzwilliam!" he called out. "Good morning, sir! I'll be with you directly." Turning to Lily: "Miss . . . er . . . Richmond, I wonder if I might pass you to my assistant, who will be very pleased to handle your registration?"

"Not at all." Lily shuffled over meekly, leaving space at the counter for the more illustrious client, and Fitzwilliam stepped forward, all bonhomie and effusive thanks. A solitary, middle-aged lady in flowered hat and laced shoes was never going to command the best attention of London hotel staff or the notice of guests and Lily had counted on this when she'd put together her identity for the next two days. It seemed to be working. She greeted the smart young woman who came to attend to her and began to fill in her details for the card from the beginning.

"My name is: Richmond . . . Vanessa. That's Miss . . . and my home address is in Yorkshire." She dictated it. "Two nights? Yes, that's right. Single room. I did book in advance. Reason for visit? Pleasure? You're asking me what am I doing in London?" Lily found an affected deafness always put people off their guard and discouraged them from listening to conversations. A shouting person had nothing to hide and nothing worth hearing, apparently. "I'm not a tourist, my dear! No, no! If you really must make such a personal enquiry you may write down: business. I'm here to work." She enjoyed the fleeting look of surprise before adding in quiet triumph, "Yes, I'm a working woman! If you can call writing work. Many do not! . . . Historical novels, dear," she confided, looking about her to ensure no one was listening in to such a confession. "Romances. I'm here at the *Castlemaine*," Lily stressed the name, "because of its connections with the flame-haired, turquoise-eyed beauty of that name . . . Barbara Castlemaine, one of the mistresses of Charles the Second, the one who became Duchess of Cleveland as a reward for services rendered . . . You hadn't connected the name? . . . Oh, the dashing duchess was strong on the wing in this part of London and I'm spending a couple of days following her traces around the Palace of St. James's . . . Yes, dear, you certainly could—they keep all my works at Hatchard's round the corner in Piccadilly . . . Now, I asked for a single room that is larger than a dog-kennel and for it to be supplied with a desk and plenty of ink. Stephens blue-black . . . You have? Jolly good."

While Lily twittered on, she was listening intently to Mr. Fitzwilliam who, like her, had chosen to check in earlier than expected. As they both turned from the desk at the same moment, he smiled and held out a hand. "How do you do, Miss Richmond. Rowley Fitzwilliam, also here on business. Pardon me, I couldn't help overhearing. I've never met a writer of romantic novels before. How delightful! We must—"

"And you've never read one either, young man," Lily said

sharply, looking him up and down. "Though you could well be the subject of such a work. Yes—tall, dark, handsome and doubt-less disreputable."

For a moment Fitzwilliam was taken aback but he rallied to slap his fedora back on his head at a louche angle and narrow his eyes. "That's just the effect of the gangster hat. All the go at the moment—the slouch—but don't be deceived! This is not a stick-up, madam."

"I see. I'm pleased to note that St. James's is still stocked with its share of fashionable—and law-abiding—young gallants. Ah, there goes my luggage . . . Excuse me—I must away to my broom-cupboard."

That should have been enough to put him off any further approach, Lily thought. Mad old bat. Harmless but better avoided. Not what she'd been expecting, though, her target. What *had* she expected? Joe had gritted out a warning that he was an exemplary Englishman while hinting darkly that he might well, under this cover, be planning to steal the crown jewels or overturn the gov-ernment. The smart, jokey chap she'd encountered in the lobby had given out no such dire signals. Lily decided that if she should ever be trapped in the Castlemaine lift she would not be dis-pleased to find Fitzwilliam trapped in there with her. Strangely, he seemed like a man who might well have a handy screwdriver in his back pocket and he'd have the athleticism to climb up and free a cable perhaps. If all else failed he'd keep her entertained. Lily hoped she wouldn't be called on to shoot him.

Her pre-judgement of the room allocated to her had been equally unjust, she recognised as she settled in. It was spacious enough for a couple and equipped with two single beds. The fur-nishings and the linen were all of excellent quality and the water came boiling out of the taps in the bathroom next door. She kicked off her laced shoes and removed the heavy spectacles that distorted her vision. Though longing to apply a slather of cold cream to her makeup, she resisted the urge, planning to make a further foray into the lobby when the rush had abated. She hung up the jacket of her heather-mix Hebe suit and, with relief, took out of her brassière the layer of padding that boosted her lissom 34 inches to 44 inches of imposing bosom. She flopped down onto one of the beds, relishing a moment to spend with the book she'd bought half an hour before. She'd been drawn by the title: *Midsummer Masquerade.* It had seemed appropriate. She'd better read it and find out how this historical novel business was managed. How taxing could it be? Lily was full of confidence. She was able to write and she knew some history after all.

Lily hadn't counted on anyone but her Aunt Phyl actually being fascinated sufficiently by this stuff to want to initiate a conversation about it. Her cover story was meant to be plausible if questioned but so dull as to deflect interest in the first place. In extremis, she would have to call on her deafness or authorial modesty to wriggle free.

She persevered for ten minutes. Ten tedious minutes of soulful sighs and side-slipping glances, fans and hearts a-flutter and—the last straw: "'Pon my soul, Mr. Ponsonby" and the book broke its spine on the wall opposite.

Back to business. Lily went to reception and began to make notes. She'd overheard Fitzwilliam booking a table for four at one o'clock. Lily rang down to the desk and requested a lunch table for herself at 12:30. She would be already in position when his guests arrived and could always linger over coffee if she needed to prolong her surveillance. Joe was going to get his money's worth. This Fitzwilliam was troubling her boss in a way that was a mystery to her. Not such a mystery to Joe, she had concluded, and wondered what he was deliberately hiding from her.

NO WONDER AT all that Special Branch had been bored out of their skins keeping a watchful eye on this bird, Lily reckoned. His three guests were respectability itself. A Tory grandee with a finger in every financial pie in Westminster, his glum wife and, last to arrive, to make up the numbers, Lily guessed, a lady who by her looks could be no other than Fitzwilliam's younger sister. Tall, slender, dark and fashionably though not showily dressed, she moved easily into her place in the group. After a loving exchange of kisses with her brother, she was presented to the other two. "You haven't met my sister Margaret, who is in her other life Mrs. Hubert Hawkes? She's so often travelling the world these days I don't have a chance to see much of her."

Lily recognised the name of an English conductor about to perform in the forthcoming Promenade Concerts. Margaret, or Meggie, as her brother called her, proceeded to keep the table entertained with a flow of conversation that skilfully drew out the rather silent wife while flirting innocently with her elderly husband, Lily noticed. A useful sister for a man like Fitzwilliam.

What was she to make of her target on this showing? Confident, amusing, attentive. She was not close enough to catch much of the conversation but he appeared to be exuding a happiness she had no way of accounting for. His happiness extended to the dull political pair and they appeared flattered and warmed by it. It had, for a brief moment, reached out and touched the dumpy, deaf old lady from the provinces he'd met in the lobby. As she watched, a young waiter allowed a fork to drop to the floor from the plate he was clearing. He stood, astonished to see Fitzwilliam leap to his feet, pick up the offending utensil and replace it on the plate with a wink and a grin. Next he'd be tap-dancing down Piccadilly. A man who was "on something"? He was definitely experiencing euphoria of some sort. In Lily's experience there could be only one possible cause for such relentless jollity. Could she be right? Lily felt a sudden need for a second opinion.

Otherwise, so uneventful was the luncheon party that Lily, who'd brought her notebook to the table in a defiantly eccentric gesture, found that between the soup and the dessert she'd sketched out the first chapter of her first anti-historical novel.

Lily decided she'd had enough. If this man was hiding himself away, he had a strange way of going about it. Here he was hosting lunch in plain sight of London society, in the company of three unimpeachable people. Lily's research had revealed he was not even lying about his name. Rowley and Fitzwilliam were his middle names. He had a perfect right to both of them. This was the simple device of a man in the public eye needing to avoid the attentions of a press who combed through guest lists these days and bribed hotel clerks to divulge the names of their famous clients. A single man, he probably had a club close by and chose to entertain mixed couples in the more relaxed atmosphere of a good hotel. Women generally did not appreciate the kind of hospitality on offer in the world of gentlemen's clubs even in those ones who were prepared to acknowledge the existence of the other sex.

Joe had sent her on a wild goose chase.

She left the dining room the moment she'd finished her coffee. On her way out she paused to bother the maître d'hôtel with a fussy old-lady question. Her arthritic left knee had detected a draught at the table she'd just vacated. Could she be certain of a seat somewhere less exposed for dinner on Saturday night? When he politely referred to his plan, she bossily peered over his shoulder and pointed. "There I am!" She'd actually been taking in the information that Fitzwilliam was booked to have dinner discreetly at the far end of the room. "You've put me in the same place but there's a much better one for me right here," she said, indicating a table that had a strategically better outlook on the pair she needed to watch. "I should like to be there, well away from the door, if it's no trouble. Oh, and could you possibly set a second place? I'm expecting a friend to join me."

The adjustments were duly made and Lily hobbled off to the

lift. The Saturday night dinner was the only meal apart from today's lunch that she'd heard her target making a booking for. She quite expected him to disappear into London for the rest of the time and she would not follow him. It was not in her brief and Joe had told her that his movements about town had been thoroughly vetted by the Branch. She was to stay at her post and report on whomever he met.

The whole business pivoted on his single guest tomorrow night, Lily reckoned. It could be anyone from a visiting Head of a Nation to a lady on the end of a telephone. In the lift she took out her London diary to check whether there was something she'd missed, some special occasion or event that might have drawn him here on this date.

Saturday the 24th of June, it said, *Midsummer's Day. New moon. Feast of St. John.*

Academic term's end. Racing at Ascot.

Lily's romantic streak interpreted these dry facts with some licence. It must be the time of year. In the green depths of an English summer—that's where they were poised. In that moment when young things found themselves set free from constraints of timetable and corset, their limbs and hearts suddenly open to the sun and new experiences. Nowadays, they jumped on a ferry and made off for Paris or Monte Carlo. In earlier times they'd have been gathering boughs in English woods and leaping bonfires to ward off evil spirits. St. John's Eve was a time of mystery and fraught with delicious danger: witches walked abroad on mischief bent, egged on by sprites and goblins. Shakespeare had staged the battle between the King and the Queen of the Fairies this evening. Beltane, god of the Celts, chose Midsummer as his moment to pay court to the Great Goddess. Gods, humans and supernatural beings, all were possessed by the same joyous urge to celebrate the return of fertility. Even in the city, all unaware of the deeper meaning, school children still danced around maypoles in June, wearing white for Whitsuntide. With a wreath of lilac blossom on her head, Lily had done this herself in happily pagan East London as a child. Her playground games, some only half understood, had crept into the city from the country and flourished like the yellow St. John's Wort in the cracks in every causeway-side. Beneath her sophisticated, street-wise exterior, a Celtic undertow ran deep and unquestioned in her blood.

There was something intoxicating and ancient about the very word "midsummer." Lily found her mind, so recently alerted to an author's sensibilities, supplying a following alliterative: "madness" or "mischief" or "malice." She searched for a word less baleful and found none.

CHAPTER 9

Joe couldn't repress a shout of laughter when Hunnyton drove up to collect him at the Garden House after breakfast on Friday morning. He walked around the dark red open-topped sports tourer expressing his approval of the motorcar and his admiration for the driver. Hunnyton was suitably dressed in waterproof cape, cloth cap with earflaps and tinted driving goggles.

"Now who's doing a Mister Toad?" Joe challenged. "Look at you! I'm afraid if I climb aboard you'll drive me back a couple of decades. We'll be bursting into the Edwardian age before you can say 'H. G. Wells'!"

Hunnyton shook his head. "Who needs a time machine? Besides—Edwardian? Pouf!—that's just yesterday. No, we're going back a few centuries. Disappearing down a tunnel of green gloom into an age where they still speak the language of Chaucer and think this young Shakespeare feller is a bit avant-garde with his expression."

"I shall be glad to have an interpreter aboard then. What is this vehicle?"

"It's a Lagonda M45. The poor man's Bentley, they call them. Very popular with undergraduates seeking to impress. I thought we'd have something with a collapsible hood so we can enjoy the views and the fresh air. It's a bit wide for the country lanes but it's got tough wheels and tyres and we won't have to blush for it when we park it on the forecourt of the Hall. If it were a horse, I'd say it was a well-shod, long-legged hunter with a deep chest, suitable mount for a gentleman."

He turned off the ignition and made to climb out.

"No, no! Stay where you are," Joe hurried to shout. "You look perfect at the wheel. It would take me at least ten miles to get the hang of it. And I did note the streams rushing down open gutters on both sides of Trumpington Street on the way here. They'd caught a Ford, two bikes and an old lady on a tricycle before break-fast, I noticed. Damn dangerous bit of plumbing! Can't think why you allow that in a civilised city. The Romans would never have sanctioned it." Chattering on, he threw his bags into the back and, hearing not even a token objection, settled into the passenger seat.

Hunnyton looked sideways at Joe as they moved out into the almost empty King's Parade, heading for the river crossing. He took in Joe's lightweight Burbury trench coat worn with an offi-cer's swagger open over a summer tweed suit; he eyed his pale grey soft hat and his black shoes from Lobbs. "I think they'll work out which one of us is from the Yard," he commented.

"I never see any point in disguising what I am when I'm work-ing," Joe said. "Some have even found it reassuring. If it scares the villains—good."

ALL ATTEMPTS AT conversation were abandoned as they zipped along the main road east leading to Newmarket and on to the North Sea coast. Joe noticed that, as with most good horsemen, Hunnyton also seemed to have a sure touch with a motorcar, and he wondered with envy why the skills had not been meted out to him in equal measure. Joe had been born on a Scottish Borders farm, and had grown up riding everything from pony to plough horse, but he was the first to admit that he was never in harmony with a car. His lack of enthusiasm to take the wheel seemed to have further confirmed Hunnyton's picture of him as a high-ranking officer who expected to be driven everywhere, a Man of the Metropolis. He had no doubt that the superintendent was looking forward to watching him submerge his shining Oxfords in something unspeakable at the first opportunity.

After a few miles of dodging dangerously around lorries and swaying haywains, they turned off the noisy road, taking an off-shoot to the left. Hunnyton slowed down in response to the narrowed road and trundled along at twenty miles an hour. Per-versely, now that conversation was possible, neither man chose to speak. Both were hushed by the silence of the thick green canopy of oak and beech enclosing the road over their heads, hypnotised by the rhythmic swish of the tree trunks as they passed through. It had the same effect on their senses as the architecture of a lofty cathedral, arousing a quiet awe.

Hunnyton broke the silence. "It'll be like this for miles now. We should get where we're going before the horse-drawn hay-carts start clogging up the roads. They'll be taking a third cut this year—it's been a good one so far."

"What's that scent? Like incense . . ." Joe answered his own question. "Of course—honeysuckle!"

"S'right. Ten minutes of this'll unclog your city nose."

"Coked up as it is with soot and fog and the spewed-out contents of the Lots' Road power station—my next door neigh-bour in Chelsea. Ears, too. Birds! I can hear real birds! We only get pigeons and raucous seagulls in London." Joe was perfectly content to exploit the image of city slicker he'd detected in Hunnyton's evaluation of him.

Once started, conversation began to flow easily along the lanes, punctuated by village and hamlet and the occasional grand house set in its own parkland, each accorded its commentary by Hunnyton.

"I notice that the grandeur of the houses increases the further we go into the dark interior. Have I got that wrong?" Joe remarked.

"Oh, where they've survived at all—and many have not—they go on getting ever more splendid right through up into Norfolk. Until you stumble on the real stunners like Felbrigg and Oxburgh and Blickling. Melsett, the house we're heading for, is not as grand as any of those, but it's the one out of all of them any man with an ounce of sense would choose to live in. Smart enough to invite royalty to stay, old enough to fascinate, well staffed and equipped. Guests never get to see the electricity generator or the refrigerators and cleaning machines it powers, though they appreciate the lamps they can turn on at the flick of a switch, the impeccable laundry and the ice cream desserts. There's abundant produce from the farm and garden. Where are we? . . . June . . . Strawberries, gooseberries, peas, beans, possibly a pineapple or two from the glasshouse . . . and the choicest lamb. Cook's favourite time of year."

"Shame we're not invited," Joe said.

"Don't worry. You'll eat well enough. We're having supper at my cottage. Yes, the old home. I bought it from the guv'nor when my parents died. My sister Annie lives in the village still—she's married to the local grocer—and she's coming in to dust about and leave a dish of something in the oven for us."

"That's very kind of her. But—supper, Hunnyton? I don't much fancy travelling down these roads in the dark and I have to be back in London tomorrow. Family event in Surrey going on this coming weekend."

"Entirely up to you, how much time you want to spend over here. I've just taken precautions. If we do get benighted you can bunk up in my spare room. And you can count on there being a good breakfast. Home-cured bacon and Newmarket sausages. Eggs snatched straight from under the hen . . ."

Joe stirred uneasily. "Sounds wonderful but—look—is there a telephone I can use out here? I shall need to contact my sister again. If Lydia's still speaking to me after my early morning call from the Garden House." He put on a crisp, cross voice: "'You're *where*? Well, you shouldn't be! Why aren't you coming down the drive?'"

"Fouling up her plans are you?"

"I'm afraid so. She's used to it. But this is to be rather a special time. Much planning has gone into it. I can't disappoint."

"The phone lines have staggered out this far," Hunnyton said drily. "You can use the one at the Hall. The butler's an old mate of mine. He won't mind. Mr. Styles is someone you ought to talk to if you want to get a clearer idea of what was going on that night in April. He doesn't miss much and he was presiding over the dinner party when the row broke out between the ladies."

"Anyone else in the household I should put at the top of my list?"

"Grace Aldred. Her ladyship's maid."

"She hasn't moved on, then?"

"No. Her family are local folk. She could have got a job in London but she preferred to stay on here, though she had to take a lowering of position to do that. Gracie's a laundry maid these days. She gets on well with the housekeeper, Mrs. Bolton, and I'd say she could train on to replace her when Mrs. Bolton retires. I've asked the staff to stand by to be interviewed after twelve o'clock. We'll be finished with the vet by then and you can take as long as you want up at the house." He looked at his wristwatch. "We've made good time. Nearly there. This is all Truelove's land hereabouts. We could take a break and offer ourselves a little distraction, I think. Your first taste of Suffolk."

He parked the car by the roadside, choosing a space under a broad oak to ward off the increasing heat of the sun and pointed across the way to a broad stretch of meadowland dotted with stately chestnut trees. "They should be still out there wait-ing for someone to come and round them up for the afternoon's hay carting." He glanced up at the branches of the tree, assess-ing the wind direction. "Come on. Get out and come and prepare to meet the best horses in the east of England."

Warily, but making no protest, Joe took off his trench coat, fanned his face with his hat and took a handkerchief from his pocket. He wiped the sweat from his face and neck and followed Hunnyton to the fence. He jumped over it and walked two paces behind his guide into the field.

"Here they come! They've caught our scent." Hunnyton gave a high-pitched whistle.

A quarter of a mile away in the distance something in the landscape was breaking loose and on the move. Hunnyton continued his swift march towards the centre of the field. Coats shining like conkers in the sunshine, ten horses were whinnying a greeting and thundering towards them. Joe counted eight fully grown, one-ton, seventeen-hand Suffolks and two smaller, but not much smaller, colts. Probably two years old and as yet unbroken, Joe estimated. They came on in a line, ever accelerating, pounding the ground. Half a minute away. Joe swallowed, unsure whether the shaking in his body was due to the tremors in the earth or his own increased heart-beat. Joe had stood up to both cavalry charges and machine gun bursts and knew that it was a waste of time to tell a soldier that the mechanised assault of a stream of bullets was more lethal than the charge of a mounted division. Every Tommy knew in his head that in terms of numbers it was. But the onward rush of heavy horses, eyes rolling, nostrils flaring, right in amongst you, way above your head height, brought with it a terror that froze your guts and your limbs as no impersonal attack from a distance ever could.

Joe found himself, ridiculously, reaching down to his side for a weapon—any weapon. It was Hunnyton's sliding glance backwards, assessing the effect the charge was having on the city gent, that roused Joe. He stepped forward defiantly and took up his place at Hunnyton's shoulder. Waiting.

With one mind the horses hauled themselves to a halt only feet from the men, carving up the turf with their braking back hooves, front ones pawing the air in a dramatic flourish. A row of rampant, Sienna-red medieval horses. Riderless and uncontrolled. Joe was aware of wild manes tossing from side to side, the smell of sun-scorched hide, the whiff and dampness of horse-foam in the wind and above all the insane cacophony of neighing and whinnying, the whole tumult erupting well over his head. He managed somehow not to flinch or cry out. He stayed very still, hands behind his back, eyes lowered, unthreatened and unthreatening.

The older horses, neighing with delight, ignored Joe and pranced up to greet Hunnyton with slathering tongues and nibbling lips while he talked to them in a language Joe could barely make out. The affection between man and horse was unmistakable. Joe could have sworn the animals knew their place in the welcoming line. It was hardly an orderly greeting queue but somehow the figure of Hunnyton, insignificant alongside the tonnage of muscled horse-flesh, managed to stay upright and unmangled and able to call each beast by its name.

The trained horses were clearly no menace to a stranger who entered the field in the company of their adored horseman but the unbroken pair, inquisitive, unaware of their strength, were where the danger lay. Jostled to one side by the older horses, they sought another outlet for their excitement. Not recognising Joe's scent, they moved in skittishly towards him, muzzles extended, noisily sniffing, inexperienced feet clumsily trampling the ground and any human foot left unthinkingly in their way. They were unaware of their killing strength, emboldened by the presence of the older members of the herd and excited by the unknown. A potential disaster.

Hunnyton broke off from thumping a big chap called Scot in the ribs and looked round sharply. Belatedly? Aware of the danger at any rate.

Joe kept his stillness but turned his head towards the bolder of the pair of colts and began to murmur a few pleasant words. He backed away, creating the space he knew a horse liked to keep about itself. "Let him come to you, laddie!" The remembered words always rang in his ear when he met a strange horse. In response, the youngster showed an increasing interest, following him with confidence, butting him lustily with his nose when Joe turned again. The nose followed up with a more intimate inspection, twitching as it moved with slobbering, sensitive lips around Joe's neck and face. A foam-flecked tongue emerged and began to lick his neck. At this point, Joe gently brought forward a hand and caressed its ears. As this gesture was well received, he leaned forward and breathed, as he'd been taught, into the huge nostrils, continuing to speak the words he'd learned so many years before. Gaelic? Latin? Chinese? It could have been anything. Horses knew no language. They were responding to his tone. It wasn't difficult to speak with delight and love for these beautiful creatures. They seemed to understand that he admired them. The second colt edged the first away, eager for its share of attention. Joe fumbled in his pocket and found a Chelsea bun. He broke it in two and gave them half each, sending the pair into ecstasies and provoking a concerted attack on his pockets.

Hunnyton, he sensed, was intrigued and mystified by this behaviour. Should he tell him that his father's head groom had been a member of the Scottish Society of Horsemen? More than just a member—a Grand Master in that secretive Masonic world. A possessor of the Word. One of the last in the land, Auld Angus had calculated; with the arrival of the new-fangled tractor, the days of the horse—and their horsemen—were numbered and his skills and knowledge would be extinct within a generation. His standing in his own community would disappear, was already disappearing. Thousands of years of acquired knowledge was laughed at and rejected by the young lads who preferred to turn a handle and steer with a wheel rather than feed, brush and harness up the great Clydesdales Joe's father kept. Virtually turning his face to the wall, Auld Angus, with the first appearance of a motorised vehicle on his land, had taken the decision to pass on his knowledge to the one youngster who'd shown a willingness to listen and believe. He'd broken all the rules of the Society by confiding it to the son of a farmer. Farmers and landowners were excluded from the knowledge but with his life and his world coming to an end he'd reckoned he had little choice.

Joe had paid careful attention, committing the words and signs to memory, writing down nothing, swearing a fearsome oath never to reveal the secrets of the craft until his own last moments. To his astonishment, the Word whispered to him over a sack of corn in a barn at midnight—a hasty approximation of the initiation into the Society of Horsemen—had been two words, two words in Latin. Though he'd made no comment at the time and made no reference to it ever after, Joe's classical education had led him to suspect, with an awe that was almost religious, that the whole ceremony and structure had been devised in a very ancient past. Romano-British, most probably. The traces they'd left behind in the landscape showed that the Roman army had had a stronger and more peaceable presence in these northern lands than was generally supposed. They'd farmed and kept stock. They'd married local girls. A good number of the soldiers were also horsemen by trade, some from far eastern lands, Persia and beyond. It had pleased Joe to think that when he'd whispered the Roman words into the ears of horses he'd ridden in India and Afghanistan that he was using a link in an unbroken chain reaching back from Britain, through Mithras, god of the soldiery, and Epona, goddess of horses, to some ancient, horse-taming homeland.

His life had taken him away from the country and finally anchored him to an office desk. The skills were not forgotten, though. Joe would say nothing to Hunnyton, as he'd said nothing to anyone, not even to Dorcas. His oath was his oath.

Lightly he remarked, "Amazing what an effect a Fitzbillie's Chelsea bun will have! I nipped out after breakfast and bought a bag of them in Trumpington Street. I say—do you think they'd have the same effect on girls? Shall we try it?"

He made no reference to the tiny bottle of oil of cloves he'd bought for an alleged toothache from Lloyd's the chemist next door. A few drops of that on his handkerchief and a discreet smear on his face and neck had done its job. Better than a calling card. Always a good stand-by in horse country.

"There's Frank come to round them up," Hunnyton said. "We'd better be off and leave them to their work."

"Well, thanks for that! I enjoyed meeting your friends."

Hunnyton peered at him. "Got a hanky have you? You might like to wipe the crumbs and froth off your chin before we encounter civilised society."

THE VILLAGE OF Melsett was indeed small. A strung-out length of timber-framed cottages, plastered and painted, with small windows squinting out under the weight of low-hanging reed thatch, undulated with the rise and fall of the land for half a mile. Each had a neat and extensive plot under cultivation at the back and the small front gardens, where there was space for one between the skirts of the cottage and the road, were ablaze with hollyhock, delphinium and foxglove. At the centre, where the road dipped into a water-splash, there was a village pub—unsurprisingly, The Sorrel Horse—and, opposite, a building which, judging by its size and the bell mounted on the roof, could only be the school. The Friday fishmonger—Mr. Aldous of Southwold, apparently, from the name painted on the side of his Morris van—had arrived to sell his wares from a box of ice in the back. They passed slowly along the high street, Hunnyton pointing out his own cottage as they drove by until they arrived at the ancient village church mounted on a slight rise above the village.

"We've time to stop here and look about before we go to see the vet," he said, showing Joe through the sheep-gate. "There's something you'll want to see, Sandilands."

Joe set off up the path, his eye intrigued by the many headstones engraved with a name he thought he recognised. As they approached the church Hunnyton caught him by the sleeve and pulled him off to the left. "No, this way. Never go round a church widdershins. If you do, the Devil will have you!" Joe doubted the Devil knew his widdershins from his elbow but if Hunnyton favoured a clockwise approach, he was happy to indulge him.

They went off beyond the church and away to the furthest perimeter hedge that divided the church land from the cultivated farmland. A solitary grave with a simple stone marker seemed to be their destination. Joe noticed before they arrived at the spot that the plot was tended, grassed over and carefully trimmed. A stone vase held a bunch of white roses. Buxom, overblown garden-variety roses. A scatter of petals over the grave told Joe that they had been placed there some days ago. Hunnyton was not the only one in the village who remembered her, it seemed.

Joe knelt and read the name. PHOEBE PILGRIM. BORN: 1892. DIED: 1908. MAY SHE REST IN PEACE.

"I noticed other Pilgrims in graves a bit nearer the centre of things," Joe said. "A Suffolk name?" Hunnyton nodded. "So why is Phoebe laid to rest here, away from her family?" he asked, knowing the answer but wanting to hear it from Hunnyton.

"There were some as said she'd no right to be on hallowed land at all. They wanted her planted out at the crossroads." He snorted with disgust. "Medieval barm-pots! You'll still find ignorant old shell-backs in these parts who think a suicide has no place in Christian soil." His voice had taken on a rougher countryman's edge to give traction to the remembered emotion. "I were that mad you could 'a boiled a kettle on my head! I gave that no-good preacher what for—right there in his own church and I got the old man to back me up."

"Good man! Glad to hear you're dragging them into the twentieth century. But—suicide? You don't have to be a country-man to find that a bit tricky. It's still regarded as a crime by the law, even in sophisticated London Town. Poor child. She was only sixteen."

Joe knelt at the grave and said a silent prayer. Deep in thought, he removed a dead flower and rearranged the rest.

"Are you ever going to tell me why you've lured me here, Hunnyton? You've managed what no official body has managed in a quarter of a century—you've got a Scotland Yard officer on his knees at a graveside on Suffolk soil. Quite a feat! Look—there were twenty-five recorded self-inflicted deaths in the Suffolk police authority in 1908 and, apart from the war years when the rate went down, it's been pretty steady ever since. I check these things! So, I'm wondering why you want the Yard here, six feet from the bones of little Phoebe Pilgrim, asking questions."

Hunnyton knelt down opposite Joe, putting his right hand on the grave and staring at him across the small plot, using the earth as he might have used the Bible offered in court. A gesture of sincerity. An accepted guarantee of truth.

"It wasn't a suicide. Someone murdered her. I've always known that. I let it go all these years but this latest—another woman in the Truelove household dying unnaturally—I had to stir myself and do something. It needs a good brain and an influential position to get to the bottom of this and sort it out. It needs you, Sandilands. I didn't just pick your name off a list. Oh, no. The insubordination and the clout I hear about appealed to me, but I chose you for a reason that's personal to *you* though you don't yet know it."

Joe shied away from things personal. "Shall we start with Phoebe?" he said crisply. "What was she to you?"

In Joe's experience, faces usually crumpled as confessions were made, truths revealed. Hunnyton's stiffened into sandstone slabs. They ground together as his mouth opened with reluctance. Difficult to read. "I loved her. Intended to marry her. She was two years younger than me but there was only one class in the little school where everybody started. She was scared when she came for the first day. She was five—a little, pale creature, all eyes. Her shoes were a size too big. Her socks were more darns than socks. I took her under my wing and kept the bullies off. Sat next to her on the bench and looked after her. I took the teasing and bloodied a few noses in return. Teacher never dared say anything to me—Miss Lackland knew who my father was." A slight smile cracked his mouth a little further. "God! I must have been objectionable! I scrupled not in those days to take advantage of either one of my fathers' positions." He shuddered at the memory. "'Diddled old Mrs. Mutimer out of her rent money, they're sayin', Sammy? My dad wouldn't like to hear that . . .' and 'That old donkey o' yours lookin' a bit scrawny these days, Noah. Will you start feedin' him properly or shall I ask my dad to come an' check up on 'im . . . ?' They were never quite sure which father I had in mind. Not sure I did myself sometimes. Still—I'm not going to blame myself for that," he added rebelliously. "Precious little else going for me."

"Phoebe worked at the Hall, you imply?"

"Yes. Housemaid. Started when she was fourteen. Eighteen hours a day, heaving buckets of coal and baths of water up and down four floors. Slavery. I saw her on Sunday afternoons, her only time off. She was looking forward to the time I could stand on my own feet and marry her out of there. Trouble was—when she was rising sixteen I was eighteen and Sir Sidney was sending me off to Cambridge for three years."

"You forgot about Phoebe in all the excitement?"

"Never! No! I reckoned I could offer her a better life if I worked hard and made my own way in the world. It wasn't to be that simple, though. As she got older she caught the eye of someone at the Hall. Not difficult to guess who. The last two times I saw her, she was withdrawn, losing weight, nervy, clinging. She kept trying to tell me something but could never get the words out. Pretty little thing she were. A young gel in her fair prime and pollen . . ." His voice had taken on the sad slowness of Suffolk speech as his mind concentrated on the distant past. He broke off to fumble in his breast pocket and draw out a wallet. Joe held out a hand to take the much-worn studio photograph he was being offered.

The young face looked back at him wide-eyed. Startled by the flash or overawed by the occasion of having her photograph taken in distant Stowmarket? Long fair hair fell in tidily combed ripples over her shoulders. She was wearing her Sunday best— possibly her only—dress and buttoned ankle boots. A large silk bow emphasised the tiny waist.

The image of that slim little frame now rotted to dust only feet below him triggered in Joe a response he suspected to have been carefully calculated, though it was none the less instinctive and inevitable. He swallowed and tried manfully to keep emotion out of his voice as he handed back the photograph.

"'Fair was this young wife, and there withall / As any weasel, her body gent and small,'" he murmured. "Though I've never been able to understand 'gent.'" When words fail you, Chaucer could always come riding to the rescue with a pithy phrase, Joe reckoned.

Hunnyton's smile was full of warm surprise. "He weren't wrong! We still use the word over here. It means neat, worthy of the gentry. Chaucer's Alisoun was lithe as a weasel and so was my Phoebe. She was proud of her eighteen-inch waist. Prettiest girl in the county. May Queen in her last year at school. Clever too. She was wasted emptying chamber pots and scrubbing floors. She could turn her hand and her head to anything. Only one thing she never learned—how to swim."

The abrupt pause invited Joe's next question. "Are you ready to tell me how she died?"

"She drowned. One summer night. In the moat behind the Hall."

Joe waited.

"She were afeard o' water. She'd never have gone near it willingly."

"The household at the time—1908?—remind me. Sir Sidney and Lady Truelove were in residence?"

"Yes. Sir Sidney was . . . oh, forty-six years old. A man in his prime, you'd say. His prime lasted him thirty years. And to prove it—his wife was heavily pregnant at the time with what turned out to be young Alexander."

"James? What of him?"

"You had to feel sorry for him. No longer the centre of attention. Down from Eton for the holidays. Rather embarrassed by his mother's late showing of fecundity, I'd say. Not easy at that age to be told you're about to acquire a baby brother or sister."

"How did he cope with it?"

"By ignoring it. He disappeared off into the woods playing with catapults and shooting off his airgun from dawn to dusk."

More and better particulars required from that source, Joe decided. Boys stalking about in the woods saw more than they were supposed to and remained, themselves, unseen.

As he got to his feet, Joe caught a stirring of foliage, at the periphery of his vision, a flash of colour. He turned his head casually to check the source. The nerve endings on the back of his neck were sending an alert, as was the sudden stillness where there had been movement.

"We're being watched, Hunnyton."

"I'd be surprised if we weren't! A stranger in the village, a smartly turned-out feller driving a showy car—he'd come in for a bit of interest. You'll have set all the lace curtains twitching," Hunnyton replied easily.

Joe nodded. No old biddies would be sneaking about hiding behind tombstones to drum up a bit of gossip and all the children were in school. His unease was not dispelled.

Hunnyton was a policeman and he knew what was expected of a willing witness. Joe asked him again for his view of the events of that summer night a quarter of a century ago and prepared to hear a professionally ordered account. But Hunnyton didn't follow with the response Joe was waiting for.

"Commissioner, I don't believe Phoebe Pilgrim had a liaison with a footman or a groom, as they said at the time. I believe she was drowned by a man of influence whose self-indulgence and carnality was a matter of record. A man who got her into trouble and ruined her." He chewed his bottom lip and Joe understood the depth and confusion of feeling that must be gripping him. An unwanted, unthinking by-blow of the Master of the household himself, Hunnyton must have been torn in two by the realisation that the same man had despoiled the girl he loved. But there was a further dire revelation to follow.

"Like father, like son? It's often said and we both know it's a load of blether but suppose . . . just suppose, Sandilands . . .

The old devil's son is now doing his best to seduce *your* girl. Planning to make her the next Lady Truelove? I doubt it. More likely the next corpse fished out of the moat. And the latter is probably preferable. I'm asking that you investigate the case to the best of your ability, Sandilands. Without fear or favour. But as fast as you can."

CHAPTER 10

"Superintendent, may I just check one detail before we proceed?" Joe replied with equal formality. "Is this your second application for an enquiry into a death? Have you already approached me by means of a recent anonymous letter to the Yard? Item number two in the file I'm getting together?"

His response was one of pure incomprehension. "'Course not! Not my style! I say these things to your face. I just have."

"Yes, yes. Exactly what I expected. I wanted to clear that out of the way. It would seem, Hunnyton, that you're not the only one keen to send me down this particular rabbit hole. Well, well!" He took on a firm tone as he continued: "Now, you're an experienced CID officer with an impressive reputation. I'd rather hear you tell me why I can take no action in the matter of Phoebe Pilgrim than listen to my own voice laying down the law in a depressing and disappointing way."

Joe tried to speak gently yet firmly when what he would really have like to do was sock the man on the jaw. Hunnyton had treated him like one of those Suffolk Punch stallions: attention drawn first—the sticky bun and the oil of cloves were represented by the portraits and the hint of a history behind them. The approach had been made with a gentle delivery, not challenging in any way. He'd let Joe come to him. He'd backed down when necessary, offering the reassurance of frequent flashes of humour and understanding.

Disarmingly, he lapsed into a Suffolk drawl when it seemed appropriate, and Joe was prepared to hear more of it now they were on his own turf. Not unexpected. Joe found the same thing happened to him, without calculation, when he crossed the border back into Scotland. He never blushed for his Gaelic growl when it escaped in London. Where an English country accent like Hunnyton's was a liability, seen as clod-hopping and ridiculous, a Scottish accent was held to be rather smart. The Prime Minister himself was a Scotsman; the Duchess of York, the king's daughter-in-law, was Lady Elizabeth Bowes-Lyon of Glamis Castle, though on the two occasions Joe had chatted with Her Grace the conversation had been conducted on both sides in cut-glass Kensington.

Joe recognised Hunnyton's verbal conjuring. All tricks of the trade. And, so far, the superintendent must think he'd been successful. True enough. But—no harm done; Joe would go along with his schemes as long as they took him in his own chosen direction.

"Rest easy, sir. No warrants and you can't slap manacles on the dead. Wouldn't expect it," he murmured, gentling again. "As you said before, it's a twenty-five-year-old case with no police enquiry worth the name carried out. No autopsy, no forensics of any kind. I just want to know the truth. I want *you* to know the truth. The same goes for her ladyship Lavinia's death. I think we might find the answers under the same roof."

Hunnyton hauled himself to his feet and dusted off his knees, still gazing at the grave. "It's not just that she was special to me . . . I don't know if it gets you the same way, sir . . . Once you're acquainted with a corpse, it belongs to you until you find out what happened to it and who was responsible."

Joe grimaced. "Know what you mean. I've had so many bloody

albatrosses round my neck I'm bent into a hairpin. I can carry one more. A little light-boned one. She's no trouble, bless her. Well, come on, other sheep's head! Let's get moving! The vet did you promise me?"

As they strode down the path Joe paused by one of the tombstones. "See here, Superintendent. There's a local family thick in the ground hereabouts, it would seem. The 'Hunnybuns.' Any relation? I like to know these things."

He had the satisfaction of watching the stony features flush red. Anger? Embarrassment? Impossible to tell.

"That was my name. It's a very ancient village name and I'm proud to bear it. There's hundreds of us in the county and in Cambridge, too. So common I didn't realise there was anything amusing about it until I was about to apply to college. The old man called me in and explained he'd taken steps to have my name changed by deed poll." His supple voice took on the tone of an aristocratic old duffer: "'Wouldn't do to have the other undergraduates laughing at you, old chap! Or calling you a nancy-boy.'" He grinned and clenched his fists. "He needn't have worried. I had my own ways of making my mark."

"Thought as much. But I'm with your old man on this—he did the sensible thing. It's amazing what a difference one consonant can make—kills off any chance of teasing and hoiks you up a class or two. Does seem a waste of a good name, though. I like it! I think you should call your first daughter 'Hunnybun.' I shall expect an invitation to the Christening."

"You'll have to find me a wife first, sir."

Joe was glad to hear a lightening of mood. "I shall give it my best attention. Carrying on the theme of 'honey,' I'm inspired to look for something in light auburn, perhaps, and very lovely as you're so hard to please."

Hunnyton rolled his eyes in scorn at this flight of fancy. "So long as she's not called Blossom or Gypsy, that'll do right well."

~♦

THEY DROVE ROUND to the vet's house, set a little apart from the rest of the village at the easterly end, its garden hidden behind a stalwart copper beech hedge. Clearly a gentleman's residence. It was Victorian, of the same period and the same red brick as the schoolhouse. Decorative cornices, stepped brick corners, contrasting black window and door details were the stamp of an uncompromising city architect who was aiming to mark out his work as something superior to the reed-thatched, ground-hugging local dwellings. A row of steeply pitched gables snapped off an angled salute and tall chimneys at either end stood to attention, giving the house more than a touch of imperial consequence, but a bower of climbing roses, which some later owner had encouraged to swarm all over the façade, poked light fun at the ruled-edge regularity and softened its severity with blousy white blooms.

They parked on the gravelled carriage sweep and got out as the church bell pealed eleven. Seconds later, the infants erupted from the schoolroom into the playground for their recreation and filled the air with their shouts and songs.

"What's the vet's name? Hartest? Must be doing well for himself. This is a very good house."

"He's a very good vet. Best the village has ever had. London trained. Not in the flush of youth. He's a widower. Came out here last summer, thinking to work out his remaining years in peace and quiet." His grin was full of mischief. "He isn't getting much! His prices are very reasonable so people don't need to think twice before calling him in and, as I say, he knows his stuff."

Hunnyton tugged on the bell-pull.

A maid answered at once, taking their hats and ushering them into a cool black-and-white-tiled hallway. "You'll be the police gentlemen for Mr. Hartest. Sorry, sirs, but you can't see him at the minute. Vet's been called out to Fox Farm. There's trouble with that new bull of theirs. But you *can* have a word with *Doctor* Hartest."

They exchanged puzzled looks but before Joe could ask a question, a door at the rear banged open and a voice called out a greeting. "How do you do, gentlemen. I'm Doctor Hartest. Adelaide Hartest. Sorry to disappoint you. My father asked me to welcome you, make his apologies and try to give you any information you might want about the death in the stables. You may see all the notes he made at the time and ... well ... we did talk about it extensively so I can pass on his comments if you wish."

The young woman looked from one to the other of the two men standing awkwardly in her hall. For mature men following a profession where words came easily, they stood in stunned silence, staring at her.

Adelaide Hartest's smile of welcome began to fade. "So long as you're not here to sell me an encyclopedia or guarantee me a pass through the Pearly Gates, you may come into the parlour and introduce yourselves. When you've remembered who you are."

Her appearance was as informal as her greeting. She was a tall girl, wearing trousers and an aged linen open-necked shirt which had probably belonged to her father or even grandfather, Joe thought critically. Lord! It could well have seen action at Gallipoli. She had wooden clogs on her feet. A pair of pruning shears stuck out of one pocket and a gardening glove dangled from the other. Joe didn't much care for women in trousers but, as she turned to lead them into the parlour, he decided to add the name of Adelaide Hartest to his list of women who *could* wear them. It was now a list of three: Marlene Dietrich, Coco Chanel and Dr. Adelaide Hartest.

Joe was the first to recover from the surprise of finding himself in the presence of a bright-faced, extremely pretty and self-assured woman. But it had been the sight of the unfashionable abundance of light auburn hair which had silenced him.

Hunnyton also had been knocked sideways. What on earth could he be thinking? Joe caught the man's eye and asked him a silent question. Hunnyton pulled a comedy villain's face and shrugged a shoulder, saying clearly: "No idea! Nothing to do with me, guv." Joe's waggling eyebrows replied in kind: "Me neither!"

Joe held out a hand and shook the doctor's, introducing himself, and then he presented Hunnyton.

"Well, I'd have been happy to welcome PC Plod up from Bury but—a Scotland Yard Assistant Commissioner and a Detective Superintendent from Cambridge? They're really rolling out the big guns! Do you two normally work together?"

"No, Miss . . . Doctor . . . just for this one outing," Hunnyton supplied.

"I've made some coffee. Suit you both? Good. Sit down, will you, and if you can stop gurning at each other like loonies, we'll get started."

While she poured coffee into blue-and-white china cups and passed around a plate of shortbread biscuits, she explained her presence in her father's house. Adelaide Hartest had only been in the village a week or two. She was taking time off from St. Thomas's Hospital in London, where she'd begun her medical career as a junior doctor and was about to enter general practice if her father could scrape the money together to buy her a partnership. Joe steeled himself to nod sympathetically through an outpouring on the difficulties that beset a woman forging a career for herself in the man's world of medicine in this post-war era, but none came. She was focussed and succinct.

Joe took the notebook she passed him and began to read through it, checking that it corresponded with the notes he'd already seen in the file. He'd deliberately handed the reins of the conversation to Hunnyton and he listened with half an ear as the superintendent held up his end. The young woman appeared to be asking more questions than the detective.

"But why? I can't understand. Why there? Why then? In the stables at crack of dawn with no company other than the two inexperienced lads? Deliberately encountering a stallion with a reputation for violent behaviour? Was the woman mad? You'll have to tell me—I never met her."

She listened to Hunnyton's explanation with incredulity. "You're saying it was done in a spirit of rivalry? Like children showing off in a playground? Lady T. was letting everyone know that when it came to horses she was more skilled than her husband's student? Ooo . . . er . . . mmm . . . Something going on there, wouldn't you say?"

Joe was beginning to wonder if the girl communicated in anything other than questions when she abruptly changed gear.

"Silly women! That's the sort of behaviour you might expect from men. *They* have more opportunities, of course, for affirming their superiority—they can always shoot more birds, pee further, drink more whisky and seduce more women."

Hunnyton froze her with a scandalised glare straight from the pulpit.

Deflected by its force, her attention slid over to Joe. "Tell me, Commissioner—you're clearly a successful member of the competitive sex—how do *you* go about establish a pecking order?"

"Oh, all of the above come in useful," he said with a happy smile. "Luckily I have a lot of gold braid to do my bragging for me these days. My other accomplishments, I'm sorry to say, have not stood the test of time and are getting a bit rusty."

"Ah! The uncertainties of middle age! Like motorcars, men need a yearly check-up. If you're seriously concerned about your declining capacity in any of the aforementioned skills, pop in and consult me. I'm sure I can do something for you."

It was Joe's turn to launch the pulpit stare, though there was a trace of laughter held in check as he replied, "Unless you're an adept with a twelve-bore shotgun, madam, I'm not sure you can help. The old eyes are less sharp than they were perhaps but—as for the other organs you questioned . . . what were they?—kidneys, liver . . ."

"Yes, yes. I understand. Tongue in good working order, too."

"I'm sure we take your point, Doctor." Hunnyton mastered his disapproval of this exchange and reclaimed his hostess's attention. "How else could the lady demonstrate her pre-eminence? Assuming she needed to. You have to admit—it would have been quite a *coup de théâtre* if she'd pulled it off. Parading with a famously fierce stallion trotting behind her on a lead and eating out of her hand right in front of the eyes of the breakfast crowd? A crowd that knows its horseflesh," he added thoughtfully. "Well, that beats a talent for flower arranging and needlepoint. Nothing like it since Professor Champion put on his show in the Ipswich Corn Exchange when I was a nipper!"

Hunnyton's eyes blazed suddenly with a storyteller's zeal. He pushed back the wayward lock of sandy hair from his forehead and launched into his reminiscence. "*Battle between Man and Stallion*, it was billed. *One night only. Vicious horse will be tamed before your very eyes by Professor Champion, the King of all Horse Educators.* Very fine show it was, too! That Champion may have been no more a professor than I was but otherwise he was all he was cracked up to be. He squared up to that horse—Draco, the Transylvanian Man-Eater, his name was. A thundering big black stallion, all rolling eyes and gnashing teeth. Took a crew of six strapping lads to keep it under some sort of control. In two minutes, the beast was eating out of his hand. After half an hour of sashaying around the arena, he'd got a saddle on him and a young lad hopped aboard and trotted him round the ring! To put the final flourish on a memorable evening, I had my first pint of Greene King Ale in the Nag's Head before my old dad and I climbed back in the cart and turned for home."

His boyish blue eyes misted over in pleasurable nostalgia, and

Adelaide's hazel eyes twinkled back her appreciation of his story. She gave him a sweetly indulgent smile.

"There he goes again," Joe thought. "He'll be breathing down her nostrils any minute."

"I'm sure you've understood it exactly, Superintendent," the doctor commended him. "But, poor woman! What a desperate thing to do. Sad and wrong-headed. And never likely to work the magic she wanted it to. When will women ever learn there's *nothing* that can bring back a husband who's determined to go astray? No demands, no persuasion, no appeals to conscience and duty." She sniffed. "I always prescribe a boot up the backside to help him on his way if anyone ever asks me. Not that they do very often. We old maids are not expected to have any useful insights into the married state. But you can bet that's what all this was about: a skirmish over an unworthy man. A tug of war that led to death. Two deaths. I add the name of the horse, Lucifer, to the butcher's bill. Now, you chaps will want to know who put her up to it."

"What makes you think she had an accomplice?" Hunnyton asked.

"It's pretty obvious. My father says she was an unadventurous woman, not given to original thought. He thinks someone planted the idea in her noddle and gave her some professional advice."

"Advice? What advice are you thinking of?"

"Pa was the first medical man on the scene—I suppose you know that. He attended to the body of Lavinia Truelove before anyone else saw it. He checked it for signs of life, of course."

Joe referred to the notes. "He stated that he shot dead the horse, which had retreated back into its stall and was stamping and quivering in apparent fear at the back. He was curious enough about this behaviour to have the carcase hauled back to his surgery for inspection and wrote a full autopsy. Very interesting. Especially the observation of the condition of the mouth."

"That made me angry! The sides of the mouth had been subject to abrasion of some sort. The wounds were not healed and the horse must have been in some pain," Adelaide said.

Hunnyton frowned at the reference. "An old country trick. There's more than one way to ruin a horse. To make it skittish and bad-tempered, they take a half-crown coin and run the bevelled edges along the soft part of the mouth. No outward sign it's been tampered with. But it can drive a horse crazy when someone tries to put in the bit and then the poor animal gets an undeserved reputation for bad temper. It lowers its price dramatically in the sale ring, of course. There's more than one scallywag groom who's hit back at his master using that trick. Still, if ever I get my hands on the bloke who did that . . ."

The cracking of the knuckles in his large hands as they suddenly became fists finished the sentence for him and won him an approving smile and a pat on the hand from Adelaide.

"I'll be there holding your coat, Superintendent," she offered.

"Father doesn't say much in his statement about Lavinia—assuming her body would be dealt with by a medical authority, I expect. Quite proper. Not his place to comment. But he did note some oddities." She reached for a small silver box lying on the table, a box Joe had taken for a cigarette container. "The wounds to her head, neck and torso were extensive and clearly lethal, but her hands were untouched. Hard to discern by torchlight in the falling rain and welters of blood but he smelled something strange on her right hand. It was clutching a mess of . . . he swears it was cake of some kind. He took a sample of it, left the rest in place to be inspected by others and brought it back to have a look under a light. He probably ought not to have done that but he always thinks he knows best and his interest in animals must have pushed him to do it. That's what I say. You're probably thinking: 'Interfering old nuisance!'"

"Not at all," said Joe politely. "If he hadn't taken the steps to preserve it, it would have disappeared with the remainder down the drainage channel on the autopsy table. Some solid evidence at last! May we see?"

The metal box was strong and airtight and Joe struggled to get it open.

"Lord, what a pong!" Hunnyton exclaimed as Joe removed the lid.

"It's not Sachertorte, I think we'd all agree," Adelaide said, wrinkling her nose.

Joe poked at the contents with a pencil end. "But it is cake. *Was* cake. It looks more like the sweepings of an ancient Egyptian mummy's tomb. A sop to Cerberus? Some opiate in there, did your father assume? A little something to quieten the horse?"

"You'll need to take it to a laboratory in Cambridge if you want to find out. My father's equipment was not up to the job. But I'll tell you something. Pa's not easily put off. He decided that if the cake was laced with something mysterious intended for use on the horse, it was probably acquired from the chemist. He went along and grilled old Mr. Morrison. Made him show his dispensing book." Her eyes gleamed and she said apologetically, "No right to do that, I'm sure you'd be the first to tell him, but Pa can be very forceful and the local . . . country shyness"—she looked with smiling apology at Hunnyton—"'foot shuffling' he calls it—irritates him no end. Faced with all that 'Don't you be asking me, sir, twern't none o' my business,' stuff he turns into a raging bully. Interesting, what he managed to extract, though. And no illegalities revealed, so no harm done. The day before the adventure, our innocent chemist had sold four bags of exotic culinary spices. To Grace Aldred, Lavinia's maid." She handed over a sheet of paper. "He took a copy: fenugreek, cumin, rosemary, cinnamon. Grace told him the cook had requested them to make up a curry."

"Sounds reasonable to me. Not sure about the rosemary," Joe said, "but the others are all constituents of Indian dishes. They do, however, as I think you've guessed, have another quite differ-ent use." He looked at Hunnyton, who understood the unspoken question and nodded imperceptibly.

The superintendent undertook the explanation. "Horse magic! In folklore, those spices are all attractants. Horses have huge nostrils and a very sensitive sense of smell. If you want a horse to love you or just behave itself in your presence you can do it by magicking it with these scents, which it adores." He grinned. "They tell me oil of cloves dabbed on a hanky works a treat too."

"That's the refined way of doing it," Adelaide said. "My father came upon a ploughman once, stripped to his skin in the shed, in the act of wiping down his armpits with a bit of stale bread. When Pa challenged him on his strange behaviour, he explained that he was taking on a new horse. This sweat business was a good way, known to all the horsemen, of making horses familiar with their handler's scent." She wrinkled her nose. "I must say, this bit of cake smells as though it's been somewhere even less salubrious than a ploughman's armpit at close of play on Plough Sunday."

Joe picked up the box, looked more closely, held it to his nose and inhaled deeply. For a moment his head reeled and his stom-ach churned. He couldn't quite smother an exclamation of distress so visceral the other two turned a gaze of solicitous enquiry on him. He put the lid back on firmly and, gasping apologetically through gritted teeth, recalled: "Trenches. Pinned down. Holed up unable to clear out for a fortnight. Plague of rats feasting on the bodies we couldn't dispose of. The men bayoneted them. Left them lying about in piles to rot. Same smell." He stabbed an accusing finger at the silver box. "Rotten rat carcass. It's the livers that go first . . . the stinkiest bit . . . Excuse me . . ."

Joe dashed from the room and, thankful that the front door had been left open, he made his way quickly to the nearest rose bed. Through his unpleasant retching noises, he was aware of a clattering of clogs down the hallway. A moment later, a white cotton handkerchief was pushed over his nose.

"Lavender. Breathe it in. Antidote."

A cool, professional hand ran lightly over his forehead. A warm, very unprofessional voice murmured in his ear, "That'll teach you to go sticking that great conk of yours into unknown substances. Poisons can be inhaled, you know. But I don't think it's poison that's provoked this reaction. It's memory. Smell and taste—they can be very acute and the mind associates them with pleasure or pain we've experienced in the past. This is very real nausea you're suffering but the brain will soon sound the all-clear and you'll wonder what on earth that was all about. I'm sure you needn't worry."

"Embarrassing, though! What do you prescribe, Doctor?" Joe managed to say, beginning to win the struggle with his heaving stomach.

"Keep starching the old upper lip and stay away from dead rats, of course. Ready to come back inside? Your friend is anxious."

Hunnyton was standing by with a glass of water when they rejoined him.

Adelaide exchanged a meaningful look with him and voiced the thoughts of both of them. "Just imagine, Superintendent—if it can do that to *him*—what must it have done for an animal with a hundred times the sensitivity?"

"Terrified the poor beast to death," said Hunnyton. "I think we understand now after that little demonstration. Is the commissioner all right?" He peered at Joe with concern. "Looks a bit seedy to me . . . Now listen. There's not many who know and I ought not to be speaking out, but . . . oh, well. We all accept that it's fear and its response, flight, that dominate in a horse? Fear is what's kept the species alive through the millions of years they've been on earth." Joe and Adelaide nodded. "Man has always tried to influence and tame horses to fulfil his own requirements. He's worked out some subtle ways of doing that. There's horse lure, like the curry spices, and then there's horse bate. Nasty stuff that has the opposite effect. Smear a trace of it on the posts of a horse's stall and it won't pass between them even if it's starving. Push a load of it on a bun close up to its nostrils and you'd send it out of its mind. Do that when you're advancing on it in a narrow space, driving it backwards, blocking its escape route, and, mad with fear, it's going to tear right through you. As its nature insists. It has no choice."

"Bate, you say? What is 'bate'? Superintendent, what exactly do you think was smeared on that piece of cake?" Adelaide asked. "What's the commissioner just breathed into his lungs? I insist on hearing."

"Decayed stoat liver, steeped until rancid in rabbit's blood and cat's urine, then dried out. Most likely," he said with relish.

"You can't get that off the shelf at Mr. Harrison's," Adelaide said. "And how on earth do you get a cat to pee in a pot?"

"Well, lacking a cooperative moggie, horse's urine is more plentiful and does the job."

"You're having me on!"

"No indeed. Believe me—this is serious magic! Produced locally, I'd say, to an ages-old recipe by someone with the knowledge. The Horse Knowledge."

"It sounds like hogwash to me," Adelaide said crisply. "Well, no, that's about the one ingredient that didn't feature in your little confection. Why do people think they need to have recourse to magic potions? My father's been handling horses all his working life without benefit of fenugreek and cumin. Rabbit's blood and stoat's liver have never featured in his *materia medica.*"

"Oh, I don't know. Horses hate stoats, even the live ones," Joe remarked. "The sight and smell of one on the road will send them into paroxysms of fear or fury—you must have noticed?"

"We certainly didn't miss the paroxysms in the rose bed, I'll grant you that," she said thoughtfully and summed up for herself: "So, Lavinia bought the lure from Mr. Harrison, helped herself to a bun from the tea table and gave it a very special frosting. It's this she must have thought she was using when she went down to the stable to make her overtures to young Lucifer. But somewhere along the way—where? and when?—the sweet spiced cake was . . . exchanged?—for a piece that had been 'bated' with a substance obnoxious and threatening to the horse. Am I getting this right?"

Time for Hunnyton to show his cards, Joe decided. Professional etiquette told him he should wait until they were alone together before putting him to the question but a glance at the doctor's face, good-humoured and quizzical, made this reticence seem unnecessary. "You're getting it right," he said. "But, Hunnyton, it's time to come clean, I think. Son of a horseman of repute as you tell me you are, you must have acquired the knowledge of lures and bates—the ingredients must be as well known to you as the recipe for fruit scones. In Scotland this knowledge is passed down to a select few initiates, never more than one or two per district. The numbers of these have diminished drastically since the war and few remain on either side of the border. Now tell us, which local man would have had the skills to mark Lady True-love's card for her? Who would have the formulae for lures and bates off by heart?"

If Adelaide Hartest hadn't been present, turning her bright, concerned face on the superintendent, Joe would have added: "Starting with your own name . . ."

Hunnyton replied at once. "Well, you can scratch my name from any list you're drawing up. My pa was one of the Horsemen, no doubt about that, but they were so darned secretive no one but the members knew who they were, not even their families. Once a month on a Saturday, he'd put on his best suit with waistcoat and watch-chain. My mother would brush his hat and polish his boots and off he'd go to Bury. Sometimes Ipswich. Dad's night out at the Whistling Ploughboy or the Great White Mare. I was a grown lad going about a grown lad's business in Bury one Saturday when I came across him with his mates. Not a drinking outing—though much ale was drunk. I asked about, listened at locked doors and discovered the meetings were the monthly gatherings of the Horse Society. As hush-hush as any Masonic do. More so.

"At home he kept his horse remedies, pills and potions in a locked cupboard in his shed. Those were the days when vet's fees were high," he said with an apologetic grin to Adelaide. "He'd dispense them to anyone needing them, but there were one or two items in there he kept for his use only. We kids never knew what the mixtures were. He had a clever way of keeping his secrets. Every now and again when supplies were running low, he give us three boys a scrap of paper. A shopping list. Never on the same day and never together. He'd send us off to local chemists. Different chemists in different towns. When he'd gathered in all the ingredients, he'd mix them up in his shed. To this day I'm not sure I could reconstitute any of his recipes."

"But someone in the village knows, evidently," said Adelaide. "The knowledge was passed to—sold to—Lady Truelove, with awful consequences. Lure swapped for bate? Now that's malice aforethought."

"I'd call it murder, Doctor," Hunnyton said.

"But murder that's almost impossible to prove," Joe warned. "I hardly like to think why we're even bothering to attempt an enquiry."

He was shot down by two focussed glares. Uncomfortably, he tried to justify his pessimism. "No evidence . . . time delay . . . lack of witnesses . . . laughed out of court . . ." He heard himself bumbling.

"All true, alas," Hunnyton chimed in in reluctant support.

"Give us some fingerprinting, footprinting, blood-typing and scene-of-crime forensic stuff to do and we're your men." He shook his head and glowered. "But this death by horse at arm's length, weeks after the event . . . I dunno!" He sighed.

Adelaide nodded in agreement. "You know, if this were a medical problem, I'd say Lavinia's death was not a solution but a symptom. A symptom of a great malaise in the family. All is not well up at the Hall, that much is clear." She got to her feet and looked at her watch. Consultation at an end. "Time you gents went off to hear what Gracie Aldred has to say for herself, I think. I say—do you mind if I tell this to my father? The curry spices and stoat's entrails? Professionally, he'll be very intrigued. Might even put some on his shopping list."

"Yes, Doctor, of course. Something may occur to him. He may, in spite of annoying Suffolky reticence," Hunnyton gave her a cheeky grin, "be handed a confidence or two—something someone would rather not divulge to a policeman." He rose to his feet. "Sadly, not everyone finds us congenial company."

She went to stand in front of him, eye to eye.

Ouch! Not a good move, Doctor, Joe thought, knowing what he did of Hunnyton's gentling powers.

"Look, Mr. Policeman, reticence is all very well in its place, which would be somewhere in about the middle of last century. You may call me 'Doctor' when I'm attending to your ingrowing toenail. 'Miss Hartest' when you see me in church. When you're teasing me in my parlour, you must call me 'Adelaide.' And your name is?"

"It's Adam. Adam Hunnybun," he said without thinking.

Her face lit up with delight as she repeated the name to herself and, for an awful moment, Joe thought she might take him for the teddy bear he much resembled and give him a hug.

"And my name's Joe," Joe said, adding a silent, "As if anyone cared."

CHAPTER 11

As they climbed back into the car Hunnyton grumbled, "How the blazes did she know I have an ingrowing toenail?"

"It's the way you walk," Joe said kindly. "You favour your left foot. Not a particularly adventurous guess—most coppers have them." He found he was reluctant to leave go of the image of the young woman they'd just encountered. "That's a wonderful girl! I wasn't happy to hear her call herself an 'old maid.'"

"Nor was I. She's wrong on the first half anyway. Not what you'd really call old. She was twenty-seven last week."

"Now how would you know that?"

"While you were being attended to in the rose garden I peeked inside the birthday cards lined up on the mantelpiece."

"So—hardly old then."

"No. And she was misleading us on the second half too, unless I mistake."

"Now how would you know that?" Joe said again but his voice now conveyed a chilly rebuke rather than a question. A woman's honour would always be defended by Joe whatever the circumstances. Whoever the woman.

Hunnyton picked up the warning and, as Joe had come to expect, backed away. Advance, retreat, concede territory, disarm, advance again, eyes averted. Joe wondered if he'd recognise the moment the superintendent was ready to throw the saddle over his back. "I wouldn't know that," the horseman said easily. "Evidence not so readily available. You might well have a better insight, city gent that you are. It just occurs to me that a woman of her quality, working at her trade, with her chances, well, it would be a bit of a surprise if . . . Just choosy, I expect. Hard to tell when she comes in from the garden looking like a rook-scarer that's been pulled through a thorn hedge, but there's something about her . . . She's friendly and yet she has a sort of shield around her. Get close and you'd bounce off."

"I noticed that, but she's very unusual. I could swear I've seen her, or her like, somewhere before . . ."

"You have. You pass her every day on your way to work. On the Embankment. She's standing with a dirty great spear in one hand, chariot reins in the other. She's hurling abuse at the Roman army and she's made of bronze," Hunnyton said, chuckling. "Boadicea! Corst, blast! You wouldn't want to get the wrong side of that one! Doctor Hartest is a corker but those pruning shears she keeps in her pocket are as much of a warning as the scythes on Boadicea's chariot wheels. 'Keep off! You could lose a limb.'"

This was a disappointing response. A crude cover to deflect the interest Joe was sure he'd noticed?

"You're too severe," he said easily. "I've remembered now where I've seen her before! She's not the Queen of the Iceni, she's a Botticelli goddess . . . Flora's her name and she takes centre stage in the painting of *Primavera*."

Hunnyton frowned, trying to recall it.

"You know the one—there's the three Graces on the left, sketchily dressed in diaphanous dresses, dancing about in a bosky dell, cupids and cherubs shooting each other and just to the right of centre, the only one who's looking at the camera, so to speak, the most amazing girl with honey-coloured hair, a deliciously wicked smile and slanting eyes. She's offering you a choice bloom from her pinny-ful of wildflowers. Or anything else you have in mind." He sighed.

"I know it. A bit flowery-bowery for my taste. If lusting after painted ladies is all the go, I'll admit to being more in tune with Peter Lely. All those Stuart beauties in slippery amber-gold boudoir gowns, pearl drops and just the odd rosebud carefully placed. There's one of the Countess of Oxford . . . or is she the Countess of Halifax . . . ?"

Joe knew when he was being sent up. "Ah, yes. Who needs 'Tit-Bits' when we have the 'Tate' for titillation? But—speaking of aristocratic ladies, I'd guess you are now taking me to the Hall to present me to the Dowager, Sir James's widowed mother. Is that what you have in mind?"

Hunnyton nodded. "She's on my list. I thought first we'd call in at my modest abode and spruce up a bit. You're covered in ginger hairs of one sort or another."

"Sounds like a good plan. Perhaps while we're at the Hall I can ask to use the telephone. I didn't think we could impose on Adelaide Hartest, though I assume the vet has one."

Joe had unconsciously stumbled into an odd pocket of resentment, judging by the abrupt increase in speed and the exclamation that followed.

"You'll need some change in your pocket. Bloody English aristocrats! They'll freely lend you their second best castle for a month, their Rolls-Royce for a week, their mistress for a night but if you want to use their telephone for five minutes that'll be sixpence please. Just leave it in the dish next to the telephone. Even if you're reporting that the vicar's fallen downstairs and broken his neck. If you want a stamp to post a letter it'll cost you twopence—"

"It's all right, Hunnyton. Calm down! I know the drill!" Joe understood the anxiety behind this huffing and puffing. "And I'm familiar with the quirks and customs of Society. I won't let you down. I shall tug my forelock and curtsey to her Dowagership and you won't need to blush for my manners. I usually find the families are reasonably straightforward. It's the butlers that terrify me."

Hunnyton grinned and eased his pressure on the accelerator.

He stopped in front of a house rather larger than the run of cottages strung out along the road and Joe stepped out to admire. Unlike the other reed-thatched dwellings, this one had a steeply pitched roof with an undulating coverlet of plain tiles of all colours from a red so dark it was almost black, fading to buff and cream. Its long front was plastered and colour-washed in the Suffolk way in the brownish-pink of ox blood, dark under the eaves where protected from the rain, bleached to almost white at the level of the brick plinth which ran around the house.

The central front door was a stout affair of weathered oak in wide planks, flattered by a lavishly carved eighteenth-century doorcase of a quality Grinling Gibbons would not have blushed for, brought in from elsewhere, Joe guessed, and scaled down to fit its more modest circumstances. Seeing his eyes on it, Hunnyton accounted for it: "I rescued the casing from Owles Hall when they demolished it ten years ago. They were about to chuck it on the bonfire. I had to take a saw to it to make it fit, but . . ." He shrugged.

"Better a fragment than a pile of ashes," Joe supplied. "And you kept the best bits." His hand went out automatically to pat the cheek of a carved cherub, who seemed to smile down an acknowledgement.

The windows on either side were of different sizes and inserted at different levels; tiny panes of ancient glass in leaded frames sat alongside more generously sized panes of Georgian glass. Precisely marking the centre of the cottage, an imposing chimney stack thrust upwards, its bulk unsuccessfully disguised by a barley-sugar twist of decorative brick-work.

Joe stood, absorbed, trying to grasp the essence of this layering of styles and materials. He realised that Hunnyton was standing tensely by his side, watching for his reaction. When caught off guard, Joe's lively features were hardly ever able to conceal his emotions. He turned to Hunnyton a face warm with delight and surprise. "Wonderful! It's a lucky man who holds the key to this house in his pocket!" he said simply.

Hunnyton seemed pleased. "Go straight in," he said. "No need for keys. The door's never locked. That's the Suffolk way."

As he put out a hand to open the door, the clip-clop of hooves down the High Street caught his attention and he groaned. "We've got company. Sandilands—you'll be needing the old bat's Christian name. It's Cecily."

CECILY, LADY TRUELOVE, hailed them in her hunting-field voice from a distance of a hundred yards. She advanced on them riding a sleek black hunter at a dignified trot, a groom following a discreet distance behind her.

The two men, caught unprepared, straightened their ties, checked each other's smile and stood ready to greet her.

"Morning, Hunnyton," she said crisply. "I see you've brought us Sandilands of the Yard."

Hunnyton presented Joe to her ladyship and they nodded politely at each other, the lady looking down critically from her perch. For a woman of her age—early sixties—Truelove's mother was wearing well, Joe reckoned. Stiff-backed in her riding gear, she presented a more youthful figure than he had expected. Her hair, collected into a glossy chignon below the brim of her shiny riding hat, was dark, elegantly streaked with grey, and her eyes, dark also, were bright and inquisitive. In her youth she must have been a stunner, Joe thought.

"Where've you got to in your day, Commissioner?" she wanted to know without preamble.

"We've just visited the veterinarian and, with your permission, your ladyship, will next undertake a tour of the stables and speak to the grooms." Joe was equally brief but his smile was engaging.

She nodded. "By the time you've finished you should have some useful insights into the animal kingdom. You may share them with me over lunch. One o'clock suit you?" She glanced with approval at Joe's luggage on the back seat. "I see you've come prepared. I trust your man has stowed away your evening clothes in there. You are expected for dinner of course. We've put a guest room at your disposal for as long as necessary. Styles will show you to your room when you arrive at the Hall."

"I do beg your pardon, madam, but I had no idea you were counting on me to stay. I've arranged to have dinner with the superintendent, who's kindly offered his hospitality and, after that, I have to return to London."

The reply was a short and sharp: "Nonsense!" A gloved hand twitched in irritation. "See to it, Hunnyton." She began to gather up her reins before Joe could launch a further objection. "Don't imagine I'm going to let you slide away, young man." To Joe's concern, her tone had taken on a flirtatious note. She leaned forward, implying that her comments were about to become confidential. "We're always short of lively company at this time of year—after the races and before Henley—and a good-looking chap like you, whose reputation for dash and diversion I have on first hand authority, is not going to wriggle out of my social net so easily. I have heard good things of you from Sir George Jardine, who is an old friend, and, indeed, godfather to my sons. I have a party coming down for a long weekend and I don't suppose many of them will have met a policeman before. They will be fascinated. You'll be able to sing for your supper . . . perhaps establish some useful connections. My son James—you know him, I believe?"

"We have met on one or two occasions, madam."

"He's travelling down from town tomorrow morning,

bringing some people with him and very much looking forward to seeing you. We don't disappoint James."

Joe was aware of Hunnyton's arm under his. Supporting him? Or restraining? The countryman's calm voice plastered over Joe's chill silence and took over for the formalities of leave-taking. He bade her ladyship goodbye and assured her everything would be arranged to her satisfaction. The Assistant Commissioner would be duly delivered to the house following on from his inspection of the stables.

The two men watched the horses trot off down the road in silence.

"One or two surprises there. Come on inside, man," Hunnyton invited. "You could do with a pint of ale. And a plate of my sister's stew to fortify you. No, no! I've not gone barmy—if you're having lunch at the Hall it would be a sensible precaution. The lady lives on nettle soup and dog biscuits and expects her guests to do the same."

"Hunnyton, I'm having dinner with you and motoring back to Cambridge tonight. Those are my plans and I shan't be changing them at the whim of an autocratic old lady."

"Ah, but it's not a whim," Hunnyton said mysteriously. "That lady doesn't go in for whims, it's plots she favours. Plots and traps and spider's webs. Come on inside. Watch the step down."

INSIDE WAS MORE delight. Joe ducked and stepped through the front door of the yeoman's dwelling into a neat and sparkling room running the length of the cottage, divided into two by an enormous central chimney which offered a double fireplace with a bread oven to the side. On the left was the living space where food was cooked and served at a substantial oak table. To the right was a carpeted room, lined with bookshelves and furnished with a sofa and two armchairs covered in a William Morris print. The walls were coloured with white-wash applied over so many generations the paint had accumulated and rounded out the corners between wall and ceiling, giving the impression of the interior surface of a silky cocoon, instilling a feeling of security and comfort. The oak beams overhead had been lime-washed to soften their massive presence and create an illusion of greater height. Vital to a man of Hunnyton's size, Joe thought, surveying them.

"I had the floor lowered a foot," Hunnyton explained. "So you can walk about without bashing your head on a beam."

The stout floorboards underfoot had been polished to a high shine and one or two red turkey rugs were scattered over. In the open fireplace, still-glowing embers were evidence that Hunnyton's sister had been in "to see to things." She had left the fire guarded and a cooking pot was indeed sitting, as promised, in the old-fashioned black-leaded oven.

Hunnyton folded up a dishcloth and took it out, placing it on the trivet left ready on the table. He took off the lid and a delicious smell of lamb stew flooded the room. A scatter of chopped herbs from an earthenware dish made it irresistible.

"You'll want to wash your hands and tidy up a bit. Those horses gave you a right going over. There's a bathroom through the back door there, in the outshot, beyond the kitchen. I have no electricity but I've made sure the plumbing's as good as it can be. There's two bedrooms on the floor above. I had thought you could have the one on the left. Up those stairs." He indicated a narrow spiral staircase that was more of a ladder. "It's not the Ritz but it's a long way from the trenches."

When Joe reappeared, Hunnyton handed him a glass of ale and disappeared to tidy himself up. While he was out of the room, Joe did what he always did in strangers' houses—sniffed about with curiosity. The photographs on the mantelpiece were of the family: wide-eyed, flaxen-haired Hunnybuns all in a row. At its most plentiful the batch consisted of five children of whom Adam, the oldest, stood out head and shoulders above his brothers and sisters. It must have been a squeeze rearing all those children in such tight accommodation, but Hunnyton seemed to love the cottage and count himself lucky to have it.

Joe always reckoned that five minutes with a man's bookshelves revealed the man and saved him hours of exploratory conversation or interrogation. Hunnyton's books were plentiful and acquired over many years. Carefully arranged on shelves by category and author, they were mostly familiar to Joe. His own shelves offered very much the same choice. Classics; philosophy; history, social and martial; a good number of novels, even one or two French ones in garish yellow covers, crowded into the space and overflowed onto the floor. A pile of *John Bull* magazines was tied up with string, ready to move on down the line to other thinking members of the proletariat. A copy of the *Daily Herald* lay shredded for fire-lighting in a basket on the hearth. Joe smiled. No *Burke's Peerage*, no *Tatler* in sight. Here at home, at any rate, the superintendent was comfortably and openly a man of the people.

When called to table, Joe kept silent about his encounter with Lady Cecily in deference to the hospitality on offer from Hunnyton. He'd no intention of spoiling a good stew. He helped himself when asked to a sizeable ladleful and, making himself useful, took hold of a large knife by the breadboard and proceeded to cut off chunks the size of cobbles, the size of lump they'd all used in the trenches to mop up what passed for gravy in their billy cans.

Hunnyton sensed what he was about and took a piece. "Glad to see you're not a delicate eater. Though my sister would mark you down for manners, I'd call it a tribute to her cooking."

They ate their way through, swapping war memories and comments on local customs and farming life, avoiding for the moment what was in the forefront of their minds. In view of the ordeal by nettle soup which was to come, Joe refused the cheese and the custard tart and sat back to smoke a cigarette while Hunnyton busied himself with his pipe.

Finally, Hunnyton decided: "You've got to go, you know. The old bird's up to something and you won't find out what it is in London. This party she's planning . . . sounds a bit odd to me." His eyes narrowed against the wreathing blue smoke from the St. Bruno old twist. "And you'd think me some kind of an idiot if I hadn't noticed that she seemed just now to be expecting you. Almost as though she'd sent an invitation and was loitering about waiting for you to arrive."

He waited for Joe's explanation.

Joe took a letter from his pocket. "In a manner of speaking, you could say that is what happened. Look at this. The anonymous letter I mentioned, delivered to me at the Yard last week."

Hunnyton read the sheet and grunted. "Woman's writing. Not girls' public school—have you noticed they always do their e's the Greek way? Secondary educated, though . . . it's nicely formed with even the odd curlicue and it's joined up properly." He puffed again on his pipe. "The phrasing's top-drawer. Short, peremptory. 'Get yourself down here and sort this out. Call yourself a copper?' Mmm . . . so you thought the Dowager was responsible?"

"I think so. Dictated, I shouldn't wonder, to her maid. I'd say that old lady enjoys a bit of intrigue."

"It's her middle name."

"This proven, I'd say, by her behaviour just now in the lane. All that: 'There you are! Dinner gong goes at seven,' stuff. Well, it worked, for here I am! I'm sure you're right and I ought to accept her invitation . . . or command, rather. I can't say I'm looking forward to it. A party thrown together at the last minute? It can hardly be a jolly occasion considering they're all supposed to be in mourning still. Look, Hunnyton—could it be that with Lavinia out of the way she's enjoying being the mistress of the house again? Showing everyone what it used to be like in the glamorous old days when they entertained royalty?" Joe suggested.

Hunnyton raised his eyebrows in speculation, then nodded.

"I begin almost to feel a pang of sympathy for James True-love—with a mother and a wife like that pair on the premises, his life must have been hell," Joe ventured.

"It was no stroll through the cowslips. They hated each other. They used him as a pawn, of course. But save your sympathy. James was never a victim. He had his ways of escaping their attentions. Uncomfortable for everyone, though, including the servants. It's never easy serving two mistresses, and both of them batty."

"Bad luck on poor James, though?" Joe persisted.

Hunnyton shrugged. "*His* choice of wife. His *father's* choice of wife, come to that. They made their own beds. They got what they wanted. Needed, I should say. That sort of man looks elsewhere for his emotional and sensual fulfilment." He paused to allow his veiled message time to be absorbed, then, wiping the distaste from his face, went on: "The men of that family have been marrying money since the Norman Conquest. Money is no guarantee of character in a wife, but it does keep the place afloat. These are hard times. Many estates have gone under, the houses bulldozed, grand old names buried with them. Where are the offspring of those old English families now? Manufacturing paperclips in Letchworth Garden City perhaps. Selling paint door-to-door? But the Trueloves are where they've always been and their roof is in tip-top condition, their moat clear as glass, their fields tilled to the last inch, their cattle and hogs as fat as any in England."

"Where did it come from, this financial parachute? Are you allowed to say?"

"It's no secret, it's just that if you want to keep your head on your shoulders you never refer to it. Midlands manufacturing money in both cases. The old girl's family made their fortune in Manchester. Cloth industry. Lavinia's lot came from Birmingham.

Metal. They prospered during the war. Any war you care to name. She was brought up in a family seat her grandfather bought for himself on the proceeds of carnage, well away from the soot and smoke and the sight of the labouring poor, in the hunting shires of the Midlands. Her father had aspirations of grandeur and the wherewithal to achieve them. He bought himself a baronetcy and his three daughters all married into the minor aristocracy."

"But Lavinia and James produced no heirs to carry on the Truelove tradition of fortune hunting, I understand?"

"None. They were married for over ten years but no luck. She refurbished the old nursery and it stood equipped and ready to go, but over time it degenerated into a spare guest room. The strain of waiting and hoping sent her a bit doo-lally, I think. She certainly got worse with each year that passed. She was a woman who'd always got what she wanted the moment the want entered her head. She could never quite accept that Nature might be thwarting her. Her mother-in-law never mentioned it, of course, but it was clear to anyone who knew them that she thought Lavinia was a hen-headed waste of time. As did her son."

"James was less than attentive, I'm guessing?"

"He was spending longer and longer periods of time away from Suffolk."

"Busy man. A rising star on the political stage—you'd expect that."

"Lavinia was accepting of his ambition. She shared it. She was already planning to do over the accommodation at number ten Downing Street. Ghastly thought! No—it was his other activities that roused her resentment."

"His philanthropic and academic interests?"

"Yes. Begun by his grandfather, continued by his father and lately vastly extended by James—at his wife's expense. Lavinia fancied she saw her money being poured into support for university research into subjects she hadn't the slightest interest in.

'Long-haired, socialist riff-raff' were having their pockets filled with her family's hard-earned cash and encouraged to while away three years of their lives making stinks in laboratories and downing pints in pubs."

"Many people would say she had a point."

"And many people would say you're trying to start an argument, Commissioner. They might even add you've got your own dark horse entered in this mad steeplechase over hedge and ditch."

"I never bet on the outcome, Hunnyton. I've been surprised far too often in this game. It's one of my faults, perhaps. I keep an open mind for too long. I extend the benefit of the doubt until the moment I'm looking down the barrel of a gun in the hand of someone I've been doubting since the whistle blew."

Hunnyton began to gather up the dishes. "Well, watch yourself up at the Hall. They're not short of firearms of one sort or another. There are people up there barmy enough to use them and you're barmy enough to provoke them."

The mild insult was accompanied by a sudden intensification of warmth in the Saxon eyes. Joe had noticed that Hunnyton was confident enough of their relationship to neglect due deference to rank when it suited him.

The superintendent looked at the clock. "Better be off." He handed Joe some pencilled sheets from his pocket. "Here's some bumf I prepared for you. Plan of the Hall in case you need to run away in the night. Names of the senior staff. Map of the grounds, distances marked. Over the page, I've drawn a plan of the stable lay-out. I'll walk you round the out buildings but leave you to it inside the moat. Oh, by the way, the drawbridge is pulled up at sunset. Traditionally and actually."

"Drawbridge?" Joe questioned, suddenly alarmed. "Where are you sending me? Doubting Castle? The lair of the Giant Despair?"

"Drawbridges, in fact. One in front, one in the rear. Both in good working order. Most nights they remember to hoist them up and lower them at dawn. Guests from London enjoy that sort of thing. They write home about it. Take my advice—before you do anything else, ask the lad on the gate to show you where the levers are—anybody with two hands can work the mechanism."

"Drawbridges! I loathe the things. They're responsible for more death and injury than the enemy they're supposed to be keeping out. Why the hell does Truelove feel he needs a moat in this day and age?"

"Moats are no big deal out here in Suffolk. Cattle troughs mostly, nowadays. Every farmhouse of any size has one, fed by underground springs. It was the main water source in the past. They're not for defensive purposes, though perhaps in the Middle Ages they might have been. The great houses keep them for show and entertainment. Some stock them with fish. Truelove keeps his weed-free and crystal clear—a sight more healthy than Byron's Pool in Grantchester, I can tell you. Everyone in the village who can swim learned to do it in that old moat. Younger guests like to splash about and squeal in the summer. Don't worry—you won't be expected to perform—it's been far too cold a season so far and the water's like ice still."

Joe pocketed the plan and looked Hunnyton in the eye. Time for a bit of aggression, he calculated. "So far, so good. It's all working out for you, isn't it, Superintendent? You've got your man on the inside for a couple of days potentially, by personal invitation of the dowager, welcomed within the drawbridge by various members of the family for reasons that wouldn't bear close inspection. I'd guess you don't intend me to leave unless I'm dragging some fiend behind me in handcuffs."

Hunnyton grinned broadly. "Not too fussed about the cuffs, sir. I just want you to ferret out the truth. I want *you* to know the truth. Nothing wrong with that, is there?"

There wasn't. Joe sensed that he and Hunnyton shared the same instinct for ferreting and could well understand why the man

wanted to get to the bottom of his Phoebe's death. A mate of Joe's
had taken a bullet in a fleshy part of his body in the war. It healed
over and for years he was able to ignore the metal he was carrying
around with him. But one day it seemed to have decided of its own
accord to burrow its way painfully to the surface again. Surgery
was required. Impossible to cut into one's own flesh. You call in
a steady hand to perform the extraction for you. He laid this out
for Hunnyton, who nodded his understanding.

"But Cecily Truelove?" Joe questioned. "She seems to think
she also has booked an operating slot with the same surgeon at
the same time. I'm sure she has no concern for little Phoebe Pilgrim—if she even remembers her. No, Cecily would appear to be
calling for an invasive procedure to be carried out dangerously
close to her family's heart. Why would she do that?"

"It can only be that she knows Lavinia's death was managed
and she thinks she knows who's responsible. She must have every
confidence that the prime suspect—who, in anyone's book, must
be her own son, James, the victim's husband—is in the clear.
Otherwise she wouldn't countenance your presence within fifty
miles. The guilty party must be someone she regards as untouch-
able by her—someone with influence—or even perhaps very close
to her. She wants the guilty party removed by an impartial police
officer with sufficient authority to effect that removal."

"This gathering she's organising . . ." Joe said, casting a fly on
the water. "She's re-creating the April house-party, isn't she? She's
re-enacting the whole show for my benefit. It's a trap for some
poor bugger. Thanks to her careful arrangements, the murderer
will be tethered here at Melsett for the next few days, drawbridge
up, ready for the strong hand of the Law to feel his collar. He'll
not have dared to turn down the invitation for fear of arousing
suspicion. He'll be giving me a rictus grin over his sherry glass
and nervously muttering, 'So, they tell me you're a policeman . . .'"
He looked searchingly at Hunnyton. "I do wonder why she

couldn't just have had recourse to the Cambridge detective division. To you, Superintendent."

"Thought you'd get there if I waited long enough. I could go on about prophets in their own country having no respect. Homegrown boy, regrettably intertwined with the family and all that. But the real reason—I'll say it now I know you've worked it out—is that you're looking at the murderer." He cast a swift glance at Joe, looking for something in his reaction and fiddled with his pipe in the annoying way pipe smokers have, using the time for thought or emphasis or just to annoy. "In her eyes, *I'm* the bloke who killed Lavinia, and she's going to do her level best to prove that. It's a risk for me but it's one I'm prepared to take to get you in there. This boil needs lancing." He waved a nonchalant hand around the room. "If you have to run for shelter from the outfall, remember the door's never locked. Consider this your retreat—your bunker if you like. You may like to know I keep a pair of guns loaded and ready up there in my bedroom. Purdeys."

"Purdeys, eh?" Joe waggled his eyebrows.

"His own guns. Made to measure. He had long arms like me. They were the old man's gift when he died."

A valuable legacy but could it ever have been appreciated by the man's oldest-born son, who had to stand by and watch the estate moving over to his younger, legitimate brother? Hunnyton showed no sign of teeth-gnashing resentment.

"Well, thank you for the offer!" Joe grinned. "Sharing a redoubt with killers—it's what I'm used to. I know how to watch my back as well as my front."

Fair warning, he thought.

CHAPTER 12

The Lagonda stopped at the bottom of the lime avenue at the point where some ancient landscape artist had calculated the visitor was best placed to be impressed by what, as Hunnyton had hinted, was one of the loveliest houses in England. Or anywhere.

The eye was led by the geometry of the row of sentinel trees straight over an expanse of deer-cropped grass, rising upwards to the bridge over a hidden moat and beyond, the grand façade. Hunnyton turned off the engine and they looked in silence.

> *"Towers and battlements it sees*
> *Bosomed high in tufted trees,*
> *Where perhaps some beauty lies,*
> *The cynosure of neighbouring eyes."*

Hunnyton's voice was quiet, as though speaking to himself.

"Milton had something entirely more medieval in mind, I think," Joe said. "It's bosomed high all right, and those tufted trees framing it look very like thousand-year-old oaks to me, but the house itself isn't very battlemented. No towers or crenellations . . . no martial intent whatsoever, I'd say. Jacobean? You'd expect it. No one feared being attacked by the neighbours any longer by that time. The Count of the Saxon Shore had long ago sheathed his sword or beaten it into a ploughshare. The nearest you get to martial is those pinnacles either side of the gatehouse, and they remind me very strongly of the ones we passed this morning on King's College Chapel."

Hunnyton nodded in agreement. "It gets even more collegiate inside. It's built in a square shape with an interior quadrangle complete with storey-high oriel window leading to the great hall."

"A house for a scholar rather than a soldier, would you say?"

"It's had its share of both," murmured Hunnyton. "But the shape lends itself to comfortable living. There's a very generous kitchen block to the northeast of the hall so the food doesn't take forever to reach the table. There are company rooms on three sides on the ground floor, with different aspects. On the east there's what they call a 'summer parlour' and on the sunnier south side another one called the 'winter parlour.' Oh, by the way, Sandilands, they don't have anything so common as a 'breakfast room.' When you come yumming down for your devilled kidneys in the morning, you'll find they're being served in the east-facing summer parlour . . ."

"Don't worry," Joe interrupted. "I'll just do what I usually do and follow my nose."

Joe wondered again what thoughts were going on behind those deceptive eyes. Here was the firstborn (according to his own evidence) of the old lord's sons. Disqualified from ever taking possession of the pile before him by the lowliness of his mother's birth. Yet, by his situation, tied to the place. A tie at first of necessity but now of love, Joe judged from a fleeting expression on the man's face. An emotion which was quickly corrected by the irony in his speech. Joe, a second son, although from much more modest circumstances, could begin to understand the envy, the anger, that the younger in line could feel. His own chagrin at the inevitable loss of his family home had been tempered by his complete lack of interest in farming and his older brother's instinctive ability for it. But what if it had been the other way around?

"I'll walk the rest of the way from here. Get acclimatised. I'll just take my notebook and a pencil."

"Good thought. Better not to arrive together, mob-handed like," Hunnyton commented. "Some of the guests may be there already. They wouldn't want to think a posse of lawmen was forming up to put a damper on their high jinks. I'll leave you then. You can find your way through the stable block over there." He waved to the right. "You won't have time to stop for a chin-wag though or you'll be late for lunch. The old girl is very punctual. You've got twenty minutes before she shakes out her napkin. I'll drop your luggage off with the butler and then, Commissioner, you're on your own."

As he started up the engine again he called over his shoulder to Joe: "Watch out for the green man! If you catch him, do everyone a favour and drown him in the moat."

JOE FROWNED AS he watched the Lagonda disappear. "Drown the green man," had he said? He tried to make sense of it. Some medieval country custom? Or: the Green man? A lawyer who'd annoyed him? A bad-tempered chap who cut the lawns? He smiled and shook his head.

Joe didn't want to be seen marching alone straight down the centre of the lime avenue. Too exposed. He preferred to come crabwise at buildings, at people, down trenches. There was no glory and no sense in a strutting advance across open ground into the teeth of the cannon. He'd learned that much. He'd saved his own skin and that of hundreds of his men, he reckoned, by simply not hearing orders of a suicidal nature passed down the line. Others had taken the same precautions. There were more effective ways of achieving your aims. Joe had learned far more from rear offices than he ever had from façades, he reckoned.

A quick glance at Hunnyton's estate map that he'd tucked into his pocket gave him his orientation and he set out across the open ground to his right, heading for an intriguing incursion into the landscape of what looked like several acres of ancient woodland which had been left untroubled to serve as an element of the framework of the Hall and as a screen for the stable block. A group of three tall elms, outliers of the wood, stood on guard. To welcome or repel? Joe made straight for them across the close-cropped grass, using them as a marker.

As he approached, he picked out oak, ash, hazel, much tangled hawthorn and a concentration of lower-growing shrubbery. Tantalisingly, Hunnyton had marked in the centre of this wilderness a tiny building he'd labelled TEMPLE OF DIANA. On a sporting and sociable estate like Truelove's there was bound to be a temple to a classical god and Diana was most suitable. Diana the Huntress, eternally young and lovely. An appealing challenge to the sporting male ego since she had dedicated herself eternally to a state of virginity. Joe had always thought it odd that her other attribute was a mismatched concern for fertility. Denying it in herself, she loved and encouraged it in women. Those who wanted to become pregnant sought her intercession and when the moment came, this goddess would even help them through a painful childbirth.

Follies, hermitages (occasionally still with hermit in residence), marble temples, they were thick on the ground in English country seats, usually put up at the whim of eighteenth-century young English gentlemen recently returned from their Grand Tour. They came back from the continent, travelling boxes stuffed with architectural designs of a classical style or Italianate nature. Some, more adventurous, brought along the architect himself if he were of cool classical style or hot Italianate nature.

Joe enjoyed harmless whimsy. He approved of follies—they made useful trysting places or a refuge from boring company. A place to retire to with a good book minutes before someone's aunt called for a fourth at bridge. He had fond memories of kisses snatched, surprising intimacies allowed, in his youth; he had less fond memories of a corpse he'd been called in to attend to, hideous flesh and blood polluting the white marble beauty. He reckoned he had time to take in Diana on his way to the stables. He hoped there'd be a statue of some sort, for choice a scantily clad Grecian lady on whose lips he could plant a chaste kiss. Sculptors quite often went into flights of erotic fantasy when chiselling out a Diana. He'd make off to the house before she could turn him into a wild animal or a bush of some sort. He remembered Diana had a quick temper and a short way of dealing with unwanted romantic overtures; her admirer, Actaeon, even her male priests had all come, one after the other, to a sticky end. Better treat her with respect when he found her. Still—a guest who took the trouble to stop off and make a votive offering to the goddess of the place on his way up to lunch might just soften the heart of the Dowager. It would certainly get the conversation going.

The heat of the open parkland changed within a few strides to cool shadow as he entered the wood. He paused for a moment to let his eyes grow accustomed to the gloom and he breathed in deep forest scents laced with the intoxicating sharp top note of the elderflower that frothed in abundance, creamy-white amongst the dark foliage. He wished he could spend the afternoon here, alone with his thoughts.

Some yards to his right, a twig snapped. A small animal? Joe moved on briskly into the heart of the wood, seeking for a rise in the ground for that would be where a temple would be sited. The trees now crowded overhead, blotting out any external pointers like the tall bell tower of the distant chapel he'd lined up his sights on. If he kept his back to the sun he couldn't go far astray—the whole grove couldn't be much more than a couple of hundred yards wide. He stopped as, again, a twig snapped, to his left this time, and slightly behind him. Could be a poacher? Joe thought not. Those fellers didn't go about snapping twigs so carelessly. Joe was used to tracking—and being tracked. Even allowing for the still air and the smothering effect of the thick tree canopy, that snap had been too loud. Not accidental. He could have sworn someone had picked up a stick and broken it with gusto. To attract his attention? Warn him off? Frighten him?

All senses alert, he continued on his way more slowly. A rustling in the undergrowth kept pace with him. A low growl raised the hairs on the back of his neck. Not an animal, he thought. But what human would be making hostile noises at an innocent visitor in broad daylight? He'd try to lure it into view. Joe took his notebook from his pocket and, humming a snatch from *The Mikado*, went to stand in the shade of a particularly gnarled oak tree and affected to be drawing a sketch of the writhing outline. A very ancient specimen he decided and tentatively reached up and tugged at one of the lower branches, testing its resilience.

He leapt to one side a split second before a log of wood crashed down, grazing his cheek, and thumping to the ground at his feet. He turned and caught a flash of green and brown behind a thick hazel only feet away. With a hideous cackle some being began to crash its way through the undergrowth, running away from him.

Joe set off in pursuit, anger and outrage and a stinging face urging him on. In ten strides he had caught up. He launched his weight at it in a high tackle learned on the rugby pitch, automatically reaching for a human right arm and, to his relief, finding one. He hauled it up behind the creature's back, shouting a dire caution in a police voice. When he sensed that resistance had stopped, he flipped his victim over onto his back and immediately recoiled in disgust. A stench of sweat and fear wafted up from the leather-clad body of a man. A wiry man, smaller than Joe but well muscled. His face was obliterated by a green mask, his head hidden under a cap of knitted wool woven through with oak and ivy leaves to produce an extravagant mass of greenery. Joe stared in astonishment. The mask was no amateur, papier maché, village-hall-drama-club attempt at stage costume. It was Venetian in quality, dark green silk, a full face mask, with embroidered slanting holes for eyes and a red-lined slit for the mouth. The eyes were dark and venomous, the teeth bared in a growl were grey and rotting.

A Woodwose! He was holding down, but barely holding down, a bloody Woodwose! Joe had seen hundreds of effigies and carvings of the Wild Green Man in wood and stone on bench ends, on architraves, hidden up in the ceiling, keeping sinister watch on the congregation in country churches. No one had any real idea where the image came from but two things were certain: they were ancient and they were malevolent. Joe was disturbed to be faced with a flesh-and-blood relic of this paganism. He resisted the urge to tear off the mask and look into the face of the coughing, winded creature wearing it. Instead he pulled him to his feet, forcing him under his arm in a neck lock, and marched him back to the pathway.

Joe stopped at the spot where his abandoned notebook told him he'd been standing, right by the considerable chunk of oak that had so nearly dropped him in his tracks. With time now to assess the weight of the object, he knew for a certainty that it could have split his skull. If he'd stood still, he calculated he would now be lying bleeding or dead—and from a wound that could have been caused by a falling branch. It would have been very simple, the work of a few moments, to arrange the scene. Remove the killer log, lose it in the undergrowth and replace it with a freshly torn down branch from the ancient tree overhead, ensuring that it bore signs of his blood. "Poor chap!" they'd say. "Killed by the very tree he was sketching! So sad . . . Still, it was a *very* old tree, rotten, quite rotten . . . Mentioned in the Domesday Book I shouldn't wonder . . ." There you had it: a death by misadventure. Another death by misadventure on Truelove land.

Keeping his voice steady, "The Green Man of the Woods, I presume?" he said. "How do you do? Or are you calling yourself the Green Knight in such seigneurial surroundings? Before I chuck you in the moat, which I am advised to do, tell me—why did you try to kill me?" He released the man's head but kept a firm grip on his arm.

"Kill you? Good Lord! Are you barmy? I didn't! If you hadn't leapt like a startled hare it would have landed harmlessly at your feet. I always aim to miss!" The voice was accentless and dismissive.

The man was lying but at least he was talking. Joe needed to hear more.

"City gent, clearly—how was I to guess you'd move like a grasshopper?" The shaggy head tilted to one side, assessing him and the voice was slick with suspicion as he asked, "Who the hell are *you* anyway?"

This was a bit rich, coming from a man in a ludicrous mask, Joe thought, and he fought back a hysterical urge to laugh out loud. He saw the eyes flick, taking in his officer's trench coat. "The war's been over a few years now, you know. Didn't anyone think to inform you, Captain?" The jibe was delivered with a derisory sneer, the use of the lowly rank insulting.

"And the Middle Ages are even more distant," Joe said, "so stop arsing about before I haul you up before the beak on a charge of buffoonery as well as attempted murder. Let's have some ID, shall we, and we'll start by taking a look at your ugly mug. Off with it, mate!"

The man pulled himself to his full height and with an over-dramatic gesture peeled the mask from his face. He shook the cap of leaves from his head and stood staring impassively at Joe.

"I'm Virbio, King of the Woods," he announced in all seriousness. "Have you come to kill me?"

Joe was lost for words. In spite of his wiry strength, the man, he now saw, was in late middle age. In his fifties perhaps. White hair sprang about his head in tight corkscrews yet his face was not the face of an old man. The brows were still black above dark mocking eyes, the practised, sardonic smile was that of a pantomime villain. He was freshly shaven, his jaw firm and in his ears he wore gold earrings a pirate captain would have sighed for. Hard to place in normal society.

"I'm Guardian of the Shrine of Diana, which, if I'm not mistaken, you were about to hunt out with murder in mind," the man elaborated.

Mad. Stark, staring. Joe was at a loss as to how he should proceed. Medical attention needed perhaps? For a moment, he had a longing for the company of Adelaide Hartest. He sensed instinctively she'd know what to do. She would identify the condition and stick a highfalutin label on it, prescribe a sedative and have him hauled away somewhere appropriate for treatment. One thing was sure—Joe could not allow a homicidal maniac to remain at large in these woods. Surely the family were . . . ?

The penny dropped and he felt foolish. His own sanity must have been knocked sideways for a moment by a perceived attempt on his life. He felt a trickle of blood dripping from his chin and dashed it away with his hand. Of course the family bloody well knew! Follies, hermitages—this idiot was a modern-day version of those poor old blokes the Georgians had employed to live a life of seclusion and poverty in romantically architected cells at the bottom of their lands. The object of an afternoon's stroll around the estate. A source of laughter and wonder for their spoilt guests. These days, with neo-Gothic, hey-nonny-nonny, Merrie England myth and legend all the rage, the Trueloves had gone one better and in their ancient woodland had installed their own rural jester.

This Green Man was tricked out expensively in an outfit straight from the stage of Covent Garden. Joe looked again with disapproval at the green tights, the leather tunic and the knee-high kid boots. He wondered how long the man had been in residence. Were the Trueloves aware that they were harbouring a log-chucking psychopath in their holy grove?

Joe resolved to raise the matter with . . . Oh, Lord! Her ladyship was waiting for him, probably tapping her little foot in exasperation. He looked at his watch. If he ran he could just do it. If he could only rid himself of this clown.

"How do you do? I'm Joe Sandilands. Now, listen, er, Virbio. I'm prepared to overlook your offence on two conditions. One: lead me to your goddess. I have something to give her. Two: get me out of this bloody wood and point me in the right direction for the Hall. I'm late for a lunch appointment with your mistress. That's: Cecily, Lady Truelove, not Diana the Huntress."

He had not taken the name of Cecily in vain. The King of the Woods reacted visibly when he used it. Unctuous servility and cooperative sanity followed. "Of course, sir . . . Come this way . . . Happy to oblige Your Honour . . . I do apologise for the churlish welcome—I had taken you for a policeman."

On the whole, Joe had preferred the rude, mad Green Man.

A FEW YARDS in front of an ornate but sturdily built wooden pavilion in a clearing, she was looking out at him, staring wide eyed over one white marble shoulder. Girlish breasts not entirely successfully concealed beneath a diaphanous shift, short pleated skirt, soft ankle boots, bow in left hand, she'd clearly been distracted by someone lurking in the bushes behind her and to the right. By Joe. He stepped forward feeling absurdly guilty that he'd startled her. She was holding out her right hand, palm uppermost to one of her hounds in the act of offering him some titbit. Superstition and a spirit of playfulness made Joe approach her plinth with head bowed. He went to stand by her side and, knowing that any seduction of the chaste goddess was bound to fail, he decided to turn his attention first on the hound. He caressed the marble head in an entirely natural gesture and murmured into its ear. "Hello, old mate. I wonder if you're Syrius or Phocion? And has your mistress detailed you to tear my throat out if I take a liberty? I'll chance it!" He reached up on tiptoe and dropped a kiss on the cold white lips. He felt about in his pocket, found what he was looking for and placed a small gold object on her upraised palm.

"*Amor vincit omnia*, Diana," he whispered. "Love conquers all. I do hope I haven't got that wrong."

HE HEARD THE stable bell ringing out one o'clock as he pounded across the drawbridge. The huge door swung open as he arrived and he prepared, hot and breathless, coat tails flapping, to face the butler.

To his dismay, her ladyship had bustled into the hall to bother her butler and enquire as to her guest's whereabouts. Instead of drawing back discreetly and allowing him to recover, Cecily stalked forward, an expression of barely contained amusement on her face.

"Take the gentleman's hat and coat, Styles, and give them a good brushing. Hunnyton warned us you were taking the scenic route through the woods." She looked wonderingly at the stains of foliage and smears of body paint the King of the Woods had impressed on the pale fabric of his coat where Joe had clamped his head against his side. "He didn't tell us you were going to take time off for a roll in the hay en route. Styles, have a word with that new dairy-maid will you?" Her eyes came to rest on Joe's bloodstained cheek. "I see she defended her honour. Styles, we'd better have a wet flannel and a sticking plaster for our guest. And I expect he'd welcome a nice dry sherry after his adventures."

Joe grinned. Perhaps lunch was not going to be the painful episode he'd envisaged. "She told me her name was Diana, madam. She's five feet tall and irresistibly lovely. When she recovers from the surprise of the kiss I planted on her cool virginal mouth, she'll probably come after me with vengeance in mind. You may well see me turn into a stag before lunch is over."

"Indeed? I've never witnessed a transmogrification before. One of your party tricks, Commissioner? I shall look forward to it—one can always find a use for a healthy young stag," she finished with an inscrutable smile.

The butler led him to a nearby washroom, where Joe removed the traces of the forest floor and accepted a rather over-sized plaster to put across his wound before rejoining her ladyship.

Styles gave them a strange look as, arm in arm and chuckling, they went into the dining room.

CHAPTER 13

The soup, as predicted, was green in colour, though made not from nettles but from peas picked in the garden that morning and introduced to a few herbs, some excellent chicken stock and a pint or two of cream from the home herd. The "dog biscuits" that accompanied the cheese were Bath Olivers from Fortnum's in Piccadilly. A taste not yet acquired by Hunnyton, evidently. "A light luncheon," the dowager had announced. "You will want to save yourself for dinner. We have an excellent cook." He managed a bowl of pea soup, a token slice of game pie with a plentiful salad and nibbled at a biscuit, cursing the superintendent for his skittish humour. Her ladyship took his refusal of dessert as an admirable masculine trait and for that he was grateful.

They ate companionably together, attended by one footman who withdrew the moment he had finished serving and clearing away. "My son Alexander is about the place somewhere, probably still in his room. He won't be joining us," she had explained. "He is one of those creatures who prefers to flee the daylight. The Romans had a word for that I think. London life proved too much for him, I'm afraid, and he's come home to recuperate and gather his strength before he relaunches himself on society. Energetic and useful chap that I see you are, Sandilands, you will not find much to admire in Alex."

Apart from this bitter remark, conversation flowed easily. His hostess was very knowledgeable about the state of the nation, and she could talk about London affairs—political and scandalous—with understanding as well as an ironic asperity which Joe found entertaining. She listened to Joe's stories of his days in India and on the North West Frontier, some of them flattering to Sir George Jardine, his friend and mentor, some sharp and comic. Cecily seemed to prefer the latter.

When the footman brought in a tray of coffee things, Cecily dismissed him. "That'll be all for now, Benjamin." Joe had noted the familiar use of the Christian name for the attentive young man. Perhaps Cecily was not the old-fashioned stickler for correctness he had assumed. "The Commissioner will preside at the coffee pot."

Joe obliged and, uninterrupted and unobserved, they settled to their coffee, free to speak their minds. She said abruptly, "So you got my message then?"

"Message, madam?" Joe said, smiling. "Would that be the anonymous letter penned by your maid and dictated by you? The letter sent to the Yard with the object of luring me down here to take issue with the man who could perhaps have had a hand in the alleged murder of your daughter-in-law?"

She sighed. "Well, I don't expect you to arrest a dead horse, silly man!" In the days when ladies carried fans, she'd have tapped him on the cheek in flirtatious reprimand. "Lavinia's death was planned. In my view, that's murder. I'm sure of that. I'm pretty sure also that I know who is responsible but I have no proof. I hear good things of you from my son James. He agreed with me that you would be the best possible man to investigate and uncover the guilty party. However—James was reluctant to be seen exercising any political authority in the matter."

Joe hoped he'd adequately concealed his incredulity.

"Astute, independent, unconnected with the family, a

gentleman, and—having the ear of the Commissioner—I thought you'd do well. I decided to lure you down here."

"You should have included hard-headed in that list of attributes. I'm afraid I can only offer discouragement. Even if I were persuaded of someone's guilt, I doubt I could interest the Crown Prosecutor in supporting a legal case which has been satisfactorily closed for several weeks. But why now, madam? Why wait so long to launch an investigation? The whole affair had sunk quietly into the sand."

"No, Sandilands. You're wrong there." At last, a note of vehemence. "It was James who first became aware of the furtive looks, the chill atmosphere . . . aware that friends and colleagues were crossing the clubroom or the road to avoid speaking to him. One day, he cornered one of his closest friends and forced the truth from him. You know what Parliament is for rumours! More reputations are shredded in the tearooms at Westminster than in the House. His fellows were remarking on the fortuitous timing of his wife's death. His own demeanour may have worked against him—James did not love his wife and failed to show much in the way of regret. What a fool! He should have moped and mowed about the place for a bit. Instead, he threw himself into his usual routine of work, appearing relieved and reinvigorated."

Joe picked up a word from this. "'Fortuitous,' madam? In what way fortuitous?"

She hesitated. "I must keep nothing from you, even the embarrassing aspects, I suppose. You may have heard it spoken of—James has ambitions of the highest order . . ."

"Next Prime Minister but one, is what they say," Joe said bluntly.

She seemed pleased that he was keeping up. "Lavinia was aware of this. She decided she would enjoy the role of the PM's wife." Cecily closed her eyes in silent pain at the thought. "She decided to help prepare his way. She made faux pas after faux pas!

She said the wrong things to the right people and right things to the wrong." And, with emphasis: "She was wrecking his career. No overriding intelligence, you see. It would not have been the first time a great man had been brought down by a silly wife."

"A great man?" he questioned lightly.

"Not yet, obviously. You're right to remind me of the dangers of maternal pride. James could be great. The stage is setting itself. He has the mind and heart for the part and he's learned his lines. The country is weary of its inconsequential political leaders. Left? Right? Who cares? The electorate is undecided because it is offered no compelling choice. Yet—rightly—people sense that stirring times are approaching and no man of character steps forward. The ship of state sails into a storm with two weak pairs of hands scrabbling to take the wheel. Churchill has a strong pair of hands and a steady vision but has been sent off duty. He's been stood down."

"But rumbling in the distance? I'm sure I catch the odd rumbling still."

"He's not a man James would choose to be seen supporting. My son wishes to present himself as a fresh political mind, unallied and without the baggage of past failures."

Joe decided to accept all this for the moment. He knew of at least two other reasons why Lavinia's death benefited James Truelove but he wished to avoid alarming the woman by showing too deep a knowledge of her son's affairs.

"So, you see, we need a solution to this unpleasantness for the sake of James's reputation but also because there is a killer—unscrupulous and effective—at large. It could be someone I speak to every day, regard as a friend . . . someone in my household or even family. I—we—need to know. The knowing is more important than the arresting."

"A large number involved. I have the police notes listing all the people in the house that weekend."

"That fateful weekend—as we say now—there were present some influential politicians. Lavinia, I remember, was making an exhibition of herself over dinner . . . rather worse than usually crass. I was seated at the other end of the table and unable to stop her launching into a shameful ragging of one of the guests—a woman. A woman moreover whom she had herself invited down for the weekend. I was mortified to catch the glances exchanged between a minister and a press baron. James's friends and supporters. Supporters until that moment when his wife revealed herself unqualified to hold a tea party for teddy bears without inspiring a killing rage among the furry guests. Imagine Lavinia playing hostess on a diplomatic occasion, Commissioner!"

"Faced with the Japanese Ambassador, flanked by a Prussian envoy and a Russian chargé d'affaires . . ." Joe made a mischievous speculation.

Cecily's eyes crinkled with waspish humour. "Lavinia could, single-handedly, have provoked a second world war, right there at the table, and presided over it if the knives were sharp enough."

"Ouch! But James is now free to remake his reputation?"

"He would have been had he not been besmirched with a much more serious accusation than making a bad choice of wife. Murder. We have to prove that he is innocent by possibly arresting, certainly making known, the identity of the person responsible. James's career depends upon it."

She turned the dark eyes of a Roman empress on Joe. Unblinking, forceful, hypnotic. "More than that. You know the state of the country. Financially ruined. Emotionally exhausted. The reins of power being tugged in all directions by the inexperienced hands of a crew of squabbling nonentities who call themselves a 'coalition.' We're hurtling towards a cliff edge, Sandilands. James sees that. He is a strong-minded man and no appeaser of bullies. He knows what needs to be done and understands that he is the man to do it. He has built up support in preparation for the moment. We cannot afford to stand by and watch that support be cut out from under him. Undeservedly."

"Are you telling me you have proof that he had nothing to do with his wife's death?"

"I know with certainty and—yes—I can prove that my son had no involvement whatsoever. But I'm his mother. Of course I would say that. We need an independent authority, trusted by all, to discover this for himself. I hand you no names, Sandilands. But I will facilitate your enquiries. You have my permission to go anywhere, question anyone in the house. Do what you have to do."

"You carefully say 'person,' your ladyship. Man? Woman? Are you hinting that perhaps I should be hunting about in the boudoir rather than the gun room?"

"I'm sure you are equally at home in both," Cecily said crisply. "But, do agree, it could well have been a woman who arranged her death. It has all the hallmarks, wouldn't you say, of a *female* mind? We are supposed to be the sex that prefers a clandestine approach to an outright assault. Women do not have the strength of mind and hand to sink knives into flesh; we tend to be ignorant of the workings of firearms, even if one should be to hand. A push in the back at the top of a staircase is perhaps the nearest we come to the physical assault. Killing at arm's length, carried out by one of God's innocent creatures—a perfect solution, wouldn't you say? A female solution?"

Joe could have demolished her argument with countless examples from real life and real death but he was enjoying hearing her nonsense, wondering where she was heading with her theories.

"Yet it has a certain sporting element about it that to me speaks of a masculine mind set," he said. "Tell me about her maid. Is she—was she—close to her mistress? Close enough to have vital information for us?"

"Oh, Grace Aldred is the girl's name. I have interviewed

Grace, of course, but she denies all responsibility. She's very loyal to her mistress—alive or dead. I've kept her on here working as a laundry maid, even left her in possession of her old room, until such time as she can be made to confess to something."

"Excellent!" Joe forced out the word. The old nuisance had probably ruined any chance of an unrehearsed testimony from the maid. "She is the first I should like to interview."

"You'll have to wait, I'm afraid. The housekeeper was so bold as to grant her leave to visit her sick mother in Bury." Cecily heard her own tone of asperity and hurried to correct it. "I'm not criticising Mrs. Bolton. Our excellent housekeeper finds herself in an awkward position—between two mistresses, you might say. Lavinia's reign is over and Mrs. Bolton will have shed no tears over that, and I am here, as you see, a power from the past, grabbing at the reins. Always with the prospect, of course, of a third mistress waiting in the wings. James will marry again. His career demands it. Meanwhile, Mrs. Bolton is a steady pair of hands and we all trust her judgement. Grace has been given a week's leave. Of course," she added casually, "there were other ladies in the house that weekend in April and I've prepared a list for you."

Joe decided to take the bull by the horns. "We always look to the motive in killings, madam. Who stands to gain? In this case, you are right to suppose that your own son, James, fits the frame very well. He loses a wife you tell me was becoming a liability. Being her heir he must retain what is left of her fortune?"

"Of course. I'm glad to hear you speak so bluntly. It saves time and allows me to be equally blunt." She gave him a sharp sideways look. "As no holds are barred I'll tell you that my own suspicions fell originally on a certain female guest. A young lady my son has formed a regrettable attachment to. The girl is his student and a pampered one at that. I know that he spoke of her frequently to Lavinia and to me in glowing terms. Lavinia became suspicious—and who shall blame her?—of his relationship with this baggage and took the bold step of inviting the girl to spend a weekend here in April. To look her over, assess the danger and warn her off. She gave James no warning of her arrangement and the whole business was a disaster. The girl was pretty and intelligent and capable of winning any verbal skirmish Lavinia cared to engage her in. But, more importantly, it was clear to all that she trumped Lavinia on a subject dear to her own heart."

"Which was horses, I understand."

"Indeed. Lavinia had established that this girl had a certain way . . . an ability . . . with animals. Horses and dogs. During the day, Lavinia took her by the arm and set off on a tour of the estate. Just the two of them. Stables, kennels—we still keep spaniels and hounds and a few herd dogs—and they returned hours later with Lavinia shaken and angry. Now, Commissioner, I looked at the pair of them with foreboding. My blood turned to ice in my veins. I saw disaster ahead. But what I feared at that time was that it would be Lavinia herself who made an attempt on the *girl*'s life while she had her under her roof. Her reason for inviting her here, Commissioner? Lavinia was capable of such a clumsy manoeuvre."

Cecily raised a hand to ward off objections that were not voiced. "No, I do not overstate my reaction. She was a woman of sudden rages. I've seen her badly mishandle her unfortunate mounts when her pride was at stake. I've witnessed her slashing a stable lad in the face with her whip. I know that she was overly harsh in her dealings with the cottagers. Adam Hunnyton and I have, too often, had to step in and repair, reinstate, reimburse . . . smooth feathers. I knew her to be—we all knew her to be—a cruel, bullying woman with what my dear husband would have called 'a short fuse.' I honestly thought she was capable of pushing someone downstairs or out of a window. And her target on this occasion was quite small and easily pushed, poor child. I'm sure no one would seriously blame her if she took steps to protect herself from an onslaught by Lavinia."

Yes, compared with the Amazon proportions of Lavinia, Dorcas was quite small. In fact she was all the things Cecily was telling him. He could hear no misrepresentation or exaggeration in what she had to say. But was Dorcas a killer? A cunning and ruthless killer who might judge that the world would be a better place without Lavinia's boots trampling it? Who might devise just such a righteous death under the hooves of an animal she had no respect or love for? Joe was shocked that he had even allowed the monstrous thought to take shape and twitch with life.

At least he was one step ahead of Cecily. He knew where she was heading with her comments. Deviously, disarmingly, towards putting the blame on Dorcas and then cancelling out the consequences. All this hocus pocus had been put on with the aim of taking Dorcas off the scene, if the worst came to the worst, on an accusation of murder. Had Cecily any idea of the girl's connection with the police officer she was now confiding in? He could have sworn she hadn't. Their names were in no way connected. Any relationship James Truelove was aware of had been explained to him by the devious Dorcas herself. Joe remembered Truelove had actually had him called to the telephone on one occasion to offer him advice on handling her. "You'll get the best out of Miss Joliffe if you don't run her in blinkers, Sandilands," he'd told Joe briskly. Truelove probably connected him to Dorcas through her closeness to his sister, Lydia, and her family. After all, she'd lived with them in something approaching harmony for eight years. She loved them and they loved her like a daughter. "My guardians," was her way of referring to Lydia and Marcus.

Perhaps that was the plain truth? Perhaps, all these years, he had been peripheral to Dorcas's life and not, as he'd fancied himself, central to it? A truly distant but, on occasion, useful uncle?

The thought startled and disturbed him.

Cecily was finding it increasingly difficult to continue but responded to Joe's concern when he prompted: "I would guess that you felt it your duty to take precautions against an outbreak of violence in the house?"

Her response had been ready to flow. "You'll think me a fussy, deluded old woman but . . . but . . . yes, I posted a footman—Ben, who waited on us just now—at the end of the corridor outside Lavinia's room that night. I told him to follow her, unseen, if she left her room and, if she went in the direction of the Old Nursery, which is out in the north wing well away from the other guest rooms, he was to alert me at once, even use his own judgement to prevent a catastrophe. He knew he would have had my backing. You will find Ben a trustworthy man with an ability to think for himself and anticipate a command. I shall look forward to hearing your impressions of him."

Good Lord! The old lady had the thought processes of a damned efficient general, Joe decided. "The Old Nursery?" he questioned, mystified.

"Yes. That is where Lavinia had chosen to put her guest. Another little calculated cruelty. She showed the girl to her room herself. I can imagine why and I'm sure *you* can imagine why . . . 'This is the room James and I had decorated last week in anticipation of a joyful and long-awaited event . . . Yes! We are to have our happiness completed, though I must swear you to secrecy, my dear . . .' I'm pretty sure she deliberately leaked news of her supposed condition. The servants were openly gossiping about it. Even my son Alexander managed to rouse himself from his stupor to ask me if I'd heard his brother's good news. But the autopsy which James had the sense to insist on showed that it was all in her imagination or calculatedly misleading."

"Did your footman follow her to the stables?"

"He did. Sadly not with any sense of urgency, however—Ben calculated that as she was in riding habit and heading for the horses, she was about to take her early morning ride a little earlier than usual and that his responsibility was at an end."

Joe understood. A footman's territory did not extend into the grounds. Their polished shoes venture no further than the tiled floor of the dairy.

"Ben knew he'd been posted to protect a guest from her ladyship. He had no instruction to protect her ladyship from her own folly. He was merely doing what I'd told him to do, staying out of sight whilst ensuring that she didn't double back and become again a threat to her guest. I have not blamed him. Nor should you. He stopped to have a chat with a kitchen maid who was lighting the fires. However, when he heard the commotion he ran to investigate. Too late. He stayed at the scene, although in terror of the horse, and sent the two stable lads she'd coerced into accompanying her back to the house to raise the alarm. The vet and the doctor were instantly called while Ben stayed on guard over the body."

"Brave chap," Joe murmured. "What a scene!"

"But why, Sandilands? Why? And why am I so certain that her death was no accident? It was all so out of character. Visiting the farm horses before breakfast without notifying the head horseman? Madness!"

"I can explain all that," said Joe. "But I agree with you that she was put up to it, her foray into the stable of an injured and aggressive horse calculatedly risky."

She listened quietly as he told her of his interview with the vet's daughter, her evidence and theories, and the conclusion he and Hunnyton, pooling their knowledge of horse-craft, had arrived at.

"Horse witchery? How very medieval!" Cecily had listened entranced, entertained, aghast. "Not sure that I can accept all you tell me, but . . . it does make a certain awful sense," she said finally. "And I would always listen with attention to your two advisers. Hunnyton is shrewd and sound and the best authority I know on the handling of horses. His father Hunnybun, whom I knew, was deeply involved with 'gentling,' as they call breaking-in horses down here, and I'm sure the son absorbed his knowledge. I have met Doctor Hartest. A sensible young woman with her wits about her. Attractive and personable too. I'd rather marked her down for my Alex." She sighed. "I've given up hope of his ever securing a rich, well-bred girl so he might as well have a competent woman who'll understand his condition and care for him."

Joe managed to reply affably, "Splendid idea! We men all dream of marrying our nurse." He resolved to find out—but not from the boy's own mother—exactly what condition was so dire the suffering Alex was thought to need a lifetime's care from a physician.

Cecily's hostess's mind was still running on matchmaking. "We shall be a lady short for dinner tomorrow night. I wonder . . . Do you think Adelaide Hartest would be insulted if I sent her a last-minute invitation? Do you suppose she has evening dress down here in the country? I've met her once or twice in church and observed her to be neatly dressed and well spoken. Though I note she stomps around the village in dungarees and gumboots. The question is: is she a lady?"

Joe should not have been surprised or irritated by her snobbery. He reminded himself that Cecily's attitudes had been formed in the Victorian Age and her perspective must always have been that of the minor aristocracy, constantly aware of status and class and seeking to improve or at least uphold what she saw as her family's place in society.

"Doctor Hartest is an intelligent, professional woman who has lived her life until recently in London. She is articulate and humorous and would adorn any Mayfair soirée." The firmness of his judgement based on one encounter surprised even Joe.

"Goodness! I'm afraid we would risk boring her to tears with our country ways, were we to invite her to dinner. A girl may be *too* educated, you know. No man rejoices to find himself seated next to grey-eyed Athena at the dinner table."

"Truly, I hardly know the lady and should not answer for her," Joe said, thinking this party was probably the last thing she'd enjoy and finding it difficult to picture rangy Adelaide in a dress, evening or otherwise. "Doctor Hartest was very ready to point the finger at Grace Aldred," he said to get her back on track.

"Ah, yes. I'm sure she's right. It seems Grace may well hold the key to all this witchery. But Grace would never have planned a mischievous assault on her mistress. She's a Suffolk girl. They don't hold with violence about here. Murders in the county are few and all committed by incomers, Commissioner. No—for the originator of this evil you must look elsewhere. But there is one person you can discount. I have already mentioned: my son, James. He has an alibi—is that what you'd say?"

"Possibly. It depends on whether he could offer witness of his whereabouts that night. And I'm remembering that this murder, if murder it was, was perpetrated at arm's length, so to speak. A suggestion was put into Lady Truelove's head, she performed accordingly and at some later time, the spiced cake was switched for a noxious offering which had been prepared in advance. Anyone could have planted the suggestion, exchanged the cake for what I'll call the 'poisoned' one in the early hours of the morning, let's say, and been fast asleep in bed by the time Lavinia was approaching the stables."

Joe fell silent, suddenly seeing the flaw in his theory.

"No. I think there must have been a simpler way," said Cecily, echoing his thoughts. "One that didn't involve to-ing and fro-ing in the night. Ben would have noticed anyone creeping about after midnight armed with a mess of stinking . . . stoat's liver, did you say? You may ask him yourself."

Just as Joe had been about to press her further on the matter of Truelove's alibi, the butler entered to warn his mistress that the first of the guests was coming up the drive. A Rolls-Royce with Surrey plates.

"Ah! Sir Basil and Lady Ripley," she exclaimed. "We're kicking off! I shall come at once. Sandilands . . ." and, with sudden intimacy, "Joe! Do come and greet them with me. James and Alex are not about the place and I do appreciate a masculine presence at my elbow."

As they got to their feet, her conversation became purposeful and fast and he recognised the tone of a commander to her aide-de-camp.

"Basil Ripley and Florence were here at the house during that frightful weekend, Joe. Basil is very influential in the House of Lords and James is keen to impress him. Florence is a bit of a gad-about—twenty years younger than her husband—and rather susceptible. Take her to have look at the Edwardian glasshouse or for a stroll in the knot garden . . . intrigue her a bit . . ."

Joe smiled and surrendered. He'd decided he would be rather entertained to play poodle—or was it tame stag?—for Cecily. He would give good value. He would establish himself as a welcome presence with an understanding smile and a ready pair of ears.

He checked his sticking plaster was in place, planned a joking account of how he'd acquired his wound if anyone asked, offered his arm to her Ladyship and accompanied her to the hall.

CHAPTER 14

It had been a demanding afternoon. The first two pairs of guests had arrived in quick succession and been welcomed with delight by Cecily. Joe had made himself useful, offering the expected staccato exchanges with the gentlemen, flirtatious chatter with the ladies, and pouring many cups of tea. He'd even found time to escort Florence on an expedition to view the pineapples in the glasshouse. Cecily had introduced him to the guests as 'James's dear friend . . . and George Jardine's associate in India, you know. Wilfred, weren't you and Maggie in Ootacamund before the war? I thought so. Joe, you must know Ooty?'"

Cecily had finally admitted that she had attempted to reconstruct the deadly dinner party so that he might have as many witnesses as possible to speak to. The three married couples who had all accepted the invitation had been present that evening, as had her son Alex.

No secret was made of his police rank; Cecily even hinted with a knowing twinkle that curled Joe's toes in embarrassment that the guests were fortunate to be meeting possibly the successor to Lord Trenchard in the service. His position was remarked on with the usual heavy hilarity and Joe had replied in kind: "No, no! Don't be concerned. I'm on holiday. The Crown Jewels tucked up in your second best waistcoat in your valise will remain undisturbed by me, Sir Basil!"

This was a waste of his time, he had decided. Just a gathering of old friends who would not have featured on any suspect list of his. This lot, though killingly boring, would never have so much as stolen a sugar lump from the tea-tray. What *was* Cecily up to? He had to admit he was rather enjoying watching her taking so much pleasure in resuming her old duties and performing them so well. He found he was slipping easily into the role she had assigned to him, astutely anticipating her needs. All the same, he would be relieved when James returned tomorrow morning and he could stop being quite so interesting.

But then the third couple had turned up. The man Joe least wanted to see from the original guest list: Mungo McIver and his attractive young wife, Alice.

Good friends of Cecily's and supporters of James. Mungo McIver was known slightly to Joe as the owner of one or two newspapers ranging from the middle ground to the right of the political spectrum. He was reputed to be a hands-on owner, actively involved in the news-making process, particularly when his own protégés were involved. His editors were not admirers of Scotland Yard and snatched at every opportunity to expose their shortcomings.

All things considered, this was a man to be given a wide berth. Joe had learned generally to mistrust, occasionally to admire, and always to avoid the Gentlemen of the Press.

Doubly difficult when one of them was striding from his Rolls, hand outstretched, broad smile on face, heartily claiming an acquaintance. "Alice, my dear, allow me to introduce the Yard's keenest hound and Head of Special Branch. We shall all sleep sounder in our beds knowing that he is here among us!"

Why was McIver here? Nothing Cecily did, Joe reckoned, was uncalculated. Did he have evidence to divulge? It was entirely

possible. But it occurred to Joe that James—or was it Cecily?—
was counting on a dramatic clearing up of the murder with a top
press man in the front row. A scoop? Wasn't that what they called
it? This would be an excellent way of restoring James's reputation.
Joe rehearsed a few possible headlines in his mind and was horrified by all of them. It might be wise to check whether Mungo
McIver had hidden a cameraman away in his entourage. What
had he brought with him? In a separate motorcar there'd been a
bowler-hatted valet—doubling as chauffeur—and a lady's maid.

In a quiet moment after tea, Cecily tracked him down to the
croquet lawn where he was trying to explain to Mrs. Somerton
that a mallet could not be used like a hockey stick. She took him
aside for a briefing. "That's the Ripleys, the Somertons and the
McIvers all safely gathered in. Six. Then there's Alexander. So
we'll sit down a modest but relaxing nine to dinner this evening.
Expect the summons for cocktails at seven, dinner at eight, will
you, Joe? Oh, and could you offer your arm to Florence? We still
do that in the old-fashioned way. She's rather taken with you. I
think your charms are probably wasted on Maggie, however. James
will be arriving just before lunch tomorrow—hoping to catch the
parade of horses on the front lawn—and he's bringing with him
three others, two female, one male. He divulged no names," she
added, her brow furrowing in concern. "It's a bad omen when
James turns secretive. It means I shall not approve of his choice
of guests."

"Bad omen, indeed. That brings the number up to thirteen
for dinner tomorrow," Joe commented.

Cecily smiled indulgently at his perception and for a moment
he feared she might pat his head. "You see my problem. No one
sits down thirteen to dinner. No! Don't think of offering to withdraw yourself, young man. Alex, as always, is the oddity." She
wrung her hands to indicate maternal concern. "We must have
that lady doctor to chaperone him. A day's notice is unmannerly

in the extreme but . . . I wonder . . . why don't I entrust the invitation to someone she'll be hardly likely to refuse? To you, Joe? I've had a cold response on the few occasions we've met and I know she's bound to spurn an invitation from me. There's a telephone in the little study to the left of the front door. Why not go and see if you can tempt her to come? Styles will give you the number . . . Ah! Wilfred! Here you are! What did you think of the orchids? Now—do we have a mallet for Wilfred, Joe?"

The use of the telephone was temptation enough for Joe. He agreed to the unwanted task without demur, excused himself and headed for the study.

First a long-distance call.

"Lydia?"

"Joe! Where the devil are you?"

"Got a pencil? Write down this number quickly before the pips go." He read out the numbers from the base of the phone. "I'm in Suffolk. Working on a murder case. Possibly two murders . . ." He gave a short account of his predicament, mentioning that he'd diced with death three times so far that day and was now in hideous thrall to a dragon dowager who was holding him prisoner within her curtilage and using him as a sort of police-gigolo. Lydia's little brother was to be pitied rather than ticked off, he implied. It usually worked but not today.

"Well, your weekend seems to be going better than mine. We were going to have a quiet time with lots of champagne to celebrate the end of term for Dorcas and neither of you can get here . . . No . . . she's been trying to contact you. Haven't we all? But no luck. You can't ring her because she's gone off in a huff, heaven knows where. Has something gone wrong between you, Joe? Well, get here when you can. The champagne will keep. I can't promise the same for the *terrine de fruits de mer.* Or the cherry ice cream."

She meant it to sting.

Joe signed off with all the dignity he could muster, replaced the receiver, then picked it up again and asked the operator to connect him with the veterinarian, Mr. Hartest.

Adelaide answered. She recognised his voice and seemed pleased to be hearing from him. She listened while he relayed Cecily's invitation for the following evening. Two seconds was all it took for her to make up her mind.

"Certainly not!" she snapped. "For about ten reasons. I don't want to. I don't like her. I wouldn't like her guests. I would almost certainly drown Alex in his soup. I shall be preparing Pa's supper at exactly that time. I shall be in church at the Evensong service. Choose whichever you like."

Joe put out a finger and broke contact abruptly, then he replaced the receiver. Pausing to count out a sixpence and a two-shilling piece to put into the box placed by the phone, he darted into the hall and flushed out Styles.

"Bicycle? Do you have such a thing on the premises?" he asked with some urgency.

"Certainly. May I enquire as to the nature and duration of the jaunt you are contemplating, sir?" The measured enquiry was laden with respectful censure. Like a good herd dog, Styles was not happy when a guest appeared to be making a run for it.

"A short errand for her ladyship." Not quite a lie.

This proved acceptable, apparently. "You'll find a selection in the garage. Everything from racers to sit-up-and-begs that don't scare the ladies." He measured Joe for a moment from head to toe with a tailor's eye and called, "Timmy!" A young trainee foot-man presented himself. "Timmy, show the gentleman to the garage and point out the *Schwinn*, will you?"

BOWLING DOWN THE lime avenue on a daringly drop-handled, balloon-tyred speedster (*the Swine*, according to a reverent Timmy, who would clearly have given his shining buttons

for a ride on it), Joe chortled with amusement. Butlers! He wondered how many decrepit old guests had been flattered into
flinging a gouty leg over this seductive killer. He felt a surge of
exhilaration, not only from the speed and smoothness of the
ride but from relief at his escape and the energy powered him
all the way to the vet's neat house. He arrived, braking silently
in front of the copper beech hedge and noting that his ride had
taken only five minutes. What right did he have to impose
himself on Adelaide? None at all and he prepared to have his
ears boxed and be sent off straight back to the Hall. He adjusted
his tie and fiddled with his plaster.

She was dead-heading the roses and turned with a smile as
she heard the iron gate creak open. Clearly expecting her father,
Joe supposed. He wished that the welcome had been for him but
the smile faded and she squinted in puzzlement when she recognised her visitor. His only recourse was to boldness. He clanged
the gate shut and pushed his bike up the path.

"Joe? What on earth?"

Well, at least she'd remembered his name. It was a start.

"Wretched telephone! We were cut off. I've come to hear the
remaining four."

"Four what?"

"Reasons. You promised me ten and had delivered six, none
of which I liked. You were saying . . . ?"

She put the secateurs away in her pocket and came to stand
in front of him. "Seven: there's a play on the wireless I'd planned
to listen to with Pa. Eight: I have nothing suitable to wear for
such an occasion. Nine: I'm damned if I'm going to rattle up to
the Hall in Dad's old vet's estate car. Ten: I don't want to risk
being put to sit next to you all evening."

Joe grinned. "Now there's the truth! I'd be persuaded by any
one of those. But listen, we can work our way around seven and
ten so we're left with—"

"No—*you're* left with. This has very little to do with me. I think you're very rude to come here and put me on the spot. You should arrest yourself for harassment."

Joe ignored this as he couldn't contradict. "The car—they've got plenty at the Hall. I'll have them send a chauffeur to fetch you and I'll bring you back myself. The dress? Hmm . . . Are you sure? It needn't be a designer number. Whatever you wear, you'll put the other women in the shade. Crocodiles in pearls!" he said in a voice bright with encouragement and challenge. "Go and look in your cupboards."

"First, I'd like to take a look at whatever you're hiding under that dressing," she said, peering up at his cheek. "Something bitten you?"

Joe exclaimed, as without further warning, she ripped the plaster off. "Good Lord! That's nasty!" She put up a hand and ran it over the bumps and creases. "There are splinters in there. Wood? Have you been hugging a tree with indecent fervour?"

"Some idiot chucked a log at me. A man with a green face and a green shirt. Yet another person in the county who thinks Joe Sandilands is a bit of bad news."

"Urgh! You fell foul of Robin Goodfellow? Rustic comedian and resident parasite? You should have run him in. Look, you'd better come into the parlour, sit yourself on a chair, and I'll get my bag. Tweezers and a spot of iodine should work wonders. You can't afford to pick up another scar—that would be extravagantly romantic. They'd have to put you in a musical comedy."

He closed his eyes politely as her swift cool fingers worked on his face, gritting his teeth against the stabs of pain from the probings and the antiseptic, and opened them again when a new dressing was in place.

"You can always tell the crocodiles you got that in a duel. Left cheek scars are all the go in Prussia, they tell me. You can say you've just been initiated into Herr Hitler's élite bodyguard of strutting thugs. They might just believe it. Some of the guests might even approve," she added darkly. "There's some speculation as to where exactly Truelove's sympathies lie. His brother-in-law, married to the older of his two sisters, if I've got that right, is a psychologist, a eugenicist or something of that nature, and he's recently defected to Germany to ply his disgusting trade, did you know?"

Joe grinned. "I'm delighted to say it was my boot up his rear that decided him to leave England in a hurry. I'm collecting enemies in high places, I'm afraid."

"Well, watch your step up there in that company then. I'm good at grazes and bruises but I have no experience with bullet wounds. Though Pa might be able to help. He served in the war and found he had to extend his skills to human patients as well as equine."

She snapped her bag closed and was clearly about to send him on his way when he began to blurt. Blurting was the only word for the reckless effusion of nonsense that seemed to be coming from his lips. "Do come, Adelaide! For me, not them! I can't tell you what a difference it would make. To see a friendly face across the table, to hear a voice that doesn't crack the glassware. To have someone whose eye I can catch in understanding. Will you change your mind?"

The urgency of his appeal silenced and concerned her. Quick and decisive as he was beginning to judge her, she said, after a questioning stare, "I'm not inviting you up to my room. The contents of it will have to come down to you. Wait a minute."

After five minutes of rummaging overhead, she clumped back downstairs and dumped the contents of her wardrobe at his feet.

"Three flowery cotton washing frocks," she announced. "No use at all." These were thrown aside to form the base of the rejected pile. A cream linen day dress followed. "Women's Institute Committee meeting . . . Now this one—long, black, formal. Bias cut. Silk. I wore this for a degree-giving dinner six years ago."

"That's certainly a possibility," Joe said. "Something at the neck, perhaps? . . . A rose from the garden tucked into a splendid bosom is always a winner."

"How lucky I am that splendid bosoms are back in fashion again," she commented drily.

Embarrassed, he struggled to excuse himself. "I couldn't help noticing the fine choice of roses in your beds when I had them in close-up." And, helpfully: "I'd suggest white rather than red. The Flamenco style wouldn't suit you."

At last she seemed caught by the idea. "I see what you mean. There's a Snow Queen. Pure white but it's a bit floppy and yellow in the middle and drops pollen. I'd have half the table sneezing into its raspberry sorbet. Ah! Got it! There's Swan Lake. Cream, cup-shaped, with the faintest flush of pink in the central bud." She demonstrated with one hand curving at her neckline.

Joe's jaw sagged and he swallowed the words he'd been about to release.

They stared at each other for a moment, and then, in a voice tight with restrained humour, she answered his thought. "No, I expect you're right. One can have too splendid a bosom. We shouldn't forget the advanced age and state of decrepitude of the guests. The sight of three nipples in a row might just bring on palpitations and I never take my stethoscope out to dinner."

"It'll have to be granny's pearls then," Joe croaked. "What a pity."

"It will do but it's a bit dull and it looks dated. Like its owner," she said, throwing down the black dinner dress. "The rest are trousers. This here's a silk lounging outfit I wore on holiday in Cannes last year." She held up a pair of flared red and purple trousers.

"Sorry, no. I'm sure they turned all heads on the Croisette but they should never have been allowed out of France without a license."

"Last item, the most expensive thing I own—and the least suitable—a pair of evening trousers. They're not by Chanel but they are the next best thing. Paul Vercors of Paris. Look—high-waisted, wide cut. If I stand with my legs together it just looks like a skirt. The drama comes when I start walking. Scandalous really. I've never dared wear them. Never had occasion to. I just longed to have them."

Joe had a sudden vision of Adelaide Hartest's slim hips and long legs stalking through the Trueloves' elegant rooms and sighed. "I like it but—what would you do about the top half?"

"My thoughts never got that far. White blouse of some sort? No. I agree, it looks like being the boring graduation black. So, that's the pumpkin and the ball gown settled," she said, "Anything else my fairy god father can help with? I think you've cast yourself in the wrong pantomime, mister. I see you as a beast of uncertain temper, lurking amongst the potted palms."

"Uncertain temper? Never. Why do you say that?"

She came to settle next to him on the sofa and for a moment he thought she might take his hand to check his pulse. Instead, she stared into his eyes, checking for whatever it was doctors looked for in eyes. Dilated pupils? Grit? He blinked nervously. "Joe, there's something troubling you, isn't there? I mean apart from murder, attacks by green shirts and threats from brown shirts. Something more important than that. Why are you really here? You could have sent an inspector from the Met. A man of your rank doesn't involve himself with country farces like this, all name-calling, tantrums and whackings with a pig's bladder, unless he has a very strong personal reason for doing so."

"Don't dismiss murder so lightly, Adelaide. But you're right. I do have a personal interest in this . . . not farce but drama—which could all too easily turn into melodrama. A girl I'm fond of . . . the girl I love," he corrected, deciding he could confide, "is tangled up with James Truelove. Hunnyton, bless the man—for

I'd probably not have leapt into action without his encouragement—lured me over here to get to the bottom of it."

"Tangled with a Truelove? How uncomfortable! Will you tell
me how she comes to be in such a spot?"

Adelaide was a receptive listener and the whole story poured
from Joe under her gentle questioning. He told how he'd met
Dorcas when she was just a young thing, how their strange relationship had developed and how suddenly after a seven years'
absence she'd flown back into his life, a beautiful young woman,
a stranger yet not quite a stranger, and claimed the love he had
always had for her. "Hunnyton says I ought to treat her as though
I'd only just met her and discount the past," he finished, dragging
the superintendent into the conversation once more.

"Sound advice," she said with an enthusiastic nod. "You could
do worse than to listen to Adam Hunnybun. He has a fund of
common sense and a good heart. And he likes you."

Joe was not very certain about any of those assertions and kept
silent. He was wondering with suspicion how she had come to
develop such a warm opinion of the man on such a short acquaintance and decided that Hunnyton must have doubled back for a
further consultation with Dr. Hartest after he'd dropped Joe off
into the clutches of the Wild Man of the Woods.

"Can I tell you something? Something of a professional
nature?" Adelaide was saying hesitantly. "I studied psychology as
an element of my training and found it utterly fascinating. *Mens
sana in corpore sano* is something all doctors should have written
on their surgery walls. Broken limbs and infections are straight-
forward stuff but the tricky—and the repeated—illnesses are not
so easy to diagnose and cure. I don't believe one-half of everything
Freud has to say, but there is much work being done—and has
been done—in laboratories which can enlighten us. Listen, Joe.
It may be nonsense or it may be of help ... Imprinting. That may
be the key. Have you heard of imprinting?"

Joe shook his head.

"Investigation's been going on for some years. If you take a batch of fledgling birds—geese, or is it storks? seem to give clear results—and deprive them of their parent birds . . ."

"Here we go again!" Joe objected. "More animal torment. But—birds? This is a new one."

"Not new, in fact. Douglas Spalding was working on it sixty years ago. Oskar Heinroth took it up. But don't interrupt. When they're ready to fly, they have to be shown how to do it or they'd remain forever earth-bound. If an experimenter runs about in front of the baby birds, waving his arms up and down like wings, they catch on straight away and do the same. They follow him about flapping and squawking, copying him with the clear conviction that he is the parent bird. He takes the process further and by even more energetic flapping and leaping into the air, or off a cliff perhaps, convinces them that they can take off. They actually learn to fly by human example. It's not perfect but it works."

Joe stayed silent, sensing she was getting to her point.

"The thing is, they grow up believing that the scientist is their parent, totally devoted to him and disregarding any other attentions, even that of their genuine parents. The same results have been recorded from creatures closer to humans—dogs, chimpanzees. It has been suggested, though not yet proven, that a similar process may take place in children. The theory is that at a particular moment in their development, a moment of change and need, they imprint on an adult or older child and follow and copy and revere this chosen one."

"You're saying Dorcas may, at a low point in her life, and finding herself without any other adult she could respect, have imprinted on *me*?"

"Think about it. It's not a very long step from 'imprinting' to 'falling in love,' which is the label we stick on a badly understood and otherwise unaccountable impulse. That's something every fourteen-year-old girl does understand. And if the chap she has in her sights is every girl's idea of a dashing hero—good-looking, energetic, chest full of medals, romantically scarred—well, poor love, she didn't stand a chance. If everything else had been normal or supportive in her background, what she felt for you would have been nothing more than a crush, soon outgrown. Poor Dorcas! I wonder if she has any idea?"

Joe longed to point out that he was suffering, too. If this psychological gobbledegook, which in spite of himself he had listened to in fascination, were halfway true, he had a worse situation on his hands than he'd realised.

"That's a very alarming condition you describe," he mumbled.

"It gets worse. It would seem that the *imprinter* himself," she poked Joe playfully in the ribs, "that's you—is not unaffected. His own behaviour changes, adjusting, through a desire for scientific knowledge (we'll rule that out) or a sense of duty and a kind nature (more likely), to what he perceives to be the needs of the creatures he is imprinting. He strives to see the world through the eyes of his subjects and modifies his own responses accordingly."

"Are you saying I've been flapping and quacking and leaping off cliffs all these years to chime with Dorcas's needs?"

"Something like that," she said, shaking with suppressed laughter.

"Am I destined to go on doing bird imitations for the rest of my life or is there a cure?" was the only thing he could think of to ask.

"No. Shouldn't think so. But you could change the condition, having recognised it for what it is. Yes. Accept it, understand it and change it for something else. I've known old gents swap their gout for arthritis—or the other way around—when it suited them. Listen to Adam. Take her for a new person. Make a fresh beginning. Flirt with her, ask her about her life—her present life—and don't rake up the past. None of that 'Do you remember when you were in pigtails?' stuff. And, above all, don't leap in and slap down a proposal of marriage at her feet. You've so far avoided this and I'm quite sure your instinct has been guiding you well. In fact, knowingly or unknowingly, I'd say your Dorcas had already started on the road back to normality by distancing herself from you for the past few years. You must hope she can love the man you are now, not the one she imagined you were when she first came running after you."

"Hmmph. Flirt and hope? You make it sound rather straight-forward, Adelaide. It's not. I had rather thought my flirting days were over. There comes a moment when audacious charm begins to look like geriatric seduction. A boyish smile turns into a sug-gestive leer overnight."

She peered at him. "Oh, I think you're quite safe. Not grey yet and no moustache. You have all your teeth. Very nice teeth. Yes— you could get away with a well-directed leer still, I reckon."

"But before I can even expose her to that—I first have to keep her safe. Get her out of James Truelove's clutches."

Adelaide's voice had lost its certainty when she replied. "Joe— how would you know that's not where she wants to be?" She looked at him, her amber eyes suddenly filling with pity and fear, and she took hold of his hand to squeeze it gently in sympathy.

"Will someone tell me what precisely is going on here?" an angry voice demanded from the doorway. "The moment my back's turned I come home to find my daughter, discarded garments round her ankles, sitting on the sofa, spooning with a complete stranger! A stranger who's parked his red racer by my front door."

Veterinary surgeon Hartest, moustache bristling with paren-tal wrath, stomped into the parlour in his socks. "Good afternoon, sir! Do I need to fetch my shotgun?" Large, red-haired, smelling of the countryside and clearly at the end of an exhausting day, he reduced Joe to quaking confusion.

"Father!" Adelaide said crossly. "Joe came seeking medical help for a face wound and psychiatric advice on a personal problem."

"Looks more like hands-on treatment he's getting," Hartest said, unable any longer to contain his mischievous amusement. "Are you billing him or is this one of your charity cases, Adelaide?"

"This is Assistant Commissioner Joseph Sandilands of Scotland Yard and he's up to his ears in a murder case. *The* murder case. He was disappointed not to see *you*, Pa."

"He seems quite happy with the substitute. Has the feller been here since eleven this morning?"

Hearing the mantel clock chime six, Joe was taken aback. He hurriedly shook hands with Hartest and made his excuses to father and daughter. "On duty at seven . . . must bathe and change into evening suit . . . Must find an opportunity to discuss the case and meantime thank Miss Hartest for filling in so effectively . . ."

He dashed off on the bicycle, but even the Swine could not go fast enough to leave his confusion behind and he arrived back at the Hall four minutes later, both cheeks aflame.

CHAPTER 15

"Stop fussing, Ducks! The kids are just fine. I left them bathed and ready to go to bed. They were boring the boots off your long-suffering Emma, reading her a bedtime story. *Swallows and Amazons* isn't really her cup of tea, I think." Aunty Phyl settled at the table, twinkled at her escorting waiter and asked him to arrange for the immediate arrival of a bottle of Pol Roger. Phyl couldn't bear lists and menus and preferred to give her requirements straight out as soon as she arrived. "We're dining unfashionably early, aren't we? Six o'clock? That's more like kiddies' tea-time. Planning to go on somewhere? The Ambassadors, perhaps? Now—who do you want me to help you watch?"

Lily's aunt, slim, vibrant and wearing with professional elegance a gown of her own design complemented by a mist of Mitsouko, looked askance at her niece. Lily's plain maroon crêpe de chine dinner dress was strained a little too tightly around the bust and drooped a couple of inches too long at the hem. The frumpish look was reinforced by an ill-considered pearl necklace and a pair of her father's reading glasses with tortoiseshell frames.

"Gawd! I hope you're in disguise, gel! I wouldn't want to think you were letting yourself go. I took you for your mother until you smiled." She looked about her at the other diners, noting their correct evening dress and general air of understated affluence with satisfaction. Phyl fitted in seamlessly. "We're a bit mismatched, you and I. Not out of the same bandbox tonight."

"That's quite all right. If anyone wants to know, I'm taking my rich publisher, that's you, out to dinner—so kill the Cockney. I'm aiming to persuade you to look favourably on my latest romantic oeuvre. I've written up the first two chapters already. No kidding! It's been pretty boring watching his nibs over there . . . Yes . . . the good looking dark bloke, fidgeting with his gardenia, at the far table."

Phyl unobtrusively located the target. "Oh. You're supposed to keep an eye on *him* all evening? Not one of your more demanding jobs, then. I see he's got his champagne chilling and his engine revving. But he's nervous. Or perhaps just excited." She flicked another glance sideways as Mr. Fitzwilliam looked at his watch for the third time in thirty seconds. "I see why he's having an early dinner . . . not so much going on as going up?" Phyl raised her eyebrows suggestively. "I expect if you checked, Lil, you'd find he has a sumptuous flower-bedecked suite booked upstairs. I've seen him somewhere before . . . Let's hope she doesn't keep him waiting long. This is fun! I didn't know you were doing divorces, Lil! Do we expect fireworks and a floor show? Anyone I'll recognise?"

They fell into a natural conversation about Phyl's exploits at Ascot as the maître d'hôtel eased by their table, leading a young girl. She looked ahead eagerly and smiled as Fitzwilliam leapt to his feet in welcome.

"Oh, my! A pair of love birds! Is that what you were expecting, Lil?"

"Well, no. I was prepared for one of Herr Hitler's generals, the Russian ambassador or Lady Astor. Possibly all three. What do you make of *her*, Phyl?"

Aunt Phyl, Cockney-born and proud of it, was known professionally as *Madame Claude, Couturière, Londres et Paris*, and could sum up a woman's character and class and tell you to a penny how much her husband had in the bank from one brief look. She was completely trusted in these matters by Lily. "Early twenties. Very pretty. A bit tricky to read. A lady, definitely, but I'd say not out of the top drawer. More Bloomsbury than Berkeley Square."

"That's a nice dress, though. Well cut, unpretentious . . ."

"Victor Stiebel, dear. Clinging but flared at the hem—that's flattering. Shows off her neat waist and ankles. Navy silk with a flash of peacock blue. A nice touch. Not expensive but it looks the part. Like the girl in it. She's no debutante. Never was. There's something about that unnatural walk they train those girls to do. As though the top of their head is attached to the ceiling by a string. Now, my mannequins—the moment they knock off, they relax and slouch about like anything, but being a deb does permanent damage to your spine. That girl swings when she walks and she's not wearing stays. No whalebone and not much elastic either under there . . . French knickers and that's about all, I'd say. I can't imagine her dropping a curtsey. Not a tennis player by any chance, do you suppose? They're beginning to arrive for Wimbledon and there's a contingent of women this year. She's got short hair and good shoulders. I can imagine her whacking a ball."

"She may need a stinging back-hand by the end of her evening. I'd say he was head over heels and on mischief bent, wouldn't you?" Lily noted the glance that sent the sommelier away, leaving the ice bucket by Fitzwilliam's elbow, and she tried to lip-read the toast he whispered as they raised their glasses.

The two women took it in turns to observe their man and reported back to each other anything that caught their interest. They'd done this before. Two females chattering together was an arrangement that never aroused suspicion.

By the time the Dover sole was served, Phyl had made up her mind. "You can come off watch, Lil. The girl's not unwilling. I thought at first she didn't want to be here—nervous, looking about her, checking her exits—but she soon settled down and they're having a really good talk. Funny pair though. This whole set-up shrieks seduction but no one's *flirting*. No eyelash batted, no moustache twirled. They're just chatting. Give and take. He's really listening to what she's saying—and that's plenty—and he's making her laugh. You know, Lil, I think they've known each other for years. She just passed him the salt a split second before he asked for it. You don't do that with a stranger. It's sort of . . . intimate." Phyl watched and came to a conclusion. "They're in love. Now, why's it taken us so long to come out with that? You can see it from here, even with your pa's glasses on." She sighed. "Lucky girl, I'd say. He's a cracker."

"Brides-in-the-Bath Smith was charming and personable," Lily said. "I'm staying alert."

"Here comes the moment critique," Phyl whispered. "They've both refused dessert and cheese and asked for coffee. He's lighting a cigar. If he calls for a brandy, assume the worst. Always beware of a bloke who finishes his evening with brandy—it perks him up where he wants to be perked and you can bet he knows that from experience. Ah, he's signalling the waiter."

A prepared tray was instantly brought to their table bearing a bottle and two glasses. A small package done up in silver paper, tied up in white ribbons and topped with a fresh white rose accompanied the Napoleon brandy. Fitzwilliam poured out the drinks then handed the package with mischievous ceremony to the girl. A birthday present? Lily tried to put an innocent explanation on the appearance of such a sumptuously decked-out offering but there was a discordant note in the girl's reaction. Her surprise appeared genuine and she shied away with a distancing flutter of her hands. Lily could only read from her lips: "But why? You shouldn't have! No need . . . really . . ." as she tucked the rose into her neckline and set about untying the ribbons.

Annoyingly, Lily couldn't make out the contents when the wrapper was discarded. It appeared to be a pair of items . . .

earrings, perhaps? She caught a flash of gold. The girl was holding the objects, one in each hand, looking with astonishment from one to the other. Fitzwilliam drew his chair closer to hers until their heads were touching, slipped an arm around her waist and leaned into her shoulder talking quietly in her ear. What he had to say stunned and moved the girl. Lily could have sworn there were tears in her eyes as she looked down at the gift, looked back at him with some tenderness, then shook her head and spoke slowly in reply.

"Whatever he's suggesting, she's turning him down," Phyl murmured. "Silly cow!"

His response to the show of emotion was to take the girl's hands in his and speak even more urgently.

She seemed suddenly to crumble under the pressure and got to her feet, picked up her bag, made hasty excuses and set off across the room heading towards the ladies' cloakroom.

Lily leaned towards Phyl. "Do you still carry a sewing kit around with you? Good. May I?"

She took the offered box and slipped it inside her own bag and, after half a minute, set off in the wake of the fleeing girl.

Entering the magnolia-scented washroom tucked away down a short flight of stairs, Lily first greeted the attendant in charge. A whispered, "I'd like a few minutes in private with my daughter if you wouldn't mind, Miss . . ." and a half crown slipped into the ready hand removed the audience.

The girl was standing, holding onto a washbasin, staring at her image in the mirror above and not much liking what she saw, Lily guessed. Sadness? Despair? Disgust? She took the rose from her dress and carefully inserted it into the small bouquet decorating the counter.

"Ah! Caught you!" Lily sang out. "I couldn't help noticing as you swept past that you've put a heel through the hem of your dress." She sank to her knees and lifted up the hem, sliding a determined thumb nail along the stitching until there was indeed a four inch tear in the fabric. "There it is! It's your lucky day! I'm an expert seamstress if I do say it myself. I always carry the necessary about with me. Black and white thread always at the ready." She produced the sewing kit with a flourish and selected the black-threaded needle. "Just as well you're not wearing yellow. This will do very well on navy."

The girl was irritated and anxious and clearly this intervention was the last thing she wanted at that moment but her good manners took over. She murmured her thanks and seemed prepared to suffer in silence until the old nuisance had finished.

Lily took off the distorting spectacles and began to stitch swiftly and neatly. "There, that's done. You'll be wanting to get back to your young man. My dear! What an elegant and handsome fellow! My friend and I were just saying what a wonderful pair you make."

A sudden rush of tears and a stifled howl of pain greeted this comment. Lily was taken aback by the grief she appeared to have caused and instinctively flung an arm around the shaking shoulders, offering a lace-edged handkerchief from her pocket and clucking sympathy. "Oh, no! I'm always putting my foot in it! Have I got it completely wrong? Look here, my dear, if the fellow's making demands you feel uncomfortable with, I can help you out of here, call you a taxi home. No girl has to suffer unwanted advances. I know a way out that doesn't take you back through the dining room. Do you live in London?"

She stifled her sobs and sniffled into the handkerchief. She managed a smile and stared at Lily as though seeing her for the first time. With the strangest of expressions she asked, "Who are you? Did Joe send you?"

Lily didn't need to simulate her surprise. "Joe? Joe? . . . No indeed. No one's sent me here. I'm having dinner with my publisher. I'm a romantic novelist and I have to confess we were beginning to weave quite a story in which you and that handsome rogue upstairs were featuring. Never guessed it would end in tears. I shall have to rewrite my ending now," she finished with a teasing rebuke. She took a chance and added, "Who's Joe?"

"My guardian angel. I'm sorry. I thought when you took off your specs to do the sewing that was a very strange thing to do. I can't help noticing inconsistent pieces of behaviour. It's what I'm trained to do," she said apologetically. "And women don't usually offer to do up my hems . . . they'd rather tread on them," she added unguardedly. "I say, are you in disguise? Has someone sent you here to keep an eye on me? To keep me out of trouble? It's just the sort of kind-hearted but sneaky thing Joe would arrange. He's a powerful man and he has a lot of people to do his bidding in London."

"Well I'm not one of them. I'm from Yorkshire," Lily lied cheerfully. "We don't hold with Machiavellian manipulation north of the Trent. Look, Miss, your friend Joe sounds more gangster than angel to me. You want to watch *him*!" She put her spectacles back on and pulled a face. "There! Do you see the change? Lady novelists make a better impression on their publishers if they look intellectual."

This raised another smile. "I do see! Perhaps I should try a pair."

"They certainly keep the gentlemen at arm's length, I've always found." She gave a stagy sigh.

The answering smile became a chuckle.

"If you're sure there's nothing I can do . . . ? Summon up your 'angel,' perhaps?"

"Lord no! I've spent the week dodging his attentions by one device or another. He'd tear my ears off if he knew where I was. But, look, if you really wouldn't mind, could you come with me to the lobby? Wait with me for a taxi? They don't much like picking up single women at this hour. You're very kind!" She put her arm through Lily's and they moved towards the door. "Now—this is bad of me—but could I impose on you further? I need some time. Could you bear to have a quick word with my companion?"

"Mr. Fitzwilliam?"

"Yes. Will you tell him I'm upset and I've gone back to spend the night with Kate? All perfectly true."

"Very sensible move, my dear. I understand."

"No, no! It's not like that . . . not what you're thinking . . ."

Lily seemed to have triggered an emotional reaction and waited to hear more, an expression of kind concern on her face.

"My companion is . . . a . . . lovely man. An honourable man. He wishes me no harm."

"Leave it to me. I'll speak to him. I'm sure I can find the right words. That's what *I'm* trained to do." They smiled at each other with mutual regard. "I'm Vanessa Richmond. How do you do?"

"Dorcas Joliffe. Thank you so much, Miss Richmond, for sticking me back together. Consider yourself my stand-in angel."

"ALL WELL, LIL? What have you done with her?" Phyl asked when she returned.

"Nothing's well, I'd say. She's done a bunk and left me to present her excuses. When I get hold of you-know-who, I'm going to fillet him!"

"You got involved with the target!" Phyl pursed her lips. "Isn't that against all the rules of undercover work? You'll catch it, gel, when the boss finds out."

"You know, Phyl, there are no rules in the kind of work I do. He employs me to think for myself. We have the same wriggly ways of getting through. I wouldn't be a bit surprised if I'd done exactly what my lord and spymaster intended—put a ruddy great spoke in the wheels of a budding romance!"

Phyl nodded. "Not sure about 'budding.' Look at him!"

Lily flicked a glance at the troubled Fitzwilliam, whose eyes were still watching the door, and prepared herself for the coming encounter. "The things I do for England! Funny, Phyl—I lost no sleep over breaking the arm of a chap who was asking for it, but I really jib at the thought of breaking a heart."

CHAPTER 16

Joe was slowly sipping a green and summery cocktail made up of gin, Rose's lime cordial and large quantities of ice when the butler stalked to his side in the Great Hall.

In his over-stimulated state Joe had decided to inject a bit of life into this dull company when he came down, bathed and fresh and evening-suited. Playing heavily on his Indian experiences, he'd taken the footman aside, relieved him of his silver shaker and, with the exaggerated gestures of a Savoy cocktail waiter, given him an energetic demonstration of how to make a "gimlet," that favourite summer tipple of the Raj. Cries of excited acclaim and an outpouring of memories from the old India hands had greeted his unorthodox behaviour and two bottles of gin had glugged their way through the silver shaker as the crowd whiled away the time waiting for the appearance of young Alex. "Well done!" Cecily had whispered. "That's not such a bad idea. The drunker the guests are, the less conspicuous my son will appear. Shall we have another round of these delicious things?"

"I beg your pardon, sir, but there's a person on the telephone requiring to speak with you as a matter of urgency. A female person. She did not give her name," Styles said quietly.

"Dorcas?" Joe said eagerly as he picked up the receiver.

"Sorry, Joe. It's me, Lily."

"Thank God! We're just about to go in to dinner. Any news?"

"Dinner's over here. In sophisticated London, they've all dined and gone on somewhere else. Aunty Phyl came and helped me watch."

"And?"

"Straight to the QED bit, Joe?"

"Please."

"Fitzwilliam was entertaining a female guest. She was happily entertained—in fact, Aunty Phyl, who hadn't a clue who the pair were, rather thought they were in love. But it all turned sour when he gave her an unexpected present. It consisted of two items I couldn't make out. Small. Gold. They had significance for her, though. She burst into tears and fled the table." She hurried to add, "They're not spending the night together."

"Identification, Lil?"

"Pursued by me to the ladies washroom, she told me her name was Dorcas Joliffe."

Lily absorbed the heavy silence and then took up again, slowly: "Upshot was, Miss Joliffe took off in a taxi, leaving me to make her excuses to Fitzwillie. She said she was going to stay with a friend . . . Kate. I heard her direct the cabby to Highgate."

Joe's voice was a growl of distress. "You said it, Lil. Romantic place, silver words—I'm sure there were plenty of those—and a meaningful gift. Yes, I know what that would have been. The Swine actually tricked me into acquiring it on his behalf the day before. He set me up to bid for it at Christie's. It cost him fifty quid; it's cost me . . ."

"What on earth was it, Joe?"

"A pair of gold-mounted miniatures. Very good ones. Great-great-grandmama and -grandpapa. A matched pair of betrothal portraits."

Hissing of a human kind filled the earpiece. Lily was quick to understand. "The shit! That was a seduction scene he'd set up all right, but more than that . . . A proposal of marriage. Don't you think? Am I reading too much into the gesture, Joe?"

"I'm sure you are." Joe's response was devoid of emotion. "He's a free man and will marry again if he is to achieve his ambitions. Future Prime Ministers are expected to acquire wives who will do them credit: they should be of high social standing, unassertive and, for choice, British. Dorcas is illegitimate and—worse—she has a French mother. The half that's not French—her father's side —is half German. Her paternal aunt, you'll recall, was conveniently murdered before she could be exposed as a German spy working at the heart of the British Navy." Sensing that he was responding a little abruptly, he added, "And, of course, she regularly marches with the Suffragettes, let's not forget."

"Then I've misinterpreted things . . . Definitely a non-starter in the marriage stakes! You've convinced me. Funny though, he seemed to me to be offering her his family on a plate. He must have been very confident that she would be impressed."

"They were impressive—all velvet and pearls and haughty stares. Now, the sight of *my* hand-hewn ancestors—bristly chins, rough tweeds and blackcock's feathers at a jaunty angle—the gentlemen were even more fearsome—would have a girl running for the exit."

"Well, that's sort of what did happen, Joe," Lily said gently. She always guessed his self-deprecating flippancy concealed distress. "She saw something there she didn't like the look of. Fitzwillie must have realised he'd misjudged things because she left the gift behind on the table when she skedaddled."

"Did he go after her?"

"No. He's still here in the hotel morosely sipping his brandy. Hoping she'll think again and come back, I expect. Do you want me to ruin his romantic prospects for a week? Albert's taught me the neatest trick and I'm sure I can borrow an umbrella . . ."

"Leave it, Lil. Just go home with my thanks. Yes, I said—thanks!

Boils are better lanced, and this is one that's been swelling for some time. Give Phyl a stiff drink and my undying gratitude, summon up old Albert and get him to drive you away from that den of iniquity . . . How did you get this number?"

"I rang your sister. Lydia told me you were down in the country chasing villains. Anyone I know?"

Joe swallowed. "As a matter of fact, you do. I'm at Melsett being the life and soul of a very dull party, at the beck and call of Cecily, Lady Truelove. Yes . . . standing in for James. Again! Does the word 'stooge' come to mind? He's expected here tomorrow morning with a mixed party. IDs unknown to me. No doubt I shall be surprised but not half as startled as he will be to see my ugly mug in the welcome line."

"Lord! What a scene! Shall I come?"

"I'm saying no for the moment. Could you stand by? Look, here's another number you can ring if you can't get me here." He gave her Adelaide's number. "That's the local vet. You can leave a message with him or his daughter. Phones out here are rarer than hen's teeth. Lily, I must go. Stomachs are rumbling. Any last comment?"

Lily hesitated and then plunged in: "Yes. There's something you shouldn't leave out of your calculations. He loves her, Joe."

A splutter of outrage then, puzzlingly, "Another poor clown caught flapping his wings and heading for the cliff edge! Hah! Serves the bugger right for tormenting the animal kingdom!"

ALEXANDER TRUELOVE, SERIAL persecutor of nannies, Oxford reject, failed banker, and consumer of dubious stimulating substances over many years, was putting on a show.

Joe could not but admire the effort the young man was making to join the party now that he had actually staggered as far as the Great Hall. Cecily had greeted him with a maternal coo of concern and, at a look from her, the footman in charge of the drinks table had stepped forward and placed a glass of something fizzy—Perrier?—with a slice of lemon into his hand. To everyone's relief, he had managed to remember the names of most of the guests he'd met before and exchanged appropriate comments and reminiscences. A genuine, clear-headed feat of memory, or had Cecily spent some time rehearsing him? Whatever the cause, they seemed flattered by the effect.

As one would be, Joe thought, by the attentions of this peacock. Cecily had misled him. In this and in how many other matters? he wondered bitterly. He'd imagined something on the lines of a Dorian Grey portrait: dissolute, lined, prematurely old, a face better hidden away. But here was a handsome youth, fair and slender, looking less than his twenty-five years when seen against the middle-aged and elderly guests surrounding him. If Dorcas had been of the company, Cecily would have sent them both off to play marbles. When he brushed aside the hair that flopped over his forehead in a blond quiff reminiscent of Rupert Brooke and turned his melting blue eyes on the ladies, they were as charmed by him as they were by the resident King Charles spaniel that skulked, quivering, about the place, begging for caresses and violet creams.

Joe had seen that unruly hair and those eyes before. Adam Hunnyton was a hand or two taller, a stone or two heavier and a decade or two older, but the two men had recognisably the same father.

The blue eyes had lost some of their openness when Cecily introduced him to Joe. "A friend of James?" he'd questioned, with a curl of the lip. "What are you saying, mother? My brother doesn't have friends. He has victims, dupes, prey. Which one are you, Commissioner?"

"I'm sure James would like to think—all three of those." Joe's tone was relaxed, his lips gently smiling, but the sudden narrowing of the icy grey eyes gave quite a different message.

Alex laughed. "Lesson one: how to duck a direct question. They warned me you'd had training with my godfather Jardine. The power behind the throne in India. Terrifying old bird! He talked me out of joining the diplomatic service, I remember."

"Very persuasive gentleman, Sir George."

"Indeed! Compelling. But you survived his ministrations to pound the beat another day? Clearly made of sterner stuff than the rest of us. Though why you'd choose bobbying over an apprenticeship in the dark arts from the master and a leg up the greasy diplomatic pole, I can't imagine. Can't say I've ever met a Scotland Yarder before . . . Socially that is."

"Can't say I've ever exchanged views over a drink with a banker before. Though I have slipped the cuffs on one or two," Joe said genially.

"Well you still haven't," Alex admitted. "The City has severed all contact with me."

"I'm sorry to hear that. Are there better prospects on the horizon?"

"No. I've auditioned several careers in what Mama calls my short life, even selected one or two for a starring role, but in the end, they've all turned *me* down. Unlike you, I've never been chosen, Sandilands. If Mama does not exaggerate . . ." The innocent eyes teased him for a moment. "Sir George rather saw you as his young alter ego—someone to be trained on. Perhaps we'd better all watch out!"

"Sir George taught me many things. One of the most useful—always check that your guests have a full glass. I note that Sir Basil is running on empty. Would you like to . . . ?"

If Joe was hoping to free himself from Alex's spiky company he was disappointed. The young man hadn't finished his interrogation. Alex paused to signal to a footman, then, tweaking Joe by the sleeve, he led him to the periphery of the knot of guests who'd gathered in the centre of the room, chattering and laughing.

"Only nine of us to dinner this evening—a small gathering—but it feels more like the Delhi Durbar!" He looked upwards to the high, vaulted ceiling. "I've always thought this place fills up fast because half the guests are already here, waiting and watching before the first cocktail's poured." He waited for Joe to raise an eyebrow. "The ancestors!" he confided, waving a languid hand towards the portraits that lined the walls. "Look at them! What would you give to hear their exchanges when the descendants leave for the dining hall!"

Joe smiled at the playful thought and cast a glance at the array of pictures of varied age and size on display. Lace and pearls and white shoulders shone out from layers of dark oils, striking a contrast with lush velvets and even the dull glow of armour. Some of the subjects stared with dreamy pride away from the painter, inviting the viewer to join them in admiring the rolling acres they possessed; some stared challengingly ahead. For an uneasy moment Joe felt himself skewered by many pairs of eyes. Most were haughty and he guessed that the next reaction of the sitters, on catching sight of him, might well have been: "Who *is* this policeman chappie? Ask what he's doing here and throw him out!"

One or two of the ladies looked more approachable.

"I haven't yet had the pleasure," Joe said. "Though I can identify one who is by no means yet an ancestor. Isn't that your mother? A Philip de Laszlo, if I'm not mistaken."

"It is. Painted when the subject and the artist were in their prime."

Joe never found this particular painter of society portraits much to his taste. Too blatantly flattering. Too sumptuous. Too much bosom and throat displayed by ladies of a certain age who should have known better. The style had fallen out of favour in a less flamboyant post-war era. He searched for an inoffensive remark. "De Laszlo must have been delighted to be offered a subject worthy of his brush. No need for the flattery of a carefully chosen angle or kindly lighting for your mother. She was then—and still is—a stunningly attractive woman."

"You see where James gets his good looks. Now see where I get mine. The late Sir Sidney Truelove." He led Joe over to admire more closely an imposing full-length portrait of his father in full Victorian splendour.

Joe was thinking anyone would have been proud to inherit the looks of this man. The best England had to offer, very likely. He stood tall and Saxon blond, ferociously moustached, hand on hip, eyes scouring the horizon to his left. He was wearing the military dress uniform of a cavalry regiment. Joe hoped it was kept for parades and suchlike formal occasions since one could hardly have done any effective fighting in that three-inch-high gold embroidered collar and the heavy epaulettes. The dark blue jacket with a white plastron were an invitation to enemy target practice, the blue trousers with an elegant white stripe emphasising the length of the leg would have been impressive circling the ballroom. The gold emblazoned czapka bearing at its crest a flourish of white egret feathers was, sensibly, carried in his hand. Worn on the head, the hat would have turned the wearer into a seven-foot-tall musical comedy hero.

"A Lancer?" Joe guessed. "I hadn't realised your father was a cavalryman."

"We mostly manage to provide them when they're needed, though the warrior strain seems to be getting a bit anaemic these days. He was in the Seventeenth Lancers. The Duke of Cambridge's Own." Alexander stared at Joe, waiting.

Joe wondered whether he was searching for recognition in his stare. Recognition of the tall, bluff, older half-brother. The similarity was uncanny. Joe had to look harder to see the connection with the impish young man at his side. "Lucky chap! You have your father's eyes and hair," he said. "But these two portraits are not a pair. This one is a Sargent, yes?"

"It is."

"A fine-looking fellow."

"Indeed. Sargent had a seeing and sympathetic eye for the elegant male form. Papa admired his work. Sargent clearly admired Papa. There's something humorous, don't you think, in that exaggerated stance? I never saw the old man stand with his hand on his hip like that in real life."

"They're sending each other up," was Joe's judgement. "Or us. It's a conspiracy. The artist and the subject are having a laugh at our expense. I always enjoy a Sargent."

"So do I. You'll find one or two of his Venetian scenes along the corridors and a couple of lake-side views with swooning ladies in white draperies carefully arranged in the foreground."

"Your father was a collector of some taste?" Joe said.

"Most of my forefathers, I understand. Even before it was fashionable, they had the knowledge to spot a budding artist and acquire samples of his work while it was still affordable. We have one of the earliest views of the Thames, painted by Canaletto when he was lured to England to ply his trade. It's in the dining room, just off the hall . . . Ah, here's our call to dinner. You'll see it directly . . ."

THE DINNER PARTY rolled smoothly along its accustomed path and Joe, from his seat at the table, was able to enjoy the promised panorama of St. Paul's Cathedral and the Thames. Here, sunk in deepest Suffolk, surrounded by strangers, most of whom seemed to require something questionable of him, Joe was calmed by the familiarity of the scene, by the cool grey elegance of the city he loved. The food was excellent, the wines well chosen. The guests were enjoying each other's company and, presiding at the head of the table, sat Cecily in her element.

When the ladies withdrew and left the men behind to undo a button of their waistcoats and run a finger round their constricting stiff collars, Joe noted that Alex was safely pinned down in a conversation about the national debt. Joe would have liked to linger and hear the exchange, having ascertained during the dinner that these men were not the old duffers he'd taken them for. They'd played an influential role in society during their professional lives and, Joe suspected, were still very close to the centre of things. Their views would have been worth hearing. He took the opportunity of murmuring his excuses, leaving the others to pass the port around. Once in the corridor, he began to head towards the kitchens, keeping an eye out for one person in particular.

He found him puffing on a surreptitious cigarette by the back door.

"Ben? It's Ben, isn't it?" Joe greeted the footman jovially. "Just the man I was looking for. Her ladyship tells me you can be of assistance." Joe looked stagily over his shoulder. "While they're all glugging their port and gossiping in the drawing room, we can make the most of a few quiet moments. Take me up to Lady Truelove's room, will you? We'll talk as we go."

Ben confirmed Cecily's account of the night he'd been put on watch. When they arrived at the door of Lavinia's room on the first floor, he stood back. "It's all right," he said. "It's not locked. You can go in, I suppose." And then, with a grin: "I'll stay outside and keep cave, shall I?"

The room was entirely orderly, vacuum-cleaned and polished. Swept clear of any useful information, Joe suspected. He went first of all to the dressing table where he knew most women left clues to their personality, their plans, their hopes. Even the silver-backed hairbrush had been cleaned. Not so much as one stray black hair remained to bear witness to its owner. Her clothes were still in the wardrobes, her underwear in the drawers, her hats all in their boxes. He wondered without finding an immediate answer why the room had not been cleared, her effects handed on to the female staff, in the traditional way.

A door to the left opened onto a well-equipped bathroom. Here too every surface sparkled. The waste basket had been emptied. A cake of Pear's soap stood ready in the dish on the washbasin, freshening the enclosed space with its lightly astringent scent. A second door in the wall to the right of the extravagantly large bed would not open when he turned the knob. Locked from the other side, he supposed.

Joe returned to Ben, who was standing to attention like a good guardsman. "Ben, I want you to show me where Grace Aldred's room is and then show me where you took up position to keep watch on the night your mistress died." He put up a hand to silence the man when he sensed he was about to launch into an explanation, a speech of self-justification or declaration of innocence. "Later!"

Ben led the way along the corridor. "This here's Sir James's room. Kept locked. No one's allowed in there except for cleaning. It's right next to her ladyship. Connecting but not connected, if you know what I mean."

Joe could imagine what he was meant to read into that and smiled but he followed up with: "Surely there's a connecting door between the two rooms?" He glanced around. "The usual thing . . ."

Ben replied rather reluctantly. "There used to be when the old master occupied the rooms but Sir James keeps it locked. He's a man who likes his privacy." Into Joe's quizzical silence he ventured to add, "If he were ever minded to take her ladyship a cup of cocoa he'd nip down the corridor. He preferred things that way."

At the end, some three doors away, Ben pointed. "That's Gracie's room. You can't get in though. She got the key off Mrs. Bolton and locked up afore she went off to see her ma. She doesn't like anyone poking about in her things."

"Is that allowed, locking up?"

Ben shrugged. "Mrs. B. and Gracie are like that." He crossed two of his fingers. "Her ladyship picked Gracie for her personal maid and she liked to keep her close by. Huh! Lucky to have a room of her own—and down here on the nobs' floor. She should try roughing it with the rest of us under the tiles . . ."

"That's ladies' maids for you," Joe said easily. "Spoilt. Goes with the position."

"You said it, m—Commissioner. Still, she deserved a bit of something, did Gracie, what with having to deal with her ladyship day in, day out. Our Gracie," he spoke with a look of affectionate indulgence, "isn't the sharpest knife in the drawer if you know what I mean, but that suited her ladyship. Anyone smarter wouldn't have lasted a week with *her*. She sacked her first three maids for what she called 'impertinence.'" Ben rolled his eyes. "Grace never complained. Kept the mistress off everyone else's back, though I'm speaking out of turn saying so . . ."

"Speak no ill of the dead, eh? That's a load of codswallop. Ben, I've always found that the dead were quite often less than angelic when they were alive. Which often accounts for their demised condition." He spoke this nonsense in a knowing, confidential voice.

"Know what you mean, sir. I expect you get a lot of that in your line of work." Ben stopped in front of a three-quarter-sized brown-painted door and nodded. "This is where the old mistress put me to keep watch, sir."

"This" was a disused slops cupboard which had once, before the introduction of bathrooms on every floor, been used to house chamber pots on their way down to and back from the sluice room. It was conveniently at the angle between two corridors. It was cramped but sufficient room had been found to insert a small upright chair. Not much chance of Ben's falling asleep on the job in this musty little space on that hard chair, Joe calculated and, for a moment, had a bleak thought of the sleepless, tedious hours of the night, watching over someone you didn't care for, unsure as to why the surveillance was necessary and with no distraction from the darkness but your own thoughts.

He looked about him. From this point, the footman had a view over Lavinia's door, James's door, Grace's door and also a clear sight of the corridor leading down the east guest wing and away to the north. Cecily was running a spy system—spying on the members of her own family and her guests.

"You must have been dying for a smoke! How often did they lumber you with that duty?"

"Not often, thank God! Once, twice a month. More often when there's company. She likes to know where everyone is," he added with a knowing look. "And why not?" he said loyally. "Sometimes they fetch up where they're not supposed to be. It helps the old mistress to know what's going on in her own house. She has a right, I reckon."

Joe grinned. "Thanks for the warning. I'll lock my door tonight. Wouldn't want to risk any illicit nocturnal visits. Not from the present company anyway."

Ben blinked and then grinned back. "This is the way to the Old Nursery. It's quite a hike. I think in the old days when there were little ones about they used to like to keep their noise well away from the rest of the house. Funny that, don't you think, sir? That she should have put someone right away down here when there were at least two guest rooms unoccupied down this corridor?" His question was clearly meant to raise an informative or speculative remark from Joe.

Joe instinctively put his own gentling techniques into operation. "I expect you can think your way through that, Ben, as well as I can. Better. You were on the spot after all and from what Cecily tells me . . ."

Ben nodded again eagerly and quickened his pace. Silently thanking Hunnyton for his plan of the house, Joe managed to keep a handle on their progress and knew they'd arrived when they reached a short corridor off at an angle. A run of four doors made up the deserted nursery suite. Day nursery, night nursery, a room for Nanny and a room for Nanny's assistant, no doubt.

"Disused, I take it?" Joe asked.

"Ever since Master Alexander went away to school, they say," Ben told him. "Though—and this is a bit weird—it's been kept as it was. In fact redecorated every year. Living in hope, I expect. Anyhow, this was where her ladyship chose to put the young woman."

"Miss Joliffe?"

"That's her. No love lost between her and the mistress. Nasty argument over dinner. The young lady stood up for herself something fine but it ended in tears."

"Whose tears, Ben?"

"Miss Joliffe's, of course. Nothing makes . . . made . . . the mistress cry. I was on coffee duty when the ladies withdrew. Miss Joliffe handed me her cup and announced she was going up to her room. There were tears in her eyes, I reckon. All that baiting by those upper-class ninnies! They behave like a pack of hounds when they think they've sighted a fox." Ben took himself in control and carried on. "She told the mistress she was leaving first thing in the morning as soon as she could get a taxi to come out from Cambridge and pick her up."

"How did the mistress take that?"

"Seemed to be just what she wanted to hear. But she said certainly not—she'd ask the chauffeur to take her to the station in the Bentley directly after breakfast. Detaining Miss Joliffe would be the last thing she wanted to do, she said, all sarky-like. Here we are. It's not kept locked though there is a key always in the lock on the inside."

Joe went in, trying to guess what had been Dorcas's reactions to the insult of being allocated this unsuitable room.

He was quite surprised to find it pleasant and spacious, the

lamps, when Ben lit them, casting a warm glow over the comfortable furnishings. The walls were papered with a lively print in
which strawberries and nightingales featured. The polished
boarded floor was covered in oddly luxurious cream rugs, a cut
above the usual practical linoleum that most nurseries seemed to
have. The child's bed—eight-year-old Alex having been the last
occupant, Joe supposed—had not been moved out; it was still
here, still made up, as though the owner was expected to jump
back in and call for a bedtime story from Nanny, who was always
on hand right next door.

Lucky little owner, Joe reckoned. He was a happy child who
had the run of this pretty space—secure, pampered, his child's
needs lavishly catered for. How very different from the childhood
experience of the young Dorcas! What *must* she have made of all
this? Alongside were an ancient rocking horse, a dolls' house, a
toddler's trundle seat and other bits of nursery paraphernalia of
a solid Edwardian grandeur. These relics of a cosseted infancy
had been pushed over to one side of the room. The rest of the
space was occupied by a fully stocked dressing table and an adult-
sized bed, freshly made up with plump white pillows and a quilt
of yellow Chinese silk.

Joe knew exactly how the insult had affected Dorcas. He had
a vision of her dark head sobbing into the pillow and felt a rush
of anger towards the dead Lady Truelove. The girl had struggled
all her life with the knowledge that she had no place in polite
society. The illegitimate offspring of a feckless father and runaway
mother, she had received only hatred and slaps from her wealthy
grandmother. Scorn from vindictive ladies was something she had
grown used to dealing with and she would have recognised this
deliberate slight for what it was. The mistress was saying: "You
are not worthy of the attention a guest would normally receive.
You have no place here." James and Lavinia were still, the choice
of the furnished nursery was suggesting, man and wife and going

about their family duties. "So there, Miss Cleverclogs! Spend a sleepless night realising that whatever claims you might fancy you had on James's attention are so much moonshine."

And all this humiliation had been doled out right under the eyes of her respected mentor and fellow academic. Joe's anger flared again. What the hell was James Truelove thinking to allow such a situation to develop! Joe would have stopped it in three words if he'd been there. If Lily's Aunty Phyl had it right, the bloke was in love with his student—how could he sit back and watch this scene play out? To Joe, it was reminiscent of the scenes of animal torment Truelove dabbled in under the name of scientific discovery in his laboratories. Joe wondered nastily if the man had been making observations—taking notes. "Influence of social criteria in display of sexual rivalry in the human female" might perhaps have been his heading. Or was he merely terrified into silence by his wife?

He went to run a hand over the pillow. Poor girl! This was a sad way to learn that a man she had admired had no spine, no decency. "She must have spent a miserable night." Lost in his thoughts, Joe had hardly been conscious of speaking out loud.

He was surprised when Ben answered him.

"Oh, I don't know about that, sir!" The tone was heavy with suggestion. "She wasn't lacking a shoulder to cry on."

"What do you mean?"

Ben took a step closer and flicked a glance to check that the door was closed. He listened for movement in the house. A show of "resident sleuth" put on for Joe's benefit? Joe didn't doubt it but he was not about to challenge for the role. He waited, as he was meant to.

"I mean as she had company."

"Company?" Joe's thoughts skittered for a moment and then he had it. "Oh! A lady's maid? Was she allocated one such from the resident staff to help her with her unpacking?"

"Nothing like that. She turned Rosie down and shifted for herself . . . Naw! She had a *man* in here. I clocked him creeping along the corridor at half past one." He paused to assess Joe's reaction.

"At one thirty in the morning? I've scanned the guest list, Ben. Now who, of that gouty unadventurous company, would be shuffling along the corridors in his bedroom slippers at that hour?"

Ben gave a scoffing laugh, enjoying the picture Joe was conjuring up. "No slippers! He was still in evening dress! I followed him to see what was going on. 'Hang on!' I thought, 'He's drunk as a skunk! He's taken a wrong turning!' Of course he wasn't and he hadn't. Knew very well where he was going. Passed all the other guest rooms and fetched up here. I think he was expected."

Trying for a calm tone, Joe asked: "Why do you say that?"

"The door wasn't locked! He didn't even need to knock. Just opened it and walked straight in."

"Go on."

"Well, words or something must have been exchanged because seconds later, out he comes again with the door closed in his face. Quiet but firm."

Joe began to breathe again.

"Well—he weren't havin' none o' that! He bangs on the door this time and calls out her name, all upset and pleading like . . . 'Dorcas, you have to let me in!' 'Lord!' I thought, 'He's going to rouse the whole house!'"

"With any effect?"

"I'll say! The lass opened up, shushing him, then she reached out, cussed something fierce, grabbed him by the shoulders and heaved him inside. Then she—or he—locked the door." Ben grinned and confided, "No idea what she did with him after that. Perhaps they had a game of Snakes and Ladders? Anyway—he didn't come back past my station for the rest of the night. When Grace started moving about before dawn waking up her ladyship

I didn't know what to do. I thought I'd better follow the mistress like I'd been told." Ben's face took on a sharp expression. "But I'll tell you what—if there's any question about the death being set up—I can tell anyone who needs to know that Miss Dorcas has got a perfect alibi." He glowered defiantly at Joe. "If anyone tried to drag that poor young gel into it, I'd have to spill the beans. Position or no position."

The bold words off his chest, he grinned lasciviously. "Miss Joliffe and young master Alex were in here together all night alibiing each other."

CHAPTER 17

"Never kill the messenger" was a reasonable rule of conduct, Joe had always thought. But perhaps he could just punch him on his cocky little nose? He clasped his hands behind his back and walked to the window overlooking the courtyard. He stared out into a dark, desolate space, out of focus and alien, a reflection of his soul. Would thumping Ben stop Joe from falling deeper into the depth below him? Joe whirled around, clenching his fists. He rather thought it would.

"Sir! Are you all right? Did I say something? I'm sorry if I did. Squealing like that ... perhaps I should never ... but Lady Cecily said it would be all right—I should tell you what I knew. And I wouldn't want someone who can't answer back to catch it for something she didn't do. They'll put the blame on the weakest. It's always their way."

It wasn't Joe's way. The footman's words punctured his swelling rage and gave him back some sort of control over his emotions. He said coldly, the policeman's reasoning taking over, "Have you thought, Ben, that on this occasion, the family might be only too grateful to accept Miss Joliffe's story? If push came to shove and they all had to come clean, that is. If she's in the clear, so is Alexander. As you said—they supply each other with an alibi for the hours before and the time of Lady Truelove's death. Though, of course, chivalry would always reduce a gentleman to silence. He would never give away a lady's secret, even when he's standing in the dock at the Old Bailey and the hangman is knotting his noose. He—they—are never going to reveal their situation to an official police enquiry."

"That's why they've sent for you, sir. Friend of Sir James and Lady Cecily, you can work it all out discreetly. No need for red faces, eh?"

Joe knew that if he were to get at the truth it would have to be extracted from the most skilled liar he had ever come across—Dorcas herself.

"Ben, did you report the, er, midnight wanderings to Lady Cecily?"

Ben hung his head. "Should 'a done, shouldn't I? Trouble if I did and trouble if I didn't, I reckon . . ."

"Ben, you are in no way to blame. You were put into a bad situation. If trouble there's been—the fault lies with others. Well—did you?" he insisted.

"No, I kept my mouth shut. I told her everything up to Miss Dorcas turning in for the night. Thing is—Master Alex is in a spot of bother at the moment." He hesitated.

"I'm aware of the young master's problems."

"Ah. Well . . . I wouldn't want to get him into worse trouble. None of us would. He's all right is Master Alex. Never any trouble to the female staff, unlike some. Us indoors—we've always covered for him. Don't like to see a bloke get picked on, even when it's his own doing it."

"And his mother's his most demanding critic?"

"Always! Especially since he came back from London this time. She's got him on a tight rein and I didn't want to say something *she*'d not want to hear and that would get *him* into further trouble. As well as doing the girl no good—her reputation would have been shot to pieces. If I'd spoken out that would have been a headache for four people."

"And you wouldn't want to be known as the spreader of gossip?"

"You've said it! We're supposed to keep quiet about what we see and hear." Ben's eyes gleamed suggestively. "People wander about in the night, like I told you. Sometimes they need a guiding hand back to their own billet. Unless we want our ears torn off by Mrs. Bolton, we say nothing. Well, over a ciggie round the back of the dairy, having a laugh with the other lads, that's different."

Joe strained to keep his focus on the job in hand when all he wanted to do was flee back to London, pursue Dorcas to Highgate or wherever she was hiding out and wring the truth from her. Professional routine rescued him from rash action. He remembered Cecily's interrupted assertion that her son James had an alibi for the night of Lavinia's death and decided to follow it up. "Lady Cecily claims that James has a cast-iron alibi for the time in question. Can you confirm . . . ?"

"Oh, yes, sir. When the house was settled and everyone in their rooms I escorted her ladyship down to the drawbridge—I always see her back safely over to her own place. That's the Dower House. About a hundred yards away down the drive. They leave the bridge up till I get back. We were just going over the bridge when Sir James comes haring up all of a lather. 'Don't you worry, Ben,' he says, 'I'll see Mama home. Tell them they can put the bridge up now. I'll be at the Dower House for the night.'"

He anticipated Joe's question. "Nothing out of the ordinary. Her Ladyship has a nice little guest suite of her own and Sir James does occasionally . . . um . . ."

"Seek refuge?"

"Run to his mum's! He didn't come back until they rang with the bad news to fetch him back over."

"Ben, there's something more you can do for me. For me and her ladyship," he thought it prudent to add. "When next you're sharing a smoke with the lads, ask about—discreetly!—if the valet that Mr. McIver's brought down with him is what he says he is. Body servant? Chauffeur? Or is he really employed in McIver's professional sphere? Has he by any chance got a camera in his kit? I like to know these things. I'm shy around cameras in the sweating hands of the press."

"Camera? Old Blenkinsop? Naw! Why would he? Known Clarence for years, Mr. Styles has. Old mates." He gave a sly smile. "But that new lady's maid his wife's brought . . . *she* has! Calls herself Chloe."

"New, Ben?"

"She's not the one they had with them last time they were here—back in April when . . ."

"*That* weekend . . ."

Ben nodded. "The other girls say she's French but I'm not so sure . . . She's been put to bunk up with our Rosie. And Rosie watched her unpack. She was very careful to warn Rose to keep her hands off her stuff, it was fragile. Cheek! Rosie checked it over later, of course. She says it's not your common or garden Kodak—it's a posh German thing. 'Leica' would that be? What would a lady's maid be doing with a Leica?"

"Thanks for that, Ben. Look—your Rose is a smart girl, is she?"

"I'll say!" Ben sighed his admiration. "Bright as a fresh-minted sixpence. Good with her fingers and knows how to keep her mouth shut. What do you have in mind, sir?"

"Ben, I think you've guessed! I think it might be to the advantage of the mistress and her family, to say nothing of Scotland Yard, if any film shot on the premises were to be, um . . ."

"Fiddled with? Exposed to the light? Before it leaves the house? I know how to do that. My uncle's got a Rollei. *I* can't be seen cruising about down the female staff's corridor but I can show Rosie what to do." Ben made his calculations and said, but without triumph in his tone, "Ah! I didn't get it wrong then—you do think someone killed her? Bashed her head in with a horseshoe and blamed the horse? Wouldn't be the first time. Someone who knew what she was up to?" He concentrated hard. He had the intelligent, absorbed face Joe had seen so often in his police recruits. Replying to Joe's uncomfortable silence, he said more firmly: "Her ladyship had no visitors that night. When Grace said good night just after midnight and left to go to her own room that was it. She was alone until Grace woke her and dressed her to go off down to the stables. She dismissed her on the doorstep and off she went with just those two poor little old lads. No. Gracie's in the clear. She came and had early breakfast with the rest of us lower servants in the kitchen. Whatever happened to Lady Truelove, it was all her own doing. She riled that horse off her own bat. Nobody helped her. Just because a fair number aren't sorry she's a goner doesn't mean any of them done her in."

The footman wriggled with a sudden rush of uncertainty. "Look, sir. Grace told me something . . . I wasn't to mention it to a soul unless it looked like they were going to kick off an investigation and try to put the blame on someone. Then I was to get hold of Adam Hunnyton and bend his ear. Adam would know what to do she said, him being the police."

"Go on, Ben, Adam and I are working on this together."

"She said she'd kept something back and put it in her own room. A memento of her mistress, or some such, she said."

"She didn't say what it was?"

"No. She said what it *wasn't*. Not jewellery, not a gown, not a picture, nothing she might be accused of stealing. You had to be very careful around Lady Lavinia."

"Ben, I need to take a look in Grace's room. Right now. Take me to Mrs. Bolton."

THE NERVE CENTRE of the whole house, Joe thought. The Housekeeper's Room. On the ground floor, it was strategically placed close to the company rooms and the kitchens and butler's suite.

Mrs. Bolton had made no reference to the lateness of the hour when Ben had signalled to her across the crowded kitchen. A quick word to deputise one of the older women, and she had come out of the hurly-burly and led them into the calm of her parlour next door. Doors were lying open to let the air circulate, one onto a still-room in blue-and-white Delft tiles where Joe glimpsed a central table loaded with pots of strawberry jam and bottles of green cordial and another open onto a capacious pantry which, he guessed, adjoined the butler's rooms. A third, which remained discreetly closed, he assumed to be the housekeeper's bedroom.

A fine set but it would be impossible to separate work and personal space, Joe thought. The Housekeeper, inevitably, became the heart of the House. Still, he knew some Metropolitan officers who appeared to live their lives in their office and sleep at their desk. He'd felt the compulsion himself on many occasions, had even, in his earlier years, been physically hauled out of his chair and bundled off home by his landlord. Ex–police inspector Alfred Jenkins had known the dangers.

"At this hour I usually treat myself to a tisane. I'm having lemon balm, gentlemen. Would you like some?"

Joe gratefully accepted for both of them. Mrs. Bolton snatched up a large handful of a sweet-smelling herb from the windowsill, stuffed it into a big white teapot and filled it with water from a kettle singing on the stove.

"Will you be staying, Ben?" she asked.

After a quick exchange of looks with Joe, Ben said, "Just long enough for a swig o' your tea, Mrs. B. Just what the doctor ordered at this time of day."

"Then make yourself useful, my lad, and draw up a chair for the commissioner by my tea table. We'll take it over there at the window. Might as well catch a cooling breeze while we can."

Ben bustled to and fro setting up a folding tray-table with white cloth and china mugs and borrowing three chairs from a large round central table already laid out for the upper servants' breakfast. Joe counted eight places. Orders for the day would be dished out with the porridge, gossip exchanged with the toast and marmalade.

Feeling suddenly clumsy amid the practised dexterity, Joe moved his large form away from the scene of action and went to stand by a dresser whose upper shelves were crowded with books. He noted the essential *Burke's Peerage*, an *Olde Moore's Almanack*, a dictionary, and smiled to see a very ancient copy of *The Accomplisht Ladie's Companion*, the essential reference book of every woman in charge of a household since 1685. His mother had had one always within arm's reach of the stove. He remembered that the title page of this book was crowded with lively illustrations of ladies in long gowns and headdresses taking delight in roasting, boiling and pastry-making as well as the more arcane arts of distilling "spirituous liquers," preserving herbs and composing medicinal ointments, some of a very dubious nature. Joe had good reason to believe that the cure for croup in infants, as laid out for the "accomplisht ladie," was decidedly more dangerous than the ailment itself. At least the recipe for macaroons did not appear in the same chapter as the one guaranteed to rid a household of *rattus rattus* and all his fleas. "Almonds" and "arsenic" were sensibly segregated.

He wondered if the recipe for gingerbread came from these ancient pages.

Stiffly corseted, though her slim figure didn't require much in the way of whalebone, Mrs. Bolton creaked down onto the chair Ben held respectfully for her and began to pour the tea. A lady approaching sixty, he would have guessed, composed and elegant. Her face was attractive but sought no appreciation from others. She was a woman who would always absorb more from her audience than she gave out. "I know who you are, sir, and why you are here," she said briskly, challenging him with grey eyes as sharp as his. "Lady Cecily has spoken to me and asked that I give you all the help you require."

Her voice had the clarity and enunciation of a governess, which he understood from Ben that she had been earlier in her life. "Schoolmaster's daughter or some such," he'd reported, "fallen on hard times. The old story! But with Mrs. Bolton it's likely true. If she catches you running she'll grab you by the ear and growl *'Festina lente!'* at you. The old dear's got a good head for figures what's more. None of the tradesmen try it on with Mrs. B.," Ben had finished with pride.

She had followed her mistress Cecily from the Midlands when she came as a bride to Melsett and in later years had taken over the duties of housekeeper. She was now looking at him expectantly.

For a moment Joe was at a loss. Where to start? They'd all recited their stories to other interested parties and must have reached that stage of tedium when people either clammed up or began to embroider on the original to avoid further boredom. Always a difficult moment.

Joe sipped, savoured, and put his cup down. Grey eyes stared into grey eyes. "Mrs. B. I've had a rough day." From the glancing focus on his sticking plaster and the accompanying twitch of the corner of her mouth, Joe gathered his encounter with Virbio, servant of Diana, had not gone unreported. "Why don't *you* tell me what help I need? I'm sure you know."

The twitch became a smile and the enlivened face took on the radiance of the goddess Minerva. Joe saw suddenly why the staff spoke of this woman with such respect.

"If you've just been upstairs with Ben I'm thinking you'll be wanting these." She hauled on a key chain attached to the belt of her skirt and selected a key ring. "Here you are. The big one

unlocks Grace's room. I doubt you'll find anything helpful in
there—it has been cleaned out regularly since the awful event and
Grace has nothing to hide. She was caught up in all innocence in
the machinations of others, Commissioner. Grace is not . . . a
plotter or an evil-doer by nature. She's a Suffolk girl with all their
admirable qualities. There's nothing more I can tell you. Mistress
Cecily gave her leave to go home to Bury. It's not an excuse,
though I'm sure you must be suspecting—collusion? Would that
be the word? No—her mother is very ill—not expected to live
out the summer, I'd say. Heart trouble. Grace has arranged for her
sister to go down and mind her mother next week and we'll see
her back on duty then. But that's not much help to you. I'll give
you her mother's address in Bury, should you wish to pursue her.
Meantime—as for me—I can only report impressions. Do you
want to hear them in the absence of hard evidence?"

Joe was thinking that any impression coming from the firm
mouth of Mrs. Bolton was worth ten times most people's idea of
evidence and he accepted gratefully.

"It was the gingerbread that made me suspicious. Grace came
in here and asked for a slice for the mistress. Just before midnight.
With her cocoa. Lady L. didn't like spicy things. Grace didn't deny
it when I guessed it was a craving of someone about three months
gone, if you know what I mean. We had a bit of a laugh over it.
It wasn't the first time I'd heard as much hinted at but this was
the first concrete clue."

"How much gingerbread did she take away?"

"I gave her enough for three normal portions. Her ladyship
had quite an appetite. I didn't want to risk her putting Grace to
the trouble of coming downstairs again for more. I was going
to put it in the pig slop bucket anyway. It had gone hard and no
one fancied it much."

"Was anything left of it?" Joe asked, feeling foolish.

"Not a crumb. No idea what she did with it and Gracie's not

saying but by morning it had all vanished. Betty, who does out the rooms on that floor, reported that there was a strange smell in her ladyship's room and she had to fling all the windows wide open to clear it."

Joe nodded. "Thank you, Mrs. Bolton. I think I know what that was. And no—it wasn't your gingerbread! Can you tell me why the room is still in its original state?"

"Mistress Cecily's orders, sir. 'Touch nothing,' we were told. 'You may clean surfaces but that's all.'"

"Mistress Cecily, ah, yes . . ." Joe said, speculation in his eye. "Back in the saddle again. Things are moving more smoothly with the old mistress in charge again, would you say?"

Mrs. Bolton's chilly expression warned him she would say nothing of the sort. Discretion even after death was the rule for housekeepers. She unbent so far as to confide, "Mistress Cecily and I understand each other well, Commissioner. Indeed, we arrived here at Melsett on the same day, over forty years ago. She brought me down with her from her father's household when she married. I was given a position of rising authority here with the task of raising the level of domestic discipline and capability. Under Sir Sidney—the bachelor Sir Sidney—things had become regrettably lax."

Joe smiled. "What I see is a credit to your efforts, Mrs. Bolton. As well run a household as I ever saw, I do believe."

Enid Bolton seemed pleased by the compliment

"Well, thank you Mrs. Bolton." Joe began to get to his feet, the interview over. "Just one more thing." He touched his plaster and grimaced. "How much per week do you pay the Green Man of the Woods to heave logs at your house guests?"

If he had thought to catch her out he was disappointed. She chuckled. "You'll not find that villain's name on my books, sir! You rightly guess I do all the payments for indoor and outdoor staff. That's been the way since we lost Steward Hunnybun and he was replaced by a Farm Manager. Albright is very good in his way, but he doesn't have Adam's insight and tact. Adam calls by and gives a hand still if ever I need him but luckily I have a head for figures and it's no trouble. You may inspect the household accounts if you wish."

Mrs. Bolton got to her feet and selected a large red leather-bound ledger, the last in a series, from the bookshelf. She placed it on the table. "Help yourself," she invited. "Lady Lavinia could never be bothered. I can't be certain she quite followed the calculations when I insisted on having her signature at the month's end. I don't believe she knew the price of a packet of pins! But no—to answer your question—'Goodfellow,' as he likes to call himself, among other things, is not on the house payroll. Never has been. 'It's a personal contribution, Enid, and none of your business,' Adam said when I asked him where the buffoon got his beer money. I don't think Adam knows either."

"Can you tell me in what ways Mr. Goodfellow bothers the household?" Joe asked as though merely requiring confirmation of knowledge he already had.

"Peeking and prying!" The answer came at once. "The maids don't like to be working in the dairy and see his ugly face leering at them through the window. They don't feel free to kick off their shoes these hot days and dabble in the moat to cool off as they'd like to. He's always drawn by the sight of a bare leg. He pushed Rose off the edge last summer and stood by laughing as she sank under—in the afternoon uniform she'd just put on all fresh from the laundry press. Just as well Ben heard her scream and came running. Pest! It's like having a hornet buzzing about all the time. Never knowing where it's going to plant its sting."

"Don't the men take some action?" Joe cast a sideways look at Ben, noting his suddenly clenching fists. "Did no one step forward to remonstrate on Rose's behalf?"

"He's too slick to do anything when the men are about.

Though I do recall that Goodfellow fell into something less salubrious than moat-water shortly after Rosie's escapade."

Ben reddened and grinned.

"The men servants work hard for their pay, Commissioner, and they don't like to see him louting about, pretending to do a bit of coppicing here and a bit of fencing there when all he hangs about for is dressing up, scaring people and getting sozzled down the pub of an evening. But their hands are tied. He has the master's ear, you might say. Lady L. couldn't stand him, though she couldn't get him dismissed either. Heaven knows—she tried often enough!"

"Where did he come from? Anything known?"

"He's been here since before the old master died. Sir Sidney knew him. From his army days? He fetched up here as a down-and-out . . . oh, thirty years ago . . . and Sir Sidney, who was a very generous man, gave him a part time job, helping with estate work, sometimes with the horses. He's been here ever since. He 'arrives with the cuckoo, that harbinger of Spring, and leaves the moment Jack Frost returns to crackle the surface of the moat with his icy breath.' That's what he tells the guests in his spirit-of-nature way. May to September, in my vocabulary. His sister's a seaside land-lady in Southend. She'd tell you she kicks her brother out at the arrival of the first summer holiday-maker and doesn't let him back until the last one has left. The man's a total fraud and an exploiter of the Truelove family's generous nature. My advice—don't ever ask him to take his mask off."

"Too late, Mrs. B.! I have looked on the true face of the nasty, blood-sucking rogue. But I see worse in the mirror every morn-ing." He grinned as he pointed to his left cheek. "And he hasn't done much to improve the landscape. I owe him one."

"Well, if you want to know more, Mr. Styles will inform you. He's been here longer than any of us."

Joe thanked her for her help and drained his herb tea. "Now

then, Ben," he said and turned to Mrs. Bolton. "If you can spare this excellent chap for another half hour, we'll get back to work."

THE WELL-OILED LOCK clicked and the door swung open on Grace Aldred's room. Cheerful and well appointed, Joe thought. In many ways a plainer version of her mistress's boudoir. Everything here was scaled down in size, subdued in colour, less sumptuous in quality. A dressing table (pinewood, not mahogany) was draped in a white machine-made lace cloth and Grace's brush and comb (tortoiseshell, not silver) were laid before a swivelling mirror on barley-sugar twist uprights. The curtains were of a pretty chintz but of a pattern too large for the room. They'd been cut down to size from some grander space, Joe thought. The bed was pin neat and made up with fresh linen but even here the coverlet showed signs of thrift; it was a patchwork sewn from scraps of silk and velvet. A square of embroidery had been left ready to be picked up again on the footstool by the one comfortable chair set beside the fireplace. To occupy the few quiet moments before the bell he noticed on the wall next to it rang to summon Grace to her mistress a few yards down the corridor.

The personal items were sparse. A photograph of two little girls in their Sunday best. Grace and her sister? A copy of last week's *Film Fun* magazine by the bedside, open at a photograph of Cary Grant. There was little of Grace herself here. She seemed to be merely an adjunct to her mistress, herself a faded scrap, a piece of the household patchwork.

Joe stood quietly in the doorway, absorbing the atmosphere with Ben moving in anxiously behind him. Joe recognised that Ben's loyalties were being stretched again. He was uncomfortable with his own presence in a maid's room and doubly uneasy that Joe was here, missing no details with his sharp, trained eye.

"I don't think this is going to take long, Ben," he said. "Don't worry—we're not going to have to search through sock drawers and read entries in diaries. If I've got this right, Grace will never know we've even been in here. Come in and shut the door. Look around. What was it you suppose Grace wanted someone in authority to see? It all looks perfectly normal to me."

"Nothing here." Ben shrugged and took a pace back towards the door.

Joe fingered the key ring. "Hang on. What's this? Two more small keys. What do they unlock?"

Ben took them, feeling the weight. "This here's the key to her maid's box. That's kept up in the attic with the trunks when it's been unpacked. This other one . . ." He glanced around. "It must unlock the wardrobe. That's where she keeps her uniform and her spare shoes."

"Have a look, shall we?"

Joe unlocked the large cupboard which, in an earlier, more glorious existence, must have been called an *armoire*. He was faced by a neat array of uniform, dark blue morning and pale blue afternoon dresses, lined up on embroidered hangers padded out with lavender stuffing. Heavier winter coats and serge dresses lurked behind them, protected from the moth by balls of fragrant cedarwood dangling like rough necklaces from the hangers. He was about to close the door when he smelled it. A base undertone, barely holding its own against the predominant cedarwood and lavender. As he shunted forward a handful of garments the smell intensified. He worked his way beyond the winter clothes to the back of the cupboard and the last item of clothing was revealed. A dark green waterproof cape of the kind ladies used to cover themselves when out riding occupied the space, looking, in its deliberate isolation, rather sinister, Joe thought. He pulled it forward on its hanger and looked around for somewhere to carry out an inspection.

"Not on the bed, sir," Ben took over. "I'll put it over here on the floorboards in case something's in there as shouldn't be. Cor!

What a pong! That's not mothballs!" He spread it out and held it down by the shoulders as though he expected it to leap up and resist arrest.

"The mistress's riding-out-in-inclement-weather coat. But what's it got in its pockets? Sorry about this, Ben." Feeling rather like the Great Magnifico two minutes into his act, Joe took a pair of rubber gloves, Scotland Yard issue, from his trouser pocket and slipped them on. "Just in case we're landed with poisons of some nature to deal with . . ." he murmured apologetically.

He felt in the right pocket and encountered a small hard lump. "Take my handkerchief from my breast pocket, Ben, and spread it here by me."

The dark brown-grey, slightly crumbling mess he scooped out was greeted with a schoolboy's exclamation of disgust by Ben. "Urgh! It's sh— horse-excrement! What's she doing with that in her pocket!"

"Not shit, Ben. No, something infinitely more evil! Horse-droppings are ambrosial in scent compared with this stuff." Joe was beginning to feel queasy and recognised that without Adelaide Hartest's sound talking-to, he would have been dashing straight for the jug and ewer on the toilet table. "Hard to believe, but that substance was once a slice of Mrs. Bolton's excellent gingerbread."

"Where did it get the stink, then? And why?" Ben wanted to know.

"I could give you the recipe for the very special frosting but you wouldn't want to hear it. I'll just say it's a mixture of decayed animal parts—stoat's liver being one. It's a magic formula for scaring horses. Yes, scaring them. They'll take fright and try to run away on catching scent of this."

"Anyone offering a lump of this to a savage horse . . ." Ben had got there and his face froze into pale disbelief.

"Anyone standing in the entrance to the horse's stall will be

cleared out of the way in the horse's instinctive effort to escape,"
Joe confirmed Ben's fears. "It will use its teeth and hooves and
frantic strength to obliterate what it perceives as the horror that's
advancing on it."

Joe reminded himself that it had been Ben, tip-toeing along
in his patent-leather slippers, who had come upon the awful scene
and had stood guard over the body with a raging stallion crashing
about an open stable. "But you were there, Ben. You saw the results
for yourself," he said quietly. He'd noticed that the lad's teeth were
chattering at the memory.

"I was lucky then," he said when he could get the words out.
"Having smashed her up, he went backwards into his stall, shiver-
ing. People say I was brave to have stuck it out down there
but—the honest truth is—I reckoned that big feller was more
scared than I was. Poor devil! Poor lady!"

"Poor *silly* lady! Where, I need to know, did she come by her
recipe? Perhaps she left it in the other pocket." Joe pulled a hopeless face. "Well, we ought to check."

"Good lord! What the hell's this? . . . These?"

He placed a folded sheet of paper on the floor and opened
it up.

"Shopping list? Recipe? 'Cummin . . . Rose Mary . . .' No, I
never saw that handwriting before, sir. Scruffy. Pencil. Not what
you'd call educated, is it?"

"Just lists the attractants. No nastiness here. But I'll show you
something that is quite stomach-churning. The second thing
Grace had left in the pocket for us to find." He placed it carefully
beside the note.

"Chicken's wish-bone? That's for good luck, sir."

A memory had stirred. Joe had heard of these things but he'd
never seen one before. "No. The opposite of good luck. This is
magic," he said. "Black magic. It's bone all right but it's from a
toad. *Method: First catch your toad.* Then you kill it and pound the

flesh to a pulp and chuck it into a running stream at midnight. Of course, the flesh and most of the bones float away downstream with the current, but one bone—this one—perversely, swirls away upstream. This is the one you want. The piece that's going to give you magic powers. Over horses. Or warts. Or sharp-tongued mothers-in-law. They do a similar bit of jiggery-pokery with frogs and ant-hills in India ..."

Ben was prepared to scoff. "Floats upstream? Naw! How could it?" Gingerly, he picked it up and smoothed it between his fingers. "Light as a dry leaf. That scooped bit looks something like the bottom of a toy boat. That wouldn't sink, but it would go along with the current."

"Look at the shape. It's like one of those Australian weapons that turn and fly back at you—a boomerang—don't you think? Some winged things do move apparently against the forces of Nature as we know them—winged sycamore seeds ... aeroplanes, for goodness sake! I don't believe in magic, either, Ben. I think the shape must be special. No time to experiment but if we popped this onto the rippling surface of a stream it might well be caught by some rule of . . . shall we say . . . aquadynamics and sweep off in the opposite direction to what you'd expect. It would be fun to try. But the men who own one of these things don't *want* to test out, cast light and explain. No—they want to believe without question and work in the dark. They also seek power by frightening and manipulating the credulous. 'Toadmen,' they call themselves where I come from."

"Toadmen? I've heard of them. Down toward Stowmarket, there's toadmen. Or used to be. Can't say as I've heard of 'em since I were a lad."

"Not since they were all given the keys to a shining new tractor," Joe said, smiling. He took the piece of bone, held it between his finger and thumb and twisted it as he would have turned the starting key of a motor. "There's more power in the turn of a piece of steel in a Fordson tractor engine than in a brittle bit of bone working inside a darkened mind. But, evidently, there's still one hereabouts who has the knowledge—and the malice—to pass on this evil piece of equipment to an unsuspecting woman and cause her death." Joe glanced at the open cupboard door. "We'll just put it back where we found it for the moment. It seems to be safe there. Did you look in the bottom? Anything else Grace left behind for us to see?"

Ben took a slender house-man's torch from his belt and shone it around the depths of the cupboard. "Yes, there is. Not much but we ought perhaps to take a look."

He brought out four blue paper chemist's bags and put them in front of Joe. "All empty. Shall I read the labels? Well, well! Cummin, coriander, cinnamon and . . ."

"Fenugreek," Joe finished for him. "Those bags contained the substance she thought she was marching into the stables armed with. We'll lock those up in the cupboard again too. But where did she get the bate that caused her death? You can't summon up a stew of stoat's liver and rabbit's blood overnight."

"*G. R. Harrison, Purveyor of Pharmaceuticals. Estd. 1882*, it says on the labels. You going to arrest him?"

"For the crime of purveying curry spices to a rich household? No, I don't think so. Mr. Harrison is about as guilty as the horse in all of this. Which is to say—not in the slightest. But there is someone lurking, someone with very evil intent, working through his own agenda. I wonder how far along he's got . . . and whether he can hear us scrabbling down the rabbit hole after him."

CHAPTER 18

Joe was awake again at five. He bathed, shaved and dressed himself in the hooray-hurrah outfit of flannels, linen shirt and Hermès cravat that he felt a summer Sunday morning in the country called for. He had no wish to undertake his next task looking bleary and unkempt in a dressing gown. 'Never frighten the upstairs maid' was another rule of country house living he abided by.

He heard her coming down the corridor at six o'clock precisely and nipped out the moment she drew level with his door. A quick: "Shh! It's only the Police, miss!" and he'd tugged her, still clutching her dustpan and brush, into his room and shut the door.

He held his Scotland Yard warrant card under her startled eyes to calm or at least distract her. "I do beg your pardon! Are you the maid who normally takes care of the rooms in this guest wing?"

"Yes, sir."

"Were you here on duty in April when the mistress was killed?"

"I was, sir."

"Then I have a few questions for you. This will only take a moment and then you may return to your duties. What is your name?"

"Rose, sir. Rose Nicholls."

"Known to Ben as 'Rosie'?" Joe smiled. At last, one thing was going in his favour. "Rose, tell me—the morning of the awful event in April—did you tidy out all the rooms along this corridor?"

"Yes, sir. Nothing interfered with the routine. The guests were still here, all of them, and their rooms had to be seen to."

"Were you also responsible for the guest in the Old Nursery?"

"I had that duty, sir." Had he imagined that the reply came less swiftly and was accompanied by a slight upturning of the nose? The very pert nose. Ben had omitted to say how pretty Rosie was.

"The occupant of the room—Miss Joliffe—was she still in residence?"

"She was. Still abed. Fast asleep when I drew the curtains back. She'd asked me to wake her at six with a cup of tea. No breakfast required. No help with dressing. A very independent young lady. Good as gold, very polite and no trouble. She left me half a crown on the mantelpiece and her copies of *True Confessions*."

"All as normal, then?"

The response came more slowly. "Yes, sir." The eyes narrowed and looked away as she added, "No harm done, I'm sure, sir."

"Right. That's enough pussy-footing about, Rose. I want you to tell me what exactly was *not* normal about that room when you did it out. I have to tell you that Ben and I inspected it last night. I'm pretty sure I know what went on in there—I would be interested to hear your confirmation. And—hear this, Rosie— I usually work in the stews of East London. You can say nothing that could possibly shock me."

He listened to her brief account. She wasted no time on unnecessary detail or speculation and he realised she'd rehearsed this speech in her mind before delivering it. She'd clearly been concerned and remained puzzled by what she'd discovered. Joe, on the other hand, believed he now had a clear idea of what had gone on that April night. He allowed himself a grim smile. For possibly the first time ever in what had been a seven-year struggle with Dorcas, he thought he had the advantage of her. What would she choose to feed him? Truth or lies?

"Rosie, your information is secure with me. Thank you for your openness and your clarity. I've heard less concise speeches from King's Counsel in court at the Old Bailey!"

"Lawyers? Oh, sir! I'm just a maid!"

"In this household, I'm surprised to hear that! You must be fast on your feet." The jovial words were out before he could censor them.

To his relief, instead of the offended splutter he'd deserved, he was rewarded with a gurgle of amusement and a very pretty blush before she bobbed and dashed for the door.

This was going to be trickier than he'd expected. He found himself in a household of well-chosen and irreproachable servants who understood and abided by the concept of loyalty. Polite and deferential though they were to the stranger policeman from London, their allegiance would go always and automatically to the family. But Joe thought he'd identified in at least two of their number a bolshy streak which gave rise to an intriguing tendency to support what they perceived as an underdog. Solidarity with the down-trodden. A third had, in the subtlest possible way, pointed to the trail of breadcrumbs that would lead him back to a murderer.

London. St. James's. 6 A.M.

LILY BLINKED, SMOTHERED a yawn and broke off a piece of her toast. She caught the waiter's eye and was about to ask him for a second pot of coffee when she abruptly dismissed him and put down her knife.

There he was. On the move again. Truelove was quietly leaving the hotel having, she assumed, taken an early breakfast up in his room. She was glad she'd disobeyed Joe and stayed on watch. Glad too that she'd thought of booking a taxi and hiring the driver to stay on call for her for the whole morning. Easing forward, she saw him look at his wristwatch and smile with satisfaction as his Bentley was brought up for him from the garage. He slid into the driver's seat, tipped the valet and set off. Luggage already in the boot, she assumed.

The streets would be empty of traffic at this hour and he could drive as fast as his great car would go. Quickly, she grabbed the case she'd packed and left under the table and nipped out to the street. She bashed the snoozing taxi driver on the head with her clutch purse and told him to follow the Bentley.

To Lily's surprise they turned west towards Kensington. Ten minutes later they had pulled up in front of an impressive white-painted birthday cake of a house. A well-dressed gentleman of middle age swept his homburg off his bald head and greeted Truelove, who'd turned off the engine and stepped out. Sir James then proceeded to take the hand of the young girl who was standing by the side of—her father?—and kissed it. They'd met before, then. Two-timing, Truelove? A jolly conversation ensued. Arms were waved. Heads were nodded. Finally, Truelove strolled over to the Rolls-Royce parked in front of the house. At the wheel sat a uniformed chauffeur and in the passenger seat a lady's maid. The car appeared to be loaded to the gunwales with suitcases and hat-boxes. Truelove spoke for a few moments with the chauffeur, pointing. Giving directions, Lily guessed.

He handed the young lady into the back seat of his Bentley, her father into the passenger seat, checked they were comfortable, and set off with the second motorcar following on.

Moving unobtrusively after them, the taxi followed on the northerly and easterly heading it had taken.

The man—if not the girl—had been familiar, Lily thought. A moment's ransacking of her mental files and she had it. Poor old Truelove! Rather him than her, she decided, trapped in a shoulder-to-shoulder situation of intimacy for the next two and a half hours with that rogue. Not the kind of shark he usually swam with. She rather thought she knew where they were going. To her surprise, they made a further stop. A third guest was ready and waiting, again on the doorstep, this time of a more modest house on the Great North Road, and was ushered into the rear of the Bentley. This identification was easier and more surprising.

The convoy moved off again and Lily decided to follow the cars to a point beyond which she could be sure they were going where she calculated they were going. Then she would find a telephone box and get hold of Joe.

STYLES WAS ALREADY up and about and ready for his day when Joe tracked him down to the kitchen. The butler's scholarly features and patrician bearing seemed out of place and out of time in what Joe saw to be a thoroughly modern working space. No sign here of Jacobean open hearths, rotating spits and water pumps; the light, high-ceilinged room was equipped with the latest in kitchen equipment laid out against sleek uncluttered surfaces. Joe spotted an American refrigerator, a Scandinavian cooking range and a French coffee grinder of café proportions, a symphony of cream, black and gold. The only concession to Suffolk heritage was the large central table of scrubbed and limed oak.

Styles was evidently disappointed to have to tell Joe that the feast of sausages, bacon and kidneys he could expect for breakfast were not served until seven thirty as this was not a hunting morning. There could, however, be coffee and tea and toast available in minutes in the east parlour if he wished. The footman was not on duty, nor yet Mrs. Bolton, but he, Styles, could oblige. He explained as he bustled about putting toast on the Aga cooker and deftly selecting cutlery that the housekeeper who was on late duty on Saturdays normally lay abed until eight on a Sunday, rising in time to go to church service at ten. This was her weekly—and her sole—indulgence, Styles confided with a lightening of the expression that in anyone else might have been called an affectionate twinkle.

"Then I'll probably see Mrs. Bolton later in church," Joe said. "Tell me, Styles, is or has Mrs. Bolton ever been—a married lady?"

"Sadly, there is no Mr. Bolton, sir. The title is the usual complimentary form of address for a lady in her position. Matrimony's loss has been our gain."

Joe located the coffee grinder, a model he understood, and set himself, without asking, to measure out beans into the funnel and turn the handle. "Aga toast and coffee! Wonderful! Join me in the parlour, won't you, Styles? I shan't expect anything more substantial until I return from my hike around the estate," he announced, trying to look hale and hearty and ready for anything. "Hard to sleep through these wonderful early mornings. The birds around here wouldn't allow it anyway," he commented. "Sure I heard a nightingale last evening."

"You are not mistaken, sir. We are favoured by their presence in the nettle patches beyond the moat to the north in the direction of the Dower House. Lady Cecily so enjoys their music she refuses to allow a clearance of their favoured habitat. If you have sharp eyes, you may well note a yellow-hammer or two in the woods, perhaps even a woodpecker. And the dance of the dragonflies over the moat is matchless."

"Excellent. I shall be on the front row of the stalls! Now I have you for a moment by yourself, Styles—a question or two. Just an eliciting of facts, you understand, carried out in privacy. But we'll wait until we're settled in the parlour." He nodded politely to two large ladies who glowered at him suspiciously as they helped each other to tie on aprons over their grey morning frocks. "I wouldn't want to put the kitchen staff off their stroke. After that, we can both get on with our day."

Styles smiled, put his head receptively on one side and picked up his tray. "The pot of honey on the dresser, sir? Would you be so kind? It's off the estate. 'Melsett,' you understand . . . I suspect this part of Suffolk has been known for its honey since time immemorial . . ."

A good butler could sail through any adverse conditions, making polite conversation the while. Even an annoyingly early-rising guest who bossily insisted on breakfasting with him was taken in his unhurried stride.

"I'LL TELL YOU straight, Styles—I'm about to pay an early morning call on Mr. Goodfellow, your resident jester. Or Virbio, King of the Grove, as he calls himself. Tell me where I shall find him."

"If that's your fancy, sir, I recommend you step carefully. He will, as is his custom, be sleeping off the effects of an evening at the Sorrel Horse or some similar hostelry. You would be wise to establish that he is alone. It is not unknown for him—against the master's wishes I needn't say—to take a companion back with him for the night. A female companion. Occasionally loose ladies make the trip out from Ipswich on the omnibus." Styles sniffed his disapproval. "He's made his home in the so-called Temple to Diana. Our guests may expect to catch a glimpse of him flashing through the trees in costume should their rambles take them in the direction of the ancient woodland later in the day."

"Is that the sort of thing that goes down well with Sir James's guests?" Joe asked, not quite managing to iron the distaste from his question. He should have realised that no criticism of the house and its guests would be tolerated by the butler.

"In a state of unbuttoned ease, some visitors, especially those of a metropolitan background, are inspired to respond to the spirit of bucolic joviality and collude in fostering what they understand very well to be a medieval—possibly older—tradition. Those with a deeper education and a love of literature are pleased to combine it—as did our national bard—with an appreciation of the classical embellishments on display."

Joe was beginning to wish he hadn't asked.

"I'm familiar with the shrine to Jove's daughter, chaste and fair, Goddess of the Triple Ways," he said, feeling a riposte in style was necessary to uphold the reputation of the Yard in the butler's eyes.

"Then you will be aware of the alleged divine powers which attract a following among the female guests?"

"The goddess has an ancient reputation for intervening in certain female conditions. She has the power to aid fertility and ease the pains of childbirth."

"Always a fruitful topic for conjecture and risqué remarks among the gentlemen! Supplications from some of our more credulous lady guests are frequently made. Votive offerings are left at the foot of her statue and pleas for divine intervention in their medical conditions are made."

"Good Lord!" Joe said, guiltily aware that he had himself fallen into the temptation of popping a token and a wish into the Maiden's hand. "It's not a parlour game! Have they any idea who might be reading their secrets? What might be made of them by an unscrupulous . . . um . . . high priest?"

Styles smiled and tilted his head to one side, indicating polite disagreement. "There have been no complaints. Indeed, sir, several lady guests have reported themselves highly satisfied with the outcome of their approaches to the goddess." The twinkle was unmistakable as he confided, "Sir James has stood godfather to one or two infants bearing the middle name of Melsett or Diana in light-hearted acknowledgement of the intercession."

"Crikey! No Virbios in the line-up I hope?" Joe spluttered into his coffee and watched as the humour faded in the butler's eyes. Struck by the same unvoiceable thought, they both looked aside and Joe returned to the safer question of the temple architecture. "The temple building is not of white marble as one might expect but something more modern and comfortable I think. It looked to me more like an Alpine chalet than a Greek temple. Steep roof and curlicues."

"Mr. Goodfellow is known to enjoy his creature comforts, sir, and his quarters have been much admired. I believe the design and the fittings originated in a Scandinavian country. Norway perhaps. That is certainly where the pinewood came from. It sits well and discreetly in its surroundings. That was the opinion of Sir Edwin when he last visited."

"Can you tell me when his employment began on the estate?"

"Indeed. Sir Sidney, it was, who took him on. Goodfellow had served in some menial capacity in the British Army in South Africa in a regiment where Sir Sidney was an officer."

"The Seventeenth Lancers?"

"That's correct. Prince George, Duke of Cambridge's Own. A very smart company they were. There has been a soldier in most of the generations of the Truelove family. The old master played a bold part in the South African war against the Boers but bought himself out immediately afterwards, not wishing to go on with them to India which was to be the regiment's next posting. He had a young wife and a family here in Suffolk by then and there was much to be done on the estate. Some five years later—1905, would that have been?—Mr. Goodfellow turned up at the Hall, seeking work. A man down on his luck would be sure of a favourable reception from Sir Sidney and a man who had fought alongside was welcomed with generosity. He was given a part time post out in the woods, where he claimed he was happiest. He declares that the noise and fury of war—along with the bullet wound he claims to have picked up—rendered him unfit for a normal occupation among his fellow men or their close society."

"Though he makes an exception to that on Saturday nights at the pub?"

"You have it, sir."

"The present master, Sir James, appears to tolerate his presence in his woods?"

Styles's face froze for a moment, his lips pursed. "He does," was all he ventured in reply. He glanced at the clock on the mantelpiece, got up from the table and began to open the window, murmuring about fresh air and the remiss parlour maid who had failed to air the room.

As the window went up Joe was startled to hear a shot ring out in the distance. Styles anticipated his question with a soothing and dismissive smile. "Bang on time! Not poachers! The rook-scarer, sir. It's one of the master's latest innovations. It's automatic. Fires itself off in the orchards every half hour from before dawn for two hours. Saves sending the children out at an unearthly hour to keep the birds off the soft fruit with rattles. You have just heard the final flourish for today. A disconcerting noise if you're not used to it but, after a while, it's like the church bells—you don't hear it any more."

Joe was further startled by the sound of feet scurrying down the corridor and young Timmy's face appeared round the door.

"Sir . . . Mr. Styles . . . Begging your pardons . . . There's a lady on the telephone ringing from London. She wants to speak to the policeman. Says it's urgent."

Joe swiftly put down his coffee cup.

"LILY! STILL ON watch?"

He listened to Lily's account, making no comment on the prospective arrival of Sir James with a mixed bag of three guests, not wishing to spoil her moment. Her identification of the three was, however, news to him—and might be a surprise to Cecily also, he suspected. "Thank you, Lily!" He spoke with warmth. "You've just passed me a winning hand! For the first time in this wretched affair, I don't feel I'm on the back foot. It may not make much sense to you down there in London but it certainly shines a light on things here. Things are coming to the boil. But knowing who're on their way, I can begin to guess where the heat's coming from. Even better—they have no idea they'll see my grinning face on the front steps."

He looked at his watch. He reckoned he had time enough to prepare for the arrival. And plenty of time to put the frighteners on the Wild Man of the Woods.

JOE APPROACHED THE ancient woodland with care, eyes scanning the bushes, ears alert for human sounds amongst the trees. The explosion he'd heard had not come from any rook-scarer. He'd not heard of a machine that boasted a dull echo a few seconds after discharge. It had been a sound he could not mistake—someone had fired off a shotgun moments before the rook-scarer had delivered its seven o'clock warning. As the blast had come from the direction of the Temple of Diana, Joe told himself that the Wild Man must have wakened and decided to pot a rabbit for his Sunday lunch. He was determined the second barrel was not going to be emptied into him.

The rubber-soled tennis shoes he'd chosen to put on made his approach soundless. He hoped no one was watching him but he rather thought someone was there, standing silently in the woodland, interpreting the unnatural care with which he eased himself through the trees as a state of fear or, at best, comical eccentricity. There was fear in his furtive movements, certainly. Fear had kept him alive; he did not disdain the natural emotion. He used it as a sixth sense but a sense moderated by reason and controlled by training.

Fear was warning him now that all was not as it should be in these woods. He stopped and with his back to a tree trunk, took stock of his surroundings. An early morning walk in June should have been a joyous experience, all senses charmed by a fresh green welcoming Nature. He analysed what was missing. No birds were calling out a warning to each other, signalling ahead the presence of a stranger. The normally vociferous ring doves had nothing to say. No animals were moving thorough the underbrush. Even the breeze had surrendered and the treetops were motionless. A lugubrious cloud of silence hung over the wood. The shot he'd heard twenty minutes ago? Were even the woodland creatures holding their breath waiting for the second barrel?

The gleam of a white marble limb through the trees as he turned his head gave Joe his bearings. Diana was pointing his way. Peering through the gloom beyond the statue he located the outline of the wooden cabin where Goodfellow had established himself as the King of the Grove. A very unappealing place to pass your time, surely? Sir Edwin Lutyens might have expressed polite approval but Joe was not an admirer. The man must be more than a little mad to be content to lead an existence out here in this spooky spot. Possibly fearful too. Joe would not have wanted to spend a single night camping out here, alone.

Fear went with the job, Joe reckoned. He wondered if Virbio himself knew the story. The Guardian of Diana's Grove was destined to reign in a state of constant terror. Not only of the goddess's vengeful temper but also in apprehension of his own violent death at the hands of his successor. By tradition, he could be challenged by some younger, more aggressive aspirant waiting for his moment. Symbolically, the challenger would tear down a branch from an oak tree and then would begin the fight to the death. At the memory of the oak branch he'd reached up and tentatively tugged at, Joe shuddered and recalled Virbio's strange question to him: "Are you here to kill me?"

Virbio had taken him for a challenger. A stalker intent on deposing him.

Poor chap! What a hideous delusion under which to live one's life! Why in hell did he stay on? How could any man allow an ancient, irrelevant and decidedly unpleasant myth to take over his life? What reality was he fleeing from? Could it possibly be worse than the fantasy? Joe decided that if he was intending to take the inebriated Man of the Woods by surprise it might be a kindness to come at him in a tactful manner. He didn't want to bring on a heart attack. Or provoke a fight to the death.

THE DOOR TO the cottage was standing slightly open. Careful to stay out of aim of anyone in the interior, Joe crept close and put his ear to the jamb. He listened for a drunken snoring. No sound. Joe pushed the door open a further inch or two and almost fell backwards in surprise as a sound shattered the silence. An unnatural, inhuman sound. The squeal of a blocked organ pipe? The smothered screech of a strangled cat? Joe discarded both of his original impressions. This was some pitiful animal caught in a trap, he decided, calculating that the brief sound was magnified by the small dimensions of the wooden hut.

He breathed deeply and moved inside, steeling himself to deal with whatever creature was in distress.

A nightmare scene assaulted his wide-eyed stare into the gloom.

In the curtained interior, sprawled on the bed in what seemed to be the single room of the cottage, lay a corpse.

The body of Virbio, Joe assumed. Lying across his coverlet. With his woolly grey hair and gnarled limbs, bunioned white feet sticking out of his winceyette pyjama legs, cup of tea half drunk on his bedside table, he could have been anyone's grandfather sleeping in on a Sunday morning. Had it not been for the copious streams of blood that covered torso and arms and the red splatter staining the white-painted wall behind the bedhead. A double-barrelled game rifle lay beside the bed, having, to all appearances, dropped from his dead hand. Nauseated by the battlefield stench of fresh blood, stale alcohol, and cordite, Joe moved closer and peered down at the remains of the face.

Fired from below, the blast had caught him on one side of the neck and made its way upwards, smashing the jaw and deflecting sideways. The eyes were intact and open. Disconcertingly, they seemed to be staring back at him. In alarm, Joe moved sideways out of their range. The eyes followed his. Locked on. From the open mouth there came the same inhuman shriek Joe had heard from the doorway. Joe steadied himself with an effort. With his speaking mechanisms smashed to pieces, all the dying man could do was make a noise through one pipe or other that remained intact. Joe reckoned that he must have survived twenty minutes in this hopeless state of paralysis and that death would come very soon. He'd cradled dying men in his arms in the trenches, in disbelief at the amount of a man's body that could be shot away and yet leave him for a few moments able to communicate.

Virbio, he could have sworn, had recognised him and was pitifully trying to form a word with his lips.

Joe repeated what he took to be the sound. "'Die?' Did you say—'Die'?" He'd had never been able to deceive a man whose case was hopeless with good-hearted lies. Quietly he said: "Yes, old chap. I'm afraid I think that's the likely outcome. Not much I can do. Look here—would you like me to pray with you? I could have a word with God on your behalf." He bent down, took hold of the lolling right hand and held it.

Whatever their professed religion or lack of one, men usually, at the end, sought after the beliefs of their youth. God, Allah, Jehova, Vishnu, to Joe they were all a central idea whatever their tribal names and he would gladly call on any of them if it brought comfort to a dying man. He watched as Virbio's eyes closed

emphatically at the word 'God.' Dismissive? In the flood of pain
the man must be suffering, could Joe possibly pick out an element
of something so petty as frustration? Was Joe reading too much
into the expression? He didn't think so. Then, blindingly, he
understood. "Not 'die'! *Diana!*"

The eyes opened again in response to his re-interpretation.

"You want to pray to your goddess!"

Joe went on holding the chill hand and, not entirely satisfied
he was doing the right thing, he began to whisper some lines of
Ben Jonson he'd been set to learn when a boy on a school bench,
his "Hymn To Diana."

> *"Queen and huntress, chaste and fair,*
> *Now the sun is laid to sleep,*
> *Seated in thy silver chair,*
> *State in wonted manner keep:*
> *Hesperus entreats thy light,*
> *Goddess excellently bright."*

He couldn't remember all three verses so he said the first one
over again and stumbled on, improvising: "Goddess excellently
bright, thou that mak'st a day of night, light the way for this your
faithful servant, Virbio, and guide him into the happy fields of
Elysium."

The eyes held his, unafraid, even mocking. Then suddenly,
with the timing of a tough East End audience delivering its judgement on a third-rate comedian, the throat emitted a derisive
gargle followed by a last gobbet of blood and the man expired, a
look of infinite scorn fixed on his features.

Only then did Joe allow himself to behave like a policeman.
First, he leaned over the body and put a finger behind the remaining ear to find the pulse spot, performing the automatic physical
checks that death had indeed occurred. Then he stood and

assessed the scene. An apparent suicide. No sign of another presence in the room, though Hunnyton and his forensics boys would
go through it with a fine-tooth comb.

The room was not at all the scene of beer-swilling debauch-
ery he'd feared. No empty rum bottles. No floozy hiding under
the bed. It was the well-ordered and austerely clean quarters of a
military man. Cupboards holding heaven knew what were firmly
closed. There were no dirty dishes or clothes lying about. Whatever he'd worn to the pub last night must be in the laundry basket.
He'd been neatly clad in striped pyjamas before the shooting. His
boots were lined up under the bed waiting for his feet. Joe's
exploratory fingernail run between the sole and the upper came
away with not-yet-dry boot blacking. He must have attended to
them on his return last evening.

Questions flooded into Joe's mind. Had he killed himself?
In London, the hopeless and destitute threw themselves off
bridges and under tube trains. In the country, where guns were
plentiful and despair rampant, self-inflicted death by game
rifle was not uncommon. Why? If not self-inflicted—who?
Would a man planning suicide have left the door ajar? Would
he have polished his boots and tidied his room? It was not
impossible.

Joe stemmed the rampaging flow of enquiry. That was not his
task. This was Hunnyton's backyard. The superintendent would,
within the hour, set wheels in motion to launch an official police
enquiry and have the place turned upside down, every item in it
examined. But Joe would take a few precious moments to absorb
his surroundings, to think and take note. He would take care not
to move about unnecessarily himself. By dashing in to attend to
the dying man Joe had already trodden in the blood that had run
down his extended hand and pooled on the floor. His finger on
the man's neck would need to be accounted for in the report. His
was the kind of presence that gave him a headache when he was

conducting an enquiry. He thanked God that Hunnyton would be in charge.

With a jolt he remembered the offering he'd made to the goddess when he'd first passed this way. Lord! If the Cambridge police discovered the shining cap badge of a fusilier regiment tucked into the palm of Diana's hand and they linked it with the regiment of a certain visiting man from the Met, he'd come in for much scorn and laughter and could waste hours of police time. He made his way to the statue intent on recovering it if it was still there. Cap badges had been a favourite thing to give out to girlfriends after the war. Some girls had them made up into brooches. Joe knew one young lady who'd collected a dozen. He'd scattered these flirty and fashionable tokens like birdseed when he came marching home. With one exception, they'd been accepted with grace and laughter. Dorcas had put hers back in his hand, he remembered, with a sigh of affected sophistication. He smiled. He'd quite expected the same reaction from the goddess. She and Dorcas had much in common, he'd always thought.

Diana had her back to the cottage and was twenty paces distant. He was almost upon her before he caught the glint underneath the pointed nose of her hound. Still there, thank God! But as he reached for it he saw that there was something else in the hollow palm. Held down by the brass token was a sheet of paper folded over and over into a small rectangle. On the outside fold was written "Sandilands."

Joe put his cap badge back into his pocket and unfolded the letter.

He knew where he'd seen the writing before. "Not what you'd call educated is it?" Ben had said. In pencil, the carefully formed but rough lettering had spelled out a list of herbs. Here? A suicide note? Feeling foolish, Joe realised that the dying Virbio had tried with his last breath to send him in the direction of the statue of Diana to find this and had not been asking for a priestly intervention on his behalf to the goddess. As the blundering policeman had subjected him to the recitation of a barely remembered ode, Virbio's final thoughts must have been unprintable.

Goddess excellently bright, perhaps. Copper laughably dull, certainly.

Not a suicide note, he was assuming. Explanations, recriminations, confessions, accusations, such notes were meant to be found and read. He'd come across them in plain sight on desks, tucked into pockets, tacked to the wall above the corpse, even, in one case, clenched between the dead man's teeth. They were never secreted away.

Dejected and full of foreboding, Joe sat down on a log that seemed to have been put there for the purpose and scanned the document. The man's spelling might not be up to much but he seemed to have plenty to say.

CHAPTER 19

When you read this, copper, I'll be long gone. He's not going to get away with it, your Lord and Master. I told him what would happen if he turned awkward and now he'll learn I meant it.

He gave me my marching orders for Midsummer Day. That's today. Got his London lawyer to send me the eviction papers. Didn't have the guts to do it himself. No more billet. No more pay. Says he hasn't the wherewithall. Likely tale, eh?

Never thought he'd call my bluff but he has. Even sent one of his tame police bully-boys to make sure I go quietly. At least I merited an 'Assistant Commissioner' from the Yard! PC Plod from the village wouldn't have cut it. Well sod you both!

I bet he's told you nothing. Eh? Aren't I right? Well it's time someone blew the whistle before he ruins many more lives. Read on, copper, if you want to know the truth about Truelove.

1908 it was when I did him the service. One of the maids—Phoebe her name was—got pregnant. Not surprised—she was a lovely lass but she was just a kid. They both were. He must have got her into trouble when he was home from school at Easter. Always wanted too much, too early, James Truelove.

By the summer holidays she was desperate. Told no one but

him. Wanted to know what he was going to do about it. The usual. He didn't want his old man to find out or his ma who was in the last month of confinement herself. But more than anything he was afeared that Hunnybun might get to hear and then the wrath of God would have descended on him. No one else to talk to, so he turned to me. Man of the world. A Londoner. He thought I'd know what to do.

He wasn't wrong. I knew a place in Ipswich where they'd fix it—for a sum. It'll cost you, I says. How much? he wants to know. I've spent my month's allowance. Pinch something then I says. House is full of stuff. Silver, gold necklace. He comes up with 2 little paintings. Silly sod! Not so easy to shift as something you can melt down, easy to trace as a signature! I managed. But I had to go up to London to do it. I even conned a receipt of sorts out of the bloke—he was a cousin of mine and owed me one. Here attached for your perusal. Wouldn't stand up two minutes in a court of law but a copper like you can read between the lines. And Alf who signed it has previous. Got sent down for five in the Pen in 1912 for fencing stolen goods so that's corroboration as you'd say. Check it—it's your job. Twenty quid wasn't near the value but then. It was enough to do the job and pay me for my troubles.

Something went wrong for him. Church-going girl, she must have refused to go through with it. She certainly never went near Ipswich. Next thing she's floating in the pondweed and who was the unlucky bloke who found her? Yours truly. Killed herself? Course she did! And that's the story I put out. But I told Truelove it would look really bad for him if I were to tell anyone what had really happened. Wasn't that the young master I'd glimpsed larking about with a young girl in the moat an hour before? Teaching her to swim? Two kids having a splash about? Oh, yer! Holding her up by the heels was a funny way of going about it. I only had to take my tale to

*Hunnybun and James would have been mincemeat. Adam H.
is just like his real dad. A ba-lamb until he's riled and then
you notice the size of his fists. I've seen the old man lay about
him . . . but never mind . . . those Boers asked for it, whatever
they say.*

*When James found himself a rich woman I asked for more.
He wouldn't have wanted the lovely Lavinia to know what
was in his past. He coughed up, good as gold. Her gold I suppose
when you come to think of it! She never knew where half of it
went, silly cow!*

*I've had a good innings and my bank book at the Co-op
will keep my sister and me comfortable. It's no life out here for
a 50-year-old with arthritis anyhow. I've had enough. I
should have shopped him to his wife and scarpered when I had
the chance. She was round here every month leaving bribes to
Diana. Desperate to present the Trueloves with an heir. Why,
she kept asking, why am I being punished? Should have spoken
out. Told her it was a judgement not on her but on her husband
that he has no son and heir. He has no trouble deflowering
virginal maids and getting them up the duff. It's the Goddess's
revenge for Phoebe.*

*But you'll do, copper. Tell whoever you want. Shout it from
the housetops. James Truelove who thinks he can be the next
prime minister is a debaucher of young girls, a thief and a
murderer. That's what you have to tell the world.*

THE VENOM REEKING up from the page was almost
tangible. Joe could hardly bear to hold the paper in his trembling
hands. "No, you swine," he muttered to himself, "if I shout anything, I shall announce to the world that the human scum who
went by the name of Virbio was a Peeping Tom, a liar, a parasitic
leach, a blackmailer and snake in the grass. And then I shall get
seriously disrespectful!"

Joe had never had so little evidence on which to base an accusation, nor yet such certainty that his suspicions were justified. He turned an angry face to the cottage. "And if someone hadn't already pulled that trigger and rid the world of a pullulating ulcer, I'd have done the job myself."

HE STOOD, GATHERED himself, and set off at a brisk trot back to the Hall. He'd covered twenty yards when the shot rang out.

High and wide to the right, it cracked past his head sending him crashing to his knees. He rolled over twice into the deep shadow of an oak tree, coming to rest, breathless and alarmed, behind the four foot thick barrier of its trunk.

Who the hell?

NOT VIRBIO'S GUN. The first barrel of someone else's. A poacher? One of his fellow guests revelling in early morning country pursuits? A resentful villager putting the wind up one of the Toffs up at the Hall? Probably their weekend sport. The comforting answers flooded in, the brain attempting to neutralise the unacceptable messages being sent by his senses. Joe rejected each one. Out there within easy range for any reasonable shooter was a man with a gun and a second shot up the spout. The gun was trained on him.

Or was it?

The bullet had smacked into the tree ahead of him, some twelve feet from the ground, he thought. He noted the place. The broad-leaved lime had stopped the bullet with all the solidity of its fine-grained wood. He didn't want to imagine what it would have done to the soft spot between his shoulder blades. Bad aim or warning shot? Joe waited, listening. No sound. Flat to the ground, he risked an eye around the trunk. No movement. He rolled over and checked the other side. All clear. Silently he wriggled to his feet and picked up a stout twig. Plastering his front to the rough bark, he took off his cap and speared it on the end of the twig. Crouched, he held it up beyond the tree at head level and waited for the explosion. A crude trick, but it had worked with helmets on bayonets in the trenches. A keyed-up man with his finger on the trigger—even an experienced soldier— would instinctively blast away at the sudden appearance of exactly what he was looking for in the place he was expecting it.

No result. Joe performed the same manoeuvre on the other side in case the shooter was moving around in an arc. His cap remained intact. Feeling embarrassingly like a boy scout on a wide day out in the woods with the troop, he next hurled the stick into a thicket behind and to one side of the tree. It landed with a satisfying crunch and a movement of the bushes. Joe was pleased with the result but the gunman wasn't falling for that either.

Joe began to breathe more steadily. Common sense was telling him that if the gunman genuinely wanted him dead, then dead he would be by now. Unarmed as he was, there was only one thing he could do.

Cap firmly back in place, imaginary swagger stick tucked under his right arm, left arm swinging with military precision, Joe marched out from his shelter. Whistling "It's a Long Way to Tipperary," he presented a ram-rod straight back to the enemy.

THE MARCH BECAME a trot as he stayed on his feet and the trot a fast zigzagging dash when he emerged from the cover of the trees and headed across the seemingly endless open stretch of mown meadow grass in front of the Hall.

Past caring who he was disturbing, he went into the telephone room off the hall, calling out loudly for Timmy as he went.

Timmy bustled up minutes later to find the policeman at the desk, grim-faced, putting sheets of paper into an envelope. "Ah, there you are! Can you ride the Swine, Timmy? . . . Thought so.

Look, go and get it out and take this note as fast as you can down to Superintendent Hunnyton. You know where he . . ." Timmy was already out of the door and running.

JOE WONDERED IF Hunnyton would come to the same conclusion as himself. It had been plain enough to Joe as he read the letter. If you want someone to swallow a thumping great lie, conceal it between two slices of verifiable truth and add a little garnish. It was a device he'd used himself. But Virbio was less skilled, evidently. He'd overdone the garnish. He looked at his watch and reviewed his schedule, which was tightening uncomfortably. Eight o'clock. His fixed points in the morning were: a visit to the stables, a confrontation in the graveyard at nine thirty, the welcoming of Truelove and his party some time before the parade of horses on the front lawn at eleven o'clock. Three hours at the outside before he greeted Dorcas. Three hours to come up with the solution to three murders. Phoebe Pilgrim, Lavinia Truelove and Robin Goodfellow. Better get on.

He went in search of Styles. He caught the butler about to carry a tray of early morning tea along the corridor. He smiled at Joe. Shiftily? No. Joe would have said rather: shyly. "For Mrs. B. I always take it along to her room myself. We do our best to relieve the staff as much as we can on a Sunday."

"A moment please, Styles. There's something you must know and I'd like you to convey it to Mrs. Bolton along with her cup of Assam."

In the quiet of the telephone room Joe delivered a brief account of Goodfellow's death.

"A case of suicide, you're saying, sir? How simply dreadful! Well, well! I'm sure the fellow had much weighing on his conscience but all the same . . . I'm surprised to hear he took his own life. He never seemed the kind who would oblige the world by leaving it of his own volition. Oh, dear! Today of all days . . ."

"I have a plan to deal with the inconvenience of it all, Styles. You must relay all this to Mrs. Bolton and you must both . . ." He swore the butler, and through him the housekeeper, to silence and ensured they would maintain a cordon sanitaire between the house, including family, guests and servants, and the wood, where discreet police activity might be expected.

Styles hurried to assure Joe that he perfectly understood and would act as prescribed until further orders. "Lady Cecily . . . ?" he began to enquire.

"I shall take it upon myself to break the news, Styles. At some time *after* the arrival of the guests," he added carefully.

Styles nodded and appeared relieved. He picked up his tray and set off eagerly with his pot of tea and his budget of news to enliven his weekly heart-to-heart with the housekeeper.

AN INVENTORY OF the guests seemed to be Joe's next most urgent task. Who was where and in whose company was something he had to establish without raising an alarm. He hurried along to the breakfast parlour where he came upon a convivial scene. The usual male breakfast club seemed to be forming up, helping themselves to bacon and devilled kidneys from heated chafing dishes laid out on a sideboard. A pair of footmen, one of them the indefatigable Ben, were standing by in attendance at the tea and coffee urns. Joe caught sight of a dish of fragrant kedgeree and was sorely tempted to join the party but he had things more urgent than smoked haddock on his mind.

Two of the gentlemen, Ripley and Somerton, were well into their breakfast, judging by the state of their plates. A third had just arrived. Alexander, to Joe's surprise, was languidly questioning the footman on the provenance of the coffee and extending a shuddering hand to reject his suggestion of sausages and bacon.

Joe sidled up to him. "Early riser, Truelove?"

"Not by nature, Sandilands. Exceptionally—on a Sunday.

Mama sent up a footman to boot me out of bed. She won't countenance my missing the Parade of Stallions. Especially not the
Midsummer parade. The whole village will be there on the lawn
with flags and ribbons and bells and babies. They may even have
put up a maypole." Alex shuddered again.

"Wouldn't miss it for the world!" Joe said, grinning.

"Good man! I say, Sandilands . . ." Alex leaned closer. "Not so
bleary-eyed I hadn't noticed . . . You might like to nip up to your
room and change your shirt. Blood-stained cuffs not really acceptable at the breakfast table, you know."

Joe stared at his cuffs in dismay.

"So that was *you* out there popping off a gun at some unearthly
hour, was it? Bothering God's creatures?" Alex delivered the reprimand with a smirk and tweaked a sprig of bracken from Joe's
tweed jacket. He dusted off Joe's shoulders with the concerned
reproof of a good valet.

"Styles sent me out to bag a brace of woodcock for breakfast,"
Joe said lightly. "They're probably under some chafing dish already
masquerading as *délice de bécasse* on toast."

"No woodcock to be had in Suffolk before they come flight-
ing in halfway through October, old man. I wonder what it was
you bagged?"

Annoyed and preoccupied, Joe muttered, "Woodpigeon then.
Excuse me—before I go up . . ." He turned and addressed the
room: "I say, you fellows . . . Has anyone clapped eyes on Mungo
McIver this bright A.M.?"

The two married men looked about them checking the company as though just noticing that the news baron had not yet come
down. Looks were exchanged and then Basil Ripley offered a kindly
but mischievous, "Last seen staggering upstairs with a half-drunk
bottle of Napoleon after losing badly at snooker. He's probably
still in bed, sharing a pot of tea or something with the delightful
Mrs. McIver. 'Do Not Disturb' and all that, Sandilands."

Joe cocked an eyebrow at Ben who nodded confirmation.

"Of course! I understand," Joe said. "It can wait. Look, I'm just going up to change and then if anyone wants to see me in the next half hour, will you tell them I'll be down in the stables?"

They all mumbled that they'd oblige, speared another kidney and returned to the racing tips in Saturday's newspaper.

A MEDDLING SCOTLAND Yard heavyweight was the last man they wanted to see in the stables at this busy time. Joe knew that and was doubly impressed by the quiet civility with which he was greeted. The head groom, Wallace Flowerdew, stepped up to deal with him, drawing him carefully aside as a great horse clumped by. A team of men and boys was moving purposefully about in the gloom in an atmosphere of suppressed excitement that seemed to have communicated itself to the animals.

The Suffolk Punches, Joe could have sworn, knew that this was a special morning. Their wise old faces had taken on an animation, their ponderous movements seemed lighter. Joe noted how a hoof would be obligingly raised to the groom's hand a second before he asked for it. They were enjoying the attention. Some oily unguent was being applied on cloths to their hides and rubbed in until their bulging sides and quarters glowed like conkers. Others, more advanced in the preparation, were having their manes and tails plaited up with red and blue ribbons. Everywhere, brass shone, leather gleamed and lads whistled cheerfully.

"That's all right, sir. We can manage. I know why you're here," Flowerdew began when they had retreated to a quiet corner of the yard. He gave Joe a succinct account of the events of the April night when Lavinia had ventured into his stables. "It was my sons took her there, sir, to her death," he concluded. "I feel responsible. Expected to get the sack. I'd have tanned their hides if the master hadn't stepped in. 'No, you don't, Flowerdew!' he says. 'It was no fault of the boys. They were just obeying a very thoughtless command under pressure. Send them to me. I intend to give them a half crown each for their trouble.' And he did."

Flowerdew's knowing old eye slid across Joe's, catching a flash of approval which emboldened him to add: "Aye! He's a good master, sir. The best. You can always rely on him to put right what's gone wrong as soon as he hears of it ... An"e loves 'is 'osses!" He delivered the ultimate accolade in broad Suffolk. "He bought four new Punches this season and cancelled 'is order for two o' them new-fangled tractor ploughs."

Joe thanked him for his account and told him he had one or two quick questions for him. "What was the condition of the stallion Lucifer when he was bought by Sir James?" he began.

"Well, first, he wasn't called 'Lucifer.' He was called 'Joey' when he arrived. Good price paid for him. He was perfect. Would have made a good breeding stallion. But then, he started playing up. Refusing the bridle, kicking about and playing silly buggers. Then he started refusing to come out of his stall and he took to biting anyone who came near him. That was when the master gave him, joking like, his new name."

"Tell me, was Goodfellow involved with his care at any time?"

Flowerdew frowned. "As little as I could manage. I like to use my own lads. Oh, don't get me wrong—Goodfellow's a practised hand with horses right enough. Cavalry groom in the South African war. But he wasn't home-trained. A bit harsh, if you know what I mean. I expect that's war for you. No time to do things the proper way. In these stables we don't 'break' horses, sir, we 'gentle' them. Master understands and wouldn't have it any other way. Goodfellow's better off larking about in the woods if you ask me. But once a horseman, always a horseman, I suppose. He's always buzzing about getting in our way. Telling us our business."

Joe took a deep breath. "Flowerdew, if I told you that the horse's crazy behaviour was caused by a deliberate laceration to the soft tissue on the sides of its mouth, discovered and recorded in his equine post-mortem by Mr. Hartest, the vet, would you be surprised?"

"No, sir. I've heard of that. Folk do it to ruin an animal at auction. Never happened around me before though. Wouldn't have thought to look even if he'd let us get near enough to look inside his mouth."

"If I suggested that Goodfellow might have inflicted the wounds?"

"No one else would have or could have done it. I had wondered. Will you tell Sir James or shall I? I think he should know. He won't be best pleased." The old horseman's normally placid features became almost animated as satisfaction vied with anxiety.

"That's all right, Flowerdew. I'll tell him. I have some other news—not unrelated—to break to him. Leave it to me."

SO DISCREET WAS the police presence Joe thought that Hunnyton had not received his message. A few yards from the open door of Virbio's cabin, a uniformed bobby stepped forward, large right hand extended to bar his way. Recognition followed and he asked, "Commissioner Sandilands? Go right inside. The inspector's waiting for you."

"Not waiting exactly," said a cheerful voice from inside. "I've just about solved this one while you were toying with your toast."

The corpse was still in place, as was the rifle. Hunnyton's murder bag lay open at the foot of the bed. The superintendent was in control and relishing it. He was making a sketch of the scene on a sheet of graph paper. Joe was about to step forward and help himself to a pair of rubber gloves when Hunnyton called out crisply, "No! Stay where you are! Sorry, Sandilands, but would you mind plonking your plates of meat on that piece of newspaper I've laid out for you behind the door?" He peered meaningfully at Joe's feet. "Ah! Changed into your brogues, have you? Those *were* your tennis shoes the constable and I found traces of in the vicinity of the body? Dunlops, ribbed soles, size twelve, scarcely worn? Your left foot was rather dramatically outlined in blood. Just stay out of the way, will you? I can't be doing with a fresh pair of Lobbs blundering on stage. I shall have to log four pairs plus any imprints the killer might have left, of course. So far no trace of *him*."

"I'm just on my way to church. Blood-stained shirt and shoes . . . wouldn't want to frighten the vicar . . ." Joe began.

"He's seen worse! The Rev. Easterby was a front line padré in the last lot. Just help me out here—I'm assuming this fingerprint in blood on the neck of the body is yours."

"I'll supply my prints for the record, of course. Yes, the man was still alive when I got here. I rushed forward to offer assistance. Nothing I could do for him. I stood there by his side and said a prayer to Diana . . ."

"Crikey! Super Plod turns up to administer the last pagan rites? That must have sent him off rejoicing!"

Hunnyton looked up, puzzled, from his notebook and focussed on Joe's face. "Good God, man!" And, more seriously, "What's happened to you, Joe? You look bloody awful! Your face is bleeding."

"The recently deceased threw a log at me yesterday. The wound opened up again when I was rolling around on the forest floor dodging bullets on my way back to the Hall an hour ago. Is this Suffolk or the Somme? Not sure."

Hunnyton listened intently to Joe's story, jotting down his estimate of the time of his arrival at the scene, the time Goodfellow had expired, and the time he'd been shot at in the woods without comment or question. "Well, kindly drip your blood type onto the paper provided. I've got a neat little sketch here and I'm not about to add any extraneous bodily fluid contributions from Scotland Yard."

"That villain tried to kill me. We're lucky it's not *my* corpse you're waving off in an ambulance."

"Everybody's lucky *this* is the corpse if I read his letter aright."
Hunnyton sniffed. "Not before time and I'll raise a glass to the
perpetrator. Those are my deathbed sentiments, if anyone wants
to hear them. Now, I hope you don't mind, I borrowed Timmy
and his flash new bike to run a few errands for me. First he sum-
moned PC Godestone from his allotment to act as guard dog,
then he belted off to the vet's with a phone message for Adelaide
to transmit to the force back in Cambridge. We're going to have to
put that lady on the pay roll. Or me on the phone line." He sighed.
"And there goes my privacy. There'll be a squad out within the
hour. I haven't alerted the Co-op funeral services yet—he's going
straight onto a slab at the morgue. I want a proper postmortem
done by a doc I can trust in Cambridge. This is one case that's
not going to come back and bite me in the bum."

"Not a suicide, then, Hunnyton?"

Joe received a scathing look. "I think you know that as well
as I do. Could easily have been, though. I've come across these
cases before. Bankrupt farmers usually. Their guns are old friends.
If your arm is long enough, you can reach the trigger and fire it
upwards into your head. Toe grip not unknown. Remote place
like this—he'd have kept his gun at the ready under the bed in
the country way. It'll be interesting to see whose fingerprints are
on the trigger."

"I'm betting—Goodfellow's." Joe sighed.

"So am I. This is murder, Sandilands; we both know that. But
it's murder by a bloke who's very sure of himself. Cool as you
please. No emotion in evidence—no fight, nothing broken. Familiar with the victim's habits. Knew he'd find him sleeping off a
hangover. Knew he kept a loaded gun to hand. This was planning
so careful, the bugger's left not a trace of his presence. I tell you,
Joe—I haven't found so much as a hair so far. That's worrying.
They always leave something . . . Perhaps the forensics boys will
see more than I'm seeing. Our careful friend would take the time

to apply the dead man's finger to the trigger when he'd wiped it clean, don't you think? He might even have been wearing gloves and needn't have bothered with the dead man's finger. What he hadn't counted on was that his target might be more alert than usual this morning. Planning an early get-away, Goodfellow might have drunk less than his usual eight pints at the Sorrel Horse.

"I was there at the Horse, Sandilands, last night. For the first part of the evening at any rate. In the public bar. Goodfellow was in the snug buying a round for his cronies. His last round as it turns out. I noted he sank two pints before I left. The barman will cast further light. We shall see. The murderer hadn't counted on the instinctive recoil of a threatened body away from a blast, what's more. Point blank range. The bullet was supposed to go straight up and take the top of the head off. But it went crosswise, through the throat and jaw. Removed his ear but left the skull intact, I'd say."

Hunnyton looked dispassionately at the shattered head. "There's so much blood and it's so fresh it's hard to tell. Are you sure it was as long ago as seven?" He tweaked the dead arm, testing again for rigor mortis. "Anyway, the doc will tell us more. I'm not an expert. Whatever—the shot only did three quarters the damage intended."

"Nothing much our bloke could do to finish him off though. A dying suicide doesn't generally have the strength to fire the second barrel."

"He couldn't hang around after the shot. He must have judged his victim had only minutes to survive. Made a fast exit and hoped for the best. Too bad for him that a nosy Scotland Yarder was taking the air in the environs and had the benefit of hearing the victim's last gasp. What the hell were you doing in the wood at that hour? Never mind," he rushed on, "Timing, Joe? Can you be precise?"

"No trouble! Styles and I heard the shot at seven o'clock exactly as I said. We were breakfasting together and he happened to open the window at the crucial moment."

"That confirms what Adelaide told me. She sent Timmy back to me with a note. She was out in the garden and heard the first shot at seven. A second at seven forty. Country folk are so used to gunfire they wouldn't notice but being just down from London, Adelaide did."

"That's exact. The second was the one fired at me as I retreated. But tell me, Adam, what did *you* make of his letter?" Joe had been aware that the superintendent had, in his rush of sympathy for him, fallen into calling him by his Christian name. It seemed polite to return the compliment and in view of the personal nature of the question, a more natural and feeling approach.

The handsome features congealed into a dark scowl. "Hardly the last note from a bloke about to top himself, was it? Had more the flavour of one who was just about to call a taxi and leg it. In fact, he'd got as far as packing. His bag's the other side of the bed. Full to the gunwales! He wasn't counting on coming back." The professional comment was followed by a more dismissive tone. "It was no more than I'd expected. And suspected for years. It's all right, Joe. I'm not one to have a fit of the vapours. I hope *you* didn't fall for his blarney?"

"I didn't. There was much truth in there but, even for me, the one lie stood out."

"The heels?"

"That's right. One detail that speaks volumes. You weren't here, Adam, when Phoebe died?"

"No. She was nailed down in her coffin and the Trueloves were presiding by the time I got here. That was a different world, pre-war. None of the right questions asked. Not even a police autopsy. A shameful, self-inflicted death, they reckoned. Better shovelled underground sharpish. A maidservant. Not worth investigating and annoying the Trueloves for. Not with her lady-ship in a delicate condition."

"But this Goodfellow, or whoever he was . . ." Joe hesitated.

"You can call him Goodfellow, right enough. I checked him out, years ago. That is his name. Robert Goodfellow, ex-army, a.k.a. Robin, Mischievous Sprite of the Forest."

"Well, our sprite describes graphically a very sure way of drowning someone. Holding the heels up forces the head down. It has the advantage of cutting off the screams as well as filling the lungs. He either did, in fact, as he says, see James Truelove holding her under or . . ."

"She had a fear of water—I told you—she would never have gone in the moat, not even for a swimming lesson with the young master. He bloody did it himself! Tried to force himself on her, I expect. She wasn't having any of his nonsense and threatened to tell me . . . He decided to silence her. Swine!"

Hunnyton lanced the corpse with a steel glare. Delivering a second death. Joe thought that if anything of Goodfellow's mischievous spirit was still hanging about the place, it would run screeching straight into the jaws of hell for shelter before meeting that implacable eye.

Limited in his movements to the area of two pages of the *Daily Mirror*, Joe had to suppress his urge to clap a comforting hand on Hunnyton's shoulder. "Well, you won't have to swing for him, Adam, and I'm glad of that. Look, I think I know who might have something to tell us about the drowning. Someone who was close about at the time. Leave it to me. By the way, I've instructed Styles and Mrs. Bolton to keep the guests away from the wood, so you'll get a clear run at this when the CID crew arrive. By the time they get here, the company at the Hall—and the whole village apparently—will be gathered to enjoy the jollifications on the front lawn."

"Ah. Yes. Of course. The Parade of Horses. Worth seeing, Joe, if you've got the time and stomach for it."

"It's the parade of humans I wouldn't miss for anything. I don't forget I'm down here to tease out the puzzle of Lavinia's death. About which Goodfellow is sinisterly silent. Don't you think? He throws a distorted light on an ancient murder but drops not a hint of the recent one in his letter."

"Eager to get off and pack? Not the world's most fluent writer—he wasn't about to embark on a further chapter?"

"Hard to believe he had nothing to say. If that chap had had mud to hand I don't think he'd have hesitated to throw it."

"You're right. There was a little something he was keeping in reserve. You'll see! Extra blackmailing ammo? He's skilled in the use of hanging threats over people. Not too much, not too little. Push a man just far enough and no further. The ones who get away with it, the ones who never turn up on our books are the clever ones, the ones who are so close to their victims they can judge their every reaction and have the restraint never to demand more than can be borne. Like the East African farmers who live on their beasts' blood—always allow the victim to recover and thrive before you open up his vein again. In connection with which—you might like to cast an eye on Goodfellow's outbuilding before you go."

"Outbuilding? He has a latrine somewhere about the place I suppose?"

"Well he was only human. It's carefully camouflaged and architect-designed in keeping with the main building. You'll find it twenty yards northeast of the rear. Have a rummage around. Here, put these gloves on. Oh, and you may want to hold your sensitive nose."

A smaller, simpler version of the pine cabin stood, door closed, hidden from all eyes by a thick screen of hawthorn bushes and tangled ivy. A shed any man would have liked to install in his back garden, at first sight. Joe opened the door and entered gingerly. On the left was, indeed, an army-style latrine of the best

continental porcelain. Scrupulously clean and scented with hanging bunches of lavender. A large enamel water jug stood by ready
for service. On the right another door opened into an allotment
holder's heaven. A potting bench ran the length of the cabin, seed
trays, used, cleaned and awaiting the next sowing stood in piles,
gardening and woodworking tools were fixed on racks on the
walls. An old, horsehair-stuffed armchair was still dented from
Goodfellow's last occupancy, a pile of *Men Only* and *Liliput*
magazines lurked underneath.

It was the range of wooden shelves with their pigeon-holed
compartments that took Joe's eye. The kind of fitting you could
see in any pharmacy, it had probably been bought in at a farmers'
auction. Some of the compartments had a name inked in on their
surface. Joe read names of herbs—hartshorne, white willow,
marshmallow . . . One of them seized his attention. It had a piece
of writing paper torn from a police notebook stuck on it with a
piece of elastoplast. "Look in here, Sandilands! This drawer was
slightly open when I entered. The only one."

The drawer must have been airtight. The smell of the contents
would have been held in check. Joe decided to leave a detailed
inspection of the scrapings of black residue to Hunnyton's forensic boys and merely noted that essence of something deeply
unpleasant lurked within. It brought instantly to mind the smell
of the offering Lady Truelove had been trying to make to Lucifer.
He slammed it shut. Lavinia had sent her maid with Goodfellow's
hand-written prescription for spices to the chemist but the second
formula, the one she had used along with the toad's bone with
such disastrous consequences, had come straight from this work-
shop.

Joe put his head round the door. "Got the message! How are
you doing, mate?"

Hunnyton sighed and looked down at his notebook. "It's
hopeless! Joe—can I be frank?" He looked up at Joe with a wry

smile. "If you were the officer in charge of this bloody case you'd have to arrest yourself! I think you know what I'm saying."

Joe stepped inside and kicked the door shut. He ignored the newspaper doormat and went to stand directly in front of Hunnyton, challenging him, eye to eye.

"No. I don't. I think you'd better elucidate for me, Superintendent."

Hunnyton swallowed and turned away, unable to withstand the challenge of his superior officer's response. "Oh, come on, Joe. You must see it!"

CHAPTER 20

H unnyton waved his notebook under Joe's nose as though it
had suddenly caught fire and he was about to get his fingers
burned. "Every word of my notes reflects procedure done by the
book. You can read it for yourself and tell me what conclusion any
sane man would come to. Any judge, any jury. Any Scotland Yard
Assistant Commissioner. Why don't you give it a go?"

The true enormity of the embarrassed half-accusation hit Joe
and, for a moment, sent his mind reeling.

Gathering himself, he began to speak slowly and carefully.
"No trace of an interloper, as far as it goes, but you have a considerable amount of evidence of *my* passage through. I have a firm
alibi for the seven o'clock shot but, as you say, death did indeed
not occur until after that time. A mischief-maker—no, let's say
simply a scrupulous reader of the notes—might conclude that the
second shot it was that did for him. Seven forty. The pathologist
may well conclude that later time to be the actual time of death.
I couldn't fault him. Though I would expect the usual umbrella
statement of 'at a time between six and nine.' I claim to have been
the target of that shot myself but where's the evidence of that? It
went skying into the trees. I take off back to the Hall where I am
observed to arrive by one or two witnesses, covered in blood and
hurrying to change my clothes. Suitably clad for church, I return

to the scene of the crime an hour later to check on the progress of the detective I have myself alerted. How am I doing?"

Hunnyton nodded. He had the grace, Joe noted, to look rather sickened by the interview.

"I have the skill, the ruthlessness and the opportunity. I deny none of that. But motive, Superintendent? Why the hell should I put my neck on the line for a man unknown to me before yesterday? For that villain? Why would I want him dead?" Suddenly understanding, Joe pointed to his face and laughed. "A log-chucking contest in the woods goes badly for me and I decide to wreak revenge? I so envy his carefree bucolic existence I decide to challenge him for the priesthood? Oh, come on!"

"No, it's not that, sir. What sort of a plodding idiot do you take me for?" Gravely, Hunnyton took Goodfellow's letter from his pocketbook and handed it to Joe. "The victim names you, sir."

"What are you talking about?" Joe looked again at the folded note addressed to "Sandilands."

Reciting from memory of the text, Hunnyton said quietly, "*Your Lord and Master,* he says—Truelove we're assuming—*got his London lawyer to evict me . . . Even sent one of his tame police bully-boys to make sure I go quietly. At least I merited an Assistant Commissioner from the Yard!*" Not exactly *quietly* perhaps. His final departure was accompanied by the blast of a shotgun heard for miles around."

"Truelove's tame police bully-boy?" Joe's anger was rising. "Is that how *you* would characterise me?"

"Not me, sir. Those are the dead man's words. I've only observed you doing Sir James's shopping for him. A judge might want to enquire into any previous association you might have had with the gentleman. He might go so far as to check the log book of your encounters at Scotland Yard. How many was it? Two? In the days before the murder . . . Oh, dear. Your secretary was present at the time? No? Pity . . ."

Joe's mouth was too dry to form the words to express his thoughts even if his shocked brain had been able to come up with some. He maintained his rigid stance, unable to contemplate the alternative of knocking Hunnyton to the ground.

"Sir! Sir! Calm down!" Hunnyton urged, sensing a coming explosion. "Always better to look the truth in the face, I reckon. We're professionals. We know how this works. We've both seen things turn very nasty in court. Some young terrier of a prosecuting council trying to make his name is all it takes. The Press love a touch of hubris as much as they hate Scotland Yard. A combination will have them salivating into their mild and bitters. A top man, war hero and one-time debs' delight being hanged by the rope he's knotted himself—they'd love it! There's a way through. Clear and obvious as a turnpike. Just slip that letter I've given you in your pocket and bugger off. I never saw it. Leave me to finish here."

He fixed Joe at last with unclouded eyes. Angry eyes. "Listen! This piece of shit flushed himself out of our lives. Not right that he should take anybody down the pan with him. Not anybody! I won't allow it. Got that? I'm telling you formally, Assistant Commissioner, that I'm scaling down the inquiry. I'll turn the men round sharpish when they get here. A few photos and signed statements from the lads—I'm not risking any charge of collusion—should do it."

He drew himself up, every inch the officer reporting to his superior. "False alarm, sir. Sorry you've been bothered. This is a suicide we're looking at. No one else is being sought in connection with the death."

Joe took his leave of Hunnyton, murmuring the official formulae. He even caught himself muttering, "Carry on, Superintendent."

He'd wondered if he'd recognise the moment. Here it was: the moment when, charmed, distracted and trusting, he'd feel the saddle slap down across his back.

Still stunned and abstracted, his mind whirling, he answered the question Hunnyton fired at him as he left the room: "Where am I going? Oh, not far." And, with a last rebellious kick of the heels: "I think it's time to hear from Phoebe herself."

HE REACHED THE grave as the church clock struck half past nine. His witness was already there in the remotest corner of the deserted churchyard, head down, occupied in tending the simple grave.

Joe came up and knelt down alongside. "White roses were her favourite flower, I take it?"

"Anything white, she loved. Summertime's easy but it's a bit difficult in the winter to come up with something. I usually manage with snowberries and ivy until the snowdrops come out and then there's the paper-white narcissi. It's a lonely site they found for her. I wouldn't like her to think she'd been forgotten."

She didn't seem in the slightest way put out to see him there. "She was murdered, little Phoebe. I suppose you've worked that out."

"I have and I know the name of the killer, Mrs. Bolton. I'm equally sure that you also know and have known for years. The puzzle for me is why you've chosen to keep silent and let a great injustice fester."

She looked down at the grave in shame and anger, words failing her. This was not the accusation she had been prepared for.

"Nothing to say? Why don't you give me Phoebe's own words, Mrs. B.? It's time we heard from her. Can you remember the last thing she confided to you?"

"She wasn't in her right mind. Mad with the worry. I'd guessed her condition. She was directly in my charge. There wasn't much about Phoebe I didn't know. Even so—I hadn't realised who'd got her into trouble. It could have been any of the footmen—they're always first on the suspect list—but for me: I'd feared the ghastly

Goodfellow, so firmly under Sir Sidney's protection. It was unreasonable that. The old master just brushed any complaints aside. I think he probably put up with it because Goodfellow had something on him—something he'd done in his army years that he wouldn't have wanted mistress Cecily to hear about.

"Goodfellow was always too interested in the maids. They had to walk miles to get around him. He was always tracking them about the place, leering out from the shrubbery. Phoebe was the one who really caught his eye. Pretty as a picture but soft and unresisting. She would never have given him a kick in the privates as the other maids did. As I directed them to do.

"But her last words to me? Full of sorrow. She talked of Adam. 'He's never going to come for me, is he, Enid? I'm going to throw myself off the roof and then he'll be sorry.'

"I told her to hold on—Adam would be down from Cambridge any minute. He'd sort things out for her. He was a good lad, Adam, and he'd understand if anyone did. Only eighteen at the time but a big husky lad with a good head on him and a sense of . . . would 'righteousness' sound old-fashioned? He'd take whoever had wronged her and beat him to a pulp."

"She wasn't reassured?"

"No. I'd said the wrong thing, judging by her outburst. 'No, he mustn't! He couldn't! We'd all of us suffer for it!' She was genuinely aghast."

"That's when the penny dropped?"

"Yes. The only man who could make the whole staff suffer was: the master."

"Sir Sidney up to his old tricks?"

"With his wife pregnant again, we wouldn't have been surprised. I charged Phoebe with my suspicions. She denied it with such amazement and horror I could only believe she was telling the truth."

"Tinkle, tinkle went the second penny?" Joe suggested.

Enid Bolton nodded. "James! He was such a *lad*! Firing off his pop gun and mooching about the place looking unhappy. All long limbs and spots. But then I thought: he's actually nearly the same age as Phoebe. I asked her."

"And she admitted it?"

"Yes. She hadn't feared him or what he was capable of, you see. She did out his room in the morning, turned down his sheets at night . . . and there was I, juggling the duties, carefully distancing her from his *father*'s lair! She went out into the woods with him on her afternoon off, helping him with his traps. Playtime, I'm sure she thought was what was going on. She liked company her own age who could make her laugh. And James Truelove has always been able to make a girl laugh. His little sisters adored him—still do. I think Phoebe was genuinely fond of him. That's always been his gift. From the day he was born, he's expected to be loved."

"They were probably observed by Goodfellow, the resident snake-in-the-grass."

"Another opportunity for blackmail and extortion. Unto the next generation."

Joe asked the next question with care: "Do you think James Truelove drowned her in the moat?"

"No. I believe she was killed. Deliberately held under. But not by James. I don't make this assertion on a basis of character. I was the one who laid out her body, you see, sir." The calm features seemed suddenly to crumple in sorrow. "She had no one else. Drunken mother, father left home years before. She looked on me as family—her auntie perhaps. I wasn't going to leave her to the ministrations of frightful old Bella in the village with her dirty fingernails."

"No police to take charge?"

"Not in those days. A quick resolution was all everybody wanted. Sir Sidney made all the arrangements. Even the Chief Constable did as he was told by Sir Sidney."

"What did you notice about the state of the body?"

"That she was about three months pregnant and just beginning to show. It was the ankles that told me what I wanted to know. There was a circlet of bruises where no bruising should have been. He'd grabbed her by the ankles and yanked them upwards, pushing her face under the water."

"He?"

"Goodfellow, of course. He had the gall to say he'd found her body. They tell me it's often the one who discovers the crime who did it. But you will know better than I. One of the footmen was crossing the drawbridge at the time he raised the alarm. Albert could swim and he leapt in and helped Goodfellow pull her out."

"Either one of them could have tugged her by the ankles to draw her to the side?"

"I checked. I asked the footman to show me exactly how they'd handled the body. No one touched her ankles. Albert confided that he could have sworn that Goodfellow was already wet before he jumped in."

Joe let out a sound like a kettle coming to the boil. "Sheeesh! Even Inspector Lestrade would have sorted this one out in ten minutes! If he'd been alerted!" He calmed himself to ask, "Did you find anything unusual when you tidied out her room?"

"You assume—rightly—that I took responsibility for doing that myself. Yes, I did. I found a ten-pound money order in her drawer. Six months' wages! Only one way she could have come by such a sum, and one purpose. I worked it out. I said nothing. Just gave it to the Reverend Easterby for the church orphanage."

"Which brings me back to my original question, Mrs. Bolton. Saying nothing?"

Anger flashed and the features were suddenly stern again. "Why don't you answer your own impertinent questions? You seem to have all the answers you want stuffed up your sleeve!

You're not interested in hearing what I have to say. You just want me to confirm your suspicions."

Joe flinched and waited in silence.

"I'm a good person, Commissioner. I try my best always to think of others and not my own personal satisfaction. I think things through. I'm sure you do too and know what I'm about to say. It would have been easy to shout and point accusing fingers and call upon the police, the vicar, Sir Sidney. The best I could have hoped for was that I should be believed. And that would have brought about the very worst reaction. If Adam Hunnybun had found out for certain that James had ruined the girl he loved, retribution would have followed. That's the sort of man he is. No one crosses Adam. He would have killed James *and* Goodfellow, handed himself in, been found guilty and gone to the gallows smiling. The Trueloves would have been publicly disgraced by association. The family was on its uppers at the time. An event of this nature would have sunk the boat. A whole household of servants as well as owners would have been cut loose to seek work elsewhere in a county that could offer them none. Farms and great houses were being sold off, businesses going bankrupt, staff being turned off the land every day. Not as bad as things are today, but bad enough. I looked about me and decided that these were people and this was a situation worth saving. I swallowed my outrage, my pride, even my craving for justice and kept silent. Phoebe would have understood."

"What were your feelings when Mr. Styles gave you the news that the villain had shot his own head off?"

"Relief and gratitude, followed by guilt that I should have such unchristian feelings. But I don't wallow in vengeance. I agree with the poet Juvenal, who tells us that revenge is the pleasure of a tiny and feeble mind. A rather unexpected sentiment for a Roman but he has many wise things to say. In my long years, I've never observed that satisfaction in revenge grows with time. It diminishes over the years, like all painful emotions, to an embarrassing twinge of memory. A momentary dyspepsia of the spirit. I get on with life, sir. Doing my best for the family and my fellows. Retribution I leave to a Higher Authority who is not obliged to suffer the consequences here below."

Joe watched as she put the remaining flowers in place, making a few adjustments to the display. The craving for revenge may have been blunted by time with the housekeeper but love and concern for the wronged was shining as bright as ever, he reckoned. He looked with understanding at the sad, wise face and found that he had, unconsciously, repeated Hunnyton's gesture at the graveside, placing the palm of his hand flat to the mound of earth that covered Phoebe and her child. Making contact. Making some sort of a vow.

"Tell me, Mrs. Bolton," he said in a tone he might have used to address the goddess of wisdom at her altar, "are people born with the seeds of evil in their souls? Is it their inborn qualities that push them into dark acts? Are they ever open to the influences of priests or policemen? Are the Reverend Easterby and I struggling against impossible forces of Nature?"

Her eyes widened, her lips quivered. "Lord! You don't want to know much, do you! Whatever's next? How do I get my strawberry jam to set?"

Sobered by Joe's crestfallen expression, Mrs. Bolton added quietly: "We all have inner qualities that dispose us towards good or evil to some degree. But sometimes—I'd say, most times—it's external, social or family reasons, that push a man or a woman to kill. The most admirable of us will wield a gun or a knife in defence of—or for the promotion of—his nearest and dearest or his country. You have been a soldier. You of all men understand that. As a policeman, you have chosen to continue to follow in the trails of violence and lawlessness. Seeking to understand? Or fascinated by it? You know the answer, Commissioner."

"Lemon pips!"

"I beg your pardon?"

"The answer to your question. My mother swears by lemon pips. Something to do with pectin I believe. She makes the best-set jam north of the Border. You see, I've guessed your secret, Mrs. B."

Joe got to his feet and held out a hand. She rose, fighting back a smile, took the arm he offered and with the sound of the five-minute bell pealing about their heads, they made their way down to the church where some unseen organist was launching lustily into "Onward Christian Soldiers."

LEAVING MRS. BOLTON in the company of friends from the village, Joe turned and headed off by himself into the woods. It was to be a short service and he guessed he could count on an hour's freedom to roam before the company began to gather for the horse ceremony. One murder had been satisfactorily solved that morning and he was confident he could in a few minutes have in his pocket the evidence that would make it two.

A further hour and some time alone with Mrs. Bolton's household record books and he would have the third and the most puzzling at his fingertips. The housekeeper had placed her accounts and day-book in front of him and invited him to inspect them. A distracting bluff? A gesture of absolute honesty? Or was this complicated woman covertly drawing his attention to something he ought to know? Joe decided to time his visit to the housekeeper's room to coincide with one of her regular absences.

Joe sneaked through the trees, retracing the steps he'd taken when he'd trotted back to the hall in the sights of an unknown gunman earlier that morning. A gunman who was still on the loose.

No use looking for the spent cartridge, he decided. The gunman would have meticulously picked up after himself. But Joe's essential piece of evidence was in a perfectly safe place. He found the large-leaved lime tree again, noting with relief that the smooth bole was obligingly spoked at intervals by sturdy branches. A climb a five-year-old could have managed. He took out his pocketknife and thumbed the blade out ready. In three hauls he was up the tree and digging out the bullet. A swift examination of the crumpled metal made him smile with satisfaction.

"You bugger!" he breathed. "Got you!"

CHAPTER 21

Cecily's patience ran out on the stroke of twelve. With a snort of exasperation she turned to Joe. "Blow the whistle, Joe! The villagers and the horses were here on time and I won't keep the children in suspense a moment longer."

Joe nodded and strode over to Flowerdew to give the signal for the start of the parade. Cecily had judged the moment well, he reckoned. The crowd was still keyed-up and good-humoured but a few minutes more and they would become restive. The children were eager for the maypole dancing and the buns and lemonade refreshments the Hall had laid out for them but, above all, they were anxious to see the horses appear. Most of them had a baby brother or sister, born in the last twelve months, being held ready by their mothers. If one of the babies cried during the pre-sentation, Cecily had explained, its screams would be greeted with indulgent laughter but also a secret shame for the older siblings who risked being plagued with playground taunts of: "Who's little brother's a cowardy custard, then?"

"Children can be so cruel," she commented.

The village boasted an ex–army trumpeter and a drummer of some skill. Between them they managed to alert and silence the crowd and give a military flavour to the occasion. The horses played their part admirably, aware that they were the centre of attention. These were no longer plough horses with bent heads and straining limbs; they stepped forward proudly onto the lawn, two by two, flanks gleaming in the midday sun, manes and tails bright with ribbons, bells tinkling. Did they know that—for this moment—they were the finest animals in creation? Sentimentally, Joe thought so and he was quite certain it had occurred to them. The crowd let out claps and cheers and gasps of admiration. Even Cecily dabbed quickly at her eyes with a lace handkerchief.

A bad moment for a cortège of cars to appear in the distance. The Rolls and the Bentley from London came purring on up the drive. Ancient and modern vying for attention. Cecily launched a hunting-field oath and seemed uncharacteristically perplexed.

"Leave the horses to Flowerdew," Joe advised, "and the motors to me."

He exchanged a signal with the head horseman, who continued with his choreography. The horses lined up, heads to the crowd, scarcely needing the guidance of their young grooms. The mothers, dressed in their Sunday best frocks, lined up also, babies in shawls held in their arms or up on their shoulders. Waiting.

Joe moved forward to greet the newcomers, telling the other guests with a gesture to remain where they were and enjoy the ceremony. He brought both cars to a halt under the porte-cochère and said briskly, "Sir James. Welcome. You're just in time. We're about to start the presentation."

The man's aplomb was astonishing, Joe thought. If he was surprised to find Joe in charge, he showed no sign of it. After a discreet nod, he herded his party out of the cars and formed them up into a group.

"Carry on, Sandilands. Sorry we're late. We stopped and took a break some miles away. Spent too long at the Angel in Bury but at least none of us needs to dash off indoors. Introductions later. Horses come first." His eye ranged, proud and proprietorial, along the line of Suffolks. "A fine display this year. Four of these are new but you'd never guess it."

The trumpet and drums, the children and the babies all fell silent and the procession began. One by one, the mothers walked the line of the horses, led by Mr. Styles, who seemed to be performing a stately introduction.

"This is Mrs. Reynolds and her son, Samuel," Joe heard him say.

"And this is his namesake horse, Sammy also," Flowerdew responded, indicating the first horse in the line-up. There was utter silence from the crowd but a series of squeaks and murmurs fluttered up from the newly arrived guests behind Joe as the baby was held with a confident smile by its mother right up to the muzzle of the great horse. The baby was tiny, the horse had a head with all the rounded bulk of a butter-churn. Even Joe tensed and swallowed nervously.

"Sammy, meet Sammy," the mother said with a giggle. She held her baby steadily while the saucer-sized inquisitive nostrils descended on the child. The horse snorted gently and with its grey-velvet lower lip nibbled delicately at the hand the baby was holding out to it. "Good old 'oss!" the mother commented and she scratched his nose and passed on with her gurgling child down the line.

Mrs. Bedford's William met William and so on until the corresponding names gave out. Then Baby Frank met Joker and Baby Poppy met Blossom, or was it the other way around? No baby cried. No horse showed its yellow teeth. As the last child was carried to safety, a female sigh of relief escaped from someone in Truelove's party. Not from the dark-haired beauty in the yellow dress, Joe thought. A sideways glance had shown Dorcas Joliffe, enraptured, standing next to Truelove and smiling at the spectacle. She of all people would have understood that the babies were in no danger from these gentle beasts. Joe looked away quickly.

The completion of the ceremony, which Joe guessed had deep roots going back to the tribes of horse-rearing Celts, was the signal for a party to break out. The horses were led off into the freshly mown meadow to offer a little bareback riding by the older boys. Some bold ones, apprentice grooms, Joe guessed, performed circus tricks, standing and pirouetting on the horses' broad backs. Three donkeys and a pair of elderly ponies made an appearance to entertain the younger children. Joe was surprised, this being the Sabbath, to hear the sudden blare of an old-fashioned wind-up gramophone. But then, this was non-conformist Suffolk, their vicar was not only present but turning the handle, and this was Midsummer, when a little madness was expected. A dozen children formed themselves into an impromptu chorus line and galloped about to the sound of 'Light Cavalry.'

Looking on, Joe's mind was suddenly filled with the image of his young son. Already a useful horseman, Jackie would have overcome his shyness and joined in the fun, Joe hoped. He turned with a sigh from the sunlit innocence of the scene, catching a wistfulness chiming with his own in the eyes of Cecily. She too was looking with the fondness of old age at the romping children. All from the village. No contribution from the empty nest at the Hall. She caught his gaze on her and, understanding, gave him a wry smile.

Hanging back, Joe braced himself to observe and then meet Truelove's guests. He thanked Lily silently once more for her phone call. All three were expected by him and he had even had time enough to calculate reasons for their appearance. None he could come up with was edifying.

From her manner, Cecily could well have been expecting these very guests with keen anticipation for a month.

"Mama, may I present Mr. Guy Despond and his daughter, Miss Despond: Dorothy. The Desponds are over on a visit from New York. Miss Joliffe you will remember, of course . . ." Truelove went through the many introductions with flawless manners and easy good humour.

Guy Despond, art dealer extraordinaire and cosmopolitan charmer, was suave and eager to enthuse about the horses. He was ready for any rural challenge, clad as he was in tweed knickerbockers, matching jacket, flat peaked cap and brogues. The man had taken over-enthusiastic advice from a Savile Row tailor, Joe thought. Or the Prince of Wales.

Daughter Dorothy was less set on being charming. She had what Joe's mother would have called a knowing eye—a pair of them, in a fetching shade of pale grey, and they were ranging over everything from Lady Cecily's pearls to the butler's buttons. Her hair was thick and a very pretty light brown. With the help of a stout straw hat, the expensive marcel wave had survived the journey in an open Bentley very well. Her emerald green suit was exactly what a rich young lady with access to the salons and modern style of New York and Paris would have chosen to wear for an outing to the country. Serviceable, unrestricting and eye-catching. Her manner was reserved but not unfriendly.

As the new guests moved off into the house, guided by Styles and a phalanx of footmen, Cecily edged close to Joe, raised her eyebrows and hissed, "Heavens! If I'd had warning of this I'd have had the Canalettos nailed down!"

"I understand the gentleman to be a most welcome and congenial guest at the grandest houses in the land, your ladyship," Joe said smoothly.

She grunted. "The fellow's as rich as Croesus. Nothing wrong with that but they say he's got the instincts of a magpie. Nothing precious is safe from a keenly judged offer if it catches his collector's eye."

"Will you require me to count the dessert spoons before he leaves, madam?" Joe asked in the tone of a stage butler.

"Not funny, Joe! A visit from that man can leave one of your grand houses looking as though a plague of locusts has blown through. I have a delicious little Lancret over in the Dower House . . . a Monet . . . a Seurat . . . Can I be certain that they are safe from his attentions? He's a harbinger of doom and decay, Joe. The last step before the bailiffs are called in, for some. My friend Miranda Carstairs sold him her great-grandmama by Reynolds one week and the next she was calling in the Removers. Why is he here? What can James be thinking of?"

Cecily's agitation was palpable. Joe set out to calm her. "I rather think you should look elsewhere for a reason for this visit. A chat with the delightful *Miss* Despond may reveal a completely different motivation," Joe suggested blandly.

Cecily stared at him in astonishment. "You don't mean . . . ?"

"A very eligible young lady, I understand from my reading of the *Tatler*. A girl with one or two broken engagements behind her on both sides of the ocean and in Europe. 'Choosy' is the word normally associated with her if you're her friend, 'fickle' if you're a disappointed suitor. Indeed, it's rumoured that the editor of the *Times* keeps a few inches of the 'Forthcoming Marriages' column in reserve in every edition to enable him to respond swiftly to Miss Despond's changes of plan." Joe sent up a silent prayer of thanks to his omniscient newshound friend, Cyril Tate, from whom he now took his script: "Since her mother's death, Dorothy has travelled constantly with her father in the very highest circles, mingling with the cream of rich, art-loving society," he confided. "She's twenty-five and presently unattached."

This exhausted Joe's stock of knowledge but it had been enough. He watched conflicting emotions chase each other across Cecily's expressive features. Astonishment, alarm and, finally, intrigue.

"Oh, my goodness! I say—do you really think there may be something going on?" Followed by a dismissive, "Surely not?

There are wealthier gentlemen about in London and certainly more illustrious titles to be had, if that's what she's after."

"But not, perhaps, titles attached to such a personable and relatively young man. Idle, elderly earls—two a penny—but an attractive man with an interesting employment and a considerable future?" Lord! What part was he playing now? Marriage broker?

Cecily was all ears and interest. "Yes, indeed. My son, who is all that you say, takes a pride in declaring that he is not a layabout but a working man."

"A situation which Dorothy is very familiar with. Her father and brothers are all busy bees who know how to keep the hives well stocked."

"You have a devious mind, Joe Sandilands. I begin to see the possibilities. But—gracious!—this is hardly the moment for James to choose to bring along his . . . his . . . raggle-taggle student, the Joliffe woman? Those two were sharing the back seat of the Rolls for sixty miles! What can they possibly have found to say to each other? What must Miss Despond think?"

"Oh, I don't know . . . Miss Joliffe is of an artistic family with many friends at—shall we say?—the business end of the art world. They actually apply paint to canvas. I dare say she was able to give Miss Despond insights into Pablo Picasso's philosophy of art— she is reputed to own one or two of his early works. I noticed the two ladies chose to walk arm in arm into the hall in a companion-able way."

"Mmm . . . Whatever else, you seem to understand that Dor-cas Joliffe is not stupid. I know she has plans of her own for James, plans in which a wealthy rival does not feature. A dangerous little creature! It may suit her well to snuggle in close with a chal-lenger. Shall I ask Styles to mount a guard over Miss Despond while she's under our roof?"

"Leave it to me. Bodyguarding is something I'm trained for, your ladyship," Joe said. "The first thing is to plan ahead—never wait for the exchange of fire. Go straight for the enemy as soon as identified, disarm and incapacitate him. I'll go and renew acquaintance with Miss Joliffe—we have met before on a few occasions. I'll try to ascertain whether her intentions are peaceable."

He drifted into the hall where the guests were being allocated footmen and maids to take them to their rooms. Stepping forward, he said, "Thank you, Norman, I'll take Miss Joliffe upstairs. The Lilac Room was it?"

He grabbed Dorcas's bag and led the way upstairs to the guest room halfway along the corridor.

"Rather more suitable accommodation than last time, I think you'll find," he said, showing her inside and closing the door. "Smaller than the Old Nursery and not so versatile but I'm sure you won't mind that." She kept her distance, white-faced and silent. Joe put up an ironic hand, as if to ward off an advance. "No, don't consider giving me a hug, Dorcas. Apart from Truelove, who treats me as your godfather or something—well, he thinks whatever you've told him to think—it's not generally known that we have a relationship of any kind. Let it stay that way. I'm working. Trying to solve three unlawful killings for one of which you are in the frame. Yes, I'm afraid there are those in this house who would very much like to put the blame for the death of Lady Truelove on you. They see you as an unimportant figure, unconnected and dispensable. They wait to see you being carted off by me to the Yard in cuffs, the arrest photographed by a news magnate who has a convenient camera to hand and a convenient hand to operate it. You may have caught a glimpse of the McIvers' maid photographing the horse parade? Avoid her lens. Mungo McIver, I believe, is intent on reinstating the reputation of the Minister for Reform in the corridors of Westminster."

"Westminster?" she asked sharply.

"The House. Where a strong cross-party faction sees him as the saviour of British politics. The only man with the will and ability to recognise and counter the threat of European aggression. He's a man whose reputation must be protected at all cost."

"A man particularly popular with a coterie of industrialists in the Midlands whose factories are poised to roll out ever more armament, I think you once told me, Joe. Did you know that's how Lavinia's father makes his millions? He provided the where-withal to take on the Kaiser in the last lot. If Herr Hitler or the Russians were to turn nasty, he'd be a very busy man again."

"It had occurred to me. Poor, generous old Papa must be a little exercised by the rumours that his son-in-law has bumped off his daughter. I do wonder what his next step might be? Denunciation? Or support and a swift crushing of the rumours by some means or other? Move an innocent pawn into the front line to take the rap? I won't let that happen! Tread carefully, Dorcas. Better if we keep our distance from each other, and don't give them an opportunity to cry collusion, I think."

"Joe! Supercilious know-it-all! I don't need your collusion, thanks! I had nothing to do with that woman's self-inflicted death, neither did James and that's what I'm doing back here. I've come to help him prove it!"

"I wonder what persuasive measures he employed to convince you it would be a good idea to revisit the scene of the crime? What did he offer you, Dorcas?" Joe's voice was heavy with hurt and suspicion.

"You don't imagine I *want* to be here, do you? I've heard the rumours circulating against James. They've been orchestrated, you know. You've got that much right. Someone wants James discred-ited or even behind bars. Someone may even have arranged Lavinia's death solely for that purpose. Smacked her on the head with a horseshoe? It would have been easy enough to arrange. I could have done it myself. I'm grieved for James—none of it was his fault and he's got troubles enough without all this sinister back-stabbing."

"So—you're here to do a little clearing of names? Sleuthing again, Dorcas?" Joe was relieved and almost amused.

"Not any longer apparently! I hadn't expected to find Scotland Yard in residence! You know your presence here confirms everyone's darkest suspicions? A policeman of your standing doesn't turn up to investigate an accident. You've muddied the waters and now, with people on their guard, I shall never get at the truth. James's wife was hateful and she's made poor James's life a misery. She lived in a slough of unhappiness and was determined that everyone close to her should join her in it. I'm glad she's dead." She concluded her tirade with a defiant, "*We're* glad she's dead."

"I could wish you hadn't lied to me about your part in all this," he said stiffly.

"So do I. I'm sorry. I should have known better than to tell you I was miles away at the time—you always find things out. I *was* here that night. We thought the least fuss, the soonest mended. No point in involving others. After all—it was her choice to confront the horse. A thoughtless, suicidally idiotic thing to do. She knew the animal was dangerous, Joe. She took me on a hike round the estate the day before." Dorcas cringed at the memory. "We inspected the stables but didn't go near—what was his name?"

"Lucifer."

"She told me he'd almost killed two of the grooms and was about to be put down by the vet. A huge waste of money, Lavinia reckoned. I asked her how many guineas. No idea! She knew nothing of the cost of things—just assumed she was paying the bills. James was to blame, of course, as the stallion had been his selection. But she intended to save him from his folly."

She fell silent, seemingly wondering if she had said too much.

Joe kept her focussed, sure that he was getting close to whatever had triggered the unlikely death. "How did she propose to do that? Tell me exactly, Dorcas."

"She claimed she had the skill to tame the brute. 'I'll have him eating out of my hand and following me about like Mary's little lamb, you'll see!' she bragged. Then, sneakily, she slipped in the suggestion she'd been working towards. Her real plan. 'Unless, of course, Dorcas, you'd like to have the honour? Here's a wonderful chance to show off those skills with animals everyone—including James—claims that you have. I dare you, Dorcas Joliffe, to parade the stallion in front of the breakfast crowd tomorrow morning, trotting at your heels like a good hound. I dare you!' She said the words again!"

Joe grimaced, picturing Dorcas's embarrassment at the juvenile challenge. "Lord! What on earth did you say?"

"I'm afraid I made a bad situation worse. I spoke my mind. I said the last dare I accepted had been twelve years ago. It had resulted in a smacked bottom and a week's gating from my grandmother. A punishment which vastly outweighed the offence. But it taught me a useful lesson. Dares are set by callous schemers to trap the naive. I told her to grow up."

"Thus sealing the wretched woman's fate." Joe sighed.

"Don't be silly! She sealed her own fate! Are you deliberately missing the point? It was *she* who planned *my* death or injury. I thought you'd have managed to work that much out! She was setting me up for a lethal encounter with that animal."

"That animal? Are you telling me you couldn't have worked your magic with him? Was Lavinia's suspicion right? Have you been deceiving me all these years?"

A scornful smile greeted his lightly delivered question. "You and many others. But I never made the mistake of deceiving myself, Joe. I don't enter into negotiations with a rabid dog or a horse that's put two grooms in hospital. There was something about the whole business with this Lucifer that bothered me. Joe, I never set eyes on him so my opinion is probably worth little but it all sounded a bit strange to me. James couldn't understand it either. The horse had an impeccable pedigree and he'd personally checked him over. James knows his horses. Suffolks are good-tempered beasts. Well, we all saw them nibbling babies with great good humour at the parade."

"Good-tempered until someone abrades the soft tissue at the edges of the mouth using the emery board from a box of matches or the serrated edge of a half crown. Something you might expect to find in any man's pocket."

Dorcas gasped. "How cruel! That's malice aforethought, isn't it? Who would do that?"

"Malice is the right word exactly. It was done by someone who had no feeling for the horse and who had a grudge against its owner. Are you aware of a man living and working on the estate who had good reason to feel aggrieved? The Green Man?" Joe lifted an eyebrow, watching her reactions.

"Oh, him! The rat-catcher! Creepy man! He was watching me and Lavinia as we did the tour. She didn't seem to mind—she even waved at him. I can't imagine why James puts up with him. He told me he'd given him notice to leave . . . Oh! There you are! That's the reason, isn't it? What are you waiting for, Joe? Go out and bring him in!"

"Listen, Dorcas. Sit down. I'll make this quick."

She listened intently as he told her of Adelaide Hartest's evidence and sketched out a ruthlessly edited version of Goodfellow's death. He made no mention of the letter or of Phoebe Pilgrim. He'd leave James Truelove to tell his own tale.

The old Dorcas was with him again as she frowned with concentration and responded with quick understanding. "Stoat's liver, you say? Yes. That would do it. But you're wrong, Joe—you don't have to be a Horseman to know that. The gypsies have the knowledge too. But they don't bother to wrap it up in cat's urine, rabbit's blood and toad bone—all that's just so much abracadabra. Whatever else, it's not magic! No—first catch your stoat! That's the vital bit. Goodfellow! He styled himself 'gamekeeper' you know. He shot birds and he trapped vermin. The kind who enjoys killing creatures. I saw a row of pathetic little corpses he'd caught and mounted on osier spikes along the edge of the wood where it meets the wheat field. Out in the open. Anyone able to identify a stoat could have helped himself and no one would ever have noticed."

"It's chilling to hear you say so, Dorcas." Again, Joe was assailed by a thought he had instantly to suppress. He forged on: "But someone would then need to be close enough to Lavinia to persuade her—or trick her—into using the horse bate—substance B, let's call it—instead of the attractant."

"Or someone could have entered her room during the night and simply exchanged samples. Well, you can eliminate James—he chose to spend the night over in the Dower House where his mother lives. He wasn't creeping about the corridors with his pockets full of rotting livers."

"I had wondered why he should choose that particular night to distance himself from his wife's room," Joe invited a comment. "Sounds very like someone setting up an alibi to me."

Again the challenge in her eye as she spoke: "You're right. It was. But you have the wrong reason. It was a deliberate choice. To avert any suspicion of hanky-panky with an unaccompanied female guest. Me. You know what these large households are like for gossip. But you can eliminate me as well. I never left the Old Nursery where the witch had stuck me for the night. It's right over the other side. I would have had to walk miles of corridor and probably got lost en route looking for Lavinia's room. It's obvious, isn't it? Are you losing your grip, Joe? Her maid did it. Quiet little thing but well-spoken. Her name's Grace. Why don't you just ask her? It was probably a half-baked reprisal for some ticking-off, some fancied slight or, at best, a hideous misunderstanding. Being maid to Lavinia would give anyone a hundred reasons for wishing her ill. She's done the world a favour—don't be hard on her. Put on your stern face and she'll come clean. Then we can all go back to London and get on with our lives."

Joe stared at Dorcas as though seeing her for the first time. Was this the girl he'd worried about for seven years? His charge? His delightful but tormenting responsibility? A pawn, casually pushing another pawn forward into the firing line? The young woman facing him was confident, argumentative and unyielding. She needed no help. She was flying by herself. She was leaving Joe behind, floundering in her slipstream, without a backward glance.

"And you can produce independent confirmation of your whereabouts during the crucial hours?" he asked with deceptive mildness.

A flash of scorn for his policeman's phrasing cut him to the quick.

"I wouldn't like to think I had to," she said, turning away from him dismissively.

"Protecting Master Alex? Or is he protecting you? What sort of arrangement have you come to, the pair of you?"

"How on earth do you . . . ?"

"I'm a detective. I've been detecting. I know that you spent the night of the murder holed up in the Old Nursery with Alexander. He came along at one o'clock, straight after snooker, still in evening dress, seeking admittance. You let him in and locked the door. Read him a bedtime story perhaps and he emerged at dawn to creep back to his own quarters."

"Joe, you know too much and understand too little. Leave me now."

"I understand everything. Well, nearly everything. I can't be certain which particular story you told him but everything else."

Dorcas looked up at him, shocked eyes seeking to read his mind.

"Young Alex was confused," Joe went on constructing his theory, "at odds with his surroundings, targeted by older, successful—and critical—male guests, falling over themselves to give him the fatherly advice he so clearly lacked. It can't be easy being the heir-but-one. The spare wheel, the afterthought who shows himself unsuited to modern life. Alex did what he's been known to do before when squashed and belittled. He stumbled along here to seek the safety of his familiar old nursery, his own bed, the one he used before life got too much for him. Sadly there was no longer a comforting nanny in residence to make it all better. Just a fellow victim of the Truelove arrogance. He must have been quite surprised on this occasion to find you occupying it, thanks to a spiteful ploy of Lavinia's."

"You're guessing all this."

"No. Knowledge of you and knowledge of him helps me to stitch together more solid evidence from Rose, the upper floor maid. Very observant girl. She noticed that both beds had been slept in. Your guest bed and the nursery bed. Alex's old bed had golden hairs on the pillow. Yours had dark ones. There was no trace of any other . . . um . . . intimacy, as far as Rosie could make out, and she's got a seeing eye for these things."

The anger was heating in Dorcas's eyes. She curled her fingers into fists and Joe feared she might launch herself at him in fury. With a mighty effort at control she finally spoke. "It was 'The Happy Prince,'" she said.

"What was that?"

"The story he asked me to read him. By Oscar Wilde. Since we're dotting the i's, crossing the t's and attributing the hairs. Alex sees himself as the young hero. It all ends in death and disaster. I'm sure you know it."

"There once was the statue of a rich young prince who had never experienced true happiness?" Joe remembered. "That one? Not one of my favourites."

"Yes. The Prince asked a passing swallow to take the ruby from his sword hilt, the sapphires from his eyes and the gold-leaf from his body to give to the poor."

"We all have our fantasies," Joe said, uncertainly. "I was Rob Roy for many a year."

"Well it's more than a fantasy for Alex. He's giving up everything to go off, doubtless in sandals, begging bowl in hand, to Africa to try to do some good or find his paradise."

"Oh, dear. That may not be the best thing for Africa. Couldn't you talk him out of it?"

"Arrogant toss pot! I encouraged him. There's nothing for him here in Suffolk!"

"Watch it, Dorcas! The helpful swallow died too, as far as I remember."

"Leave me now, Joe. I'll talk to you when we're back in Surrey. If I can go on dodging your suspicions and you let me get that far, that is."

Unsure of himself and doubly unsure of her, Joe started to do as she asked. He paused at the door and looked back at her. Left to herself, she suddenly seemed small and dejected, a girl unhappy and out of place. Still his responsibility? No longer, he felt. It hadn't escaped him—her frequent and unconscious use of "we" instead of "I." But, now, the second person making up the pronoun was not Joe Sandilands. It was to Truelove she looked for support; his needs were paramount. Joe stopped his thoughts right there. If the details he'd gleaned from his examination of the household and estate records in Mrs. Bolton's office had told him anything, it had sounded a warning that Dorcas must be carried, kicking and screaming if necessary, out of Truelove's orbit as soon as he could manage it. Joe couldn't leave her in this troubled house surrounded by these scheming people. He knew what he had to say.

"I've got a car on hand, Dorcas. Why don't we grab our bags and just make a run for it? We could be back at Lydia's in time for supper." He was about to add a joking reference to cherry ice cream but remembered Adelaide Hartest's advice to avoid nostalgia. "I don't like or trust any of these people you're involved with. I believe they wish you harm and I'm going to take you, by the scruff of your neck if you make a fuss, right away from here. We could do what I know you've always wanted to do—chase about the Continent hunting down your French family. We can hire an open-topped car and be on the road to Provence in no time." Too late, he realised that it was nostalgia that had him by the throat and was shaking desperate clichés from him. "The warm south, pitchers of red wine, cicadas, violet evening skies, battlements if you hanker for them still—I know just the battlements. We'll meet up with your painter friends . . . fast-talking rogues—poseurs the lot of them—but entertaining poseurs. They make you laugh, Dorcas. It's a long time since I heard you laugh. A smile would be a start . . ."

A smile would have triggered it. Even a weak and watery one would have justified a lunge towards her. He'd have sunk to his knees and seized her hands. He'd have thrown away his uncertainty, his reserve, and blurted that this time they would travel with a marriage license and to hell with everything else.

She looked back at him stonily, unable to respond to his emotion.

Joe controlled his desperation and said more soberly, "We've no worthy part to play here, Dorcas, you and I."

At last a smile but the comment that accompanied it was barbed. "Part? I thought you were playing Major Domo perfectly, Joe. How ever would we manage without you?"

Disgust with himself and anger with Dorcas provoked a brusque response. "Time, perhaps, to let you find out!" He began to walk to the door.

A stifled gasp made him look back. The familiar face was wearing an unfamiliar expression—saddened and disbelieving.

But it was the expression of a girl who's just been given the news that her favourite dog has to be put down, Joe judged, distressing enough, but hardly the emotion of a girl whose lover is leaving.

They stared at each other in silence for an uncomfortable moment as seven years of intimacy crumbled between them. Joe resisted the urge to stride back and seize her in a comforting hug. This girl, suddenly a stranger, might well have screamed for help. He began to speak to her urgently, confidingly, appealing to a quality he knew she still possessed: her enquiring intelligence.

"Listen Dorcas! You've always been my equal in 'sleuthing' as you call it. Join me in one last combined effort will you? Working together, we can flush out the person really responsible for Lavinia's death. You do want to know, don't you? You *have* to know!" He waited for her reluctant nod before he continued. "It will involve trickery, lies, floods of tears and possibly fisticuffs. How about it? What do you say?"

"Not sure about the tears, but all the rest I can manage," she said dubiously. "And I'll do anything I can to clear James's name. I told you—that's why I've come back here to this terrible place. I would much rather have worked it out for myself without benefit of your conjuring tricks but . . . Oh, go on, Joe."

Joe went on, eager but uncertain, his plan evolving as he talked. It sounded ridiculous to his ears but Dorcas began suddenly to smile and the smile widened. "Same old Joe!" she said. "Still the Fusilier! If in doubt stage a controlled explosion!"

Finally: "It'll never work. And, if it does, you'll be thrown out of whatever clubs you're still a member of. You'll lose your job and they'll cut off your buttons with a ceremonial sabre."

"Lucky if it's just my buttons," he said, managing a rueful grin.

CHAPTER 22

All he could do was get on with his job. Finish, point an accusing finger, pose for the camera and leave. He'd had enough. In fact he rather thought he'd talked himself into a solitary dash down into France, where he'd always found a balm for his emotional abrasions. Just one more piece of evidence and he could be reasonably sure he knew who had tricked Lavinia Truelove into walking into her death in the stable.

All was quiet in the telephone room. Sunday lunch time in the outside world. He was surprised there was even an operator on duty.

"A trunk call please, Miss, to a London number ... Julia! Oh, I'm so sorry to bother you on a—"

"Joe! At last! Ralph was just wondering where you'd got to. Here he comes. Don't keep him talking—he was just about to carve the leg of lamb and we've got my mother-in-law for lunch."

There was a clunk as Superintendent Cottingham seized the telephone. "I managed! Not easy—you know what these high-falutin lawyers are like. Upshot is—no surprises. Lavinia Truelove's last will and testament turns out to have been her first and only will and testament. Drawn up at the time of her marriage, on lines agreed by her father, it has remained gathering dust on a shelf, unaltered since the day she signed it. No attempt was ever made to look at it again. She retained control of what I'll call her 'resources'—sounds more modern than 'marriage settlement.'"

"These resources, Ralph? Any indication . . . ?"

"I tried to find out how much we were contemplating. I gave their discreet Mr. Brewer a choice of 'plentiful/comfortable/ adequate.' He picked 'plentiful.' Throughout her married life she spent freely, to the advantage of the Truelove estate, apparently. Nothing we didn't know in all this. No dramatic changes in her will of the kind we favour, like—all to my lover, Vicenzo, the second footman, or to Pets' Paradise, or the Communist Party. Nothing of the sort. 'Everything of which I die possessed' etcetera goes to husband, James. Full stop."

"So James finds himself in undisputed sole possession of the plentiful resources. Hmm . . . Ah, well. Rather dashes one of my theories to the ground. I've been going through the account books. All the same—that's something we needed to know. Another piece of the jigsaw. One more piece of blue sky but the picture builds."

Joe must have sounded despondent. Ralph hurried on, in a voice trying to suppress a triumphant chortle: "But there is something more. Perhaps even the four corner pieces? Something old Brewer let slip right at the end when he shouldn't have. Something in response to a remark I made with a dash of low cunning as I thanked him and signed off. That's when pompous prats let their defences down, I find. Right when they think they're getting shot of you and you've sportingly admitted defeat. That's the moment! What I do is think of my best judgement on the situation and then I completely reverse it, however ludicrous it may seem. I make a throw-away remark on these lines, assuming the bloke I'm conning is in the know, as am I."

"I think I follow. Not trying some mind trick out on *me* are you, Ralph?"

"Never! Usually I get a stunned silence while they work it out and the length of that can be revealing. Other times I get an outraged denial and correction. Even better. But just occasionally, I get a wondering agreement and a spluttering: 'Now how the devil did you know that? Our Police are getting to be a force to be reckoned with!' This was one of those occasions. It's word for word the response I got from Mr. Brewer when I flew a very chancy kite in his face! . . . Just finishing, darling! . . . Now—listen to this, Joe!"

JOE REPLACED THE receiver and instantly reconnected with the operator. He looked anxiously at his watch. Cyril Tate was probably well into his second dry sherry at the Cock in Fleet Street. But no. He was still at headquarters and Joe's call had him on the line in seconds.

"Of course I'm here! It's still Ascot weekend down here in the Metropolis. Another hour's copy to write up before I dash off to the next event—tea with a duchess. Make it quick, Joe."

Matching Joe's own urgency, Cyril answered his questions with the curt, pared-down sentences of the airman he had once been and ditched the society commentator's persiflage. "In the last year? I'm fishing my diary from my pocket as we speak. It takes me back as far as last January."

Joe heard pages rustle and he pictured Cyril thumbing through his large-sized, heavily scrawled over and full-to-bursting record of social engagements. "February . . . here we are . . . You'll have to depend on my memory for this one. The birthday ball out in Wiltshire of Amanda Seacombe . . . As well as the many royal cousins clustering round, there was present your person of interest: Dorothy Despond. Attending with her father. Don't ask me why. I didn't write down the whole guest list but I'm pretty sure the Trueloves were there. James and Lavinia."

"Evidence of this? I can't afford to get it wrong, Cyril. Lives at stake."

"Make that 'certain' then. I can send you the shots if you like. Otherwise a back copy of *Tatler* will confirm. Hang on! Come to think of it . . . skipping on a bit . . . Here she is again in March. Literary and Arty jamboree in Hertfordshire." Cyril flinched at the memory. "One of those god-awful shows where they expect you to roll your sleeves up and paint a watercolour, write an ode and stuff an owl. All in the space of one wet weekend."

"What was Miss Despond doing there?"

"Leading a snappy little art appreciation group, if you can believe it. Subject: 'Dada and all the other -isms . . . How to hold your own conversational end up when all about are losing their marbles' sort of stuff. James Truelove was not only a fellow guest— he was in the front row, lapping it up! Without the missus, this time. Ho, ho! I see where you're going with this! You clever old sod! Those two knew each other before the wife died. Good enough, Joe?"

"It'll do, Cyril. Many thanks!"

"Have I just hammered a nail in some poor sod's coffin?"

"No, no! But you may just have saved a girl from a fate worse than death—a life with James Truelove. I owe you a pint in the Cock when I get back to civilisation, old mate!"

THE PHONE RANG as he left the room. Joe looked about for Styles, then, thinking it might be his superintendent ringing him back with an afterthought, Joe closed the door and picked up the receiver himself.

"Hello. This is Melsett Hall here," he said carefully.

A young woman answered. "That's not Mr. Styles," she said in a voice slow with suspicion.

"No indeed, Miss. Will you wait until I find him or will you leave a message? I think he's officiating at the teapot in the east parlour at the moment. Sudden influx of thirsty guests."

"Who are you?"

Joe explained who he was.

After a long pause, she began to talk. "I've only got threepence and I'm ringing from Mrs. Crispin, the grocer's next door so I'll have to talk fast. It's Grace. Grace Aldred."

"Oh, hullo, Gracie! I was just talking about you with Ben. How are you getting on? Or, more to the point, I ought to ask— how's your mother doing?"

"Mother? Oh, she's fine, thank you for asking, sir. She's back on her Iron Jelloids and her Pink Pills. Look, can you tell Mr. Styles or Mrs. Bolton I've decided to come back? There was no need to stay here a whole week. Monday's my busy day and I ought to be back at Melsett. And now my sister's here with her two little 'uns . . . well, it's a bit crowded and I've never got on with my ma. Not like Sarah, they're thick as thieves those two . . ."

Joe listened to at least sixpenn'orth of family intrigue and drew his conclusions. He cut her short: "So, you're packed and ready. What time is the next bus? . . . Two o'clock . . . In half an hour . . . Get on that bus, Grace. What time do you expect it'll arrive in Melsett? . . . Right. I'll come and collect you myself at the bottom of the drive. Don't worry. I'll tell those who need to know."

FOUR O'CLOCK FOUND Joe lurking in the shade of a chestnut tree at the end of the drive. The bus braked, pulled over and parked. Joe leapt forward to greet the sole descending passenger with a smile and an extended arm. He introduced himself briefly. "From the Hall, Miss Aldred. I'm a friend of Adam Hunnyton. My name's Joe Sandilands. We spoke on the telephone earlier. Let me take your bag."

Grace was self-possessed enough to smile back and pause to wave a showy goodbye to the gaggle of young faces peering at her from the bus with astonishment and speculation. She claimed his arm, enjoying the intrigue of being seen in the company of such a smart gentleman and, without further ado, set off with him up the drive.

"You got away with no trouble, then?" he asked politely.

"Yes. They were quite glad to get shut of me. I'd rather be here with the other girls. We get time for a good gossip on Sunday afternoons. I'd miss that, Mr. Sandilands."

As soon as the bus had rattled out of sight, Joe pulled her to the side of the drive into the shade and put down the bag. He turned to face her. Neat, brown-haired Grace had the plain but bright features of a robin, he thought, and she carried her head slightly cocked to one side, which increased the illusion.

"Listen carefully to me, Grace. I must give you my full title and explain why I'm here at the Hall at the invitation of Cecily, Lady Truelove."

Grace nodded without surprise to hear his explanation.

"Now tell me—who exactly gave you permission to be away from the Hall?"

"It was Mrs. Bolton, sir. Last Tuesday . . . She asked me how my mother was getting along and I told her she'd been having these pains in her chest . . . Yes, it was Mrs. B. She's strict but she's a kind-hearted lady. She told me to take the whole week off if I wanted to. I said no need for that—I'd got behind with my gophering and would never catch up. I expect she'd cleared it with Lady Cecily. Nothing happens without her ladyship knowing."

"I've visited your room, Grace. Thank you for so discreetly preserving the evidence. Were you expecting someone like me to come along and rake it over?"

"No. Can't say as I was, sir. No one so grand as you. I had hoped Adam Hunnybun might come and set everything straight. I wasn't sure quite how he'd manage it—he doesn't often visit these days. I was waiting for him to come back."

"How did you come by the rain cape your mistress was wearing that night?"

Grace looked affronted at the question. "I was her personal maid, sir. Who else would have the sorting out and cleaning of her things? It came back from the hospital with the rest of her clothes. They went on the bonfire."

"Cleaning? You had preserved the cape in its uncleaned condition. Why?"

"I wasn't happy about that rubbish she was meddling with. Witchcraft, she called it. Monkey-business, I thought. I had bad feelings about the whole silly scheme. I didn't want to get the blame. They always go for one of us when someone high and mighty takes a tumble and I was the one who'd been to Mr. Harrison's and bought the stuff she had me smear on that gingerbread. I thought someone ought to know the truth of the matter. How I tried to put it right. Tried to stop her getting hurt."

Grace frowned and paused, wondering whether to go on.

"Tell me what happened that night, Grace. I should like to know what you did to protect Lavinia from herself."

"She swore me to silence, sir. Told me what she was planning—to tempt that great savage horse out of its stall where it had been holed up for a week and attract it to her with those oriental spices. Horses love them, she said. They call them 'drawing herbs.' Sounded a bit dangerous to me so I . . ." She sighed and was uncomfortable in telling the rest of her story. "So I disobeyed the mistress. First time I'd ever gone behind her back. I told someone. Someone I could trust and who knew all about horses. 'Can that be safe?' I said—luring a beast towards you like that? She'll get herself killed. And I don't want to be blamed for it."

"What advice were you handed, Grace?" Joe proceeded with caution. Gentling. Leading her on. She knew where she wanted to go; all he had to do was reassure her that she was on the right path.

"Good advice!" she said defiantly. "It made sense to me. Lady

Lavinia must have gone and done something wrong . . . The horse wasn't supposed to even come out of its stall . . . 'He must not be drawn,' I was told. 'You're right, Grace, that's madness. That animal has a bad record. What you need is something to keep it well *away* from the mistress. A smell that will repel it, not encourage it to venture out. Leave it to me. I know just the thing that'll have it backing off. You must find a way to smear the substance I'll give you onto the cake instead of the spices from the chemist. Can you do that?' Well, of course I could. Nothing easier. It was handed to me sealed up in an old jam jar. I did all that nonsense about making a paste of the spices from the chemist and smearing the gingerbread I got from the pantry like the mistress told me to. She wasn't paying much attention because she doesn't like strong smells and—mixing and cooking—all that's servants' work and she wasn't interested. I chucked the spicy slice away in the pig pail and put the muck from the jam jar on another slice. That's the one I stowed away in her pocket ready for the morning. It smelled disgusting, even to me. 'That'll keep anything at a safe distance, man or beast,' I thought. Was I to blame, sir?"

"Not at all, Grace. Don't concern yourself. You did your best. What any dutiful maid would have done. But, sensibly, you kept the cape as evidence that you'd tried to avoid a disaster in case someone like me came calling? Your little insurance policy?"

"That's right, sir."

Joe's voice was authoritative but kindly as he asked for his last piece of information. "Grace, I need to know whom you consulted in your hour of need. Who was it who supplied you with the good advice and the bating mixture?"

Her eyes skittered from side to side and he thought for a moment she was about to refuse this last fence. At last, she told him.

Joe's response on hearing the name was instant and decisive. He grabbed Grace by the shoulders and pulled her further into the shadows. "Grace, I'm taking you straight to Adam Hunnyton's cottage, where my car is parked. I'm going to ask Adam to drive you back to Bury right away to your mother's house and there you are to stay until he comes to fetch you back again. I'll tell them at the Hall that there's been a telephone message from you: your ma's taken a turn for the worse and you've got to stay on. That will be perfectly acceptable."

He didn't add: "Indeed, something of a relief for one person up there." Arranging another murder so soon after the last might be a bit tricky with a house full of guests. What would they come up with? A garrotting in the drying ground? A sudden surge of lethal current from one of those new-fangled ironing machines? He didn't want to terrify the girl.

But Grace was thinking things through. "Not the sharpest knife in the drawer" had been cocky young Ben's assessment, but she was by no means the dullest, Joe guessed.

"Am I in trouble?"

"Possibly. Though you haven't deserved to be and I shall say so."

"Will I get the sack?"

He must have hesitated a fraction too long.

"Worse than the sack? Is that what you're trying not to say, sir?"

"I think it's not impossible that steps might be taken . . ." he started to say with annoying imprecision. "Look, Grace, there is much at stake. Things you have no inkling of. Not very certain I do myself. Come with me. We've no time to lose. Adam will know what to do for the best—I'm no more than a stranger here."

HALF AN HOUR later Grace Aldred was safely—and happily—stowed away with Adam's sister. Rather than make the journey back to town and into a family situation Grace had just left, a stay with her old friend Annie was much to be preferred.

Having gone without the 'light collation' on offer for lunch at the Hall, Joe had wolfed down a piece of fruit cake and a mug

of tea at Hunnyton's cottage. Grace had accepted a biscuit, listening nervously as the two men spoke to each other in short sharp
phrases, looking constantly at their watches, calculating times and
distances and making plans. Grace, while not managing to follow
much of the professional-sounding conversation, seemed to sense
that everything stemmed from the action she had taken on that
ghastly April morning and she twitched with feelings of guilt and
foreboding. It was not over yet and someone was for the high
jump. But these two men who spoke over her head in soldiers'
voices seemed to have her welfare at heart and they assured her
it would all soon be dealt with and she wasn't to worry. Joe had
seen her safely off to Annie's house in the company of the superintendent, whom she seemed shyly to adore.

Joe strolled into the hall and greeted Styles with the self-
satisfaction of a man just returned from a post-luncheon
constitutional. He walked swiftly about the corridors for a
while, smilingly avoiding conversation with anyone and finally
headed for the telephone room. He emerged after a few minutes, leaving the door open and calling for the butler. "Ah,
Styles! There you are. Sorry, I seem to be treading on your toes
today . . . I was in there talking to the Yard. The phone rang
as I put the receiver down. Thought it must be my superintendent with an afterthought but no—it was for you. The Aldred
household ringing from Bury, courtesy of the grocer. A three-
penny bit to hand and time of the essence so I took a message."
Joe's eyes went slightly out of focus as he recalled a piece of
lightweight information. "Grace's mother's taken a turn for the
worse. Heart trouble. Grace won't be back until Wednesday at
the earliest. Apologies and all that. Oh, and would you please
tell Mrs. Bolton she's sorry about the . . . gophering? I say—
does that make sense?"

Styles smiled. "Perfect sense, sir. Mrs. Bolton will be relieved
to hear there's been a communication. Tea has been cleared, I'm

afraid, sir. Shall I summon up another pot? No? The dressing gong will sound at seven for dinner at eight."

"Thank you, Styles. I shall be on parade at eight."

BEFORE THE GONG sounded he would set in motion the plans he'd made with Hunnyton, and he'd start in the kitchen. He looked at his watch. The lull between tea and drinks. This was the right time to catch Ben and Mrs. Bolton and explain what he wanted from them.

Two hours to go before he could disappear to his room and be certain he would not be disturbed. At seven he would go up and do his packing, preparing for a quick exit. Lagonda back to Cambridge and then whatever train was available to get him back to reeky old London. He could be back at his desk by mid-morning on Monday, checking one last time the wording of the resignation that he kept permanently in his drawer undated and ready to be delivered to the chief commissioner. He could be taking one last look at the plane trees lining the Thames Embankment. Like them, he'd absorbed year on year the contamination of his surroundings and finally, in a moment of release, he'd throw off the whole layering of filth to reveal the pristine white trunk beneath. If his core did indeed remain unsullied. He couldn't be certain that the rot hadn't begun to penetrate.

In an odd mood of self-doubt and nostalgia, spiked by an edge of excitement and anticipation of change, he first made his way to the Great Hall. He passed the crowd of disapproving ancestors in review one by one, countering their superior stares with his own knowledgeable gaze. He moved on down the corridor to the dining hall, where he annoyed a couple of footmen who were putting the finishing touches to the dinner table by taking up space in front of the Canaletto landscape of the Thames. Saying a quiet farewell? There hadn't been much he'd enjoyed at Melsett but he'd been glad to see this.

The enchantment was broken by a confident voice at his elbow. A low and intimate voice that sent a shiver down his side. "So here it is! I'd never seen one of his views of London before. It's superb, of course. Though I have to say, once one has seen any of his sunlit pictures of Venice, the contrast with a grey northern cityscape is striking but unwelcome. The dome of St. Paul's seems reduced, the architecture uninviting, the water murky, don't you think?"

The voice was accompanied by a trace of perfume matching in its sophistication. *Cuir de Russie?* Masculine tones of birch and amber were sharpened by a top note of jasmine. It spoke to Joe of Paris, of leather jewel cases spilling over with diamonds, tickets for the Opéra and champagne. He'd last encountered it in the plush, enclosed comfort of a first class sleeping carriage on the Train Bleu heading south. The women who wore it gave and expected no quarter. They relished an armed flirtation and they knew how to deal with irony.

"If the subject is dear to one's heart and the artistry sublime, I claim no disappointment, Miss Despond. If I had the resources to buy it, I would think I'd died and gone to heaven."

"Call me Dorothy. I remember that you're Joe. Anyway, Joe, I don't think it's for sale so we both have to put heaven on hold."

Joe had the clear impression she was trying to provoke him.

"There are others perhaps more attainable . . . Did the Stubbs take your fancy? The Gainsborough? Cecily Lady Truelove is, as we speak, locking up her Lancret, secreting her Seurat, I believe."

He meant it to sting and, hearing her sharp intake of breath, he guessed he'd been successful. She disengaged with a fencer's flourish and stepped between him and the painting. Her eyes locked on his in disdain. "What are you? Cecily Truelove's guard-dog? You are very rude, even for a policeman!"

"I apologise. I acknowledge that the goods you deal in are vastly more expensive than a pound of pippins. The last thing I'd want to do is ruin Truelove's chances of selling off his birthright. Suffering from straightened financial circumstances, as he is at the moment, he may be minded to do just that."

She had not known.

The pallor of her face, the long silence before she replied told Joe all he wanted to know. Was he being an utter cad, revealing Truelove's position? Yes, he was. He could make out a case with no difficulty. It was a caddish thing to do and far outside his usual meticulous manners. But the rebellious streak in Joe took up arms alongside his unfashionable belief in the rights of women to live their lives with the freedom accorded their male counterparts. The men in Truelove's world could learn of his imminent destitution by the simple exchange of information from one deeply buttoned arm chair to the next in a St. James's club, between the rows of leather-covered benches in the Houses of Parliament, between shots on the grouse moor. Who would whisper a life-saving truth in Dorothy's ear? No one. She and her father were not on the circulation list when it came to scurrilous confidences, distanced from the English establishment as they were by class and nationality. Even set apart by their wealth, which brought with it a certain mistrust and, in these hard times, envy. If Joe slipped away into the dark now and left this girl, however worldly and uncongenial, to be hoodwinked by Truelove, he would hold himself guilty of neglect of duty for ever more.

At last, Joe had chosen to pick up the gauntlet thrown down at his feet some time ago. *A l'outrance,* Truelove! To the end, however bitter!

"What are you trying to say?" she asked.

"That Lavinia Truelove, who largely—and generously—financed her husband's activities during their married life, died having almost exhausted her resources. James may have been her sole heir but he inherited no more than the few thousand that remained of the marriage settlement with which to run his estate and his academic and altruistic concerns." He kept his voice level, the tone that of a trusted family lawyer. "A Lavinia remaining alive might well have been able to intercede with her father on her husband's behalf when the bottom was reached, but with her death in questionable circumstances being whispered about on all sides, it's unlikely that he would find himself able to help a man suspected of killing his daughter. The pay of a government minister will hardly maintain a staff of five in Town, let alone the fifty he presently employs in the country. You will be aware of the present straightened circumstances of the English land-owner, indeed, the whole nation? James Truelove, I think, will have calculated to the nearest thousand what he can get for his Canaletto and all the other glories. I suggest that if you have an interest, you seek out the man himself and verify what I have just told you. If I correctly understand your circumstances, the truth ought not to be kept from you."

He would have sworn she hadn't known about Truelove's dire financial circumstances and he thought, from her silence, that she was in confused retreat but her answer, when it came, parried his attack. It was delivered with a growing assurance, even scorn. "Oh, old news! Yes, you're right. James is contemplating auctioning off one or two of his paintings, but we're hardly talking of a closing-down sale. He'll be buying others to replace them. More modern in taste maybe. Pictures degenerate. They have to be moved on before they near the end of their useful existence. Before boredom and decay set in. I would certainly advise James to dispose of this Canaletto. It's of England but it's not English. It's . . . displaced. Rootless. A refugee. Like me," she added, revealing an unexpected crack in her confidence. "Maybe you'd like to buy it? You don't seem to be a friend of his, but he could probably let you have it for . . . ten thousand pounds. Do you have ten thousand pounds, Commissioner?"

"If I had cash to spare I'd spend it on a Whistler," he said blandly. "Tell me, now you've done your audit—how do you value the ancestors in the Great Hall? There are some impressive signatures on those canvasses."

At last a feeling look and a half smile. "No idea. I've looked, of course. But I'm not very keen on selling off . . . people. One's own people. I have no ancestors I can name, let alone look at. My father doesn't even remember who his grandparents were. I feel the lack of background acutely. At home, I drink cocktails with men whose people crossed the ocean aboard the Mayflower; here, I take tea with the bony descendants of the Norman Conqueror. I expect you know—we are . . ." She reached for a word and came up with two—both of them French. "*Parvenus . . . arrivistes . . .* Why does it sound so much less insulting to confess it in French?"

He realised she was waiting for a response. An acknowledgement that she had just surrendered more than a confidence: an advantage. "I can't for the moment come up with an English word for what you're describing, Miss Despond. 'Johnny-Come-Lately' doesn't quite do it—he's a character from a nursery rhyme, surely? Perhaps that tells you something of our national character. We have always accepted that talent, wherever it has its roots, will transplant and flourish in our soil." He added, teasingly, "Handel . . . Disraeli . . . our Royal family . . . and, yes, Canaletto, for starters."

She listened patiently to his burbling, still getting his measure, he thought.

"But surely there were painters in your homeland? Hungary, it's rumoured. Somewhere in eastern Europe?"

"Refugees travel light, Commissioner. If I had portraits of my ancestors I would never sell them. It smacks of the slave market. Oh, I know that they are no more than dabs of oil on canvas but I can't bear to see faces and figures that must once have been dear to someone coming under the hammer. Being valued by the likes of Clarence Audley, ogled in the sale-room by any rag-tag-and-bobtail." Her sneer made it clear that he answered this description.

"Were you aware that two miniatures of Truelove's came up at Christie's this week? Ancestors who disappeared from the house nearly thirty years ago?"

"Yes. It was I who drew Papa's attention to them. I research the catalogues for him. He decided to buy them and present them to James as a token of our esteem this weekend."

"A delicate gesture. A 'sweetener,' as it's called in the trade."

The half smile became a full one. "He was thwarted on the day by a low-down trick—a 'spoiler,' as it's called in the trade. Performed by yourself, I believe?"

"I was, indeed, the bobtail in question."

She appeared to relent slightly. "Anyway, no more of James's pictures will suffer that ignominy. It was wrong of me to dangle the Canaletto in front of your nose. There are more ways than one, Commissioner, of righting a listing ship and getting it safely to harbour."

The implication was unmistakable. Joe sighed. How could clever girls like Dorcas and Dorothy be so taken in? Why would they refuse to see the truth when it was spelled out to them?

"Shovel on fresh cargo? Or jettison the existing load? Both?"

"You'll have to wait and see, won't you, Commissioner?" She left him with a smile he could have sworn she'd learned from Leonardo.

He could almost bring himself to feel sorry for Truelove. This girl was no Lavinia. She had in seconds taken aboard news any other girl would have found devastating, evaluated it, made her calculations, and come to a decision. She intended to go ahead with her plans to marry a future prime minister, acquire a ready-made set of ancestors and a country estate. Cecily might even be allowed to keep her Lancret. In spite of her undisguised contempt for him, Joe admitted to himself that he admired Dorothy

Despond. Beauty, a quick wit and a buccaneering attitude were a combination which always seduced him. Altogether Truelove could congratulate himself on a match made in heaven. On the debit side, Joe could not count on an invitation to the wedding. And Dorcas? She could count on heartache at best.

The forces were gathering fast, the noose tightening, he realised, now that so much else was clear to him. Dorcas had been chosen as the victim, just as he had originally suspected. She had been lured into making a second appearance at the Hall and the way had been prepared for some sort of grisly unmasking. The deranged student in love with her mentor: it was a familiar story that would slip down with a knowing chuckle in the clubs of St. James's. Wasn't the girl in question a Joliffe, after all? That rackety family so discredited by the behaviour and dubious death of this girl's aunt a year or two back? The Wren at the Ritz case? James should have known better than to encourage such a fragile personality. Still, that was the Trueloves for you—all heart and philanthropy. Too good for their own good—what!

There were factors in this affair that would have convinced any Scotland Yard officer of Dorcas's guilt. With a chill, he calculated that Truelove, familiar with Joe's relationship with the girl, must have been aware of Joe's knowledge of her skills and of her character. He was well placed to know that she had the capacity to commit such a crime. It had certainly crossed his mind, he recalled with a flush of embarrassment. But, because of this very association, Joe was less likely than anyone to charge her with murder and haul her off to the Old Bailey for public trial.

"This could surely all be resolved within the family, so to speak?" Joe could almost hear the suggestion being put to him. Slyly and with bluff bonhomie. "Come on, man! No need for uncomfortable denunciations, prison sentences and the rest of it!" Nothing that would weigh heavily on the Truelove conscience. Nothing that would spoil the Truelove reputation for public service and philanthropy. No need either for a black cloud of suspicion to smudge the horizon of Truelove's romantic prospects, which seemed to be brightening briskly from the west. And all this convenience came with the bonus of a grateful assistant commissioner of police firmly in the politician's pocket and in his power.

Joe had made his plans. He'd done his best to protect Dorothy. He had now to concentrate on saving Dorcas from herself. Dorcas might be lost to him, but she was not going to be lost to the world. One last flap of his wings was called for.

The seven o'clock gong sounded. Time for the last act.

THE WHOLE COMPANY dazzled. Assembled in the Great Hall, champagne glasses in hand, they chattered and laughed. Diamonds winked, pearls glowed, rich colours and fabrics shone out against the sober background of the men's evening dress. The ancestors, ranged up around them seemed at last to approve. The only cloud on the horizon was the face of Cecily, who was advancing towards him.

"We are now thirteen!" she said. "Well, twelve and a half if you count Miss Joliffe. She hardly considers herself one of the party, I think." Cecily nodded in the direction of Dorcas who was lurking moodily on the fringes of a group, preferring to stare at the pictures rather than join in the conversation. "Joe, are you quite sure you delivered my message to Miss Hartest? She certainly did not have the civility to send me reply and reassurance."

"Half past seven for eight. It's not yet eight. I sent the chauffeur down at seven thirty. I'm sure . . ."

At that moment Styles appeared at the door, raising his eyebrows for attention.

"Oh, it seems you're right, Joe. Look at Styles. Something's exciting him. Let's hope it's Adelaide."

She went over to the door and the butler announced, "Miss Hartest, your ladyship."

Adelaide came in with all the aplomb of Cleopatra entering Rome in the sure and secret knowledge that its mighty ruler had been in her bed the night before. Conversations were put on instant hold as everyone turned to stare. Joe gulped. One of the women gasped. It was Alexander who reacted. He dashed over to ease his mother out of the way and welcome the last guest. Joe heard his voice, animated and friendly: "Adelaide! Alex Truelove—we met at the Church Mothers' Waste-Not-Want-Not sale three weeks ago. You helped me decide between the knitted cat and the stuffed owl."

"I remember. And is he giving satisfaction, your choice?"

"I'll say! I put Olly up for target practice in the orchard. So poor is my aim these days, so jittery my fingers, I have to report he's still intact. Not a feather out of place! Adelaide, you're looking quite splendid! For a moment I thought myself back at the Palace. Come and meet another Londoner. Joe Sandilands is about the place somewhere . . ."

On cue, Joe came forward to take Adelaide's hand. The fingers were trembling despite the smile on her face. He leaned towards her and spoke quietly in her ear. "Not the Palace. I'd have said rather an ambassadorial reception on the Right Bank in Paris. Every man in the room has his eyes on you, thinking lecherous thoughts, and every woman has her eyes on her man, thinking murderous thoughts."

The black silk trousers which had appeared outlandishly daring when waved in front of him in her sitting room, now—filled with her willowy frame and topped off with a short jacket of military cut—were stunning. A white blouse, frilled at neck and cuff, softened and made fun of the masculine assertiveness. As did her chestnut hair, which billowed out exuberantly about her head in loose, barely-in-control curls. Adelaide Hartest was showing all the tongue-in-cheek sexual allure of a thigh-slapping pantomime prince. She murmured back, "What do you think of my buttonhole, Joe? Swan Lake came up with just the right bud today."

Joe dared to bend and nuzzle the rose. The smiles they exchanged seemed to puzzle and annoy Alexander, who took Adelaide firmly by the arm and led her into the centre of the room to perform the remaining introductions. "Come and meet Dorcas Joliffe—she knows a great deal about animals and doctoring, too. You'll have much in common."

CHAPTER 23

Cecily, in the end, must have been pleased with her arrangements.

The guests were, for the most part, animated and witty, the conversation sparked by an undercurrent of tension and mystery. The candlelight flattered the company and the food on their gold-rimmed plates. The dishes chosen were superb, the accompanying wines impeccable. Course followed course with Edwardian opulence, served by deft, handsome footmen wearing a parade uniform of fairy-tale splendour.

Excessive, Joe judged, accepting a helping of *bavarois à la framboise*. He saw a trap being baited with honey. The last scraping of the jar? Surely Dorothy wasn't taken in? From her chatter and laughter, he could only assume this display was no more than she was used to and expected. Seated between a saucy Alice McIver and a saucy Adelaide, Joe found himself talking rather too freely and more entertained than he would have thought possible with the depressing load of a forthcoming denunciation on his mind.

He glanced around the table as the evening closed in between dessert and savoury, checking the faces. Almost all were flushed and relaxed. Only Dorcas had remained aloof from the gaiety. She was wearing an elegant dark silk dress which flattered her slim figure and doing her best to bat into the ground the overtures of her immediate neighbours. Mungo McIver had quickly given up on her and talked to the lady on his other side, as, eventually, did kindly Basil Ripley. She cast the occasional dark glance at Joe, followed by an equally dark shaft of recrimination in Truelove's direction, and cut up her food without actually eating much of it. She drank three glasses of wine, Joe noted. Of all the people at the table, innocent and guilty alike, it was Dorcas's behaviour he needed to be able to forecast as things reached their climax. If she reacted badly and abandoned the script, his plans would come to nothing. The thirteen diners he was dealing with had to be handled with the caution and cunning you'd need to control a herd of half-tamed horses. It would take one ill-chosen word, one hasty action to spook them.

He looked anxiously at his wristwatch.

With the meal drawing to its close, Cecily began to glance around the table, catching the eye of the lady guests and preparing to announce that they would withdraw, leaving the gentlemen to enjoy their port. After that would come tedious rounds of snooker or cards and the evening would run into the sand though, for the moment, the company seemed still sprightly, the buzz of conversation animated. Joe judged his moment had come. With a swift gesture of the hand to Cecily, he held her in her seat and himself rose to his feet.

One of the male guests, more tipsy than the rest, interpreted this as a familiar movement. Joe was about to make a speech. Wilfred knew what to do; he tinkled merrily on the side of his claret glass with a spoon. "Pray silence for the commissioner!" he announced. "Speech! Make it funny, Sandilands!"

"Not a speech, you'll all be relieved to hear—the Plod are not known for their light-footed levity. Indeed, there was once a policeman so achingly dull, all the others thought he was Noël Coward. But I have to announce—for your further entertainment—

and with the gracious collusion and dramatic flair of Lady Cecily . . ."

Cecily chased the expression of astonishment from her features and replaced it with one of knowing amusement as all eyes turned on her.

" . . . an after-dinner game. No—don't run for the door, Ripley! I have in mind something a little more sophisticated than Sardines. I'm calling it 'Deceive the Detective.' All the rage in London Town. At least half of the people gathered around this table are old hands, in the know, so to speak, and have been playing the current round of the game for some time. The others will be surprised—but I hope not alarmed—by the sudden appearance out of the shrubbery of policemen in uniform, clanking handcuffs, possibly a judge and hangman."

Glances were exchanged, eyebrows raised. Well, at least this promised to be livelier than a round of piquet, more entertaining than the Music Hall Medley they knew Maggie Somerton had in store for them. They listened on.

"The aim of the game is to solve a murder puzzle before the detective does. You must come up with the answer to two questions: Who has been murdered? Who is the murderer? Evidence will be presented, witnesses called on. You may make notes and confer but there must be a decision arrived at by the stroke of midnight. We'll need to withdraw from this table, of course, and take a breather. I've arranged for coffee and brandy to be served to you in the Great Hall in—shall we say—half an hour?"

Joe caught Ben's eye and he smiled and nodded.

Murmuring and giggles broke out around the table. Florence Ripley reached into her bag and drew out pencil and notebook and looked up with the alertness of a prize pupil, ready to start. Dorcas stared at him with foreboding. Dorothy and her father exchanged looks of indulgent incredulity. The English and their parlour games! Mungo McIver showed some agitation. He seemed to have heard a whistle blow in the enemy trench and patted his pockets. Seeking what? Gun? Camera? He caught Truelove's eye and his query was returned by an amused shrug of the shoulders. Adelaide put out a hand below table level and patted Joe's thigh.

They rose with varying degrees of enthusiasm to his smiling invitation and went off to powder noses, find a flowerbed to pee into, take a breath of fresh air and hiss whispered speculation to each other. Under cover of the disruption, Adelaide leaned close to Joe and whispered, "You're nuts! You'll get a unanimous decision: it was the horse that did it, in the stable, with his teeth."

Joe went straight to the Great Hall to check his arrangements. The ancestors, he thought fancifully, were not pleased to see him. A chorus of harrumphs would have run around the walls if they'd known the real purpose of his unscheduled invasion of their family territory.

Nervously, the thirteen entered on time and gathered together in the centre of the room, too strung up to commit themselves to taking a seat at the table he'd had laid with a carafe of water, glasses, notepaper and pencils. Coffee on trays followed them instantly, supervised, surprisingly, by Mrs. Bolton. A cross Mrs. Bolton who whispered words of protest in Cecily's ear. "Short handed—sorry, ma'am."

"Glad you could join us. Do stay, Mrs. Bolton. We're sorry to inconvenience you," Joe said. Cecily set about playing hostess alongside Enid Bolton, dispensing coffee as she remembered her guests liked it. Truelove and McIver had instantly stationed themselves, an alert and menacing presence, on either side of the doorway. For their easy retreat or to block Joe's exit? Cecily was having none of it.

"James! Mungo! Stop louting about over there and come and help me with the cups. Then settle down, will you? I know Joe has something important up his sleeve for us and I insist you play nicely."

Adelaide carried coffee over to Dorcas, who refused it with shake of the head.

No one would sit. Cups were put away on side tables, behind potted plants, all, in their agitation, chose to keep their hands unencumbered, their feet ready to move off fast. Ben entered with a refill jug of coffee and Joe asked him to wait by the door.

"Joe, will you get on with it?" Cecily demanded. "We're all ready."

"Well, I have before me a mixed bunch. I have something approaching a very informal and entirely illegal Court of Justice. You are thirteen in number. Unlucky for one. Twelve good men and true—and women!—will make up the jury who will assess the guilt and decide the fate of the thirteenth member. The one among you who will be here accused of the murder of an innocent woman."

"Ooh! The game's afoot," trilled Alice McIver. "Bags I not be the thirteenth—I couldn't keep a straight face. You'd all guess it was me."

Joe smiled and forged on. "Last April, Lavinia Truelove was tricked into confronting a dangerous horse—you all know most of the circumstances. What you may not know is that the maid, Grace, who assisted her in the scheme, in a good-hearted attempt to mitigate the effect of her mistress's folly, consulted someone she considered an authority on horses, a person of understanding and wisdom whom she trusted. This person chose, for personal motives, to give exactly the wrong advice and also supplied the means to provoke the attack."

A frisson ran round the company as they realised they were involved with not a game but a real and recent death. A tricky moment. If one of them called his bluff and shouted, "Blow this for a game of soldiers! I'm off!" the rest would follow. Joe relied on the strength of a very human quality to keep them listening: ghoulish curiosity.

"We are looking, ladies and gentlemen, for a person who sought to destroy Lavinia. I put it to you that her death was not an accident. It was willed, engineered and carried out at a distance. The tool was an innocent animal." Joe filled in as briefly as he could for the benefit of those not in the know how this had been managed. He explained how the horse bate substance had, by trickery, been secreted in the pocket of Lavinia's cape, triggering the attack on her. "But why? Always the first question for a detective. Several motives were explored and rejected. One—and one only—stayed with us. With his wife disposed of, Sir James was once again a free man. Did someone wish perhaps to supplant Lavinia in Truelove's affections?"

Joe waited for a spluttering objection from Truelove—"I say! What utter nonsense!"—to roll away and carried on.

"I have in mind a person who was smarting from the insults Lavinia dished out over dinner that evening with such malice. Someone who had formed a secret and hopeless affection for her hostess's husband. Someone who had the knowledge of country horse-witchery . . ."

He waited for this information to be absorbed and watched as the audience looked from Dorcas to James and back again with round eyes and an audible intake of breath. He waited for an explosive response from Truelove. But James Truelove made no further protest. He failed to see the disbelief in the eyes of Dorothy Despond standing at his side because he could not bring himself to look at her. Dorothy's father, Joe noted, moved closer to his daughter and put a protective arm around her shoulders. Dorcas Joliffe had no such comfort, standing by herself, as aloof and friendless as Joan of Arc at her trial.

It was Dorcas who made the first response. Faintly, she pleaded: "James . . . Won't you tell them the truth . . . ? Why don't you speak up for me? Please, James!"

Truelove looked down at the floor and said nothing.

Everyone turned to stare at her. Dorcas had eyes for no one now but Joe. Judging the force powering those dark flamethrowers, he thought he probably had only seconds before he was struck down with paralysis or the plague. Even Adelaide was watching him with incomprehension and disgust. Cecily, on the other hand—always on his wavelength—had shown herself ready to respond to his promptings. She moved straight away to obey him when he requested that she open the door to the vestibule.

Three men who'd been waiting behind the door now strode in and closed it behind them.

"Who the hell is this?" Joe heard Guy Despond protest. "Where'd he get these fellers? Back stage at the Adelphi?"

Superintendent Hunnyton stood, a tall and satisfyingly dramatic presence, flanked by two uniformed constables. He introduced himself in measured police tones and paused for a moment, surveying the company.

"Miss Dorcas Joliffe? Is she here? Good evening, Miss. I'm taking you into police custody so that you can help us with our enquiries concerning the unlawful killing on these premises of Lady Truelove in April of this year. My apologies, Sir James, Lady Cecily . . . It seemed better to remove the accused quietly. Not good form to drag anyone away from the dinner table."

He nodded at Joe and walked out, Dorcas following uncertainly with a constable on each side. Her backward glance was for Joe. It told him that, if she was taking her first steps to the Tower of London, that bleak place would be a more agreeable situation than the one she was leaving.

In the Great Hall trembling hands distractedly picked up coffee cups. "Helping with enquiries, eh?" Everyone knew what that meant! The herd began to relax, each member thankful that his or her innocence had been recognised. McIver asked Ben to fetch a tray of brandy. Lady Cecily called for lemonade. James exchanged long looks with his mother. Alex turned for comfort to Adelaide who gave him a hug and a handkerchief and patted his back.

After a moment, Alex freed himself from the doctor's embrace and jumped to his feet, overthrowing his chair. The crash turned everyone's attention on him. Red spots of anger glowing on his cheeks intensified the blue blaze of his eyes. He looked desperately from Joe to his mother and Joe's heart sank as he realised that he had failed to factor into his plans a reaction from Alex.

"She was with me all night!" he yelled. "Dorcas couldn't have done it! She let me into her room and I stayed. In all honour, I'll have you know. Oh, it's not what you think! She took me in and tucked me up in my old bed and read me a story. She was still asleep in her own bed when I crept out at dawn."

Joe was aware of the masculine reaction of revulsion as eyes flicked in acute embarrassment to the ceiling, the floor, the nearest candlestick. The women, apart from his mother, looked at Alex with pity.

"I'd have gone to my grave before I endangered that poor girl's reputation but I cannot stand by and see this disgusting calumny heaped on her by a policeman. You're a cad, Sandilands! And a useless detective!"

"Calm down, Alex," said Cecily. "I'm surprised but reassured to hear you have some human instincts after all. But you're not showing much acumen. Weren't you listening to Joe? The damage was done by the time you were wandering the corridors. Now, thanks to Grace, we know the gingerbread was already loaded earlier in the evening. It was charged with a substance supplied by Dorcas Joliffe. The girl could have spent the night in the footmen's dormitory and it would have had no more significance!"

The crowd absorbed Cecily's comments in silence. One or two nodded regretfully. They silently approved the boy's showing of loyalty while reckoning that it in no way cancelled out Joe's accusation. Playing the detection game, they had calculated that the villainous Dorcas must have seized on the alibi unconsciously offered by the blundering young Alex and tucked it away to be used as a last resort. She was probably at this very moment, with a delicate flush of embarrassment on her cheeks, regaling the superintendent with this lesser confession. Dishonour was, after all, to be preferred to death on the scaffold.

"All the same—good man, Alex!" murmured Basil Ripley. "That was well spoken. We understand."

Joe puffed his cheeks and blew out a sigh of relief. "I say, Ben, can you squeeze another cup out of that pot?" he asked, sinking onto a chair, and Ben obliged.

"But what . . . ? Why did she . . . ? Why didn't she . . . ? What the hell's stoats's liver . . . ?" The chorus of questions poured out and by unspoken consent, the company followed Joe's example and settled down at the table to compare notes and thrash out the meaning of the extraordinary scene. Mrs. Bolton and Ben remained aloof and dutiful at the door.

Truelove listened to the encouraging burbles of support that came his way with pained gratitude. At last he felt strong enough to voice his dismay and disbelief. "Look, Sandilands, old man," he remonstrated, "I know what you're up to but did you have to stage this . . . this . . . pantomime so publicly in front of my friends? Have you any idea what excruciating embarrassment you have subjected us all to? To say nothing of the distress you have caused that poor girl!"

Then it began. Sorrow followed swiftly on the heels of anger. "You've all seen her—she's nothing more than an impressionable child. Emotionally quite immature and inexperienced in the ways of the world. But look, it doesn't have to end like this. That poor little person was carried away by a moment's madness. You must blame me, I'm afraid. She was an outstanding student. I made something of a pet of her, made promises regarding her future that perhaps she over-interpreted. If, as you say, Joe, you've set us up as judge and jury . . ." He looked around the table, gathering support. "I'll speak for all by saying that Lavinia was killed—as any good man and true would say—as a result of her own folly." He appeared to be satisfied with the number of nods this raised and carried on: "That she was the author of her own misfortune, as the lawyers say. Not the brightest, my Lavinia." The loving, indulgent smile that accompanied this thought triggered a clenching fist in Joe. "Surely you don't have to put Dorcas through a court hearing?" Truelove shuddered. "The Old Bailey, black caps and a thrill-seeking public? Huh! Blokes like you, McIver, with cameras flashing! I won't have it! Much though I admire your professionalism and punctilious attention to the finer points of Law and Order, Sandilands, I must tell you to call off the hounds."

Seeing the tightening of Joe's jaw, he hurried to add in a conciliatory tone, "Forgive me. In my concern I go too far. A police officer is under no obligation to obey a government minister. He is employed by the people to serve the people. We ought all to remember that. But I still say, as a matter of humanity—will the people be served by the punishment of a thoughtless girl? You know as clearly as I do, Sandilands, that, realistically, this business will never come to court. For fifty years now, we've had a Crown Prosecution Service which, as part of the Home Office, does a very useful job. You are well aware of this; I mention the matter as some of us gathered around this table—law-abiding citizens, all—may never have encountered it. The system weeds out cases it judges a waste of public resources. This is certainly one of these cases. The family uphold the decision already taken by the magistrate at the time of the accident—which, in spite of your evidence, I still believe it to be—that we are dealing with a death by misadventure. I don't ask, I *beg* you to declare here before my friends that you will pursue this no further. You have gone far towards clearing up a mystery which would not bear the increasing weight of speculation that was being heaped upon it to the detriment of my good name and for that I am grateful."

Cecily turned to Joe. "Well done, Commissioner! It's never easy lancing a boil. Bystanders inevitably risk being contaminated by the effluent. I will say it—since James, in his rush of soft-hearted solicitude neglects to—we're grateful that you have wielded the scalpel. Grateful that you have proceeded through to the truth with such delicacy and concern for the reputations in question. No heavy boots, no handcuffs. Only *friends of the house* here present to witness the misguided girl's downfall."

Her sharp look around the table was unmistakably a swearing to silence on the part of everyone, their understanding nods a guarantee of the reinstatement of her son's reputation and career.

Joe watched the pious sorrow gathering, listened to the murmured compassion being offered to Truelove and his stomach curdled. Only Adelaide was looking puzzled and angry. She got to her feet in a marked manner and murmured something to Cecily as she went by on her way to the door.

Joe followed her clicking heels and managed to cut her off before Ben could open up for her. He hissed, "Stop right there, Adelaide. Don't leave me alone with these swine! They may need you to sew their balls back on before the evening's over!"

CHAPTER 24

J oe turned to Ben.

"Did you bring it, man?"

Ben picked up a brown paper package from behind a plant pot and handed it to Joe.

Joe turned his attention back to the gathering. They fell silent, eager to hear him apply the soothing ointment of compliance and understanding. A police officer, a high-ranking one destined for the top position at the Yard, a man now shown to have the confidence and trust of a minister of Truelove's promise, was a man they would listen to.

He stayed on his feet between them and the door.

"First things first: Miss Joliffe, for whose fate I observe you all to be exhibiting so much sympathy, is as we speak, on her way to enjoy a cup of cocoa with Adam Hunnyton. She will have already heard an apology for the treatment she has just received at our hands. That scene was enacted with her knowledge and consent, her contribution voluntary. It was, nevertheless, an unpleasant experience. I hope one day she will find it in her to forgive me. I know she will never forgive you, Truelove."

He paused for emphasis. "Yes, you, Truelove! That was a farce, not a pantomime, you have just witnessed. But the first act only. A scene played out to reveal to me—and to all in this room—the depths to which the Truelove household was prepared to stoop to protect its own. Its reputation, its very existence have been—still are—at stake. With one woman dead already, two more women's lives and happiness were to be sacrificed without a second thought to keep a Truelove in place and in affluence. That's what this is all about. You have shown yourselves in your true colours. I'm now going to hold up a mirror so that you can see yourselves in all your dishonour."

Pompous rhetoric, perhaps, but calculated. An Englishman, even a rogue, still had his attention caught by a challenge to his honour.

Jaws dropped, two men leapt to their feet uttering threats. Again, the only thing that saved Joe from a revolt was curiosity. Wives tugged their husbands back down into their chairs, clucking and fussing. What on earth was this fiendish policeman going to come out with next? They had to know.

Alice McIver, more prescient than the rest, spoke sharply to her husband: "Don't interrupt, Mungo! He's just smashed up the wristwatch, now he's going to pull it in one piece out of someone's ear."

Alexander managed a delighted grin. "She didn't do it, did she? Ha! Told you so! You've been having us on, Sandilands! Poking us with a stick to see which way we'd jump."

"No, she didn't do it, Alex. Dorcas Joliffe is entirely innocent of any attempt on Lavinia. The only thing she has been guilty of is trusting James Truelove. The man who connived at the murder of his own wife. Lavinia produced no heir and had, after many years, dished out the last of her fortune. Her character and conduct were increasingly showing themselves unsuited to life at the side of a man of Sir James's political ambitions. She had become a worthless hindrance to the Truelove line. With her off the scene, James, still youthful and destined for a glowing future, could attract a rich, socially adept woman of childbearing years. He had one such in mind.

"But how to manage it without drawing down suspicion on himself? The notion of allowing his wife to follow her own stupid fantasy to its inevitable grisly end occurred to a Truelove mind that disastrous weekend. There was even a love-lorn student on hand to take the blame, should anything go wrong and blame become a feature of the case. Dorcas Joliffe, in her blind attachment to her mentor, was a useful insurance policy. As was a recently appointed and ambitious Assistant Commissioner of Police. Conveniently, he was known to have connections with the Joliffe family and could be depended on to deflect suspicion from the Trueloves while ensuring that the blame-carrier escaped any serious trouble at the hands of the law. How thoughtful . . . How neat!

"Grace was the only one who tried to avert a tragedy. Unfortunately, in her dilemma, she sought advice from not Dorcas but from one she trusted and who knew something about horses. I've discovered that in this household, everyone considers himself or herself an expert. But in this case, the authority consulted had access to a very ancient source of information."

Joe slammed the brown paper parcel down onto the table and slid out of it a leather-bound book.

"Dr. Hartest. Please be so good as to open this tome at page three hundred and seven, will you, and read out the recipe you'll find there."

Adelaide reached forward and took the book. "It's something called *The Accomplisht Ladie's Companion*," she said, mystified.

Mrs. Bolton gasped and glowered at Ben, who was beginning to look a little shaken.

"And here it says: *Receit for the bating of horses. A sovereign receit for keeping a horse in its rightful place. Will stop a horse in its tracks on the open road. Caution: will rouse ire and acute ill-temper in the creature if used against it in a confined space. Require your servant to collect together the following ingredients . . .*" Adelaide looked up, sickened. "They're all listed if anyone wants to see them . . . Stoat's liver, cat's urine, rat's blood . . ."

"We'll never know at whose instigation the ingredients were collected together. No difficulty in harvesting the essential one—the stoat remains. These were freely available to anybody walking about the estate, where they were regularly displayed on a spiked fence by Goodfellow. In the few hours available to our conspirator, the recommended maceration time in noxious fluids had to be ignored. Not a problem to a mind unimpressed by magic, a mind that saw through the hocus pocus to the essential effective ingredient. I'd have harvested half a dozen stoat livers, added a few rat entrails for bulk and stirred up the whole mess with a touch of urine from a house chamber pot. Perhaps our modern-day apothecary can inform us? I do know from Grace herself that the authority she consulted was . . ." Joe turned, not for cheap emphasis, but to do the accused the courtesy of looking her in the eye. "You—Cecily, Lady Truelove.

"And you, in turn, Cecily, consulted and conspired with your trusted friend and retainer, Enid Bolton.

"The plan devised by the two women was known to Truelove . . ." Joe asserted a fact for which he had no evidence and left a pause in which Truelove might have registered a denial. He did not, in the end, have the gall to leave his mother and his housekeeper to carry the can. "They arranged for James to be seen by the servants crossing over to spend the night at the Dower House."

The group had fallen silent.

"This was murder. Nothing less. A plot which led to a shocking and painful death. We have the answers to the two questions I set you: The victim of murder? Lavinia. Her killer? The Truelove Household. A conspiracy of three: You, James; you, Enid; but principally, you, Cecily."

Loyal old Sir Basil Ripley had heard enough. He got to his

feet and pointed an accusing finger at Joe. "Not another word, young man! So this is the new policing you were so keen on, James? Is this truly a sample of your appointees? Where *did* you recruit him? Auditioning for a part in the latest shocker on the wireless? Sherlock Holmes with his dubious detective skills? Or was he trying for Inspector Lestrade with his clumping feet and his clunking logic? I can see no more advantage or entertainment in listening to this man's ravings. What are you waiting for, James? Have him thrown out."

Support for Joe came from an unexpected quarter. "Siddown, Ripley! You'll do no such thing, Truelove! Now—carry on, Assistant Commissioner Sandilands." Guy Despond pronounced his rank with careful emphasis.

"Hear, hear!" said McIver. "Let him at least get to the end. I do enjoy a good story."

"Yes, go on, Joe." Cecily's voice. Sweet and reasonable. "I do hope you're going to do justice to my motive for indulging in all this chicanery. You're very nearly there."

"A wasted lifetime? Is that strong enough? How it must have irked your ladyship to see all your sacrifices—your money, your years spent fostering the family of a man of dubious fidelity—come to nothing. You did your duty by him. You produced four children. You made a considerable investment in the line and to see it shrivelling away in the hands of a daughter-in-law you despised was more than you could bear. Her degrading behaviour at the dinner table that night in April signed her death warrant as far as you were concerned. You had to secure the future to validate your own past. I attribute the inspiration for the plot to you. As you told me candidly early on in my investigation— it's a woman's crime.

"You, Enid. For you, Lavinia had to die to preserve the household. To keep the house, as you always have. If Truelove failed, the whole establishment would have faltered and gone under, as other neighbouring estates have done, and been sold off, their staff released into a cold world with no chance of re-employment. The prospects for the older servants—I speak of you and Mr. Styles—were grim. Weighed in the balance against Truelove's sparkling prospects, an injection of cash and a new heir to the family, Lavinia's life counted for little. She represented a deficit in your book and you are a meticulous bookkeeper. You believed it the right moment to do a little judicious balancing. You had the means and the knowledge, and the practical aspects of the plot from the gingerbread onwards were left to you. I believe the lives of Dorcas Joliffe and Grace Aldred would have been at risk if a further adjustment had become necessary."

Enid showed no emotion. She stared straight ahead, back rigid, hands folded.

But emotion finally got the better of Dorothy Despond. "And my life? What of that? Where do I figure in all this? A brass weight in a scale pan?" She jumped to her feet and glared at Truelove. "You haven't even got the guts to do your own murdering! You leave it to Mummy and the servants! You're nothing but a cheap chiseller!" She grabbed a glass half full of brandy and hurled it, glass and contents, in Truelove's face. Her father rose with her and the two strode to the door.

As she drew near to Joe, Dorothy whispered in a voice surprisingly in control, "Thank you, Joe. Canaletto had it right about England. Cold, unwelcoming and very murky. Worth collecting, though, if you get the chance—and it begins to look as though you may . . ."

"Couldn't agree more." Joe smiled. "I'm off to the south of France and glad to shake off the mud and the gloom. Why don't we step outside, Despond, and leave the assembled jurors to come to a decision?" He offered his arm to Adelaide, who seemed eager to leave with them.

"I ought not to care, Sandilands," said Despond, closing the door behind him, "but there are villains at large in there, free to stay or leave, and I'd like to know what you propose to do about them."

"I?" Joe said, waggling his eyebrows. "Nothing at all. Nothing I can do. Unless Cecily and her son are prepared to write out a confession and sign it, British law would never allow me to bring such an insubstantial case to court. The Crown Prosecution Service would turn me down in five minutes. I've always known that. At best, they'd consider putting Grace Aldred in the dock on the evidence we have."

"But you stuck with it anyhow." Despond smiled. "And my daughter and I are eternally grateful. Not used to being taken for a ride, Sandilands. I'm used to being the biggest shark in the pond. What will you do now?"

"My bag's packed. I thought I'd leave them in the company of their dear friends to hear their judgement. I'd hope to hear the question asked: 'How can we accept the fact that the forthcoming Home Secretary, destined to be in absolute charge of Law and Order in the land, has been complicit in the killing of his wife and other forms of skulduggery?' I wonder what sentence they'll dole out."

"Ten years' exile? Blackballing from his clubs? In Ancient Athens they'd have written his name on a potsherd and got the guy ostracised. But, don't raise your hopes, Sandilands. He's among friends back there." His eyes narrowed in mischievous speculation. "Not sure of the newsman, though . . . He's the weak link. Too good a story to keep under wraps, are we thinking?"

Joe smiled. "You're forgetting the ladies, Despond. My hopes rest with Maggie Somerton, Alice McIver, who has the country's most influential newspaper magnate wrapped around her little finger, and Florence Ripley. Florence was scribbling notes throughout. A man's reputation can be preserved in the safe confines of a St. James's club but . . ."

"Not in the tearooms of London," Dorothy supplied with an unladylike chortle. "That's where *I'm* planning to make a start on the demolition!"

"Well, I'm off now to have a cup of cocoa with the superintendent and Dorcas. They'll be wanting to hear the outcome. Such as it is." Joe held out his arm. "Won't you join us, Adelaide?"

CHAPTER 25

In the cocoon of his lamp-lit home, Adam Hunnyton's comment on the affair was, predictably, a grumbling protest on behalf of Ben, the footman. "You tricked him! He's a good lad. He deserves better."

"I know Ben's worth! Yes, I did deceive him because I am also aware of his sense of loyalty. I never like to put a man's loyalty under stress. It does no one any good. But I did give him my card with a scrawled message on the back. The police college at Hendon can use such a man. He's wasted smoking Woodbines to pass the long watches of the night in a slops cupboard spying on Cecily's guests."

Joe stayed on with Adam when Dorcas and Adelaide left. Dorcas had gratefully accepted the offer of Adelaide's spare bed for the night, before returning to Cambridge and the railway station in the morning. She had broken her silence to say only that she wanted to go home to Lydia and Marcus. Joe gathered that his company would be unwelcome for the moment and mentioned tactfully that he was planning to stay on in Cambridge for a couple of days. Forms to complete, statements to make, liaising to be done . . .

Before he crept up to the sleeping quarters in the loft, Joe agreed to a snifter of apple brandy and a smoke with the superintendent and settled with him at the table. He reached into his pocket and took out a shining object. He placed it on the table in front of Hunnyton.

"Recognise it? No, why should you? There must be thousands like it scattered around the Truelove estate. But this one is special and very identifiable. For a start I witnessed it missing my fleeing form—deliberately missing, I hope—and lodging itself in the trunk of a lime tree. I marked the spot and later retrieved it. Attempted murder? That's the first charge. When I hand this to our ballistics blokes they'll be able to tie it to one of the Purdey guns you keep on the premises, Hunnyton."

Adam smiled. "And what's the second charge?"

"Murder."

"How come? I see you sitting here in front of me as large as life and twice as ugly . . . I must have missed you. Someone's bound to point it out."

"No. I have in mind the murder of Robert Goodfellow, lately resident on the Truelove estate. You shot the bugger at seven o'clock precisely as he lay in his bed. Forty minutes later you fired at me, establishing a second possible killing time. More plausible, as it couldn't be connected with any rook-scaring explosions. It sent me off back to the hall, blood-stained and dishevelled, looking every inch a wild killer. The scene of crime also was, as you pointed out to me, innocent of any trace of a third man. No one else had entered the cottage, according to the best evidence you could find. Of course there was none. Just my bloody foot and fingerprints. Perhaps a stray hair or print from the investigating officer but—there—you'd expect and discount that, wouldn't you? The fact that the man lived on a further twenty minutes and really did die in my hands just added more credence to your story."

"You may have noticed that I didn't charge you with anything formally or informally. Why on earth should I want to pin a killing on you, Joe?"

"A trade-off. Knowing what the risks were, I would be more likely to rush to accept the alternative you so nobly offered me. Suicide. Goodfellow is buried with a suicide label attached to him and no one will ever know the truth. Just as Phoebe was branded a suicide. Poetic justice? Symbolic but hardly lyrical. The man died in revenge for Phoebe. This was always about Phoebe, wasn't it? You could not be sure. You always thought it was a Truelove who drowned her—a suspicion so unpalatable you chose to bury it with her corpse. It was another death of a woman in suspicious circumstances that gave you the leverage you needed to get—at long last—a CID detective down here to sort it out for you. You could hardly go about arresting your own much-admired, unimpeachable half-brother. The exemplary Englishman. Get some other poor fool to do the dirty work for you . . ."

Adam smiled again and refilled his brandy glass. "Good story so far. Carry on," he invited.

"You were keeping the villain Goodfellow under surveillance. You trailed him back from the pub, intrigued that he had had much less to drink than he normally did. A break in the behaviour pattern. Your professional eye would have taken that in. You watched as he prepared his departure. You saw him put his farewell letter to me in Diana's hand. You read it and in it found confirmation of your girl's killing and James Truelove's seduction. You guessed—it could be no more than a guess—that it was Goodfellow himself who'd drowned her and for that he was going to die.

"Next morning, you returned, armed. The old steward striding about the estate with his father's Purdey tucked under his arm was a familiar sight. But you never intended to use your gun on the Green Man. You took his shotgun from under his bed, fixed up the firing angle and pulled the trigger. Unfortunately, he woke and moved his head a split second before the bullet struck. You must have been in a quandary, Adam. Leave him and hope for the best? You could hardly administer a second shot! As his throat was a wreck, you took the chance that he was not about to make any deathbed accusations. But you hung about just in case, watching.

"And a few minutes later, in response to the earlier shot, tripping along through the bluebells comes the London Plod, who proceeds to put his feet right in it. You see him off with a shot up his bum and put together a bargain he'd be mad to refuse. He even feels grateful to you. Do you know, Adam, it was some time before the penny dropped and I worked out what you were up to. You bugger! You even had the gall to shove a crumb or two of the horse bate you were given by Adelaide into one of Goodfellow's drawers—leaving it ever so slightly open with a sticker on it so that I'd couldn't miss it. Establishing a tangible link between the dead rogue and the guilty family. In case I needed a little shove in the right direction. That's the third charge: supplying false evidence."

Adam grinned. "All correct but for one detail, Joe. He didn't wake up of his own accord. I woke him. I take no chances. Dish out no injustices. I offered him his life in return for the truth. He confessed that he'd dragged Phoebe to the moat and drowned her in a rush of carnal lust that was repulsed. She threatened to shop him to Sir Sidney. She said she'd tell the old man his pet Spirit of the Woods had raped her and was the man responsible for her condition. Thereby incriminating *him* and exonerating the young master. A version that would have been much more palatable to the old man. I told you she was quick-witted. But it got her nowhere with that brute. The man condemned himself out of his own mouth. His sins, in the end, found him out."

The old-fashioned phrasing recalled to Joe Mrs. Bolton's estimate of the man's character. She'd mentioned, in approving tones, his "righteousness." Joe replied in kind. "You wanted him to see the face of Retribution looming over him before the lights went out?"

"He recognised me all right. Killing him gave me more satisfaction than accounting for a whole squadron of the Hun."

"You put on the breastplate of judgement, reneged on your offer of his life for the truth and pulled the trigger."

"So? What would you have done, Sir Gawain? Slapped him on the wrist and handed him over to a bunch of his drinking cronies for a decision on his fate, going by present form! My word against his on an uninvestigated death that happened a quarter of a century ago—that doesn't get attention from any police department in the land and you know it. You are only here, looking more closely because you had strong personal, present-day reasons to do that." Less angrily, he added, "I'm not ungrateful—never think it. You've done your job. But—let's be clear—I'm glad he's no longer on the face of the earth, festering and spreading his malice."

"Too late. It's already spread. It's touched you, Adam. Take care you don't pass it on like the flu."

"What are you going to do about it? They say you're a man who takes a hard line when it comes to ethics in the Force. You've fined coppers on the beat for drinking, sacked officers for taking bribes . . . I'm ready to hear what you propose for a superintendent who commits murder."

"Tricky." Joe paused to marshal his thoughts and took a moment, as he often did in a tight spot, to select a diplomatic formula of the kind his old friend Sir George Jardine would have used to oil an unpalatable response. "I don't give a shit," he said finally. He picked up the bullet and tossed it over to Hunnyton. "Stand off! I suggest you do with that what I did with the letter.

"Now, Adam. It's been a long day one way or another and I'm turning in. Early start for Cambridge in the morning and I have to get a young lady onto the ten o'clock London train."

"Then I'd better drive you. Um . . . If it's no bother, Adelaide's expressed a wish to spend a day or two in Cambridge. Hope you

don't mind, Joe, but I sort of suggested it myself. Your Dorcas was
more hurt than you supposed by that charade. She may well have
agreed to it but it still knocked her back to find the man she . . .
um . . . respected . . ."

"Loved," Joe corrected. "I'm not a fool."

"Well, she doesn't want to talk to you. Not ready yet to forgive
you. She's rather clinging to sensible Adelaide for support. In fact
I think she's hiding from you behind Adelaide's skirts. She senses
this is a moment when she needs a doctor rather than a detective
and if the doc's another woman who's very ready to agree with
her that Joe Sandilands is a complete arsehole—all the better.
There's a fence there that, just for once, you may not be able to
mend with charm and a glib tongue. It's got a dirty great hole
right through the middle of it."

"You'll be glad to see Tommy again? Does Adelaide like dogs?"
This was the feeble attempt of a tired man to change the subject
and extract information and Adam was not deceived.

"Adelaide? No idea. The woman's a mystery to me. She doesn't
have a dog of her own, though her father has the usual pair of
Labradors," he said genially. "Tommy'll be waiting behind the
door when I get back to Maid's Causeway. There'll be eggs and
bacon and a basket of mushrooms on the kitchen table and Mrs.
Douglas at the hob. You're very welcome to stay for breakfast.
Hannah would insist. I told you my landlady was the best cook
in Cambridge—she's also the handsomest. In fact—she's a corker!
I'd make an honest woman of her tomorrow if she'd have me but
she's waiting for something better to turn up. When I'm feeling
cheerful, I tell myself it must be that she prefers the spice of an
illicit affair."

Joe grinned. "Don't kid yourself. She just doesn't want to be
'Hannah Hunnybun.'"

"It had occurred to me. But I don't stop trying. Look, Joe . . .
Don't mess your life up out of pride or misplaced loyalty. We do

a nasty job. The nastiness can rub off on you. What you need is a loving dog who's never going to notice and, failing that, a good woman who does see it and helps you scrub it off."

"One more apple brandy and you'll have me agreeing with you," Joe said doubtfully.

CHAPTER 26

J oe trailed a hand in the cool green water, snatching at a strand of weed for the pleasure of feeling its slippery smoothness between his fingers. The punt he was lounging in surged forward at a kick from the pole and he cut his hand on the plant's sharp edge.

"Watch it!" he growled. "I'm supposed to be spending a relaxing afternoon recovering from my exertions. All this swooshing and heaving about makes me feel like a badly stowed cotton bale. Where am I supposed to put my feet? This cushion's soaking wet! Call this fun? Isn't it my turn yet to have a go with the punt pole?"

"Not until you've fully appreciated the demonstration I'm giving you."

"I've been watching. And—I've been meaning to ask for the last mile—aren't you standing in the wrong place? Why are you balancing precariously on the platform at the back? It would make more sense to put your feet down here in the body of the boat. You'd have much better control, surely?"

"You know nothing of the mechanics of punting. Oxford ignoramuses punt from inside, Cambridge men stand up here on the stern. I don't want to attract rude shouts and possibly a dunking from the local chaps—they get very picky about style. But I can see you're the sort of man who can't bear to be pushed around by a girl. Look—there's a deep, grassy indent in the bank over there and a convenient willow to hitch the punt to. I'll make for that. We're not all that far from Grantchester meadows now. It's a wilderness of buttercups and tall-growing Queen Anne's Lace. Plenty of shade. We could be thinking about landing for tea."

She nodded down at the hamper Joe was struggling to prevent from overturning. "I asked them at the hotel to forget about the flask of tea and put a bottle of champagne in there. For consolation or celebration? I'm not sure yet. Depends on what you have to say for yourself. Or there's apple juice if you want to keep a clear head. And some ham sandwiches, some spice buns from Fitzbillies and a chocolate cake. That do you?"

The promise of chocolate cake and the sight of Adelaide Hartest's sunburnt bare feet right in front of his eyes produced a sigh of pleasure and a stir of excitement. Her damp summer frock was clinging in a very indecent manner to her legs and her face was pink with exertion, her eyes alight with humour. Perhaps there was something to be said for punting after all.

"Watch it, Adelaide," he warned. "I can work magic with spice buns."

"Joe," she said with a smile that was uncomplicated, warm and for him alone, "you don't need the buns."